BLACKWATER
FALLS

ALSO BY AUSMA ZEHANAT KHAN

ESA KHATTAK AND RACHEL GETTY MYSTERIES

A Deadly Divide
A Dangerous Crossing
Among the Ruins
A Death in Sarajevo (a novella)
The Language of Secrets
The Unquiet Dead

THE KHORASAN ARCHIVES FANTASY NOVELS

The Bladebone
The Blue Eye
The Black Khan
The Bloodprint

BLACKWATER FALLS

AUSMA ZEHANAT KHAN

MINOTAUR
BOOKS
NEW YORK

First published in the United States by Minotaur Books,
an imprint of St. Martin's Publishing Group

BLACKWATER FALLS. Copyright © 2022 by Ausma Zehanat Khan. All rights reserved. Printed in the United States of America. For information, address St. Martin's Publishing Group, 120 Broadway, New York, NY 10271.

www.minotaurbooks.com

Designed by Steven Seighman

Library of Congress Cataloging-in-Publication Data

Names: Khan, Ausma Zehanat, author.
Title: Blackwater Falls / Ausma Zehanat Khan.
Description: First edition. | New York : Minotaur Books, 2022.
Identifiers: LCCN 2022023243 | ISBN 9781250822383 (hardcover) |
    ISBN 9781250822390 (ebook)
Subjects: LCGFT: Detective and mystery fiction. | Novels.
Classification: LCC PS3611.H335 B55 2022 | DDC 813/.6—dc23/
    eng/20220518
LC record available at https://lccn.loc.gov/2022023243

Our books may be purchased in bulk for promotional, educational, or business use. Please contact your local bookseller or the Macmillan Corporate and Premium Sales Department at 1-800-221-7945, extension 5442, or by email at MacmillanSpecialMarkets@macmillan.com.

First Edition: 2022

2 4 6 8 10 9 7 5 3 1

In memory of my father, Dr. Zehanat Ali Khan,
who taught me everything I know about grace,
compassion, and the fight for justice.
You will always be in my heart,
loved, and deeply missed.

BLACKWATER
FALLS

CHAPTER ONE

No death could have been more profound.

The girl's face cold, the injury precise, the small town waking to grief on Sunday. He'd framed the death as poignantly as the image that inspired it, the girl's arms wider than the heavens, the gold-and-crimson shawl falling to her shoulders, her head held in place by a scarlet ribbon that swept across her nape to loop around her pale white wrists. A separate ribbon bound her feet in their neat red shoes, her legs locked together at the ankles, her blue dress hitched up.

No fresh blood, but even with the missed detail, perhaps this served her better. Her body was stiff, her blue eyes open and unseeing, a touch of frost on her delicately formed brow, another pale dusting on her lashes. The frost would melt under the hot summer sun, and then the girl's skin would glow with her inner radiance.

Her clothing enhanced that radiance: the blue dress, the two-toned shawl. The diamonds pinned to her breast and shawl, the kerchief tucked into her belt.

If it had to be done, he would pay her the homage she deserved.

Her body in the foreground against a field of bright gold.

The door that beckoned worshippers to pray.

Ah, holy Mother of God. Those pensive, staring eyes.

Why had he done this to her?

CHAPTER TWO

Inaya Rahman parked behind the sheriff's rig, an oversize SUV with a massive push bar upfront and a shiny Starling County decal on the hood. The cars parked across the street had left a gap behind the mobile lab and ambulance. The sirens were quiet, the rack lights turned off, a hush around the perimeter, where the police were setting up a cordon.

She slid out of her car neatly, her Denver Police badge conspicuous on the waistband of her slacks. As a detective, she was not in uniform, dressed formally in a sharp blue blazer and a buttoned-to-the-throat white blouse. She had to be. She was forcing her way into an insular group, as wary of the sheriff's reputation as the sheriff would be of hers. The Community Response Unit of the DPD was about as popular with law enforcement here as police oversight had been in Chicago, her former placement. The CRU was small, floated outside the existing police structure, and could be assigned to any case that called for police accountability. In the aftermath of national protests against police brutality, the thinking behind CRU was to offer complete transparency to overpoliced communities. And to bring in new investigators where complaints had been filed against an officer whose conduct was under review.

Inaya's presence would inform the sheriff he was about to be removed because of a backlog of complaints against his substation. The complaints weren't just about excessive force by Blackwater deputies; they also encompassed sustained harassment of minorities that the sheriff had refused to respond to. He'd object to being taken off the case, and he'd probably resist. She wouldn't let that stop her. She was ready to do her job, and eager to get back to real police work. For the past few months, she'd been working on community outreach, visiting expos and fairs, talking to students and local council members to get a feel for how effectively the police were serving the public. It was important, trust-building work, but it wasn't what she had trained for—it was what she'd had to accept. Maybe she'd needed the change; events at her past placement had led to the collapse of a case of national importance, followed by a very public breakdown. The fallout had caused her to flee to Denver, but now she was growing impatient with the downgrading of her duties, eager to put her skills to use. Enough of being condescended to. Enough of being overlooked.

She straightened a seam on her blouse, her shoulders back, her chin raised. She couldn't undo past mistakes; she could only use what she'd learned to move forward.

This was a new city, a new job. A chance for her to start again.

As she neared the building, her steps faltered in her court shoes. A tent screened the front of the two-story building from view, a house with narrow dormers, its porch in need of repair. Inaya knew this house. It was a local mosque that served the Muslim community in Blackwater Falls, Castle Pines, and several of the smaller mountain towns. A crowd was beginning to gather on the sidewalk; she acknowledged a few of the women she knew before moving past them.

A muscle-bound patrol officer was guarding the entrance to the tent. His bulk made him perfect for the job. He shifted to block her entry, despite the fact that he could see her badge.

"And who might you be?" He made the most of his limited authority, his arms crossed over his chest.

She ignored his attempt to discourage her, showing him her ID. "Detective Inaya Rahman, CRU. I was called to the scene."

His ID was obscured or she'd have used his name to emphasize his lack of courtesy.

He scowled down at her, crowding her a little. "I'm not sure the sheriff would feel the need to call you."

He was right, but she wasn't going to tell him she was here to take over. Instead, she countered, "*I'm* not sure why you're standing in my space."

She did know why, of course. She was young, female, and dark-skinned, a newcomer or an outsider, depending on how he saw her. He'd rely on that, boxing her in, and ignore the fact she outstripped him in rank if she gave him any leeway.

"If you're in any doubt, please call the sheriff. Or you can check with Lieutenant Seif, the head of Community Response. He knows Sheriff Grant. I'll wait while you confirm his orders."

She turned back to face the crowd, pretending to be at her ease. Privately, she worried she was late, which would put her at a disadvantage.

The officer lost interest. He pulled back the flap with a flourish, aiming another dig.

"The sheriff will put you in your place."

"No need." She chose to misunderstand him. "I can find my own way."

As soon as she sealed the flap behind her, the hum of activity from the sidewalk subsided. Law enforcement officers congregated in the outer area, blocking her view of the mosque's main entrance, a beautiful golden door imported from Morocco.

The sheriff of Blackwater Falls, a formidable man in his fifties, stood by the women's entrance, surrounded by his officers. After a glance at her badge, he ignored her. The uniforms followed suit, speaking in hushed tones.

Sweating a little under her smart blazer, Inaya smoothed the tight French braid that had taken the place of the headscarf she'd worn most of her adult life. As a cop, the scarf put a target on her back, and though it wasn't as modest, keeping her hair confined made her feel as if some part of her courage had survived. She scanned the tent, hoping to catch sight of Lieutenant Seif, her immediate boss. He reported to higher-ups, but was always in charge at the scene. She turned as the huddle of men at the front parted, giving her a clear glimpse of the mosque's main door. She looked up. Then farther up.

She caught the dead girl's eyes, stared at the sweet blank face.

The girl's arms were stretched out above her head, her blue dress slightly raised to display a pair of neat ankles bound with fine blue satin. A shawl over her hair trailed down to a gash at her side. The arrangement of the body was unmistakable, the cloak an inadequate substitute for the young girl's hijab.

Merciful God in Heaven.

Her recognition of the girl was instant.

Her name was Razan Elkader. She was a Syrian girl from the local community whose scarf had been stripped from her head, the shawl substituted as a travesty. It left the girl exposed in a way others could never understand.

Inaya's hand trembled as she raised it to touch the hem of the robe.

Go with God, be with God now, little sister.

She stopped short of touching the girl, her entire body racked with tremors. Lieutenant Seif came into view, heading in her direction. She swallowed the constriction in her throat, her pulse erratic, her eyes burning with the urgent need to cry.

A soundless scream scraped her mind.

Not this, not this, not this.

Her tattered composure gave way. She fainted at the dead girl's feet.

CHAPTER THREE

Inaya splashed her face with cold water in the mosque's restroom, shaken by the scene she'd caused. The sight of the girl's body shouldn't have shocked her; she'd seen death before. She was experienced, even hardened, yet she couldn't be detached—she saw her own fate in Razan.

Her mind reconstructed the scene. The icy flesh of a girl nailed to the door of the mosque in a gruesome emulation of the Crucifixion, wrists and ankles pinned, a broad gash to the right side of the body, the five holy wounds mapped out on the girl's body, anointed by a scarlet ribbon. If not a desecration, then a hate crime, perhaps both.

She was shivering despite the summer heat when someone rapped at the door.

Her mascara was smudged in patches beneath her eyes, her head was sore from where she'd struck it when she fell, but the knock was insistent. She opened the door to find Waqas Seif frowning down at her. His cold dark eyes dissected her appearance as she slipped into the hall. He shook his head at one of the patrol officers who'd ventured inside, the gesture telling him to leave, the door to the women's entrance still ajar.

"What was that, Rahman?" The clear bite of Seif's voice cut through the fog that shrouded her. She blinked several times, scrubbing at her cheeks with the remnants of a paper towel. She firmed her shoulders, though she was far from recovered. She had to move past it if she was going to prove herself. She'd prepared to work in the field again—she couldn't let herself be intimidated.

Maybe Seif sensed her reaction, because he repeated the question, the edge sharper this time.

Seif was much taller than she was, the color of his eyes densely black, his well-cut hair the same shade, with just a hint of curl. The modeling of his face reminded her of the portrait of a famous Persian mystic, otherworldly and enigmatic. The image was dispelled when he spoke in the incisive tones of a cop.

Inaya focused on the knot of his gray tie. He tended to dress in monochromes, as if that minimized his restless energy. He was five years older than she was, but his unforced authority made that distance unbridgeable.

They'd interacted very little over the six months she'd been in Denver. She didn't know the details of his work; though they were on the same team, their cases didn't overlap. Apart from community outreach, she was working through a stack of complaints filed against cops who used force to subdue kids in school. They were called "school resource officers," and as in the world outside of school, excessive force was usually applied to Black or brown students. The complainants in these cases called out not only police bias, but the policy itself.

Inaya was meant to either retrain or remove the officers who were named in these complaints, a task that could blow up in her face.

"That wasn't the impression I was hoping you'd make on Sheriff Grant."

Seif's acerbic comment brought her back to the present.

If he'd asked her to account for her loss of composure with a hint of empathy, she might have explained herself.

Her stomach clenched and a familiar blend of guilt and self-loathing rose to the surface of her thoughts. She deliberately slowed her breathing, letting her lungs fill with air while she counted down in her head.

It's not going to happen again. I'm safe; my family is safe. There's nothing he needs to know, nothing I need to confess.

"You're right, I'm sorry. Blackwater Falls is a small community; I knew Razan a little." She wiped her forehead. "We've taken over—why do we have to worry about the sheriff?"

Seif didn't move, but somehow his presence encroached into her space. The line of his lips was flat, the groove at the edge a warning.

"He's an important man here. Be careful about throwing your weight around."

Inaya experienced a flutter of alarm. She hadn't handled the crime scene well, and Seif could probably tell she was nervous, but it was reasonable to want to know what his plan of attack was. She wasn't going to let him bully her just because she'd asked a question.

"Fair enough, but my priority is this community. That's why we're here, right?" She made a sweeping motion that encompassed them both. "Hiring people like us isn't just window dressing, is it? Because no police department can afford that in this day and age."

He ignored the buzzing of his cell phone. "Subtlety is more effective than a frontal assault. Didn't they teach you that in Chicago?"

She flinched from the harsh words. Oddly, her reaction defused his temper.

His voice was a shade less sharp when he continued, "You're a resident here. You know the community. Liaise with them; speak to their concerns. Be careful about sharing too much about the investigation, as with any other homicide." He underlined the last words.

"You're not staying?"

He smiled a sharklike smile. "Can't you handle things on your own? You live here, don't you have any insights?"

"Of course." She turned to look at Razan, her body on display. "The obvious conclusion is that this was a hate crime."

His gaze settled on hers, probing, judging. "Do you usually accept the obvious?"

Inaya stiffened her spine. "You may not be aware that there's been some trouble with the Resurrection Church here in Blackwater." She spoke with a forced calm.

"The evangelical church?" Seif looked beyond her to the window. In Denver, the church complex would have occupied an entire city block; here, it took up a stretch of land near the foothills, west of Titan Road. The church paid for officers to regulate traffic on Sundays, a connection

Inaya had noted as a matter of course. It was one of many things she'd observed about her new home.

"The church has an outreach branch, though its members operate more like vigilantes. They're called the Disciples."

Seif showed no reaction. Perhaps he already knew.

"And you think these vigilantes are capable of this murder?"

Inaya shook her head. "No, there hasn't been anything like that, that I know of. Some of the younger members harass mosque-goers here on Fridays, but mostly the Disciples herd underage kids out of parties in the foothills and enforce community service on offenders who've vandalized church property. I'm not privy to their other activities."

Seif's posture relaxed. "Maybe nothing to concern us, then."

She wouldn't charge into a case headlong again, but neither would she overlook the nature of this crime. "This was a crucifixion, sir. Of a victim who appears to be Muslim."

The headscarf stripped from the girl had to be relevant. Inaya touched her own braid self-consciously, still unused to the absence of her scarf. Seif followed the gesture, as if he knew her secret—why she'd worn the scarf, why she'd given it up. He hadn't raised it at her interview, or opened up a space where she could get to know him. He kept his distance, coldly formal.

"The sheriff briefed me on the victim—he knows his community. Razan came here from Syria. That's background we'll need to dig into."

His voice dropped a little. If Inaya didn't know better, she might have thought he identified with Razan or with the community she came from. But she'd made that mistake her first day on the job, when she'd guessed his background from his name, and offered him a shortened salaam. He'd looked through her at the greeting, so she'd never done it again.

But any decent person would mourn a young girl's murder, and grudgingly, she decided to credit Seif with that much feeling.

"Get out there," he said now. "Make your own observations."

She didn't protest. Razan needed someone to speak for her, to fight for an answer to the insult of her murder. Someone who understood who she was growing up to be. Inaya was at the exit when Seif murmured her name.

"Inaya."

It surprised her that his pronunciation was perfect. He either called her "Rahman" or he didn't address her at all.

"Sir?"

Her heart stuttered when he asked, "Is there anything you want to tell me? Anything you think I should know?"

Seif studied her in a way that made her think he could read her mind.

"About your competence to work this case."

Inaya closed her eyes to consider. When she opened them again, Seif was watching her, waiting for a misstep.

"Not at present." She sounded unconvincing to herself.

She leaned against the doorjamb, spying Jaime Webb talking to a deputy. She worked well with Jaime, another new recruit. He was candid, funny, and unsullied by policing, eager to be mentored by Seif, and just as eager to be partnered with Inaya.

The sheriff signaled Seif, who nodded, pulling the door wide. He paused for a moment to look down at Inaya.

"Talk to the community. Follow up on the church, bring anything you find to me. And watch your step, Rahman. Don't alienate Addison Grant."

"My first responsibility is to this community. I have to do what's right for them."

"Pay attention, Rahman: that's what I'm telling you to do."

CHAPTER FOUR

Water from last night's rain rushed through the creek, background noise to the whispers Inaya did her best to ignore. The creek wound around the little town set deep in the Rampart Range, homes tucked away in the hills. Some of the houses were ski chalets, others were terra-cotta-roofed ranch-style dwellings. The higher up they were, the better the view of the Chatfield Reservoir, a gleaming shaft of blue against a mud-green horizon. Fat and swollen from the rain, the creek rolled down the hills to empty out at the falls that had given the town its name. At the center of Blackwater Falls was the historic old town, its flower-lined streets leading south to the narrow rim of the falls that spilled over into a pond.

Moving outward from the center in a loose grid were the exclusive gated communities that gave the town its immaculate facade. Farther out from these were battered little clumps of housing, laid out for seasonal workers.

To the west lay the great factories and plants and the massive Lockheed Martin complex, a combination of sprawling concrete boxes and glass towers. Picturesque ranches and the richly green grounds of the Cottonwood Riding Club boxed in the town to the east. The city of Denver was a twenty-minute drive north, a shiny, made-over cow town that bustled with noise and activity while Blackwater Falls slept to the south, now the home of an unspeakable crime.

Inaya met briefly with the families who were waiting for news, telling them they would be notified of developments as soon as there was any information. She was grateful her parents didn't know she was on site. She'd half expected someone from the mosque to call and give them the news. Observing a professional distance would have been harder if they'd shown up to offer support. As it was, she'd had to turn aside questions from women she prayed beside in the mosque.

Now the outside world was closed out, save for the roar of the creek. Inaya stood next to a somber Jaime Webb, assessing the position of the body. The normally talkative Jaime was writing in his notepad, while Seif and the sheriff conferred. It looked like Seif had decided to handle the sheriff himself, not trusting Inaya's tact.

"What was up with you and the lieutenant?" Jaime asked. He sounded like a child concerned about his battling parents.

"He doesn't like me much. I must have done something to get his back up."

"You haven't been with us long, what could you have done? The most exciting thing you've handled is giving out candy at the Expo."

Inaya gave an inelegant snort. "Fainting at the crime scene probably didn't help."

A man who looked hot in his plastic coveralls stepped around them, greeting them with a smile. Inaya could see a hunter green tie through the small opening at his neck. Instead of a mask, he wore a face shield over his glasses. His name tag identified him as Julius Stanger, MD, a pathologist with the Denver police.

"Don't feel bad." The man had overheard. "There's always that one person who adds a personal touch." His tone was gentle. The green eyes behind the glasses crinkled at the corners, inviting her to share his humor, but with Razan's body staked to the door behind his head, Inaya couldn't bring herself to smile.

"Dr. Stanger." If she started to work homicide, their paths would inevitably cross.

"You knew her?"

"Just by sight." The congregation was spread out. Muslim families socialized mainly within their own ethnic groups. So far Inaya had met only other Afghans and Pakistanis.

Stanger's glance fell to the badge pinned to her waistband. "You're DPD?"

Realizing she'd been remiss, she made introductions. "Detective Inaya Rahman and Officer Jaime Webb, Community Response Unit. We're taking over." The sheriff's team went quiet at her words, his deputies alert. Seif had yet to give the command to clear them from the scene. And as long as he was present, she would keep his warnings in mind.

"Is there anything you can tell us about the body?" she asked Stanger.

"There's the obvious. The victim wasn't killed here. There has to be a staging ground."

"Because of the lack of blood?"

"This isn't official, you understand." She nodded to encourage him. "From early signs, I'd say the body was preserved. She wasn't killed this morning, and likely not last night, either."

Inaya looked across the tent to the door. "Her body hasn't decomposed. Somehow she looks cold."

Ice crystals on her brow. Lips and fingertips blue.

"Not talking out of turn, are you, Stanger?"

The sheriff had finished his discussion with Seif. His presence eclipsed Dr. Stanger's, his uninflected voice just that bit louder, his physical presence bullish next to a man of Stanger's lean build. Everything about him was hearty: his thick neck, his florid tan, the incipient jowls that hinted of self-indulgence. He wasn't dissipated—not quite. Perhaps his responsibilities didn't weigh on him as heavily as they should, though he'd have seen his share of darkness. There was a word for the differences in their experience. It eluded her for the moment.

Grant made a move to exclude Stanger, who ignored his cue, offering introductions. Inaya had dismissed Julius Stanger too quickly. While Seif had slipped away, leaving her to deal with the sheriff just as he'd promised, Stanger stood his ground. She took another look at his mild expression—the pale green eyes had turned steely at the sheriff's warning.

"These detectives are from the Community Response Unit."

Stanger remembered their names as he introduced them, another mark in his favor. "This is Addison Grant, sheriff of Blackwater Falls."

Grant took them in with sharp-eyed curiosity, and a suggestion of . . . what? It couldn't be menace. He sounded out her name with less affinity than Stanger had.

"So this is CRU. We've got your mysterious Lieutenant Seif, and you're what—Mexican?" The words were blunt, but spoken without hostility. Grant was testing the waters.

Inaya considered her response. She was dark-eyed, her hair a thick brownish black, her skin brown and unblemished. Despite her distinctly different features, she was often mistaken for Latina and expected to explain her origins. She could have told Grant she was from Illinois—she knew he was asking something else. She was mixed, her roots straddling Central and South Asia, so as a shortcut, she said, "I'm Indian."

When he narrowed his eyes at her, she realized the term meant something else to him. But how could he mistake her for native when he had to be familiar with the state's indigenous peoples? Or was he just playing with her? She clarified to be on the safe side.

"I'm half-Afghan, half-Pakistani." With a conciliatory murmur she hated herself for, she added, "And all-American."

"Is that so." Grant pointed to the body, which was still being photographed. "Sounds like you'd know the victim, then."

Inaya feigned surprise. "The victim is Syrian. That's quite some distance from either Afghanistan or Pakistan."

The sheriff's smile was all teeth.

"All-American is what I meant. Just like you said." Stanger murmured something to him; he gave his assent. "We're going to take her down. You can meet us at the morgue if you like, or you can stay and talk to these folks—your call."

The photographer was nearly finished. It was time to make her position clear, but there was something hovering at the edge of her consciousness—something important.

"Is there a profiler on site, Sheriff?"

"Why? Can't handle this on your own?" He clucked his tongue. "Seif said you could."

She stiffened, catching Stanger's frown from the corner of her eye.

"It's too early to rule anything out, but if you don't have a criminal profiler"—she knew a county substation wouldn't—"I'll call in ours.

It's important Detective Hernandez sees the body in situ, nothing disturbed or rearranged."

The sheriff leaned down a little, light glinting off the stars on his collar. "Will she be another one like you?"

"I don't understand."

"Is she going to come over all . . . ladylike . . . when she sees the body?"

A few of the men laughed, and Inaya felt her face warm, her palms sticky against the fabric of her slacks.

Dr. Stanger spoke up. "Wasn't it last summer that Deputy Perry thought the entrails of a deer he found were actually human remains? He passed out at the sight, as I recall."

Inaya flashed him a grateful glance. Jaime closed his notebook and tucked it away.

"Detective Hernandez is bound to see things we've missed." She read Cat's text on her phone. "She's fifteen minutes away, so I'd rather the body was left as it is. CRU has the scene."

She gave the sheriff a courteous nod. He watched her for a minute without speaking, and she let him make his own assessment of her determination. Abruptly, he emitted a short, sharp whistle. He stepped back, and the look of approval on Stanger's face told her she'd won this round. Activity around the body ceased, and the tent began to clear.

Inaya's relief was fleeting. Grant's head swiveled to the door, his eyes pinned to Razan.

"Be careful," he said, close and low. "I'm not a man you want to cross."

CHAPTER FIVE

Outside the mosque, a commotion was growing. Other families had joined the Somali women who had gathered there in the morning. Deputies from the substation were aggressively moving the barriers back to expand the perimeter. Farther down the street a group of Somali teens raced to the scene, drawn by the cries of the women. They'd come from Main Street, two blocks over; some were carrying take-out cups from a local café, which they dropped as they hurried to confront the police, who swiftly closed ranks behind the barriers.

It took less than a minute for everything to change. Batons came out. The Somali teens chanted at the cops at the barricade. They tried to force the women back out of harm's way; the women linked arms, trying to push the boys back. An officer rushed to his patrol car, turning the siren on. Others rushed to the sheriff's rig, unloading equipment from the back.

Inaya and Jaime ran from the tent to the sound of metal crunching bone. Cries of fear filled the air. There was a concerted push against the barriers by the teens; then they were through, caught up in skirmishes. A woman and a boy fell to the ground, boots kicking at their heads. The boy was wrestled onto his stomach by two Blackwater cops; one put his knee on the boy's back as the other restrained him, then struck the boy's head with his baton. It made a horrifying sound. The boy continued to fight, and when he turned his head to the side, Inaya saw blood on his face. The second cop leaned in, lining up his baton against the boy's dark throat. Both ends of the stick were grasped in his strong hands, exerting pressure on the boy's larynx.

Other confrontations had broken out down the line.

The bright glare of the sun gave the scene an air of unreality, as if a film were being recorded, the sound at a muffled distance. And indeed, there were witnesses who held their cell phones up, recording the naked brutality.

The sheriff wandered out of the tent, making no move to interrupt. He bowed to Inaya, a smirk at the corner of his mouth.

"Call your men off!" she shouted.

"It's your scene," he said with relish.

Jaime plunged into the melee to rescue a woman being trampled. Inaya followed at his back. A blow bounced off her shoulder as she wriggled her way between the blue line and the members of the crowd who had pushed through the barricade. Nearly everyone was taller than she was, but she had Jaime at her side as a bulwark. She shouted herself hoarse. It did nothing to stop Grant's men, and she saw with horror that a woman's shawl was stained with blood, the side of her face badly bruised. She called to the women to fall back.

Jaime threw himself at the cop who was choking the boy with his baton. The stick went flying from the officer's hand, skirting the hot pavement. Someone in the crowd picked it up and waved it, and in slow motion Inaya watched as a young officer reached down to unholster his gun. The whole scene had narrowed to the gun in his shaking hand. Either he couldn't hear Inaya's orders, or he chose to ignore them. His gun hand came up, sliding past Inaya's waving arms to focus on another target.

Frozen with dread, she waited for the shot, sweat trickling down her back.

A bullhorn sounded instead, two sharp blasts.

The combatants fell back as a tall Black woman stepped onto the scene.

"Enough!" she said through the bullhorn. She stepped onto the curb to give herself added height, her back to the crowd, her hand pointed in warning to the sheriff. "You know who I am. Get your boys back, Sheriff Grant."

She pivoted on her heel to face the other way.

"We've got this," she told the crowd. "We're not going to let this slide." She pointed at a few individuals who were recording with their cell phones. "Let's get that evidence secured."

When she turned to face the sheriff again, Inaya's mouth gaped at her beauty. Bronze skin and beautifully expressive eyes, cheekbones set at a high slant, lips colored a rich cherry, curls brushing her shoulders. She was poised between two highly charged groups yet had total command of the scene.

To the sheriff's men, she said, "This community is not the enemy, so I suggest you stand down. We'll be reporting your actions; expect a lawsuit to follow."

Grant ignored her, calling for arrests. "Round 'em up," he bellowed.

Inaya stepped into his path.

"Your team is off this," she told him. "There won't be any arrests unless they're for violation of the use-of-force guidelines."

He checked himself, his head jerking between the Black woman and Inaya. "You wanna make nice with that pain in the ass, you have my blessing, but those boys threw the first punch. No one attacks my men."

"They're just kids." Inaya lowered her voice. "They want to know what's happening at their mosque. We should be talking to them."

Grant jabbed a finger at Inaya. "You're deluding yourself if you think they don't see you as the enemy." He spoke into his radio, calling off his team.

He shoulder-checked her as he brushed past her. Expecting it, she held her ground, glad to see him go. Ambulances arrived amidst the chaos. A handful of CRU officers were all she had to work with to keep control. She gave them instructions and left them to it, searching for the boy who'd nearly been choked to death. She found him sitting on the sidewalk next to Jaime, who'd taken the time to uncuff him and apply basic first aid.

The boy was breathing harshly, his shoulders bent over his knees. She didn't try to question him, surprised by his red-rimmed eyes. This muscular young man—not a boy as she'd thought—was crying. He wore a white cap over his curls and had a wispy goatee. She did a quick scan of the rest of him. No tattoos that she could see, no weapons, no gang colors. A white T-shirt with a graphic that said "Malcolm was right" and tapered Adidas pants.

Before he could fire up at her, she gave him a calm salaam.

He offered her a grudging "Wa alaikum salaam." Then he couldn't contain himself and burst out, "You're on the wrong side, sister."

Seif had told her she was uniquely placed to respond to the concerns of the mosque community.

Not CRU as a whole, just her.

That was working out well.

CHAPTER SIX

Seif answered his cell phone, recognizing the number as his source on a case he was working. Less frequently than he liked, the source called in with tips for Seif to follow up.

"You have something for me?"

"A warning only, this time."

The voice was bland, almost robotic, Seif couldn't guess at the age or race of the caller, though he knew it was a man.

"Fire away."

"If you start with violence, you'll end the same way."

Impatiently, he checked his watch. "I don't like riddles—be clear."

"Ask yourself why the sheriff preys on the Somali community."

"What proof do you have of that?"

"Look outside the window."

He strode through the interior of the mosque, absorbing the details of the scene. Crime scene techs were at work under Dr. Stanger's direction. As he neared the exit, he heard the noise outside. He paused before a window and saw Inaya and Jaime sitting beside a Black teen. They were consoling him, even as a crowd gathered.

He canvassed the street for the sheriff. Grant and his men were gone, but not without sabotaging the start he'd hoped to make. The seeds of a headache formed behind his temples. Another mess to sort when his focus had to be elsewhere.

"I hear you," he said into the phone, but his source had ended the call.

Whoever he was, he had eyes on Seif, because he knew Seif was at the scene just as he'd been a front-row witness to a dose of police violence.

Seif scanned the scene again, searching for someone who stood out. He saw members of the mosque community, and the neighbors who'd come to support them, plus the few boutique and café owners whom Grant had pointed out earlier.

It would be a huge break in his case if he could identify his source. He should see if he could smoke him out. But that could also spook his quarry, who'd cooperated until now.

He slipped out the back, heading to his car. He'd put Inaya in charge. It was time for her to step up.

CHAPTER SEVEN

"Let's talk."

Areesha Adams handed Inaya a card, and reading it, Inaya felt her stomach tense as if she'd been punched. The woman was a community organizer, a civil rights lawyer with a cause. She'd already threatened a lawsuit.

Areesha gestured at the mosque. "There's a room inside we can use, and I think it's important to feel each other out."

The scene outside had quieted after Areesha had spoken with leaders of the Somali community. The women had herded their sons home because Areesha had promised to get answers for them.

"Give me a moment."

Inaya walked back to the tent and ducked through to call Seif. He answered on the first ring. She brought him up to speed on the confrontation, and then asked, "Did you know there's a lawyer on this case? Her name is Areesha Adams. Have you heard of her?"

She held the phone away from her ear as Seif swore.

"She's a pain in the DPD's ass. If she's involved, the investigation is fucked."

"Sir, I think Adams is ahead of us on this." She noticed that Jaime had followed her, and she motioned him closer. "She seems to know the community, and if I had to guess, I'd say she's built trust with them."

"Don't guess, Rahman, find out. Let her in, but keep your guard up. She'll be looking for mistakes."

They were already past that point, so she told Seif the rest.

"There was a kid in the crowd, sir. A Somali kid named Omar. I don't know him from the mosque. He was worried that the body we found could be that of his sister. Do you know anything about a missing teenage girl? Someone other than Razan?"

This time Seif's curse was inaudible. He gave it a beat, then told her, "I'll look into it and get back to you. Stay sharp, Rahman."

She could tell he was about to cut her off. With the way Grant's officers had ignored her orders, she needed her position spelled out. "Sir, to be clear, am I the officer in charge?"

"What the fuck do you think?"

The call went dead with that.

"Always a pleasure," Inaya muttered, sliding her phone into her bag. She'd forgotten about Jaime, who'd been hanging on her every word. A slow grin spread across his face like he'd just been handed a gift.

"No love lost?" he teased.

Inaya made a chopping motion.

"I said nothing, you heard nothing."

Jaime continued to grin, so Inaya made him write down her instructions.

"We need DPD officers securing the perimeter. See who might be willing to loan us a few; use my name if you need to. Ask Dr. Stanger when we might have a time of death, and back up Cat if she needs some time with the victim. Tell her to take her own photographs."

Jaime's writing may have looked like chicken scratch, but Inaya knew he hadn't missed a word. He was amiable and eager to please; he was also sharp enough to have been recruited to CRU by Seif. He even managed to crush on her without making her uncomfortable.

"One more thing."

"Name it." Jaime looked up, and for a moment his expression was unguarded, his eyes hopeful on her face. Inaya pretended not to notice.

"I need you to find a prayer space that can stand in for the mosque. We have to start delivering on our promise of community response."

CHAPTER EIGHT

"You're in the wrong game, lady." Areesha's observation held no malice.

It was almost the same thing as Omar had said. Inaya moved closer to the tent, where the bustle of activity continued. Jaime came up to join them, his pleasant face flushing as he took in Areesha up close.

"No." Areesha waved Jaime away. "This is just your detective and me. I'll have plenty to ask you about your role in this confrontation later."

Jaime cleared his throat. "Boss?" he asked. Inaya had tried to break him of that habit, but had gotten nowhere. He called all his superiors "boss." Better than "ma'am," she figured, though she was hopeless at sounding officious. She told Jaime to make himself scarce.

"Detective Hernandez will be here soon," he informed her.

"Good. I'll join you in a few."

He looked at her hopefully, his thumbs tucked into his belt. "Thought I'd learn something from the best if I stuck around."

"We need a few minutes, Jaime."

"Boss."

Both women watched him go. He turned his head and caught them at it, flashing Inaya a smile.

"That boy is sweet on you, Detective."

Inaya dismissed this out of hand. "He's just young." She didn't have much time. She wanted to catch Dr. Stanger before he left. "This community seems to have put their faith in you. I'd like to know why before I give you anything."

Areesha crossed her arms. Her handbag slid down her shoulder to her elbow.

"Zero-sum game, huh? Give to get."

Inaya shrugged. "You said you wanted my help."

"I did *not* say that. I said, 'You're in the wrong game.'"

"Meaning?"

Areesha pulled back the sleeve of her jacket to expose her arm. She held it up to Inaya's, making a comparison.

"You're the wrong color for this job—you'll burn out faster. I've heard about you, you're new. Which means you have no idea what's been going on here. The sheriff is going to skin your carcass and leave you out to dry."

Inaya winced at the description. "I can handle Grant. And I'm no stranger to homicide."

Areesha tensed up. "You've confirmed this is a homicide?"

Thinking on her feet, Inaya lifted the tent flap. "See for yourself."

"Holy Mother of God, she's white," Areesha breathed.

There was something in the statement that puzzled Inaya, but she nodded. "She's Syrian. But what I think you're missing is that she's Muslim, and her family came here as refugees, a vulnerable, under-served group, and that's why CRU is here."

Areesha was shaking her head, a stunned look in her eyes. "You came here because she's white. The sheriff set up this investigation be-cause that girl is white."

Something pinged in Inaya's mind, something she had to pin down. "Why is the color of the victim important? Why did Omar think the victim was his sister?"

Areesha bit her lip, a little of her cherry lipstick staining her white teeth.

Inaya didn't know she'd been so tense—her body relaxed at this sign that the other woman was fallible.

"We can't talk here, not properly." She nodded at the card Inaya held. "When you set up a meet with me, don't bring Officer Webb."

Inaya slid the card into her pocket. "We haven't done a next-of-kin notification. So you need to keep what I've told you quiet."

"That won't be a problem." She looked Inaya over again and came to a decision. "Listen, whatever path they direct you down, ask questions about the Resurrection Church. It's a cornerstone of this community."

Inaya had seen that for herself—the huge, imposing structure backed onto Rampart Range, traffic stretching all down Titan Road for Sunday service.

"Why Resurrection?" she prodded.

Areesha jerked her chin at the tent.

"Because the hate we face in this community trickles down from the church."

CHAPTER NINE

"Detective Hernandez is here."

"Good."

She walked down with Jaime to meet Cat at her car.

Catalina Rivera Hernandez was Inaya's unofficial partner at CRU. They'd been assigned to numerous outreach programs together, and had developed an easy working relationship based on an understanding of the things they had in common, outsiders in a world hostile to the communities they came from. Cat had come to CRU from Nogales, a town that straddled the border between Arizona and the state of Sonora in Mexico. She'd run an NGO called We Rise Together that offered legal and medical services to those who crossed the border without official documents. And those who crossed the border in search of work weren't her only constituency. She represented many of the undocumented who had been in America for decades, but who were now swept up at Border Patrol checkpoints that tunneled into Arizona, or ICE raids in communities where the rent was cheap enough for seasonal workers to be housed.

Most of the people she worked hard to serve were Mexican. Cat herself was a third-generation Chicana. The rest came from places like Guatemala, Honduras, and Nicaragua. We Rise Together provided the same services to all, and had opened a second chapter in Denver, which her husband took over when Cat had defected to the police.

Cat had been recruited to their small team by Seif, who to Inaya's surprise had convinced Cat to sign on by quoting her the stats on the arrest and incarceration of Latinx individuals in the county. Seif told Cat she would do more good working within the system; he gave her carte blanche to develop community-centered programs with whatever budget they had. Before the George Floyd protests, this budget had been nonexistent. Now money was raining down on CRU, and Cat had put it to good use.

That wasn't the only reason Seif had brought her on board. Cat was a former trauma therapist who'd transferred to criminal psychology. As a profiler, she was frequently loaned out on cases, but in the case of Razan Elkader's murder, they'd need to keep her in-house.

Inaya hid a smile as Cat jumped down from the SUV she drove. She was tiny, shorter and more rounded than Inaya, with an irresistible warmth. Her car seemed huge beside her.

"You're early," Cat said by way of greeting.

"I'm lead on this."

"Excellent." Cat showed her dimples to Jaime. "Hey, Jaime, *mi pequeño*, you good?"

Jaime was six foot three.

"Better once we get her down."

"Dr. Stanger is waiting on you, Cat," Inaya said.

When Cat saw the body, she crossed herself, bowing her head out of respect.

"Come," she called the others.

A rustle of amusement ran around the tent. Mockery of Cat's somberness or her diminutive stature. The same man who'd called out "Fuckin' A" now said, "Looks like we got a diversity parade going on here." He added a few epithets. A few of the other men laughed.

"Shut it," Jaime said, red-faced and belligerent.

Cat ignored the byplay, shaking hands with Dr. Stanger.

"The poor child." She grimaced at Inaya. "I need to sit and study her." She turned to Stanger. "You'll have photographs?"

"Of the position and scene," he confirmed.

"Then I'll just observe."

Jaime procured a plastic chair from somewhere, and Cat settled in, breathing slowly, her hands folded in her lap.

Inaya didn't disturb her. She was studying the body herself, looking for things she'd missed. The scene was deliberate, the body too delicately styled to be the work of vigilantes. If the Disciples escalated from harassment to murder, they'd do it execution-style and dump the body in the reservoir. Unless they were meant to think that.

Cat whispered, "*Madre de Dios.*"

After a respectful pause, Inaya said, "We'll get forensics on the ribbon once she's down."

Inaya had become deeply fond of Cat as they'd worked together these past months. Her pragmatism was a good foil for Cat's fertile imagination, as Cat believed the dead confided in her when the silence of the living turned to stone.

She rose from her chair, pacing from one side of the body to the other, pointing to the girl's scarf. Most of the girl's hair was exposed, defeating the purpose of the headscarf, as she'd explained to Cat.

"The scarf is draped like the Virgin Mary's."

"Mary wasn't crucified," Inaya whispered. At her side, Jaime looked sick.

Cat's hand touched the blue dress. "'*Mary folds round him her mantle of blue.*' The symbolism is unmistakable. The positioning of the body is equally deliberate. He sees the girl both as who she is and who she isn't. Muslim *and* Christian—hence the allusion to Mary. Young and chaste, unless he touched her."

"We won't know that until Dr. Stanger gets her on the table," Jaime put in.

"Is the stab wound above her ribs the only wound?" Cat asked. He gave her a slow blink. Inaya had caught on. Jaime still wasn't there.

"The holy wound. So a Christian death for a Muslim girl."

Inaya's face tightened in acknowledgment.

"Possibly a connection to the local church, if he's superimposing one identity on top of another." Inaya briefed them on what she knew about the Disciples.

Cat looked thoughtful. "Vigilantes might be involved—someone strong had to heft her up that high. But the mind that directed this—that arranged a tableau for us, in effect—belongs to someone who thinks of himself as an artist."

"You're sure it's a man?"

"The strength involved to hoist her up on the door? Wouldn't it have to be? It's strange, too, that the pose seems almost worshipful."

Jaime looked confused. "Boss, Christians don't worship Mary, they worship Jesus."

Cat crossed herself again. "They—we—revere her, which is a different thing." She squeezed Inaya's hand in a gesture of consolation. "That's what this killing is. Not a crucifixion—a veneration."

They looked up at the girl on the door, at the tragedy of death.

The sacrifice of God for man reflected in the Virgin's endless grief.

CHAPTER TEN

After finishing with the scene the previous day, Inaya was ready for work the next morning when her mother met her at the door, a familiar light in her eyes—the light of battle. It was time to discuss Inaya's marital prospects, her least favorite subject, and she knew the conversation wouldn't end well. She rehearsed it in her mind. She was failing at the task of being an eldest daughter, and worse, she was setting a bad example for her sisters. If Inaya resisted marriage, why should Noor or Nadia agree to it? There would be no distinguished sons-in-law who would expand their clan, no long-awaited grandchildren to comfort her parents in their old age.

Even if Inaya had been willing to argue the subject, she didn't have time for it now. She was supposed to lead a team briefing, and was rushing around collecting her things while her mother chased her, her kind face anxious yet imperious. It was the particular gift of Pakistani mothers to calibrate doses of guilt alongside maternal affection.

Inaya stopped her search for her keys to pat her mother on the cheek. They were the same middling height, but other than that, there was nothing that would indicate they were family. Sunober Rahman, like Inaya's younger sisters, was slender and light-skinned with pale, clever eyes. Inaya's father fit the same mold, whereas Inaya was dark in her coloring, more rounded than her sisters, but given the nature of her job, also more physically fit. She took after some distant member of the family, but among her own small clan, she looked like a foundling.

This didn't bother her. Only her mother's attitude toward her striking non-likeness did.

"*Beta*," her mother said now. "You are killing yourself for this job, and why? It's dangerous, it's unsafe, you could be making much more money as a lawyer, your colleagues don't respect you—"

"Only my boss," Inaya interjected. "The rest have been very kind."

"And not only the criminals—the public hates you." Her mother carried on undeterred as Inaya shrugged her jacket on, scooping her purse from a console in the hall. Down the spacious hall from the kitchen, she heard her father boom, "Leave the girl alone. She needs to focus on her job."

"Some job," her mother railed. "Murder and madness make her happy. Your daughter is almost thirty, and is there a man in her life? Is she willing to meet one? No, of course not. She prefers the company of criminals, and God knows what she does at night."

Gently, Inaya caught her mother's arm. "Hush, Ami. You know I'd never do anything to make you ashamed of me. All I'm doing is working at a job I'm good at, a job that makes me happy, so can we just let this go?"

"No chance!"

The words were shouted down the stairs by Inaya's sister Noor, whose bright head appeared around the banister, mischief in her eyes.

"You're not helping," Inaya shot back.

Tears began to gather in Sunober's eyes, but they'd been used against Inaya too often for her to be discomfited.

"All I ever wanted was for my daughters to find husbands who would be good to them, and give them children as beautiful as my own. Yes." Her mother nodded emphatically. "You *are* as beautiful as your sisters, even though—" She waved a hand at Inaya's face. "You are my Black Beauty. I'm still very proud of you."

"Mum, that's racist," Noor shouted down. "You can't say things like that. Plus, you're going to give Inaya a complex."

"Too late," Inaya shouted back, a hint of laughter in her voice.

"You know what I mean," her mother said impatiently. "There's nothing wrong with being *saanvli*—I'm saying I like it. All these rules of your country, I don't understand."

"Your country too, Ma."

Noor sashayed down the stairs to join them. Their mother was right—Noor was stunning, and she knew it. She wore skintight jeans that faithfully traced her curves, teamed with a lemon silk blouse that drifted off one shoulder, the color a perfect complement to her auburn hair and tilted-at-the-corners green eyes. Her makeup was applied with an expert hand. A tangle of gold chains at her throat matched the earrings that glinted through her hair. Today she'd pulled it back with a soft yellow ribbon that drew attention to her smooth forehead.

"Baba's driving you to school today," Inaya told her. "I have to get to work." She slipped her keys into her bag, her hand pausing by the navy blue scarf that hung on a peg by the door. Noor jerked the scarf out of Inaya's grasp.

"You don't need it, *baji*. You've been doing so good without it. And you look gorgeous with your hair out, no caveats." She offered their mother a glare. "Though I really hate that braid. You should let me style you sometime."

"Don't even think about it." Inaya kissed her sister on the cheek. At twenty-two, Noor was seven years younger than Inaya, in her senior year of college studying fashion design, but in terms of brushing up against the darkness of Inaya's job, they were worlds of experience apart. Just like their youngest sister, Nadia, who despite being prelaw was just as unworldly as Noor. "It's only hair. It's not that important."

That wasn't true, but it wasn't true in a way she couldn't explain. She was the only woman in her family who'd worn a headscarf until she'd given it up when she moved to Blackwater Falls. She still felt naked without it. Not in the titillating sense of being exposed, but in terms of what it said about her spiritual commitment.

Without the scarf on her head, she felt like everyone could see her internal struggle. But she knew the scarf didn't make her who she was, so how could its absence *un*make her?

If Inaya hadn't come up with answers to these questions, how could her mother or Noor understand? Her mother was relieved Inaya had given up her scarf. She thought it made her a target, but Inaya refused to consider herself a victim. When it came to her sister, Noor disagreed with Inaya on everything. She styled herself beautifully for her social media accounts, which wasn't a problem in itself, but she was secretive with her phone, which concerned Inaya. Even so, they weren't at the same place in their lives; they didn't worship in the same way. Inaya didn't begrudge Noor her choices, she just didn't want to have to justify herself. After all, she wasn't a child. But in her parents' home, she was always subject to correction.

"Fix your shirt, *budtameez*. What if your father sees you?" Her mother's sharp voice drew Inaya out of her thoughts. Noor drew up her blouse with an air of nonchalance, covering her exposed shoulder. She glided down the hall to the kitchen with a wink at her older sister.

Inaya's hand was on the doorknob when her mother spoke behind her.

"Your sisters don't understand because they're young, but you should listen to me, *beta*. This time in your life won't come again. You're missing all your chances. I could understand if you were still practicing law, but this work you're doing now—anyone could do it. And you're such a bright girl. I'm not saying don't work—I live in this century. I'm saying work at something that matters. Something that won't send your father into an early grave."

"We've been over this—"

Her mother threw up her hands. "Fine, fine. But tell me this." She picked up the headscarf that had fluttered to the floor. "You wore your hijab to proclaim your faith to strangers. That is your duty, you think. But you know that marriage is half of faith. So explain to me why you obey some duties, but forget the ones that would please your father and me."

The charge was unfair. Inaya had tried her best. She'd had a proposal from a man named Yusuf who didn't mind that she wasn't a doctor, a man she'd grown to care for, but when he'd told her she'd had to give up her career to focus on building his, she'd realized that though

Yusuf might have loved her, he didn't understand who she was at her core.

"Mum, I can't discuss this again. And please don't drag Baba into this. He supports my choices."

Sunober nodded her head, but there was something ominous about the gesture, and Inaya braced for the rest.

"This is selfish of you, *beta*. You've gone your own way with your work, though your father wanted you to work with him at his firm. Fine. I accept that. But your sisters will never have a better chance than now to find suitable partners, and you are standing in their way. I say no to everyone who asks for them because I have an older daughter who refuses to get married."

Inaya balked at the accusation. "I'm not standing in their way. I'd be nothing but happy for either of them, if marriage is what they want—though they're too young to figure that out. And when you don't have time to figure yourself out, that's when you make mistakes."

"And what about *your* mistakes? A *rishta* has come for you, and at your age, they're harder to come by. He's a physician from a good family, he's well-known, and he's responsible. So what do you want me to do? There's a family that wants to meet Noor next week."

Inaya sighed. "Then let them meet Noor. I'll make sure I'm home to help."

Hope brightened her mother's eyes. Inaya felt sick at the sight of it.

"And what about your *rishta*?"

Her father came into the hall to stand behind her mother. He was dressed in a navy blue suit for work, his tie neat and elegant, his polished leather briefcase in one hand. He wrapped his arm around his wife's shoulders, and as Inaya looked into the gently aging face that bore the marks of his journey from Afghanistan to America, a rush of affection washed over her. Her father would never throw her to the wolves; he would talk her mother around.

"You are speaking to my daughter about marriage when she needs to keep her mind on her job? What she does is important, *khanum*. And with this case—" The lightness left his tone. "She's serving our community. You should admire that in her."

Her mother was lost for words. She shrugged free of her husband's hold. "Admire that my daughter is mixing with the most dangerous people she could find?"

Haseeb cut her diatribe short. "What if it was one of *our* daughters, *khanum*? Nailed to the door of the mosque? Wouldn't you want someone like Inaya working to give us answers?"

"*Astaghfirullah.*" Sunober spat out the word. "May a day like that never come."

"Then let our daughter do her job so no other family has to face that."

Sunober turned on him fiercely. "You find someone to marry her, then! A *rishta* like this won't come our way again. He's Pashto-speaking, he's handsome, and his mother says his character is beyond reproach."

"His mother *would* say that," her father said with a twinkle. "Besides, Inaya doesn't speak Pashto, so why should that matter to her?"

Inaya was struggling to learn her father's language. As a child, she had spoken it well, but as with anything left unused for too long, her affinity for Pashto had faded, a regret she still felt, though her father had never minded. Her mother's native tongue held sway in the home, and all three of her daughters were fluent in the Urdu language.

Inaya's phone buzzed in her purse. Probably her boss demanding her ETA: Seif wasn't the patient sort, and she couldn't see herself tendering an explanation about her family dynamics. To cut things short, she asked, "What do you think, Baba?"

His twinkle became bolder. "My darling child, any man who meets you will fall at your feet and be dazzled like Majnun for the rest of his natural life."

"Haseeb!" his wife reproached him. "No more fairy tales. Make the girl see sense!"

Inaya's father stood between his wife and daughter, his kind face lit with sympathy.

"There's no harm in a meeting, *jaanum*. After that, the choice will be yours, not ours."

Inaya's phone buzzed again, reminding her this was no time for a discussion about a world where women didn't age out of the possibility of marriage when they hit thirty, or need to get married at all. Her father had extended her all the grace he could.

She gave in, reaching for the door again.

"Arrange for Noor to meet her *rishta*, if she's keen. And I'll meet this handsome doctor of yours, but I'm not making any promises."

Delighted to have gotten her way, Inaya's mother was all smiles as she fluttered a hand at Inaya. "Go, go. I'll call his mother at once."

When they were alone, Inaya confided in her father, "You know I haven't sorted out my future plans. I'm not ready for this, Baba. I need to make myself whole before I consider getting married. I only agreed to meet this guy to get Ami off my back."

Her father passed a gentle hand over her head, his way of blessing her.

"The work of this world for each one of us is to make ourselves whole. You aren't alone in that, *beti*." He touched his forehead to hers. "But do not speak of yourself as incomplete, hmm? You are the reason the sun shines, the reason God created daughters. Now please, for me, be careful at your job. And take your time making your decision."

His eyes were on the scarf that Inaya had placed on the console.

He wasn't speaking about the stranger she'd just agreed to meet.

CHAPTER ELEVEN

The CRU was housed in the Police Administration Building, a complex whose architectural style was characterized by plenty of concrete. The narrow windows choked off the light, which took some doing in a city with so much sunshine. Glass doors opened onto a patchwork of cubicles and desks, a color scheme of mostly gray and beige, though some thoughtful individual had dotted sweet-smelling potted plants around the floor. One wall held a community notice board beside another that displayed action items for their team. Beneath this, the team's command structure was pinned, but in bold letters beside it was a mantra that had flowed down from the top: "NEW USE OF FORCE GUIDELINES IN EFFECT."

Inaya's and Cat's desks faced each other, Jaime's was set off to the side behind Cat's, so that whenever Inaya looked up from her desk she encountered Jaime's moon-faced stare. She couldn't understand what he saw in her—she was six years older than he was, which placed her in another galaxy, not to mention they had different vocabularies when it came to policing: Jaime eager and optimistic, Inaya burned in the crucible of police accountability.

The public hates you.

You're in the wrong game, lady.

She shook off her mother's complaint even as Areesha's warning burrowed deep.

Seif had called a team briefing, and officers were staged all around the room. Inaya had the floor, going over the actions she'd taken. She was followed by Cat, who gave her initial read on the nature of the crime. "It's too early to draw any definitive conclusions, but the killing is so carefully staged that I'd be surprised if it was his first. We should rule out any similar homicides."

Seif was leaning against the wall. He hadn't taken issue with any of Inaya's actions, but now he pinned Catalina down.

"Anything like this would have been flagged by now."

"Sir." Inaya held up a hand. "I spoke to Areesha, at the scene. She hinted there was some history to the crime in Blackwater, and the youth I told you about—Omar Abdi—was searching for his sister."

Seif frowned at her. "Did either of them mention the discovery of a body?"

"Well, no, but I'm meeting Areesha later to follow up."

"No," Seif said sharply. "In case you haven't heard, she's threatened us with a lawsuit. She's looking for mistakes; we're not handing her any."

The team's eyes came to her. Flushing, she persisted, "She knows something."

"I don't care. This is non-negotiable, Rahman." His eyes cut back to Cat. "Finish what you were saying, Catalina."

Inaya was "Rahman" to Seif, and other members of the team were addressed by their surnames, but with Cat he used her first name, giving it a liquid Spanish pronunciation. Inaya resented the favoritism. Maybe if she had a doctorate in psychology, he'd speak to her the same way.

Cat's glance flashed her way, warm and sympathetic, the dimples firmly suppressed.

Sounding like she was thinking aloud, she said, "I don't know that this killer limits himself to Blackwater or even to Colorado. With an MO this detailed, we should be broadening our search. I'll have more to tell you once I've seen the pathologist's report."

Seif assigned the search to a junior officer, who walked to his desk to get to work.

"Any other possibilities?"

Cat tipped her head to the side. "If it's not a serial, then I can't quite explain the care with which the body was arranged. I'll need to think about it."

"We have time," Seif agreed. He addressed the whole team. "We've located the parents. I'd like Catalina and Rahman to do the notification, and to turn that into an interview. We need to know how long Razan had been missing, and why the parents didn't report it."

"Maybe they did," Inaya offered. "The sheriff was angry at being sidelined. That could be about more than just ego."

Seif turned on her. "You lead with assumptions like that, you'll fuck this whole case up."

"It's a legitimate line of inquiry." Inaya looked to Jaime to back her up. He jumped to her defense.

"Grant was uncooperative, sir. His men were a lot worse, insulting the detectives. They provoked the community, and left us to clean up their mess."

Seif was gentler with Jaime, their youngest team member, than he'd been with Inaya. "There's a lot of personalities in law enforcement, Webb, and we're stepping on their toes. Try to keep an open mind."

Jaime set his jaw to stubborn. "I won't about the racism, boss."

Neither Cat nor Inaya had mentioned to Seif the racial slurs they'd encountered, and now Inaya felt a sudden fondness for Jaime. He was decent down to his bones.

"Fair enough." Seif moved the meeting on. "Other things we need to dig into once you've spoken to the parents. A timeline of Razan's movements. Who saw her last, and where? The clothes she was wearing: the shawl, the brooches, the ribbon—where did they come from? What about her personal effects: her cell phone, laptop, and so on? Are they at her home? We also need to track her family, her friends, any and all of her contacts. We follow her life online. We'll narrow our lines of inquiry down once we have a time of death from Stanger. Stay sharp, think ahead, and get to work. And keep this tight. No one speaks to outsiders. If inside information is leaked, I won't hesitate to kick you off the team, and that will be the least of your worries."

His gaze came back to Inaya as if he expected her to protest. She'd already moved on.

"Sir, instead of Cat and me doing the notification, maybe you should handle it."

Impatience flared in his eyes. "Why?"

"As part of our community outreach efforts. The Elkader family is Syrian—Arab—so you might make a stronger connection."

A collective silence filled the room. Seif pointed one finger at Inaya. "You. With me. Now."

Seif stalked to his office at the opposite end of the room.

Angry herself now, Inaya moved to join him. Cat put a cautioning hand on her shoulder, giving it a little squeeze. "Try not to kill him," she said. "I like having you for a partner."

In spite of herself, Inaya's lips twitched. "It might be the other way around."

She joined Seif in his office, where he banged the door shut, galvanizing the whole team to get back to business. The door might have afforded Inaya some privacy for her dressing-down if the entire office hadn't been paneled in glass. Seif liked to keep an eye on things.

Seif flung himself into his chair, but didn't invite her to sit. She took the bit between her teeth, refusing to wait with her hands folded behind her like a troublesome child. Plus Seif had once joked with the team that his surname was proof that CRU was a safe place to work. The verdict was still out on that.

"*Now* what have I done?"

His eyes narrowed, and he stood up, setting his hands on his desk. "Don't take that tone with me." He shoved a file on the desk toward her. Her eyes came to rest on an upside-down picture of Razan still mounted to the door. From this angle, she looked like she was floating.

"Do you pray at the Blackwater mosque?"

Immediately, Inaya's back went up.

"Not that it's any of your business, but yes."

Seif leaned forward. "We learned from interviews Grant's deputies conducted that Razan's family worships at that mosque. So if you need a 'connection' to do a death notice, you have one. You don't need to out me in front of the team. That's the first point."

Inaya couldn't help it. Though Seif hadn't moved again, she took a step back in dismay. She noticed now that despite his dark coloring, Seif's skin was as light as Grant's.

"'Out you,' sir?"

She didn't know it, but her expression was troubled.

"That I'm Arab or Iranian or anything else. If I wanted people to slot me into a box, I'd do it myself."

"But your name—" She found it difficult to hold his eyes. "Your name gives it away."

"Only to you, and that's how I prefer it. Now to the second point—"

"Are you ashamed of your background?"

She said it disbelievingly, knowing that if he admitted it, she wouldn't just be disappointed, she'd lose all confidence in him.

He glanced past her to the team. To Cat sitting at her desk, working up a profile.

"Identity politics aren't part of our job."

At Community Response? Inaya couldn't leave it alone.

"All politics are identity politics. It's just that some groups hold all the power."

His gaze flickered. His voice changed as he said her name, his tone low and confiding.

"There are things I want to do in this job, Inaya. I need the tools to do them, and this is one of those tools. Do you get what I'm saying?"

He sounded frustrated at having to explain it, as if he thought she'd understood.

And she had. She felt like a fool at the way she'd overstepped, too quick to make things personal. With a wry attempt at humor, she said, "So you don't want to meet the parents?"

His grin disarmed her. "Funny, Rahman," he said. "I'm on another lead."

She raised her eyebrows. "Do tell."

"When I'm ready." He hesitated. "Your family—they're religious?"

This time she didn't make the mistake of assuming any personal interest. "They worship at the same mosque, if that's what you mean. They may even know the Elkaders."

"Okay. They ask questions, you don't answer. Nothing about this case is open for discussion, I don't care how close you and your parents are."

Of course he didn't. And he was calling her professionalism into question.

She never discussed her cases with her family, but the news about Razan had spread through the community. She hoped they reached the Elkaders first.

A warning bell sounded in her mind about the Disciples.

"Does the community need to be warned about these vigilantes?"

"I'll put out a statement."

"In person?" She tried to think of a meeting place. The mosque would be best, but depending on what they found, it could be an active crime scene for weeks. Maybe the community center or the sheriff's station. They could post a notice outside the mosque about the statement, or send it out through the online newsletter.

"What about the sheriff's station?" The look of officialdom might give the community a sense that something was being done.

"Leave the sheriff to me."

"Will you debrief me on how that goes?"

"If necessary," he said coolly.

Inaya found this odd. They were working the same case, so why was Seif so secretive? Was it just her he didn't want to include?

"If you don't want to brief me, you can tell Cat; she'll bring me up to speed."

It was the wrong thing to say. His mood altered, the air in the room growing heavy. Even then, she wasn't ready for his aggressive response.

"You think I'm focused on personalities? That you're my main consideration when a sixteen-year-old girl has been murdered? You think a lot of yourself."

Inaya's mouth went dry. She hadn't overstepped that far, had she?

"For God's sake, learn to act a little more like Catalina. Now get out of my office and get on with your job."

"Sir," she said woodenly.

She left his office and went straight to the bathroom. Catalina joined her there.

"Was it as bad as you thought?"

"Not really. He's got a temper, but we know that. He seems a little off about this case."

"He's sensitive about his background."

Inaya had gleaned as much. "Why? I came up in a hard school, and I don't give a damn what others think. He should be proud of who he is."

"Just because he's private doesn't mean he isn't proud."

"If I understood him a little better, we wouldn't butt heads so often."

Cat's pretty face softened. "That will come in time. Now, shall we take Jaime with us?"

"He's too clumsy. The Elkaders might feel crowded by his size."

"Then you have to let him down."

Inaya groaned. "No, you."

Cat had succeeded in lifting her mood. Her focus returned to Razan.

"Let's do this. I'll take lead—you'll observe?"

"Cat and mouse," Cat replied.

Inaya pushed open the door. "They're not guilty of anything, Cat."

Cat looked thoughtful. "Then why didn't they report their only daughter missing?"

CHAPTER TWELVE

Fatima and Hassan Elkader lived outside the gated communities of Blackwater, on the fringes of Rampart Range. Good views, but poor housing, small bungalows lumped together on zigzag trails, paint peeling, corrugated tin stacked up on dry, dusty lawns where only weeds survived.

There was no meandering creek here, no Kentucky-style white fencing for the pastures and corrals that expanded from Castle Pines to the reservoir. Just a bus stop at the end of the twisting hill road that collected passengers from the fringes and dumped them off downtown or at Lockheed Martin, the county's biggest employer.

To their credit, the Elkaders had made an effort with their home. A colorful braided runner ran the length of the porch. Ceramic pots filled with geraniums framed a freshly painted door. Tucked under a rusted mailbox was a small Syrian flag. The sight of it caused a lump to rise in Inaya's throat. The Elkaders had come to America as refugees, fleeing Syria's civil war. They'd come in search of safety. Razan's murder was proof they'd failed to find it.

Inaya pointed out the flag to Cat. "Dangerous?"

They looked down the hill to the shadow of the Resurrection Church.

"Maybe," Cat admitted. "Depends if the Disciples could identify it as the Syrian flag."

Cat had once told Inaya that apart from Mexico, many of the volunteers who worked at We Rise Together in Nogales were unable to identify countries in Central America on a map. Inaya had had a similar experience. Some of her colleagues had been strongly in favor of the invasion of Iraq, yet couldn't place any of Iraq's neighbors.

Inaya's knock on the door was answered by a gaunt man in his fifties. His hair was a thick thatch of white that grew past his collar, his eyes ravaged as he stared at their ID. Numbly, he motioned them into the interior of a room crowded with cushioned sofas. Small nested tables housed a variety of knickknacks. Photographs of the family were absent from the room.

On the wall behind the sofa was a framed map of Syria, and on either side of this were mother-of-pearl plaques with Arabic script that denoted the names of Muhammad and God. Sandalwood burned in a censer on the windowsill of the window that faced the yard. The room was small, hot, and crowded, but it was spotlessly clean.

A woman entered the room, hastily drawing on her scarf. She relaxed when she saw her visitors were women, letting the scarf rest in her hands, her curly brown hair cascading down her back. She was several years younger than her husband, her face marked by worry, pain at the back of her eyes. Had she guessed what they had come to say?

Cat guided her to a seat, and the woman said her daughter's name on a gasp. Her husband grasped her hand, and Inaya noticed that his right arm hung limply at his side, the hand and wrist bound with a thick white bandage.

She offered the formalities of notification in a soft, compassionate voice, making space for the parents' grief. They hadn't heard from community members about the body at the mosque, and they needed time. The father's face puckered and the mother's body heaved with soundless sobs as she said again and again, "You must be wrong, you must be wrong."

Their sorrow was so immense, so suffocating, that it overshadowed the questions Seif had told Inaya to ask. Yet the analytical part of her mind noticed the absence of surprise in their grief. They tried to deny they had lost their child; they couldn't imagine how such a fate could have befallen them.

Cat made consolatory conversation, and eventually the Elkaders calmed.

"Where is my daughter?" Fatima Elkader said. "I must see her."

Her lightly accented English was strong enough to suggest she had either learned it in Syria or put in a determined effort once she'd been granted asylum. Her husband didn't speak.

Cat explained the coroner's process, delineating the timeline.

Hassan Elkader had sunk back against the sofa, his dark eyes filled with despair. When he spoke, his accent was much stronger than his wife's.

"Where did you find our daughter?"

When Inaya gently disclosed the location and the manner of Razan's death, a terrible cry broke from Fatima. Her fingers tore at her hair as she began to wail. Cat leapt from her chair to stop her, but impelled by a force she couldn't control, Inaya knelt at the woman's feet, looking up into her ravaged face.

"She was left in a holy place, sister Fatima. She died in a state of grace. *Inna lillahi wa inna ilayhi rajioon.* She's at peace now."

Fatima's frenzied movements checked. She spoke to Inaya swiftly in Arabic, and regretfully, Inaya shook her head, cursing Seif for avoiding the interview.

She repeated her name, and the other woman nodded.

"You are one of us? You know us?" The words were wondering.

"I am, sister Fatima. I pray at the Blackwater mosque."

The tightness in Fatima's body loosened. She touched Inaya's knee. Then her eyes skated over Catalina.

"You are both . . . ? You are not . . ."

She and Cat took their seats. She had wondered when it would strike the Elkaders that neither detective was white. Many new immigrant communities associated whiteness with authority. In large, multicultural cities, their presence as police officers would have gone unremarked. In Blackwater Falls, the two women stood out.

Inaya patiently repeated the information she had given them at the outset.

"Detective Catalina Hernandez and I are from the Community Response Unit. That means we're here to serve *you*. To answer your questions and provide any support you might need as we investigate Razan's death."

At the mention of her daughter's name, Fatima's face crumpled again.

Inaya glanced around the room again. Some effort had been made to personalize it, yet she noted the absence of family photographs, or of any of the strewn-about paraphernalia that would indicate the presence of children.

"Is Razan your only child?"

Fatima's mouth began to tremble. Neither parent answered.

Inaya tried again. "Do you have a photograph of Razan? Any family photos, perhaps?"

Hassan Elkader stood up. He went to the dining room that connected to the small sitting room. With one hand, he fumbled about in the drawer of a walnut cabinet with glass doors, striking for the absence of any china on display.

He came back to show them a photograph sealed in laminate and further protected by a zipped sandwich bag. Inaya took it from him with thanks. Despite the lamination, the photograph was cracked, fine white lines appearing down the middle of a family grouping. The Elkaders, three young boys, and Razan. The parents were seated in the center of the group in a well-appointed family room saturated with light, Razan standing to their left, the three boys ranged behind them. Both mother and daughter were without their headscarves, suggesting that the photograph had been taken by a close relative. Razan's hair was the same texture as her mother's, falling in long, loose curls to either side of her neck, her blue eyes bright with challenge. She was younger than the girl Inaya had seen in person. Her brothers ranged in age from eight to fifteen, perhaps. Two had curly dark hair, one was chestnut-haired and blue-eyed like Razan. No one in the photo was smiling.

Inaya looked to Fatima. "May I?"

At the woman's nod, she removed the photo from the bag, touching it with careful fingers. Without a word, she passed it to Cat, who saw as she did that the well-appointed room was in fact only half of a room. The wall behind the family was intact and hung with exquisite artwork, delicate hexagonal tables with bone inlay patterns placed around the room. But the roof of the room was missing, one wall crumbled, the room open to the sky.

"Razan?" Inaya checked. Both parents nodded.

"And the boys?" Her eyes searched what she could see of the house before coming back to the parents.

Holding his bandaged wrist to his chest, Hassan Elkader answered for them both.

"The youngest was lost at sea. The second is with my brother, who was stopped in Turkey. My eldest, Luqman . . ." He choked on the name. "He was captured by the regime when they took our city."

In a hushed voice, Inaya asked, "Your city?"

Fatima spoke up. "Halab. Aleppo." Her voice cracked. "We lost our children to the war."

She began to cry again. Inaya left her with Cat and found her way to the kitchen, where she made tea from a small, silver-plated samovar that was gently steaming. She added copious amounts of sugar, and returned to the room with four fragile tea glasses on a tray she had found on a shelf above the sink.

Fatima gripped the tea glass like a lifeline, oblivious to the heat. When she had finished her tea, Inaya handed her a second glass.

Once she judged the moment was right, she said, "Tell me about Razan. She looks very bright and spirited in this picture."

Maybe a Syrian family didn't want to hear that about their daughter, which was why Inaya had said it in a tone of frank appreciation.

"She was a good girl, and so brave, like her brother Luqman."

"They were close?" Inaya probed gently.

"He was her twin. Everything he did, she wanted to do also. He joined the resistance in Aleppo. She wanted to fight too, but of course, he didn't let her. When he was taken away, she tried to cross to the regime side to see if she could find him. Her cousins brought her back—if regime soldiers had found her, you know what they would have done."

She broke eye contact with Inaya, ashamed, and Inaya thought of the terrible fate of many of the young girls who had strayed across the path of the destroyers of Aleppo. There were reports that Syrian women had committed suicide to escape that fate.

Hassan Elkader decided to spare his wife the rest. "We come from a country that drinks the blood of its young. We had no choice. We had to think of our daughter. And now you tell us our beautiful, brave daughter is dead."

Though every instinct Inaya possessed cried out at her to console them, another part of her mind observed that this was twice her parents had made note of her courage.

"Was she brave in America as well? Or was she like any other teenage girl, busy with her studies and her friends?"

"She missed her brothers. So much." Fatima held her arms open. "So much, she couldn't talk. She had a picture with Luqman. She carried it everywhere, but she didn't speak about Luqman. Then she began to make friends, learn English."

Inaya made a note to check on Razan's belongings.

"Go on," she encouraged. "Did she have many friends?"

"Girls," Fatima said stiffly. "Not boys. You understand this."

And Inaya did, of course. Young Muslim girls were often segregated from their male peers, other than members of their family. They were not permitted to date and were unlikely to have boyfriends, let alone relationships with the same sex. But Inaya thought of her own sisters, and she knew there were ways of getting around even the strictest rules. She couldn't dismiss the possibility that Razan had been involved with someone her parents wouldn't have approved of, no matter how innocent the relationship.

She asked several more questions about Razan's friends while Cat took down their names, plus the name of Razan's school, a private school with an excellent reputation that catered to Blackwater's more affluent families. Cat nudged her, and she knew they were thinking the same thing. How had the Elkaders afforded the tuition at Blackwater Academy? When she asked the question, the Elkaders spoke of a scholarship Razan had won.

Razan's after-school activities proved harmless—she was interested in computers and was learning to play the piano. She had joined the physics and math clubs. She helped with the student paper and managed the audiovisual requirements for the school's drama department. Bit by bit, she managed to extract from Fatima the picture of a lively and engaged young girl who had embraced the opportunities offered by her new country, but the details of her life at school, and her personal interactions, were unknown to her mother. Few of her friends had ever been to the house. Fatima earned money by sewing Syrian crafts and selling them to an artist's boutique. Hassan Elkader worked at the local meatpacking plant. Razan had been selected for an internship at an up-and-coming aeronautics firm. Nothing remarkable or out of the ordinary. Fatima mentioned in detail the extreme kindness of a sponsorship group affiliated with a friendly Baptist church. The Baptists had helped the family to settle, had found Hassan his job and enrolled Inaya in school.

For six months, they had seen to the family's every need. Then the Muslim community had taken over. Across the country, churches were hands-on when it came to refugee sponsorships. Mosques were slow to get organized or to respond in any structured way to the desperate need of their coreligionists. Muslim communities excelled at donating to overseas relief efforts; on their home ground they still had work to do.

Blackwater Falls' small community had been inspired, or perhaps made ashamed, by the efforts of the Baptist church to assist with refugee resettlement. They'd worked in tandem with the church to help families get acclimatized to their new homes, arranging drivers' tests, social security numbers, language classes, and more. Razan had been quick to take advantage.

There was still a question mark in Inaya's mind. What had happened to the passionate young activist who had stood against the Syrian regime? The girl who had tried to rescue her brother from forces loyal to the regime in the streets of a bombed-out Aleppo?

Maybe the refugee journey and the family history in Syria were relevant, but Inaya didn't think so. Not with the way the girl's body had been displayed—intended to play on existing tensions within Blackwater Falls. Forensics would give them more, and once they were available, Cat would be able to fill in the profile.

What *was* relevant to Razan's murder was that they were dealing with a Syrian Muslim refugee family, outsiders on two fronts, in a community dominated by the Resurrection Church, and its vigilante arm.

Maybe Razan had been targeted, either because she was a refugee or because she was an Arab Muslim. Early days to develop a theory of the crime, but the religious overtones of the murder were hard to discount.

She asked Fatima how her husband had injured his hand.

"Did it happen at work?"

If Fatima had been pale before, she was a ghastly color now.

Faintly, she said, "A little while ago, there was an accident with the machines."

Cat fetched her a glass of water that she took with trembling hands.

"Forgive me if this sounds insensitive, but how are you managing without your husband's salary? Will he be able to return to work?"

"'S-salary'?" The word was unfamiliar. Fatima gripped her knees.

Inaya indicated the house. "Did your husband receive compensation for his injury? Where did you say he worked?"

Round-eyed, Fatima stared at her. Inaya relieved her of her glass, setting it on top of a table. She took the woman's trembling hands in her own, wondering if the family's status was an issue. If the Elkaders hadn't been granted status yet, it might explain Fatima's reaction.

"Razan. Razan was earning money at her job."

Loath though she was to do it, Inaya seized her opening. She leaned in close, her knees nearly touching Fatima's.

"Sister Fatima, our pathologist thinks that Razan was killed several days ago. So why didn't you tell the police that your daughter was missing? Because she *was* missing, wasn't she? When did you last see her?"

Tears drowned the bright blue eyes. "Wednesday morning when she left for school."

Then Razan would have missed two days of school before her body had been found on Sunday. Another day had passed since then, and still the Elkaders hadn't spoken.

"We didn't want . . . we didn't *think* . . ." Fatima shook her head from side to side.

"I'm sorry, but I don't understand. What didn't you think?"

Fatima was sobbing openly. When she was able to speak, she whispered, "I thought Razan needed time to herself. I didn't know she was like the others."

The air in the room went electric.

"What others?"

Fatima had begun to rock herself, a keening cry in her throat, her nails tearing her knees.

Cat called out to Hassan. Met with an eerie silence, she got up and searched the house.

"He's gone," she told Inaya. Neither woman had heard him leave.

Fatima sank down on to the floor. The keening became a wail.

Inaya had no choice but to restrain her while Cat called for medical help.

A shadow fell across the glass-paned door, blocking the light from the room.

When Inaya looked up, the ghost of a girl was standing there.

CHAPTER THIRTEEN

When she glanced at the door again after calling an ambulance, the girl she'd seen haloed in gold had disappeared.

"Did you see?" she asked Cat.

She'd arranged for someone on the mosque's steering committee to meet Fatima at the hospital. An alert was out on her missing husband, but not to flag him for arrest. Fleeing his own grief, in whatever manner he'd sought his escape, wasn't a criminal offense.

With Fatima attended to, the two women had searched the immediate surroundings for some sign of the girl who'd appeared at the front door. But the little clutch of houses stood empty and bereft, the weeds growing tall between abandoned plots of land. The paramedics hadn't seen anyone on their approach up the road, making Inaya question what she thought she'd seen. But Cat had seen her too.

Catalina crossed herself again. "*Not* Razan," she said firmly.

"Unless we start believing in ghosts."

"You tell Seif that," Cat suggested.

Go gentle, Inaya, he'd said.

One of the dead girl's parents was in the hospital, the other had been driven from his own home. She could just imagine how well Seif would think she'd followed his instructions.

Not feeling too "safe" now, she thought, knowing she should call in, but hoping to find something in the house that might mitigate the disaster of the interview.

"Did you find anything when you went looking for the father?" she asked Cat.

"Nothing. Two rooms, and no one in them. We should search Razan's room."

Inaya agreed. Hassan had given his permission at the outset of the interview, Fatima nodding along.

Cat caught at her sleeve, her gentle eyes questioning. "Inaya—'others'? Other *girls*?"

Inaya thought of Omar thinking the murder victim might have been his sister. She swallowed down her sense of horror. She'd been in Blackwater only six months. She'd heard nothing through the rumor mill, seen no reports in the paper. Nor had the sheriff flagged anything for their attention, and he couldn't be so disdainful of CRU's intrusion into Blackwater that he'd neglect to mention it. There would be no coming back from an oversight like that.

Sabotage, a voice in her mind whispered.

Yet Seif had made nice with Addison Grant, reducing it to an issue of personalities. Maybe this was where Areesha Adams came in. Shining a light on truths others were concealing.

"After we left the scene yesterday, I did a search on missing persons. There were no results in the database. So whatever is going on, there was no official report." She drew a finger across the surface of a spotless table. "You've lived here longer than I have, Cat. Was there anything in the news?"

Catalina set down a knickknack. "Nothing. Not about murdered girls, at least."

Inaya picked up on this as the two women methodically sifted through the sitting room.

"There's something else?"

Catalina swept her heavy brown bangs aside. A strand of hot pink touched her face, a clue to Cat's inner complexities. Sedate, grounded, warm, friendly, but also unexpected and imaginative, ready to take a leap. She was Inaya's favorite kind of partner—one who followed her instincts. Seif went easy on Cat, had even told her that the hot pink streak in her thickly bunched hair would make her an instant hit at the Community

Expo. In contrast, Inaya had received a full duty inspection that lingered on the absence of her headscarf. Then Seif had told her to remove a ring with a mounted turquoise block because he thought it was it too showy.

Cat cut into her thoughts. "Remind me to tell you when we have more background on the father. Not here. We can meet up at our usual place."

Their usual place was a bakery called Marhaba in Blackwater's prettified old town.

"We're overdue," Inaya said now. They completed the check of the sitting room and the nearly empty dining cabinet.

She called in to report, listening to Seif's displeasure in her ear. She offered her excuses and told Seif that Hassan Elkader had gone AWOL. She asked him to put someone on a background check into the family.

"What are you looking for?" Seif's sharp voice asked. It would be attractive, Inaya mused, deep and rough, if he wasn't always barking at her.

"Immigration status. We've been told they came here as refugees, but is there paperwork to back that up? Were they sponsored? If so, by whom? What was their port of entry, and where did they arrive from? They mentioned a journey by sea. Which sea?"

She heard the scratch of Seif's pen on paper. She'd seen that pen; it was much more ostentatious than the kuchi ring he'd told her to remove, with its stone that warded off the evil eye. The barrel of the pen was a sleek dark amethyst, the grip patterned in silver, the cap and nib a bright gold. He wore it clipped to the inside pocket of whatever jacket he was wearing, and used it to the exclusion of any other. Inaya wondered if it was the gift of a particular friend. Maybe a woman he was seeing.

"Did you get that, Rahman?" She'd missed something in her mini-reverie.

"Sorry, sir, say again?"

"Stay out of the girl's bedroom. I'm sending techs from the crime lab now."

"We have permission to search," she argued.

"If the father is involved in Razan's murder, we can't risk contamination."

This was why Inaya had delayed calling him. She knew he'd go down this path, and now she tried to backtrack.

"Listen, sir, he's not on the run; his reaction was perfectly normal given the circumstances." She barreled on, not giving him a chance to disagree. "Did Jaime know about the Elkaders' other children?"

She heard Seif rustling papers. "I'm not seeing anything."

"Razan isn't the only child the Elkaders lost. There was a boy who drowned 'at sea.' Another son they claim was disappeared in Syria. A third left behind in Turkey. And now they've lost Razan. So Hassan needed a moment. That doesn't mean he's involved."

"It also doesn't mean he isn't. Get out and secure the house. I'll get Grant to lend us some men for the search."

"Qas!" His first name slipped from her, and Cat's eyebrows went up. "We haven't vetted Grant's officers—you didn't see their behavior at the crime scene. I don't want them running Hassan down—they'll arrest him without a second thought. Think about the optics of that."

She held the phone away from her ear, expecting a furious blast. What she got instead was icy disapproval.

"But you're not in charge, are you, Detective? So I make the calls, and that's my call, because you can't assume prima facie that Elkader is not involved."

Inaya held her phone in a white-knuckled grip.

"Take a breath," Cat mouthed at her.

She didn't listen. It took her only seconds to run through various possibilities in her mind.

"Thinking this is an honor killing is an Islamophobic leap," she said to Seif.

Dead silence. Then, "I'm not the one who made that leap."

Inaya said nothing.

"Are we done?" Sarcasm from Seif.

Inaya rallied. She told him what Fatima had said about "others," though she didn't mention the sighting of the girl at the door. "If you want me to really work this case, you should let me speak to Areesha and find out what's going on."

"And what do you think *I* should do?" More sarcasm.

Inaya gave him a straight answer. "You should find out what the sheriff knows about any missing girls in this town. There's a connection here we're missing."

"You don't ask for much, do you?" Seif sounded milder now, maybe even admiring.

Inaya was distracted by the roar of pipes coming up the road. She looked to Cat, who peered through the stained glass.

Alarm clear on her face, Cat motioned for her to look. Inaya saw a convoy of bikes, giant tricked-out Harleys, speeding up the road and coming to a stop outside the house, where they left their engines to idle. The bikes were ridden by a dozen or so big, gruff men, some with grizzled beards, white lines cracking sunbaked skin, blue or red bandannas wrapped tight and low across their heads. A few stragglers at the rear wore red caps with "MAGA" stitched in white across the front. Some of the riders had black fuel tanks stenciled with a stark white cross that looked menacing stretched out on its side. One flew the Thin Blue Line flag, another had gone even further. The wind caught at the flags on the biker's handlebars, on the right the Colorado state flag with its distinctive yellow "C," on the left the Southern Cross. She must have missed a history lesson somewhere. Colorado wasn't part of the Confederacy.

"What's that noise?"

Inaya had forgotten that Seif was still on the line. "I think we're about to meet members of the Disciples. We need to find Elkader before they get their hands on him."

The bikes split up. Two came up the drive, spraying gravel with their tires. Others rode into the yard and circled to the back of the house, blaring their horns as they went. The rest fell into formation, a line of sentries along the road. No one could pass from either direction.

The noise was overwhelming.

Inaya heard Seif shouting orders to someone.

"Lock yourselves in, and—hear me, Rahman—don't fucking leave the house."

He'd gone, but neither she nor Cat were listening. She darted past Cat, who opened the door, her mind on the Syrian flag pasted up under the mailbox.

The Disciples got to it first.

CHAPTER FOURTEEN

The man who strode up the Elkaders' porch crushed the small flag in his hand.

"That's not your property," Inaya told him. He was much taller than she was and bulky with it, but the bulk was muscle, not fat, unlike his brethren, who were mostly men in their fifties and sixties with loose-hanging bellies. There was one woman with them, a hard-living blonde whose lipstick was starting to run. She was wrapped around the back of one of the riders.

All the bikers in her immediate vision wore identical black leather vests over T-shirts, the vests adorned with patches: the American flag, a cunning-eyed bald eagle, the number 45, the starkly imposing Fallen Cross. On the front left of the vests, each biker wore a Disciples patch above his heart. The man who had crushed the Elkaders' flag also had a patch on the right that said "Road Captain." His bare arms told more of his story, camouflaged by remarkable tattoo art. Snaking around his right bicep were the words "Wretch Like Me." The left bicep bore a similar design, this time the words saying, "Disciple of God." There were no skulls on his arms, and no Nazi paraphernalia, but on his right forearm was a giant cross, stabbed through with five wounds.

Inaya gasped, drawing his attention. His head dipped down to hers and she saw the words "CHRISTIAN WARRIOR" stamped boldly across his thick throat. He was attractive in a rough sort of way, with uncombed hair to his shoulders, heavy stubble rather than a beard on a strong square jaw, lazy hazel eyes that folded in at the corners. He'd clearly done some hard living too, though she guessed his age as under forty.

She put out her hand for the flag he'd stolen; he held it out of reach. The bikers laughed.

She and Cat stood shoulder to shoulder blocking the Elkaders' front door. Now they both moved to display the badges clipped to their belts.

"DPD," Inaya said. "Please identify yourself."

"This is still America, isn't it?" His teeth were very white against his stubble. "Cops can't just stop you anywhere and demand to see your ID."

"They can when you're trespassing on someone else's property."

He opened his palm and let the flag fall. Inaya caught it as he said, "The only flag we fly in this country is the American flag. Our neighbors need to know that."

She could hear Cat breathing beside her, rattled, but trying to conceal it. Any show of weakness and the pair of them would be finished.

Deliberately, she let her eyes cut through the motley assortment of bikers before bringing them back to his.

"I see a Thin Blue Line flag. And someone's whistling 'Dixie.' Looks like you might be breaking your own rules."

He threw his head back and laughed, his muscular throat rippling. When he'd finished, he said, "Some folks still think the Confederacy *is* America."

"Does that include you?"

He shrugged, straining the seams of his vest. "I say live and let live."

Inaya flattened the Syrian flag in her palms. "Shouldn't that apply to your neighbors?"

That wiped the humor from his face. His gaze turned thoughtful, switching between her and Cat. "Maybe, maybe not. We watch out for our own around here. Same as you, my guess."

No need to speculate that the Elkaders weren't included in this group.

Cat shifted suddenly, gazing up at the top of the road, opposite the way they'd come. A sheriff's vehicle was coming down the road, moving at a snail's pace to avoid the bikers' roadblock. Flashing lights, no siren.

Thank God. Seif had scrambled backup for them.

Road Captain—she didn't know what else to call him—swiveled his head to watch. The car reached the barrier. A window rolled down, the pipes of the Harleys too loud for Inaya to catch the exchange. Then the patrol car reversed, speeding up the hill out of sight. A chill settled in Inaya's bones. If they were relying on the sheriff, it looked like they were on their own.

Road Captain read her mind. "You two ladies by yourselves?"

Some instinct impelled Inaya to state, "*Detective* Inaya Rahman, *Detective* Catalina Hernandez."

"Detective?" Road Captain's brows came together. "We got trouble here?"

The same instinct made Inaya tip her head in a way that was mildly flirtatious. His eyes warmed as she said, "That depends on whose side you're on."

Road Captain's hands formed into fists. Heart racing, Inaya held her ground.

He didn't crowd her. He dipped his head to his fists, and just beneath his knuckles she read on one hand, "JESUS SAVES," on the other, "SO DO I."

"Mind if I ask you a question, Road Captain?"

"Name's Ranger, Detective."

"Mr. Ranger—"

He grinned at her. "Just Ranger. That's my club name. Ask what you want."

Inaya pointed to the bleeding-cross tattoo. "What does your tattoo mean?"

He stiffened. An older man came up the steps, his beard so luxurious it curled. His patch said "Sergeant at Arms." He muttered in Ranger's ear. Ranger shook him off. The Sergeant leaned against the porch railing, which looked too frail to support him, his eyes fixed on Cat. She pulled out her phone and sent a text. The bikers throttled their engines in response to her action.

Ranger held out his arm for inspection, the bicep deliberately flexed. If she wasn't in the midst of a showdown with a group of vigilantes, Inaya might have laughed at the ploy.

"Yes." She made herself sound impressed. "That's the one. What's it mean?"

"Wounds of Christ. Don't you know your Bible?" Before she could answer, he went on, "'Hernandez' I get, but your name, babe . . . where's it from? Don't think I've heard it before."

She didn't doubt it. She'd been asked the question before in a few different scenarios, her least favorite being at the airport, where she had to choose between saying "Afghanistan, Pakistan" or "It's a Muslim name." None of those were good choices at the airport, and they weren't any better here.

"It's Brazilian." Maybe she could pull that off.

His lazy golden eyes went sharp. "You think I'm a bigot?"

Inaya felt Cat tense at her side, her hand slowly moving to the gun tucked in at the back of her pants. She knew why. The Sergeant at Arms had gone solid.

Guns wouldn't help them here, when a sheriff's vehicle had driven away instead of coming to their aid. They were out of sight, out of mind. But every dangerous situation that faced a police officer called for the same thing.

Deescalate. Do it now!

She pressed the tiny flag to her heart, stroking it with her thumb, her other hand free and clear where the bikers could see.

"The family who lives here didn't mean any disrespect. They just wanted to keep a little piece of the home they've lost."

"ISIS," the Sergeant barked, sharp enough to startle her. "An American patriot doesn't stand by when ISIS comes to town."

The flag slipped from her hand. Ranger swiftly recaptured it. He didn't offer it again until Inaya said, "They were *running* from ISIS. They thought they'd find safety here."

"Burn 'em!" the dissolute blonde screamed. "Burn 'em all!"

Pipes began to roar in assent.

Inaya murmured low to Ranger. If he wanted to hear her, he'd have to step in front of the Sergeant, and he did.

"They lost three children getting here. We found the body of the fourth today. Murdered here in Blackwater. Do you know anything about that?"

Ranger's face went hard. "This is a good Christian army. We don't want outsiders here, but we didn't touch the girl."

Cat leaned against the door, masking the move for her gun.

"How did you know we were talking about a girl?"

CHAPTER FIFTEEN

Road Captain didn't like Cat, that much was evident. While Inaya kept Ranger's attention on her, Cat checked out the other bikers. They were white to a man (and woman), though sometimes a club would include a lone Mexican or two. He'd be given a name like Hombre or Diablo where he rode at the rear of the formation. She was glad there was no Diablo here, because they worked extra hard to fit in, to flatten their racial differences, and in this case would have called her out just to demonstrate they'd washed the Mexican off their skin.

The Sergeant at Arms rolled up to her, and said, "You got papers, spic?"

"Hardtack," Ranger warned low. Another club nickname, Cat guessed. They'd have to dig up some background on the bikers' actual names.

The humorous part of her wanted to pull out her gun and say, "Here's my papers, old man." The smarter part was reminding her about the use-of-force guidelines. She'd be doing paperwork for days if she unholstered her gun.

So she said blandly, "I don't think our Lord and Savior would appreciate your tone."

"You a Christian?" He planted his hands on his hips. Like Road Captain, his biceps and traps were huge, his stance intended to straighten her out.

For answer, she pulled her fine gold cross out of the neck of her shirt.

It was the wrong move, because he rounded on Inaya for similar proof.

"What about you, Brazil?"

Inaya hesitated, but she covered it by saying, "Jesus is a light unto the world."

Cat smothered a snort. It struck her as ridiculous that the Disciples were asserting their testosterone-fueled Christianity to Mexican and Afghan-Pakistani detectives at the home of a Syrian family. She'd texted Seif an SOS. Officers were on their way.

So she felt emboldened to say, "It seems to me that decent Christian folk wouldn't want to terrorize a family who lost their child today."

Her words rippled through the ranks of riders. The idling engines stopped. The woman who'd screamed "Burn 'em all" refused to meet Cat's eyes.

Good, Cat thought. *She's human.*

She turned back to Ranger. "Did you come here knowing this family's daughter was dead? Were you thinking of offering condolences?"

Ranger called Hardtack off.

"Word got out. Thought we'd see what we could do." He made a snap decision and tossed the flag to Cat. "Open the door. Let 'em know we're here."

Cat made her body a bulwark, her arms at a diagonal, the flag tucked into her pocket.

He shifted so that his body eclipsed Inaya's—if Cat needed to get off a shot, she couldn't. His smile was so smooth, she knew to fear it. Probably he'd get himself a photo spread in *The New York Times* like Richard Spencer. "The Well-Dressed Arch-Conservative Slash Neo-Nazi."

Road Captain wasn't dressed like a well-heeled preppy, but he'd clean up as nicely.

"Now isn't the best time, I'm afraid." She brought out her dimples, though she couldn't have felt less like being friendly. Charm or no charm, Ranger gave off a chilling vibe.

His big hands descended on her shoulders.

"Move, *chica*. I'm asking nice. I got something to say to these folks."

Inaya slipped around him, wedging herself between him and Cat.

"Please," she said. "Don't make things worse than they are by mistreating an officer."

Cat noted his eyes got soft when he looked at Inaya. He wasn't as careful with her.

When her shoulders tensed up, he felt it. His fingers bit into her flesh. She made a sound of pain, and Inaya shoved at Ranger's chest. "Get your hands off my partner right now."

He didn't budge, but he eased up on the pressure.

Paperwork be damned. Cat unholstered her gun.

The moment the Sergeant at Arms saw it, all hell broke loose. Men came off their bikes, the blonde cheering them on.

Inaya's gun was in her hand too, both women's backs to the house. Cat heard the sound of a shotgun being loaded, and she flinched. The Sergeant at Arms yanked out a gun from his jeans; it looked like it had been customized. But she and Inaya weren't wearing any kind of body armor. They'd come to do a next-of-kin notification. They hadn't expected this.

She was shocked when Ranger advanced, pushing Inaya back against the house with one meaty arm on her chest, just beneath her shoulders.

Her hands were free to move. She kept her gun hand down.

Hardtack raised his gun to Cat's face.

Someone was going to get hurt.

Hardtack's gaze shifted past her face to the door. She heard the hinges creak.

Please, Jesus, not Elkader. The Disciples had come here for him.

A girl wearing a white hoodie stepped out onto the porch. On the back of the hoodie was a stylized rendering of the word "Resurrection." She yanked the hoodie down, and dark blond curls spilled out.

"Hardtack!" A command to the Sergeant to lower his gun, who sent a spiky glare Ranger's way. He backed off, tucking his gun away. The cordon of bikers stood down.

"Dad, what are you doing?"

The girl's eyes were on Ranger. He dropped his arm from where Inaya stood pinned and stepped back, his focus shifting to the girl.

"I told you not to come here, Mercedes."

"And *I* told *you* I'd be checking on my friend. You and your goons should leave."

Hardtack scowled at her. "Fuck, girl. You're one of us."

"I hope not," Mercedes said clearly. She'd placed herself between the two detectives and Hardtack. Cat slipped her gun back into its holster. Inaya did the same. "Terrorizing someone who's half my size isn't who I want to be."

"Girl." Ranger's tone held a warning. "Get yourself gone *now*."

Mercedes stood toe to toe with him until he groaned a whispered "Fuck." Then his arm stole around her waist.

The girl pulled up her hoodie and Catalina saw the pure line of her profile, the girl's skin brown, her eyes like ink, and then she understood.

She'd seen the girl through colored glass.

Inaya shared her discovery and asked, "Are you the Virgin in gold?"

The girl looked at them, puzzled. Sirens sounded down the hill.

CHAPTER SIXTEEN

Sheriff Grant had blown Seif off. He'd sent a patrol car out to the Elkaders' house, then just as quickly called it off. Or the officer had made the determination on his own, another possibility. Blackwater police had left Inaya and Catalina to face down a group of bikers on their own in the back end of nowhere, characteristic of how they operated. Too much attention when it wasn't warranted, or total neglect of legitimate complaints.

Seif had done his own digging into Grant, getting the feel for Blackwater long before Razan's murder had come to light. That was his way. He was thorough; he was meticulous. Any other way, he'd be dead, and getting killed on the job was a luxury he couldn't afford. He was the head of his family. No mother, no father, just him and twin brothers in their twenties.

In another culture, the boys would be on their own. Moved out, independent. Maybe hooked up with a girl. Scratch that, with an unspecified partner. Not in his culture. A Palestinian father who'd been killed. An Iranian mother who died of cancer. Both of them devout, unlike Seif. He wasn't lost, searching for God or himself. He'd made choices, and he owned them. His brothers didn't like those choices. They'd gone the opposite way. Prayed five times a day, no alcohol in the house, no pretty girls on their arms. They didn't get drunk or do drugs.

No, their high came from something else. The two young fools were activists, hyped up on the suffering of the *ummah*. They were anti-military, anti-FBI, anti-police, anti–the Iraq war, anti–boots on the ground any-fucking-where they shouldn't be. One was the editor of his college paper. The other was the co-president of his college's Free Palestine chapter. They were bound to every cause but his.

They loved him, both of them, like only boys raised by an older brother could. But they called him out on everything he stood for. He didn't care. He loved them back like they were all that mattered on this earth. Which was how it had been since their parents died, and he wasn't about to let go of the reins now. His job was to make sure they got settled. Got their education, got married to good women, then got on with their lives. After that, he'd think about himself.

And what he was doing in a place like Blackwater, when he should have been in D.C. That was where he belonged, working on anti-corruption with the FBI. He'd paid his dues; he'd cut himself off from his history, going so far as to substitute his mother's surname for his Palestinian father's, grateful his first name wasn't common among his people. He'd been named after a family friend from the Gulf, and his self-sabotage had worked. He had no political opinions, no cause he would live and die for, except the FBI, who'd farmed him out to Denver. Light-skinned, brown-eyed, clean-cut Qas was on the inside, and that's where he wanted to stay. He could make things happen on the inside. Like justice for Razan. Like bringing Grant down.

So he was giving Grant rope, like he'd been told to do by the FBI, but things were playing out fast and loose, and Catalina and Inaya had nearly paid the price. *His* people. The ones he was meant to protect. He'd fucked up, thinking Grant could be trusted. He wouldn't do it again. Catalina would understand—they'd become close, because she never pushed too hard. She didn't coddle him, didn't overdo it to get on his good side. She was just who she was. Competent and caring, good at reading his moods and giving him the space he needed. He offered the same to her. She was the one person on his team who deserved that respect.

And Inaya, fuck, *Inaya* was getting under his skin. Too much like him, too good at what she did to be stuck here. Her choices, what she wanted, how she believed—fucking brave, worthy of respect. He didn't want to feel this, but he did. They'd say he had too much hot Arab blood in his veins, too much honor tied up in women, and maybe he did, but Inaya wasn't his. He didn't want her to be, so he shouldn't be thinking these thoughts. He found he couldn't help it. The way she looked at him, not quite able to conceal her curiosity. The fact she didn't back down when he was out of line. Or that she'd once greeted him with a salaam he'd coldly rebuffed.

She didn't give him space. She didn't respect boundaries he thought were etched in steel, the wall he'd built up, warning everyone off. He didn't like it, but he couldn't deny Inaya got his blood pumping. It wouldn't take much for her to push her way behind that wall. That couldn't happen, because Seif had a job to do. Though his hotheaded younger brothers didn't know it, they were fighting the same war.

Elkader had been picked up. No arrest, but he was safely squared away, while the crime scene techs worked the house. He'd spoken to the man in Arabic, read his shock and grief as sincere, taken him to his wife at the hospital, where he'd left them under guard for their own protection. Patrol officers had swarmed the house, taking down the names of bikers who had trespassed into the yard. The ones on the road had fled. The rest were cautioned and let off, except for two that Inaya had pointed out: a rough-looking man who hung over a girl in a hoodie, and the Disciples' Sergeant at Arms, who owned the unregistered firearm he'd used to threaten a cop. Hardtack. Real name, Monty Frisch. He didn't seem too worried about his detention, probably wore it as a badge of honor. He'd shouted at Seif; Road Captain had silenced him.

Road name, Ranger; real name, Lincoln West. Mercedes West was his daughter. He'd moved her away from Catalina and Inaya, off the Elkaders' property, the pair of them detained at the edge of the road.

Cat and Inaya were in the yard. They'd given him a full debrief, telling him two things of note. West had a five-wounds-of-Christ tattoo on his forearm. And his daughter had come to see Razan. She'd come from inside the house, though Cat and Inaya both swore they'd first seen her through the stained glass panel in the front door, her hoodie up, her hair spilling out, so she'd looked like Razan, mounted on the door of the mosque. They thought they were seeing double.

The women were good detectives, not given to fancy; they wouldn't have made that up. It was too big of a coincidence to ignore. They were taking both father and daughter to the station—not for a comfortable chat, but for a proper interview. He'd sent Jaime to set that up. West argued that his daughter was a minor, he wouldn't let her be questioned on her own. Mercedes cut him off at the knees. "I'm seventeen. I'll be glad to help."

She didn't know Razan was dead, or didn't seem to. He would have to tell her.

But one thing he wanted to know. Where was the girl's mother?

Inaya and Cat hadn't got that far. Seif's arrival had cut their conversation short.

"Sir." Inaya caught up with him. He didn't care about rank. He made them call him "sir" because it created the distance he needed to do a job no one knew he was doing. If he was unapproachable, no one would question his absences, no would call him on the fact that he still hadn't dealt with Grant and his monumental fuckups. "Elkader didn't give us a chance to ask about reporting his daughter missing. His wife said she thought Razan needed space. It just doesn't track, sir. It's a religious family—they wouldn't let their daughter wander off."

He noted the way the wind caught at tendrils from her braid and whipped them against her face. Her hair was long and shiny, the braid thick enough to wrap his fist around. He wondered how it felt to leave it exposed when she'd kept that part of herself hidden for so long. With an effort, he focused on her words.

"Give them a day or two. We should have Stanger's postmortem report by then, which will give us more to ask them."

"We won't have a timeline to work with. That's setting us back."

She looked so earnest he wanted to smile. Instead, he made his tone brusque. "We've got plenty to work with. Interviews with West and his daughter. The church, Razan's friends. The community here." He jerked his chin at the house. "Whatever we find inside."

"I'd like to interview West."

"No." A patrol officer came up to notify him they'd completed the cordon around the house. He gave further instructions, ignoring Inaya's impatience. "I'm doing the interviews. I'll need Catalina with me. Especially for Mercedes. They'll connect better, because with her name I'm thinking her mother was Latina."

He waited for Inaya to remind him he'd had the option of connecting on the grounds of similar ethnicity and language with the Elkaders. Wisely, she decided not to challenge him.

"Loose talk, all these leads. Someone needs to talk to Grant for a read on the town."

"The sheriff is off limits to you. He'll only deal with his superiors."

"Then let me talk to Areesha," she persisted. "I'm working in the dark here, when I could be gathering intel."

The corner of his mouth quirked at her use of spy-speak. She probably watched shows like *Homeland*. But he had to give her something. She was building up a good head of steam.

"You have to watch yourself with Adams," he told her. From the gleam in her eyes, he cottoned on to the fact that he'd just been played. She didn't care about the sheriff. Areesha Adams was the interview she wanted. He shook his head, not letting his amusement show.

"Adams is good at ferreting out the things she wants to know. Things you may think you have no intention of telling her."

She tutted at his use of the word "ferret," and said, "I'll bet you wouldn't say that to her."

His face finally eased into humor, so Inaya took it further.

"Sounds like you have some experience with Ms. Adams."

It sounded like a double entendre, which wasn't what she'd intended. Her skin began to heat, beads of perspiration forming at her hairline. He was tempted to erase them with his thumb.

He ran a hand through his sleek black hair, watching Inaya watch him do it. "Adams is one of the lawyers who handed the DPD its ass over Elijah McClain. She says cops shouldn't get to investigate cops, that we'll always exonerate ourselves." Colorado's record on officer-involved shootings wasn't impressive, either: it was the fifth highest in the nation.

The Elijah McClain killing had rocked the city of Denver. The young man had been stopped while walking to his home because he'd worn a ski mask, then injected with ketamine to subdue his struggles, dead at the hands of the police within hours. The police had been cleared of wrongdoing in the first investigation; the public outcry led to a second review, and the officers involved had been held accountable. After that, the guidelines had changed.

Anything could be justified by the police to show that the use of force was necessary. But Seif had seen enough to compare the violent takedown of often unarmed Black men and children with armed members of militias storming state capitals and surviving showdowns with cops without a single shot being fired. De-escalation was possible; it just depended on who needed it. De-escalation alone wouldn't satisfy Areesha Adams, who was demanding nothing less than defunding the DPD and reinvesting its share of the city budget in disadvantaged communities. Parts of that made sense to Seif, parts didn't—when a drunk came at you with a knife, you wouldn't hesitate to call 911. Plus, to his way of thinking, cops were part of the community too.

It would be a good test to see if Inaya could handle Adams without blowing things up. Leaving him clear to follow through on his own investigation into Grant.

She returned to her earlier theme.

"What about the sheriff? If there's background here as to why the parents didn't report that Razan was missing, or, say, why parents didn't report *other* missing girls, that's something we can't ignore. His fingerprints will be all over that."

"Jesus, Rahman, you're like a dog with a bone. We don't need an in-house Areesha, I told you I'm dealing with Grant."

"We're Community Response." She was getting agitated. "We represent the community."

"Don't forget we're also cops. We owe Grant a little respect."

Her lips firmed in annoyance. She had more to say, no doubt. She'd been tentative in her dealings with him those first few weeks after he'd brought her on board. Now she was starting to come into her own, no longer invested in hierarchy or in remembering her place. All of that was good. All of that was exactly what he wanted from a member of his team. But not here, not now on this case, when he needed to keep things locked tight.

So he pointed her to Razan. "Get more background on the girl, set up your meet with Adams. Record the interview, if she agrees, and see what you can find out about Razan's personal effects—we didn't find anything with the body. Once forensics is done with it, do a search of her room. That should be enough to keep you occupied." He made his tone dismissive. Her brown eyes sparked in response, her disapproval plain. Maybe she thought he was dirty. So be it. Then she'd stay away. Because he couldn't afford to let Inaya get close.

CHAPTER SEVENTEEN

Catalina was talking to the girl, her gentle voice deflecting the cell-like containment of their deliberately bleak interview rooms. Gray walls, a black table, bottled water on the table, the temperature low, the girl snuggled into her hoodie.

Seif had put Jaime in with Lincoln West, who, no fool, demanded a lawyer, refusing to speak until she arrived. So he'd told Jaime to leave West to cool his heels. Next, he sent Cat in with the daughter to get background, and now he joined them in the room, hooking his suit jacket over the back of his chair.

He studied the girl, who showed the natural anxiety one would expect when cornered by two cops, no matter how gentle Catalina was. He introduced himself and told the girl to call him Qas. He made it sound like "Cass" instead of "Qaas" with its hard Arabic "Q," something that wouldn't sound foreign to her ears, establishing a comfort zone. The girl had pulled up her hood, her face shrouded in shadows, but Seif still couldn't see the vision Catalina had described. He asked her to lower the hood, and in the yellow glare of the lights, his suspicion was confirmed.

This girl looked white, same as he did, but just like with him, there were gradations of white. Neither of them was milky, neither had the ethereal glow of a Nicole Kidman or the suntan of local Coloradans. Under the light skin, there was a warm, golden-brown tint. His denoted his Arab-Iranian identity; hers would be something else.

He braced his elbows on the table, not leaning in too close.

"Would you like your mother to be present?" he asked.

The girl looked surprised, like he should already know everything there was to know about her. Her backpack was at her feet, her purse slung across her body, her cell phone peeking from a pocket. She was wearing skinny jeans and neat white Converse sneakers with her hoodie, her casual attire setting off her youthful beauty.

"My mother's back in Mexico," she told him. "Waiting for her papers to come through."

"Your parents are married, then?"

She looked offended by the question, but all she said quietly was, "They're good churchgoing people." He checked for a purity ring on her finger. Her hands were bare, but there was a tiny rose tattoo spiraling up both her middle fingers. So she had some attitude.

"Are they?" He leaned in, Catalina shifting to give him room. "Your father had one of my detectives pinned to the house, and his friend had a gun pointed at Detective Hernandez. They were at the house to harass the Elkaders. And if I had to guess, I'd say that wasn't the first time."

The girl frowned, considering this information. She'd been there. She'd seen her father in action. She'd tried to call him off, so nothing he was saying was likely to be a surprise.

"I know that's what it looks like, but that isn't what they mean by it."

"They?" he clarified.

"The Disciples. They . . . proselytize." She checked his face to see if she'd used the right word. He gave her a nod of encouragement. "They try to spread the good news."

"On Harleys that circle the houses of people like your friend Razan Elkader? You don't think that might be designed to scare them off rather than to welcome them to share in the message of Christ? Is that how you would do it?"

"I guess not." She looked flustered, playing with the strap of her purse. Confidingly, she said, "I did tell my dad it wasn't the right way to go about things. I said Razan and her parents wouldn't feel welcomed by bikers buzzing their house. But it's a Disciples tradition. They don't mean any harm. It's a way of testing whether people belong here."

He cut through her rationalizations. Point-blank, he asked, "Like you? Like your mother? Does your father think you belong?"

Catalina drew in a breath at his side. He waited, not turning down the heat.

Color filled the girl's face, and she put her hands to her cheeks.

"You sound like you think—do you think my father is a bigot? Would he have fallen in love with my mother if he was?"

Fair enough. But some people hated Mexicans, while others reserved their bile for Arabs. And these Disciples might see themselves as engaged in fighting the new Crusades.

"What did your friend Razan think of your father's 'welcome'?"

Mercedes looked down at the table. The color leached from her face.

Catalina spoke up. "We'd like to know about Razan, Mercedes. You were at her house today. How did you get in? Why did you enter from the back?"

"I knocked," Mercedes said. "No one answered, so I thought I'd just check at the back. I haven't seen Razan in a few days, so I wanted to ask if she was sick. Or if she'd just taken a couple of days off for the sake of her mental health. She often camps for a day or two out at the reservoir—it helps her get away from everything."

Both detectives tensed up. "By herself?"

"Sometimes she needs to be alone." Mercedes slumped back in her chair. "But she always lets her parents know if she's going to the reservoir."

The Elkaders had made no mention of this. Neither did it fit with what he expected from cautious Syrian parents. Their daughter would have been their treasure, although the journey out of Syria may have made them lower their guard. The necessities of survival could have demanded they allow their children a greater degree of independence. And if Razan had exercised that freedom to camp alone at the reservoir, she could have met danger there.

"Do you know where she camped?" he asked.

"Up at Marina Point. She likes to be close to the lake."

The easiest thing to do would be to check at the park, which required site reservations to be made in advance; an online booking would even give them the site number.

Catalina followed up with the next logical question. "We've heard that Razan was devoted to her studies—would she have taken the time off from school? How long has she been absent?"

Mercedes shrugged. "I don't know. Maybe two or three days? She wasn't at school last Thursday or Friday." She peered curiously into their faces.

Razan's body had been discovered on Sunday. They were two days into their investigation, but where had she been last week?

"When was the last time you saw her?" Seif couldn't keep the edge from his voice.

Mercedes stopped fiddling with her purse, her eyes catching his, wide and inquiring.

"On Wednesday. We hung out at the library."

"Just the two of you?"

"There was a group of us. We were at the library for a while, then went to get ice cream."

Catalina pushed a notepad and pen at Mercedes. "Could you write down the names of your friends who were there, and the name of the place you went to get ice cream?"

Mercedes looked at them, alarmed. She'd finally caught on to the significance of their questions. "Has something happened to Razan? Is she *missing*?"

So she hadn't heard the rumors, though the leap she'd made was interesting. He left it to Catalina to answer.

Catalina reached across the table for the girl's hands, enfolding them in her own. Mercedes clutched onto them like a lifeline.

"I'm very sorry to tell you Razan was found dead on Sunday."

"What? She committed suicide?" Mercedes whispered, holding on to Catalina's hands so hard that the skin around her knuckles blanched. Cat and Seif exchanged a glance.

"Was Razan having suicidal thoughts? Did she ever express that to you?"

Mercedes shook her head wildly, curls flying. "No, no, nothing like that. She would never do anything like that to her parents, not after her brothers . . ."

"So you knew about her family?" Seif asked.

She turned her gaze to him, but he knew she wasn't seeing him. She was sorting through images of Razan, snippets of conversations they'd had, her mood the last time she'd seen her. All this to hold off confronting the reality that her friend was dead.

"Yes, like I told you, we were really close. She told me about her parents, her brothers, her journey here from Syria. She did a project on the war in Syria for our history class. She loved school, loved her job, loved being here."

"Then what made you think of suicide?"

She looked at Seif helplessly. "I don't know. Razan was happy and she was thinking about her future. She liked raising her voice, making change, being an activist, which, you know, is not exactly easy in a town like Blackwater Falls. She thrived on that kind of stuff. But underneath it, she was also sad all the time—I mean, who wouldn't be? She watched her little brother drown. She doesn't know—didn't know, I'm sorry—when her other brother would be able to leave Turkey to join their family. She was saving up money for him to come. And her twin—you know she has a twin named Luqman?"

Both detectives nodded.

"Well, she thinks her twin is either dead with his body thrown in a mass grave so no one can find it, or that he's alive and being tortured. She lived with that night and day. She's had trouble sleeping because she dreamt about him so much. She felt like he was calling out to her, telling her he wasn't dead, that he needed her to go back to Aleppo and find him."

She drew in a quick breath, and Seif didn't interrupt. "So it was like she was living two lives, do you know what I mean? She was Razan, happy at school and home and work, glad to be here in America because she thought it was a great country, you know? But also sad and stressed underneath, going home every day to parents who couldn't hide their grief. Especially after Mr. Elkader lost his job. He was trying to save up the money to bring his brother and other son from Turkey."

Tears flooded her eyes. Her voice broke before she continued, "Like, I couldn't go home to that every day—did you know her parents had a habit of calling for the twins at the same time? 'Luqman, Razan, come here. Luqman, Razan, *yalla*.' And they still do it, they can't break the habit, so Razan has to—had to hear that every day. Like half of her was missing and she was always being reminded. That's why she sometimes took off to camp by herself."

Seif noted this unexpected sensitivity in Mercedes, a depth of insight beyond her years. And the words burned themselves into the secret place where he sheltered his rage.

Luqman, Razan, yalla.

He thought of the way he often called the twins, running their names together. *AlirezaMikhail.*

He had no illusions about Luqman's fate in Aleppo. Luqman and Razan were lost to the Elkaders. He saw his thought echoed in Mercedes' vulnerable face.

She let go of Catalina's hands, wiping the sleeve of her hoodie across her eyes. Slumping back in her chair, she said, "That would make *me* suicidal. I tried to be there for her because she was such a good friend, but I guess it wasn't enough. In a situation like that, I don't know what you're supposed to do."

Seif couldn't leave that on her shoulders, couldn't let the thought sink in like cement.

"You cared about her, Mercedes, and you haven't done anything wrong. Razan didn't commit suicide. You'll hear it sooner or later, so I'm telling you now—Razan was murdered."

Her lower lip began to tremble, her pupils dark with shock.

"*What?* Why?"

Seif looked down at the notes he'd scribbled while she was speaking, questions that urgently demanded answers. This was the moment to get them, when she'd refused the counsel of her father. But he couldn't do it to this girl, who'd just exhibited such compassion for her friend. He discreetly nudged Catalina, who asked, "Mercedes, do you need a moment? Would you like us to call your father in? Or we can arrange for a grief counselor to speak to you."

Mercedes didn't hear her. She was staring at the notepad in front of Seif, seeing the hard slash of his handwriting, the questions numbered in a row. She pressed her lips together, waving a hand at the page.

"Ask me your questions. I don't want to forget anything you need me to remember."

Seif looked to Catalina. She'd know if he was taking advantage or if he should proceed.

"Please," Mercedes interjected. "I *need* to help."

Catalina gave him the signal to go ahead.

He ran through the questions quickly, confirming the time and location Mercedes had last seen Razan, where they had parted ways. She hadn't checked sooner because their teachers hadn't made an issue of her absence, so she'd thought Razan's parents had called in and told them she was sick. She'd left messages for Razan on her cell, none of which were returned. Seif asked her to turn in her cell phone for their review. She looked uncomfortable, but she pulled it out of her purse and slid it across to him.

"You won't—you won't look at other things?"

He gazed at her steadily. "Do you mean photographs?"

She blushed a fiery red. "I don't send nudes! I'm a member of the church, and anyway, that's not something I would do. You can't trust boys. They show them off to their friends, and when they break up with you, they post them on social media."

The rage in Seif's gut stirred again at the thought that a teenage girl had already learned how to protect herself from the predators among his sex. It was a tangent, but he followed it up. "What about Razan?"

"Never!" she said in a deathly whisper. "She was Muslim. She wore hijab, she never showed her arms or legs or anything. She didn't even have a boyfriend."

That wasn't a guarantee of anything, in Seif's experience. He thought of his own rowdy brothers, who were pious and practicing, but thought about girls all the same.

"Do you have pictures with Razan?"

She nodded uneasily. "Just normal stuff. Selfies with our friends.

You can look at those if you want, but I have some private texts with my boyfriend. I could just delete that string?"

He felt a sudden warmth toward her at her obvious embarrassment, as he tried to fathom how this girl could be the child of Lincoln West, who was living the biker life. Bikers lived rough and hard, with no limits on their freedom. Perhaps Christian bikers were different, though evangelicals were as scandal-prone as anyone else in the church.

He slid her phone back to her, not telling her they could recover that data if any of their leads led them in that direction. Catalina wasn't on the same page.

"You don't have to surrender your phone, Mercedes. You can keep it if you want and ask us to get a warrant."

Of course Catalina would act to counsel the girl. He spared a brief moment to wonder if Inaya would have done the same—seeing herself as the girl's advocate, not adversary.

Mercedes pushed a few buttons on her phone, then passed it back to Seif. On the notepad where she'd jotted down the names of the friends who had been with Razan at the library, she neatly printed the password. The phone was an older model, not keyed to facial recognition. "I said I want to help you, and I will. Some things are private, but I don't have anything to hide." She blushed again, and quickly Seif directed her onto another subject.

"You mentioned that Mr. Elkader lost his job. Did you hear that from Razan?"

"Well, everyone kind of knows."

"About Razan's father?" he prodded, a little surprised by this statement. Catalina looked alert. She signaled to him, and he let her take over.

"You mean everyone knows about the plant where he worked? Was it Natural Foods?"

"Yes, the meatpacking plant. A lot of kids in Blackwater have parents who work there—mostly their dads, but a couple of the moms I know too."

It was clear Catalina knew the answer, but she urged, "So *what* does everybody know? About the plant, I mean?"

Mercedes looked puzzled. "I thought it was common knowledge. You get an injury, you're out. There's no compensation or anything, and they won't hire you back. They know people like Mr. Elkader don't have the money to sue."

"It was a work-related injury, then?"

Seif had seen the bandage, and he'd filed away the possibility that in the process of mounting a dead weight on a door, whoever had arranged Razan's body could have sustained a serious injury. He'd send Jaime to follow through with that, look into Hassan Elkader's medical records. And he'd read Cat right. She knew more about the plant than he, which was why she'd raised the question.

"So there was additional pressure on the family," Catalina mused.

"Well, that was one of the reasons Razan had to work. To help support her family."

Another question on Seif's list. He posed it now. "Where was Razan working?"

Mercedes' fingers closed around her pen. "At the ice cream shop on Main Street—do you know it? We went there a lot with her because she could get us a discount. And Mrs. Wendell, who owns the store, didn't mind. She's one of our church leaders, and she said it was good Razan brought in so much extra business."

"Razan didn't mind working at a place where she'd have to serve her classmates?"

Most of the families who sent their kids to Blackwater Academy were in an exclusive financial bracket; their kids didn't work unless it was some highly prized internship that would get them into a good college, and most of those internships were unpaid.

"Nobody hassled her about it. And even if they did, she'd been through a lot. So she didn't even notice the little things."

"What about your father and his friends? Did they ever stop in?"

He grinned when she rolled her eyes at him. "Can you imagine someone like my dad, or any biker for that matter, hanging out at an ice cream parlor?" The visual made Catalina smile, and Mercedes went on, "Bonebreakers Bar is more their speed. Besides, just because someone rides as part of a social club doesn't mean they're a bigot."

Seif had his own thoughts on that, but he didn't push it.

"So no harassment at work," he concluded.

Mercedes' eyes shifted away from his.

"There *was* something, then?"

"Not from my dad," she told him. "And not exactly harassment. Razan's dad didn't like it that she was working at the store."

"Because he liked his daughter at home? Or did he want to limit her exposure to members of the opposite sex?"

"Neither. Razan was a really good student—like top of the class, even genius. Her dad was worried she wouldn't be able to keep up her grades with her internship *and* working at the shop. It was a lot of hours. She didn't have much free time. That whole day we spent at the public library, the rest of us were blowing off our work, but Razan was really studying."

Seif was taken by surprise. "Her English was good enough that she was offered an internship?"

Mercedes nodded vigorously. "She picked it up in six months, and then there was no stopping her. But English wasn't her favorite subject— she was more into physics and math." She gave a delicate shudder. "The boys thought that was really cool."

Seif intended to return to this, but first he asked, "Where was she interning?"

"Apex Dynamics—do you know it? It's some kind of tech firm, but it's doing really well because it's a subcontractor for Lockheed."

The Lockheed Martin aerospace complex was one of the largest in the state.

"What kind of work did she do?"

Mercedes grimaced. "Well, they billed it as getting girls into STEM— you know, science, technology, engineering, and mathematics—but she said she was basically a coffee girl. After that, the guys didn't mind as much losing out on the internship."

Seif's antenna went up. "There was some resentment about Razan getting the job?"

Mercedes gave a bitter laugh. "Guys are so entitled. The job at Apex was such a hot opportunity—think about how good it would look on a college application. They thought one of them would get it for sure, even though Razan was president of the physics and computer clubs. She also did all the AV stuff for our drama productions—did you know?"

Catalina had told him as much.

"Can you tell us the names of the other competitors for the internship?"

Mercedes' lovely eyes filled with dismay. "I didn't mean to get anyone in trouble. It was just a stupid internship. No one would have hurt Razan just because she got it."

"But there *will* be a vacancy now."

"Maybe so, but like I said, all she did was get coffee for the boss. They gave her some extra homework, but as far as I know that was it. So the boys weren't all that upset in the end."

Maybe, Seif thought. Or maybe someone was itching to fill that vacancy. He kept that thought to himself.

Underlining the words now, he asked, "So no harassment at school, by students or teachers, as far as you know. None at work, either, by any members of the community who might be less than welcoming to . . . outsiders—and keep in mind that Razan was Syrian, Muslim, and a refugee. None from your father or his Disciples. Is that a fair summary?"

"Well . . . mostly."

A retraction. She was stepping back from her earlier unqualified position. And she'd mentioned something else that he'd set aside for the moment. Mrs. Wendell, ice cream parlor operator, was also a member of the Resurrection Church.

Another connection to the Disciples. But he'd better get that on the record.

"The Disciples follow the teachings of the Resurrection Church?"

"Yes?" She said it as a question.

"And Mrs. Wendell of the ice cream shop—she's a church leader at Resurrection, is that right?"

Mercedes beamed at him. "One of the best. She's cool with all the girls and parents."

He was trying to picture Lincoln West at a parent-teacher conference and failing. They'd be interviewing Mrs. Wendell, and could work that out for themselves. He pushed a little harder and got Mercedes to write down the names of the boys who might have resented losing the internship. Then he took on her retraction.

"What does 'mostly' mean, Mercedes? Was someone bothering Razan? Did she talk to you about that?"

"It only happened the one time. We sorted it out."

"What happened precisely—can you tell us? It might be important."

She bit her lip uncertainly. "I'd be getting people in trouble."

Seif was on the losing edge of his patience. Maybe Catalina sensed that, because she spoke to the girl gently, convinced her that if someone she knew *had* hurt Razan, she wouldn't want to be part of covering that up.

In response, Mercedes asked him, "How do I know I can trust you? How do I know you'll help?"

He bit back a cynical reply. He knew what he thought of his job, but if he confessed anything close to the truth, she'd terminate the interview and take her teenage secrets with her.

"You have my word that that's what we're here to do."

That was all it took for the story to come out.

CHAPTER EIGHTEEN

Razan was heading into gym class, dressed in her sweats, her headscarf loosely wrapped. The class was girls only, so she usually left her scarf on the bleachers. She was early and picked up a basketball, trying to do a layup.

The ball bounced away from the rim. Jeers sounded behind her. Her mouth turned down at the corners. It was Campbell Kerr and his friends, Matt and Dylan, seniors at their school. They called Campbell "Superman" because his initials were "CK," like Clark Kent. Razan wasn't sure how she felt about him. He wasn't as arrogant and entitled as some of the other boys who got off on bullying others, but he'd wanted the internship she'd gotten. His friends had taunted her, calling her a diversity hire. She didn't even know what that meant, so she'd asked Mercedes, who'd gotten so angry when she told her that Razan had to make light of the episode.

She faced Campbell and his friends warily, hoping the teacher would arrive at the gym soon or that the other girls would hurry up and join her.

"You're in the girls' gym class?" she asked them.

It might have been unwise to provoke them, but showing her fear would be worse.

The three of them came at her. Matt got her hands behind her back. Razan had dealt with Syrian security forces, eluding them when they'd given chase, once pushing one of them away when he'd caught her, fiercely grappling with her body. Now she leaned back against Matt's wiry frame, bringing her legs up and kicking Campbell in the chest. It was like shoving at stone. He grunted, but he didn't budge. His eyes were on her hair.

He made a grab for her headscarf. She saw it coming and ducked. Matt's arms were around her chest, wiry but strong, pinning her hard against him. She knocked her head back hard against his and saw stars. His grip loosened and she tumbled free, rolling back to her feet.

The four of them were still alone. She ducked around Campbell, racing for the door. He caught her before she got there, both hands coming up to capture the tail ends of her scarf. She jerked against his grip, and the scarf caught her at the throat, choking her. She let out a gurgling sound. He moved quickly then, releasing his hold on her scarf so he could whip it from her head.

She heard the sound of the scarf tearing, and she gasped.

Matt and Dylan laughed. Campbell stood there watching her. Her dark blond hair tumbled free, falling to her shoulders in waves. She struggled to gather it back into its ponytail, shoving it into the neck of her sweatshirt. Matt reached for her again.

Sweating, she saw that Campbell had taken out his phone. Matt wrenched her hair free with a rough jerk of his hand, combing his fingers through it. She swore at him in Arabic, landing a kick on his thigh. Her foot came down hard, his knee buckled, and then they were wrestling on the floor.

It took him two minutes to subdue her. He was panting above her, her hair flying everywhere, when Campbell leaned in with his phone. Matt grinned into the camera and called her something foul, her curls gathered in his hand.

She was too furious to cry. She leaned across and viciously bit his wrist, drawing blood. Humiliated, he cuffed her across the face.

Smugly, he said into the camera, "No ragheads in America. Score one for the USA."

The arrival of the rest of their gym class put an end to it. Matt scrambled off her body, holding his bleeding wrist like a badge. Campbell's phone disappeared from sight. Mercedes rushed in and helped Razan to her feet, finding her scarf and tossing it onto her head, too late.

The boys were suspended for a week.

But the video posted by Campbell was seen by everyone at school, then racked up thousands of views. Eventually, it was taken down, though it kept reappearing in private chat groups at school. A still of Razan without her hijab had been posted in the boys' locker room.

They'd intended to humiliate her, and maybe, in part, they'd succeeded.

But Razan had played it cool, mocking Campbell and the others in a video of her own, coached by Mercedes, who'd told her what to say.

"I didn't know Campbell was so into me—he was panting to see my hair." She paused and looked into the camera, her guileless eyes wide. "It's only hair. No need to be so desperate."

And with that, she'd scored a win over Campbell that had made him the butt of the joke.

CHAPTER NINETEEN

Seif let the silence build, digesting Mercedes' description of the incident.

"What you're describing is an assault. Did Razan report it?" Catalina probed.

Fire burned in Mercedes' eyes. "Yes. To the guidance counselor, the principal, even to the sheriff. Cam and his friends were suspended for a week, and then, like, it was done. It was hushed up, because no one wanted Cam to lose out on his future. Razan didn't matter as much."

"Wouldn't that give the boys license to harass Razan further?" Cat asked. "If the consequences they faced were so minor?"

Mercedes drummed her fingers impatiently. "Cam's parents are lawyers. They turned the screws on the school."

Seif considered this from the perspective of a teenage male's place in the pecking order at high school. A lawsuit based on an injury inflicted by a girl would be a hit to his Superman ego. He put that conclusion to Mercedes.

"Cam's posse always finds a way to make him look good. His parents' money solves his other problems, though he doesn't usually ask for their help."

"You sound like you know him well."

"We used to date, but it never got serious."

"Why was that?"

Mercedes hesitated. "I didn't have a problem with Cam until he did what he did to Razan, but I didn't like his friends all that much. They used to hit on me when Cam wasn't around. I asked him to drop them and he didn't." She shrugged with classic teenage cool. "So I dropped him instead."

Seif admired her self-confidence in standing up for herself.

"Did the bullying continue?"

Mercedes must have read his anger, because this time she volunteered freely, "Not from Cam so much, but whatever there was, my father put an end to it."

"Your father?" Catalina sounded surprised, and no wonder. The Disciples made for unlikely heroes, especially given the way they'd stormed the Elkaders' house. "What did your father do?"

"My dad set Cam and his posse straight. They never bothered Razan again." Her eyes were wide and wondering. "I don't know if it was just my dad, though. Being scouted for college was important for Cam, but he went kind of quiet after."

"Did he feel guilty? Was he ashamed of what he'd done?"

"I wish I knew." Mercedes sighed a little. "It would be nice to have a reason to think well of him again." She flicked a glance at the door. "What about my father? Will he be all right?"

"That depends on what he tells us."

CHAPTER TWENTY

Inaya could tell Seif was reconsidering whether to include her in the interview with Lincoln "Ranger" West. She suspected Ranger would be gentle with Cat, as most men were, but she also knew she hadn't imagined her own rapport with him. She shivered a little. Rapport with a possible white supremacist wasn't exactly what she'd signed up for. On the other hand, she didn't intend to back down.

She didn't rush Seif, letting him come to it in his own time, and he did.

"Can you handle this?"

"Absolutely."

Cat offered to check on the pathologist's report.

"Later," Seif said. "I want you to oversee the interview from outside." He indicated the surveillance room. "And when we're done, I need you to run down a map of the Chatfield Reservoir. As detailed as you can find. Get Jaime to check the bookings for the last month."

Inaya's interest was piqued. They'd had no reason to flag the reservoir during the course of the investigation. Did Seif have a lead he hadn't shared?

"Coming?" He held the door to the interview room open for her.

Ranger was sitting at the table, leaning all the way back in his chair, his thick forearms crossed over his chest, the veins running like rivulets beneath the ink of his tattoos. His long legs were stretched out, the ankles crossed in a casual pose that was altogether too studied.

Inaya and Seif took up seats across from him.

Bluntly, Seif asked, "Did you assault my officer?"

Ranger grinned at Inaya. "Don't think I did. Did I, babe?"

"Maybe not," she conceded. "But you were trespassing, and you did aim a gun at Detective Hernandez and myself. Was that a legally registered firearm?"

"Not hard to get a gun in Colorado."

"That doesn't answer my question."

He jerked his head at the two-way mirror. Seif's brows went up, yet he didn't seem all that surprised, as if a private signal were moving between the two men.

Ranger stood up and moved close. He wasn't handcuffed, because Seif had wanted him to have room so they could see how things would play out during the interview. Seif didn't back away from the taller, bulkier man. The biker whispered something in his ear. Seif looked to the window, then to Inaya. He paused. Then he left the room.

Inaya stared at Ranger, who grinned at her.

"You should go too, Brazil."

Inaya gritted her teeth. "I'm *not* Brazilian, as I think you know, Ranger."

"Name's not Ranger."

He strolled back to his chair, spreading out with a sigh. When Seif returned he sat up straight, all business. "You call it in?"

"I've heard your name, but I checked you out to make sure." Seif jerked his chin down, the dent at the corner of his mouth dark and deep.

"Yeah, I've heard of you too." He jerked his chin at Inaya. "What about her? You trust her? There's a lot riding on this."

Seif's endorsement was hardly unequivocal. "Enough to continue for now."

"Someone's leaking information to the sheriff, keeping him up to date on your progress."

This time Seif was more emphatic. "Inaya is safe."

Safe for what? She looked at the two men, confused. "What's going on? You sound like you know each other."

Ranger's laid-back manner was suddenly a thing of the past. He slipped a hand into the pocket of his jeans, and flipped his wallet onto the table.

She peeled it open, incredulous.

To Seif, she said, "Did you know Ranger was undercover?"

"Not exactly. But he's not unknown in certain circles. He's with the FBI."

"Joint Terrorist Task Force," Ranger clarified. He morphed from biker to federal investigator in the blink of an eye, addressing Inaya with calm professionalism. "And for God's sake, don't call me Ranger. When I'm not a Disciple, I'm West."

"How long have you been embedded with the Disciples?" she asked as Seif pushed his credentials back at him and Lincoln West returned them to his pocket.

"Three years. I'm in deep," he told her. "Investigating their involvement in domestic terrorism. They sent members to storm the Capitol."

Still finding it hard to believe, Inaya asked, "State or federal?"

"Both." He was serious now, the teasing manner discarded.

"Finally," Seif muttered. Inaya ignored this to ask, "What about Mercedes? Is she a plant? You wouldn't risk your daughter anywhere near insurrectionists."

"She's not at risk," West said firmly. "I make sure to keep her clear."

"Does she know?" Inaya asked, surprised.

He shook his head, regret plain on his face. "That's what would put her at risk." He shrugged. "Better she thinks I'm a criminal than be in a position to be used against me. The backstory—my entry into the Disciples—that's as close to the truth as possible. I've been a Christian biker most of my life; that's how I got recruited to the task force. Now tell me about my kid—how did her interview go? I'm thinking you knew better than to strong-arm her."

"You have nothing to worry about there," Inaya replied. "No one could go hard on such a tenderhearted kid."

West's face softened with gratitude, a warm look in his eyes for Inaya. She gave him an encouraging smile, and his gaze grew more intense, all his focus on her. There was no denying West was attractive—she'd thought so even when she'd believed him to be a criminal. Now, with the shine of his FBI credentials and the news of his undercover mission, his pull was even more powerful. She drew in her breath, and Seif gave her a scalding look. But rather than letting it cow her, she stubbornly kept her attention on West, thinking, *Can't a girl look?*

West's smile was different this time—a little wicked, as if he'd guessed his impact on her. Inaya's eyes glinted with challenge—she wasn't any man's prey—and his smile deepened.

Irritated, Seif returned them to the matter at hand. "What kind of crimes are the Disciples involved with? Razan Elkader's murder?"

Inaya had the sense he resented something about West—maybe being played for a fool. But it felt personal.

"There's no talk about Razan among the club." He rubbed the rough growth on his jaw. "I think their involvement is unlikely. They sell drugs, run guns—you probably know about that—to fund their insurrectionist activities. They don't want the attention of the cops, and the girl's death is nothing if not a spotlight."

"Then why buzz the Elkaders' house?"

"They've been engaging in the routine harassment of outsiders since the club started up. Hardtack said reining it in now would look like we have something to hide."

Inaya's thoughts darted off on various tangents. There was so much to get into about the Disciples, including why West expected Seif to know about whatever the Disciples were into, but she began with, "So your encounter with us was staged?"

"Mine was, yes," he agreed. "Not theirs." The lines in his face deepened. "Mercedes wasn't supposed to be there. I had to get things under control."

If that was his intention, he'd blown it, Inaya thought. "We had four guns out. You need to pull your daughter out of this, Ranger."

"How do I do that? Her mother's in Mexico, and we don't have any other family. No." He pounded his fist, and Inaya jumped. "She's my daughter, my responsibility."

"She was close to Razan, and if the Disciples aren't involved with her death, someone else is. Maybe someone at the Academy or the church. There's a cloud hanging over her head."

"Protecting her is my job. I'm not turning that over to anyone else. And didn't I tell you to call me West? 'Ranger' works for the Disciples."

"West," she obliged, and he relaxed. "Is that why you stepped in when Campbell Kerr and his friends were targeting Razan?"

"No man worth the name would give those guys a pass. Plus Razan was a friend of my daughter's. Teenage boys are posers. It didn't take much to scare the shit out of them."

Inaya wasn't fooled by his nonchalance.

"Did you ever meet Razan?"

"I couldn't. Too fine a line to walk between Mercedes and the club. My kid will be devastated."

Inaya made a sympathetic sound.

"Why the tattoo if they didn't kill Razan?" Seif fired the words like bullets. West gazed at him, surprised. He turned his forearm over and, close to, Inaya noticed that the tattoo was like a painting—a gorgeous example of religious art in blue and gold and red.

"What's the name of the artist?" She flicked open her notepad.

West frowned at them. "I don't see the connection."

Seif explained about the arrangement of the body, and West growled low in his throat.

"Christ."

It wasn't an allusion to Razan. He glanced down at his tattoo, rubbing at the cross absently. He gave her the name of the artist to write down.

"I don't know that that will help. Getting tattooed was part of my initiation into the Disciples. Some part of their Christianity is real."

"Not the parts about welcoming refugees and cherishing the poor, I'm guessing."

West's eyes lit with humor. "No, not that part."

"So you chose the design yourself?" Seif interrupted. He seemed averse to their rapport.

"Yeah. Thought it would make me one of them. The Disciples may be nothing more than low-rent hatemongers, but their ties to the church are deep."

"If they stormed the Capitol on January sixth, I wouldn't call them low-rent."

"They weren't instigators, they didn't plan it, Seif. They just went along for the ride."

"Quite a ride." Seif didn't hide his contempt.

"Do we have a problem here?" West demanded.

"Yeah," Seif batted back. "If they're not instigators, and you're with the Joint Terrorist Task Force, why have you been in with them for three years?"

West looked impatient. "It takes time to build cover, you know that. You don't show up and make Road Captain overnight. More, there was chatter about their intentions and I had to sound it out to make sure it was nothing."

"Then why are you still here?"

A bright, burning energy filled the room, so hot that it seared Inaya. The two men were in a standoff she didn't understand, undercurrents rippling. Nervously, she cleared her throat. West glared at Seif for a full minute, but he was the first to back down.

With a sigh of frustration, he told them, "You can question my motives all you like, but you've already checked me out." He paused, considering his next words. "Let's just say that the Disciples are branching out, getting serious about their evangelism."

Seif didn't meet him halfway. He snarled a single word. "Meaning?"

West gestured at Inaya. "If you can't understand, maybe Detective Rahman will. Christian evangelism has taken a nasty turn. Or it could be it was always that way. It's anti-Black, anti-immigrant, anti-Muslim. Like I said, outsiders aren't welcome, and they're getting invested in keeping them out through hazing and harassment. I'm embedded in the plot."

Seif's response was sarcastic. "But they didn't kill Razan, as far as you're in the know."

"No, you're right, they didn't. I'm on them, and I'm in with them, so if it was a Disciple, he was acting on his own. I'll keep an eye on things, though. Tell them the questions you asked me were about Razan. That might flush something out."

Seif and Inaya paused by the door, ushering West out.

"You've got me in the system," West said. "You need to keep me there, and keep my identity locked down. Hardtack is tight with the sheriff, and word is that Grant's getting his info from somewhere. That's why his hands are clean. Grant knows how to look out for himself."

Inaya's stomach tightened when she saw Seif make a quick motion with his hands, warning West to shut up. "Go on ahead," he told her.

She slipped outside the door but didn't leave, straining to hear what he said.

West's deep voice rumbled incomprehensibly.

Seif's, on the other hand, was clear. "If you'd let me know you were undercover, I could have kept you out of this."

Inaya pressed closer to the door and heard West say, "You don't advertise it—that's why they call it 'undercover.' You of all people should know that."

A long pause. What were they doing? Why didn't they speak?

She held her breath until she heard West speak again. "Watch your team," he warned, his front of geniality gone. "The sheriff has someone on the inside. I like her, but what if it's Detective Rahman?"

CHAPTER TWENTY-ONE

Cat waved Seif and Inaya over.

"I've found the video." Her gentle face was grim.

They crowded into the surveillance room, Cat's computer screen on pause. The lights were dim, the window looking out onto an empty interview room, the scene bare and antiseptic. The hum of the computer was loud in Inaya's ears.

Cat hit a button and the video began to play. Campbell Kerr must have had the latest smartphone, because the picture quality was excellent, though the video wavered with the movement of his hand.

The episode of Razan being assaulted in the gym by three burly football players was uglier than Mercedes had been able to convey.

Bile rose in Inaya's throat, acrid and hot, the taste trapped in her throat.

Cat had paused the screen on Razan's stricken face. The girl had lost something in that moment, and it wasn't just the belief that she'd found a place of safety fleeing Syria.

Plain as day on her face was the knowledge that no place was safe for her. Yet the bitter curve of her lips appeared to take that in stride.

But more than that, beyond that, there was a look in those dark eyes that Inaya knew well. A toxic combination of shame and doubt, her self-respect shattered. The assault had involved a chastening of her pride. Maybe even a humbling of who she was.

A wave of sickness swept over Inaya, worse than what she'd experienced at the sight of Razan's body. In death, there had been a solemn dignity. In this, there was only pain, a pain that caught at Inaya's throat, choking off her voice. She had an intimate awareness of Razan's vulnerability. As a newly minted lawyer in Chicago, COPA—the Civilian Office of Police Accountability—had been her training ground.

She went into work every day with her head held high, ignoring bacon sandwiches left in her desk drawers, beer spilled in her locker, the trashing of her personal effects. She couldn't ignore the disappearance of key supporting evidence from her files, or the silencing of her complainants, cases suspiciously dropped just as they were coming together.

There were reprimands in her personnel records on minor technicalities. She rapidly acquired a reputation not as a whistleblower or troublemaker, but as a traitor. She didn't bleed blue. She didn't know whose side she was on. She was a brown face in a very white police force—she was someone who didn't belong.

And she was Muslim, with that rag on her head.

Ultimately, it was all about the rag on her head.

Her headscarf, or more accurately, her hijab.

Her promise of decorum in her conduct before God.

Her choice. Not imposed on her by her father, as some supposed. Nor dictated to her by community pressure, or this or that imam. Something she chose for herself, something personal and intimate, that nonetheless proclaimed her ideals to anyone who saw her. A conflict between her inner and outer worlds. A conflict that nearly led to a complete breakdown.

Racist taunts became racist deeds. Graffiti on her locker. Pornographic emails. Headlights blazing through her parents' house, a pig's head left on their doorstep. A flyer sent to her parents' mosque with her picture blown up in the center, Inaya in uniform, under the words, "Does Officer Rahman represent you?"

If it was intended to isolate her in her community, given the powder keg that was race relations with the Chicago Police Department, it worked. She was a traitor twice over, too brown for the badge, too blue for her coreligionists. Inaya had known what she was taking on when she decided to put her legal training to work at COPA. What she hadn't expected was that she would experience the dichotomies so explicitly.

Her parents were well-respected and she herself was popular in the community, so she'd held her ground, made her explanations, told them what she was fighting for and why. She'd seen good cops at work, seen her colleagues make a difference in both COPA and the Civil Rights Unit. Something could be done. She could be one of those officers who changed the system from the inside.

But she was still in the Laquan McDonald period, before the George Floyd tide had flooded over them. The communities she served were vulnerable; she was vulnerable too. She'd learned the extent of her weakness when she'd moved forward on a complaint against a popular officer, despite being warned to drop it. She'd learned a brutal lesson. Seeing proof of Razan's assault brought that lesson back.

"Inaya, what's the matter?" Cat's voice broke into her turbulent thoughts. She turned away from the video with an inner admonition to remember that this was a different time, a different place. She'd survived her humiliation by running away from it, leaving her work undone, lacking the courage to explain things to those who'd deserved better from her before she disappeared. Her judgment of herself was harsh: she was locked in a moment of terror, unable to make another choice. Her desire to change the system from within had taken a serious hit. What was she doing as part of an institution that had proved itself incapable of reform?

But then she thought of people like Cat and Jaime, and maybe even Waqas Seif. They had stepped right in to fight for justice for Razan. If they didn't do it, who would?

To Cat, she said wryly, "Just feeling sorry for myself."

Sympathy shone from Cat's kind dark eyes. She'd told Cat the entire story, and Catalina had listened without judgment, without pushing Inaya to return and finish the job she'd started. She suspected there was a reason Cat didn't see things in black and white—her own past confronting ICE agents couldn't have been pretty—yet something was holding Cat back from confiding in Inaya in turn.

"It was brutal." Inaya wasn't talking about herself. "Razan looked like she'd been catapulted back to the worst days of her life."

She hadn't asked Fatima Elkader about the dangers she and Razan had encountered fleeing Syria, partly because she thought she might not be able to stomach the answer, partly because she hadn't wanted to shame a woman who'd already suffered so much.

"Look at this, though."

Cat pulled up a second video on Mercedes' phone. It showed a confident young Razan with a fashionably styled hijab and a touch of lip gloss on her lips, delivering her kill shot.

"I didn't know Campbell was panting to see my hair."

Her accent was lovely and lilting, her pose defiant, and Inaya wondered if she was the only one who could see the strain behind the posturing.

"No doubt this was a hit to Kerr's ego. I wonder what he did in response."

"We haven't interviewed him or his friends yet," Cat told her.

"You're not going to, either," Seif said as he joined them in the room, swiveling the screen so he could watch Razan's takedown of Kerr. "The sheriff tells me he's a football hero—the big man on campus at Blackwater Academy, the blue-eyed boy all around."

"We can't play favorites," Inaya pointed out.

He straightened, turning the screen back around. "I wasn't planning to, but a big part of Kerr's makeup seems to be taking women down—proving he's a man." His gaze moved between Inaya and Cat. "I'm not subjecting you to that."

He overrode Inaya's instinctive objection. "He'll be more cooperative with me. First up, though, we need to do a deep dive into Razan's background—I want to know about her friends, any problems at school, or with her family."

"What about the church? Or the company where she was an intern?"

"Like I said, before we rattle any of the power players in this town, we need background. I put someone on that like you asked; when we're done here, check in with the team. Also, make sure any necessary inter-

views have been set up for you while you go through what we've got."
He checked something on his phone, then raised his head. "Dr. Stanger
needs a few more days on the postmortem, Catalina. When he's ready,
use what he has for your profile. Webb is reporting to me on the reservoir. Once he's done, he can canvass people at the public library and
check in with Mrs. Wendell at the ice cream parlor. We should be able
to nail down the last time Razan was seen." He waited while they scribbled notes. "Rahman, you can tackle the school, but when you head out
to Apex Dynamics, I want both of you on that interview."

Inaya had noticed before that Seif ensured that neither she nor Cat
went out on their own, unless it was to an innocuous event like a county
fair. Yet Jaime, who was their junior, was often given solo assignments.
It could be that Cat and Inaya's work was more serious and required the
insights of two senior detectives, or it could be that Seif was protective
of them, something he wouldn't admit to. She should have resented it,
but she didn't. It would take a while to build up her nerve to the point
where she felt safe on the job without a partner.

"The sheriff might interfere if we start stepping on toes," Inaya
warned.

"Then I suggest you be more diplomatic than you were with the
Elkaders."

"You could have taken that interview," she said sweetly.

She should have known better than to taunt him. His comeback was
sharp and to the point. "If you need me to do your job, feel free to let
me know."

"Like hell," she muttered under her breath, all sweetness abandoned.

CHAPTER TWENTY-TWO

For the next two days, Cat and Inaya did as directed by Seif, putting together the early pieces of Razan's life, tracking the Elkaders' immigration status, while Jaime searched bookings at various campgrounds, trying to corroborate the last known sighting of Razan. The use of Razan's library card proved she had been at the library in the early afternoon on Wednesday, when the Academy had a half-day. Razan's friends at school confirmed they had entered and left the premises together, though Razan had studied in a quiet room by herself. A quick chat with Tori Wendell at the ice cream parlor verified that Razan's group of friends had stopped in for ice cream between five and six that night. Razan had left the parlor on her own. No one they'd spoken to yet had seen Razan after that, which would put the time of death between Wednesday evening and the Sunday morning she was found.

Double-checking with the Elkaders, Cat discovered that Fatima Elkader was still in the hospital: the family's latest tragedy had exacerbated underlying health issues. Hassan Elkader said that he hadn't seen his daughter after Wednesday morning, and had not been unduly alarmed because Razan sometimes chose to go camping by herself. She should have let them know, yes, but cell phone reception around the foothills was hit-or-miss.

Jaime headed into Seif's office, probably to confer about the campsites up near Marina Point. Cell phone location data had come in on Razan's phone and everyone else's they'd interviewed thus far. Inaya was sorting through the data now with the help of a few junior officers. Cat offered to help.

"You focus on the profile; we can manage this."

Cat perched on the edge of Inaya's desk. "Anything so far?"

Inaya gestured at the others. "From what these tech whizzes have explained to me, Razan shut her phone off at the library on Wednesday around two p.m. She never turned it back on."

A sharp pain burned under Cat's ribs. "Premeditated," she said. "Someone knew her schedule." She thought for a moment. "She didn't turn it back on at the parlor?"

Inaya shifted through a pile of statements. "Mercedes said she liked to be present when she was with her friends—she had it on the table, but she didn't keep it on all the time." Inaya's sorrow was palpable. "As awful as this is, it helps us with the timeline."

Cat's exhale was like a soft cry.

"Go home, Cat. You have an early appointment."

Inaya was just as tired, but this time Cat agreed. Emiliano had been complaining about her late hours. He'd been even less thrilled about tomorrow's early start, so she'd cook him his favorite dinner before she fell into bed.

"I'll see you tomorrow. Say good night to Seif for me."

Catalina's early morning appointment was with Julius Stanger. She'd met him briefly at the crime scene and liked him immediately. He gave off an air of cool competence, but didn't bother with the professional detachment that was second nature to most people who did the kind of work they did. You might need that emotional remove to do the job properly, but Dr. Stanger ruled his mournful kingdom the way he wanted—fully invested in the victim.

When he finished the call he was on, he met Catalina in the hall, wearing a suit beneath his lab coat. He took her to view Razan's body, then brought her back to his office.

"Did you finish more quickly than usual?" she asked him.

"Just the preliminary report. Cause of death was the wound between the fourth and fifth ribs. The lateral entry pierced the abdominal aorta. That's how she bled out."

Cat leaned in a little. "How long would that have taken?"

"No more than a few minutes. To put it simply, she bled to death, though the body didn't decompose. I can tell you the medical side of it; the rest is more your purview than mine."

"I'm not following."

"She wasn't killed where she was found—there was no blood on site, and there would have been a great deal of blood. Her clothes were clean too, so she was dressed in fresh clothing after the kill, before rigor could occur. From the temperature of her internal organs, her body was frozen. My guess would be she was kept in a large freezer, since none of her limbs were broken. There were particles in Razan's lungs—they might tell us more about where she was held and for how long. We're doing cell deterioration tests as well, to pin down the time of death."

"How does that work?"

A long analysis followed on the science of water molecules transforming into the ice crystals known as freezer burn or frost, and the comparative differences with blood. Cat grimaced at the comparison of human flesh to animal decomposition, but the long and the short of it was that Stanger estimated the body had been frozen for less than seventy-two hours and had begun the process of thawing during transportation from a freezer.

Cat's team had already discussed other factors: the kill site, the absence of blood at the scene, the transport vehicle that must have been used. All questions without answers.

"What about the murder weapon? Is there anything you can tell us?"

A noise clanged in the hallway beyond—the sound of a drawer in the cold room closing? A moment later, there was a heavy knock at the door. A tall, angular man in a thin suit pushed the door open before Stanger could answer.

The man's blue eyes skated over Cat. Stanger introduced him as Russell Pincher.

"Sheriff's expecting a report," Pincher told the pathologist. It came out like a demand.

Stanger shook his head, and the way he did it told Cat he took a certain pleasure in refusing the man who'd interrupted them.

"I'm only authorized to share my findings with the detectives from CRU." He waved a hand at Cat. "Which I'm doing, as you can see."

"Grant won't like it," Pincher warned him, ignoring Cat.

"I can't help that." Stanger's voice was firm.

Pincher didn't swear, didn't move. His cold gaze traveled around Stanger's office, pausing on his computer. He tipped his head at Cat.

"They'll be gone soon enough, Stanger. Grant and I will still be here."

The threat stood on its own. Pincher closed the door behind him.

Stanger gave Cat a rueful smile. "Sorry about that. It's the price of doing business here."

Cat's head turned to the door. "A heavy price, it seems to me."

"I can handle Pincher. And Grant for that matter, if I have to."

"You *shouldn't* have to," Cat said gently. "When they make the job political, they dirty it. I take it Pincher works for Grant?"

Stanger made himself busy with his computer. "He's Grant's fixer."

There were whispers about Blackwater Falls, whispers about those who worked with Grant, whispers that left them oily. Julius Stanger didn't have that oily sheen—he was capable and direct, handsome in a bland way, though he had an edge.

"Don't let him fix you," she murmured.

"Count on it, Catalina."

He didn't say her name like Seif did; he made the "t" sharp. Gently, she corrected him. Embarrassed, he made the adjustment at once.

"We were talking about the murder weapon," she said, to get them back on track.

He angled his monitor to face her. A sketch appeared on the screen. Catalina removed her reading glasses from her purse and perched them on her nose.

"This is what the angle of penetration tells us, along with the internal damage."

She was looking at a long, thin blade—more a spike than a blade with the way it veered off at the tip like an extreme right-angle triangle.

"Have you identified it?"

"I think it's a tool," Stanger told her. "The kind you attach to a military knife, though I haven't seen one like this in these parts. Members of my team are running it."

Cat was doubtful. "A blade like that doesn't look like it would have the strength to do that kind of damage. Wouldn't it snap off, if it was a tool?"

"Not if it was military-grade. It's not one of our military's, though."

She made a mental note to do some digging on Apex Dynamics and its military contacts. No one else connected to Razan had a military background, unless it was her brother in Syria.

Stanger's glance at her was keen. "You haven't found the murder weapon."

"Or the kill site, or a place where her body may have been stored, or the vehicle used to transport Razan's body. There were no witnesses to the crucifixion."

"I'm sorry. I was hoping to be of more help."

"The sketch helps," she assured him. "Are you finished with the Elkaders' house? We need to do a search."

"Officially, we'll release the scene tomorrow. Unofficially, I can tell you, Razan wasn't killed at home. There's no blood at the house, no appliance large enough to hold her, and no other signs of struggle or a disturbance. I'm not sure where the parents are staying, but they can return home soon."

"Mrs. Elkader is in the hospital; I believe her husband is staying with friends. We'll notify them after we've completed our search."

She returned her glasses to her purse, standing up.

Stanger beat her to the door. He gripped the knob to hold it closed.

"There's one other thing I should mention. Your terrain, I'm afraid."

"There's quite a bit of overlap, Julius. I'd like to hear what you think."

The dead speak, she wanted to tell him. *Only a few of us listen.*

"I mention it because of the way you gave the body time."

"I was showing Razan the respect she deserved, just as you did."

When he had taken her to view the body, she had wanted to protest the bleak responsibility until she'd seen what Julius had done. Razan was fully covered, the wound alone exposed. Her hair and throat were concealed by a dignified headcloth. The act of maintaining Razan's hijab told Cat a lot about Julius.

His eyes warmed, and he hurried into speech. "That's just it, Catalina. The entry wound indicated something similar."

Catalina pursed her lips. Murder wasn't respect.

"The wound was precise, the injury acute," he went on, oblivious to Cat's thoughts. "The killer couldn't have approached her from a distance with that particular weapon. He'd have had to be standing right next to her. He may have been . . . close . . . to her."

"It's possible," she agreed. "Or he approached in the dark when she couldn't see him."

Stanger leaned against the door. "I don't think so."

Cat looked up at him, curious. "Why not?"

"Death was nearly instantaneous. He didn't want her to suffer."

Which led Cat to wonder if the killer had cared.

CHAPTER TWENTY-THREE

By that afternoon, their team had completed background checks on the Elkaders and been out to the reservoir. Search teams had gone to local campgrounds and reported back to Seif: there was no sign of Razan. If she'd gone camping, it wasn't at Chatfield State Park.

They'd also familiarized themselves with the major players in town. Inaya had established links, mainly through campaign donations, between most of these players and the sheriff, though he'd stonewalled her wherever he could. He'd refused to turn over paperwork, acted as if he hadn't been removed, and was generally resistant to any pressure she or Seif tried to exert. Though, truthfully, she wasn't altogether certain Seif *was* exerting any pressure.

It was late Thursday afternoon, and she and Cat were on a break, catching each other up at Marhaba, the bakery whose name translated into a welcome, before they returned for a briefing.

Marhaba was run by a friendly Lebanese couple, and had highly coveted seating under a picture window that looked out onto the falls, the foothills silhouetted behind them. The mouthwatering scent of *kanafeh* drifted down the street to the old town stores, an irresistible draw. Inaya and Cat met there once a month to catch up on their personal lives. Cat shared tidbits about her husband Emiliano, a proud and fiercely handsome Mexican-American. Emiliano hated that Cat had given up her career at the NGO she'd founded "to work from inside the system," a phrase Emiliano loathed. He wasn't quiet about this, and the wrangling between them dampened Cat's otherwise sunny demeanor. When it was Inaya's turn to confide, they picked over her nonexistent love life, and the challenges involved in keeping an eye on her younger sisters.

"Why does everything reek in this town?" she asked Cat, her thoughts returning to the sheriff. Cyrine Haddad, the Lebanese proprietor, stopped by their table to take their order before Cat could come up with an answer. Cyrine was a sweet-natured woman in her fifties, with an unlined face and the most beautifully groomed eyebrows Inaya had ever seen. They lay like sleek pelts across her brow, a dark contrast to her dyed golden curls. She wore flawless makeup that suited her tawny skin, and had gold chains swathed around her neck, a showy Maronite cross dangling from one. She was glamour and artifice on the surface, warmth and simplicity at heart.

Lebanese music played lightly on the stereo, and the scent of *kanafeh*, rich, cheese-filled, and syrupy, saturated the room. Cyrine had a strong artistic sensibility, and had decorated with vintage posters of Lebanon, most with place names in French, including one for Messageries Maritimes advertising a cruise with stops in Egypte-Syrie-Liban. Behind Inaya's head was an advertisement that invited tourists to "Visit Baalbek," a city in the Beqaa Valley known as Heliopolis in Greek and Roman times. Across the room was Inaya's favorite poster, a sweeping view of the wide arc of Beirut's Corniche done in Art Deco style, with blocks of green and white and blue. Not a single camel was featured, and nowhere was the script in Arabic.

Once, Inaya had been shopping at a cleaned-out local grocery during the holidays, and a man in the same aisle had said on his phone to his wife, "This looks like downtown Beirut." He hadn't noticed Inaya, who managed not to roll her eyes. Clearly, the man knew little about the cosmopolitan city often described as the Riviera of the Middle East.

She and Cat loved Cyrine's bakery. It was the kind of place that washed their worries away. Most of that was due to the genuine warmth of its proprietor.

Cyrine unloaded their drinks from a tray, saying, "Pakistani chai for my darling girl, and Mexican café for my daughter, yes?"

Inaya's tea was milky and sweet, the milk and tea boiled. Cat's coffee was rich and dark, almost bitter. She considered sugar a sacrilege when it came to her brew.

The drinks were followed by two enormous helpings of *kanafeh*. Both women could eat no more than a quarter of a slice, taking the rest home to their families. Cyrine had already placed pretty white boxes with green and red trim by their plates. She had beautiful hands, with balanced, capable bones.

"Gather your strength, my darlings. For this is a terrible thing, *non*?" She clicked her tongue at them. "You must be working very hard."

Inaya invited her to sit, and Cyrine called to a handsome, dark-haired boy to bring her a cup of spiced tea. The boy, Elias, was her son, and he'd inherited her elegant eyebrows and tawny skin, though he lacked her sunny demeanor. He had the brooding-teenager thing going on, his cell phone glued to his hand and his conversation limited to a phrase or two. But he liked Inaya and Cat and could be counted on for a nod in their direction.

He placed his mother's tea on the table and sauntered off to a corner, where he hunched up his shoulders to read something on his phone.

Inaya took a sip of her tea. Heavenly.

Fortified, she asked Cyrine if she knew the Elkaders. The Haddads were Christian, so they wouldn't have met at the mosque, but they could have met at the bakery.

"A terrible thing," Cyrine said again, her face suddenly drooping. "One child and I would be inconsolable. But *two* of their boys, and now that sweet child Razan? What devil followed them from Syria?"

Inaya knew she didn't mean it literally, but she hadn't considered that angle. Could the past be at play? How likely was it that an enemy from Aleppo had made his way to Blackwater Falls? Still, the boy, Luqman, had been in the resistance. What about the father?

Cat tipped her head to the side. Inaya followed her gaze to where Elias was no longer leaning against the bakery case. He'd straightened, and his hands were in fists, his cell phone abandoned. He'd been eavesdropping on their conversation. He'd been with Mercedes and Razan on Wednesday, and at the ice cream parlor, too. The police had spoken to him to confirm Razan's movements: he was one of the last people to see Razan, and Inaya wondered how he was bearing up. Inaya nodded at Cat, who wandered over to the boy.

"Have you been to see them?" Inaya asked Cyrine.

"Of course. The community arranged a Qur'an *khatam* ceremony for Razan, and the parents are anxious for a quick burial, as is their custom."

Inaya sympathized. The delay in burying Razan would be anathema to devout Muslim parents, yet she'd had no choice but to put Fatima off after she'd collapsed with grief, even as she'd promised her Razan's body would be treated with respect. Nonetheless, the body was evidence and would remain with the pathologist until they were certain there was nothing more to learn from the way she'd been murdered. A *khatam*, however, required nothing more than a gathering of friends prepared to complete a recitation of the Qur'an as a blessing for the deceased.

"Was Razan having any problems that you knew of?" She lowered her voice. "Did she have a boyfriend?"

Cyrine's gem-studded fingers traced the rim of her cup. She looked up at Inaya.

"Do you know about the incident at school? With the football hero?" When Inaya nodded, she went on, "That was the only thing, as far as I knew. She was a good girl, a very hard worker. She wasn't easy to intimidate or to embarrass."

"How do you know this?"

"Elias told me. She organized the multicultural night at their school, and after that, some of these"—she made an expressive gesture with her hand, choosing not to finish her comment with an epithet—"these *children* would follow her home from school or to her place of work and call her names. She didn't even notice it." Cyrine marveled at the thought.

Inaya frowned to herself. How could Razan not have suffered if she was being bullied? How could she have dismissed it—the same way she'd dismissed the assault by Campbell Kerr? What kind of teen was that certain of herself, that self-assured about her place in the world?

"Elias attends Blackwater Academy?"

"Of course," his mother said proudly.

Inaya glanced over to where Cat and Elias were engaged in earnest conversation.

"How is he taking her death?"

Cyrine sat back in her chair. Her gaze flicked to an old-fashioned clock on the wall, the numbers on the dial circling a three-barred cross at the center—a Maronite cross like the one she wore at her neck. Her voice sounded very different when she said, "Are you asking me as a friend or as a police officer?"

"A friend, of course." There were no circumstances in which she could imagine a teenage boy like Elias devising or carrying out such a complicated—and though she hated herself for thinking it—and *artistic* murder.

"Listen, Cyrine, have you heard anything about a Somali girl going missing in Blackwater? You've lived here much longer than I have."

Cyrine's rosebud lips formed an "O," and she said, "You don't know?"

So there *was* something to know.

"When you come here as an immigrant, there's a lot they don't tell you." Cyrine looked at her with a meaningful expression. "Rights you're entitled to, others that don't exist."

"I'm not following."

Cyrine sighed. "If the girls were white, the police might have done something. The news reporters might have come around and asked questions."

Hairs rose on the back of Inaya's neck. "Cyrine, what girls? Was there more than one?"

Cyrine carefully unfolded a paper napkin. She grabbed a pen from the counter and scribbled something on the napkin. She folded it into a square and passed it to Inaya, sliding it under her hand.

"There are some things in this town I can't be associated with. Not if I want to keep my livelihood."

"Cyrine, what—? Why didn't you speak to me if you were having problems?"

Cyrine shook her head firmly, blond curls dancing. "I couldn't do that to your mother."

Cat signaled to her to come, and Inaya leaned down to Cyrine, kissing her on the cheek.

Trying to make it sound humorous, Inaya said, "Don't worry about my mother. Worry about *me*. I'll need to talk to you again."

She was just about to slip the napkin into her purse when something loud and heavy crashed through the bakery's front window, shattering the pane. Other projectiles followed it, accompanied by the riotous noise of flash-bangs. For a moment, Inaya couldn't see. She shouted at Cat to get Cyrine and Elias into the back room behind the counter and to take cover herself. Pipes roared down the street.

A flaming bag of something hit her shoulder and bounced off. She smelled the putrid scent of excrement, felt the lick of flame. Her vision came back. Giant pieces of glass hung at jagged angles, some scattered across the brick that had broken the window. The fire roared along the floor to the table where she and Cyrine had been sitting. She ripped a tablecloth from the table to smother the flames, coughing up smoke. Elias came running with a fire extinguisher, wrestling with the nozzle. She took it from him and expertly flipped it, bracing the cylinder against her torso, to douse the rest of the flames.

Flash-bangs continued to go off as PepperBalls came through the window. Then Cat was at her side, and the two women yanked Elias back from the window, where he was trying to get to their assailants.

"We need you safe," Cat snapped.

She joined Inaya on the pavement, both women with their guns drawn and the necks of their blouses pulled up over their mouths. Tears streamed from their eyes, an effect of the PepperBalls. Inaya's heart was like a trip-hammer, pounding hard in her ears.

She couldn't see much through the smoke, but she heard the roar of motorcycles racing away. A couple of the bikes trailed at the end, and she recognized the colors of the Disciples. She tucked her gun away to give chase.

"Inaya!" Cat called after her.

Her head swiveled back. "Tell backup I'm on foot going west." She'd picked up one of the bricks, and as she ran fleet-footed through the street, dodging gawping passers-by on the street, she raised her arm and hurled the brick at the rear tire of a silver Harley.

It hit the spokes hard, and the bike spun out, tossing its rider in a heap.

"Freeze, police!"

Though adrenaline was pumping in her veins, everything seemed to slow down, her mind breaking down the composite elements of the chase, as if she had all the time and clarity in the world. Cat huffing behind her on the street to catch up. The cries of frightened bystanders. Flash-bangs and PepperBalls still going off in the background. Cyrine's plaintive cry. The engine of the motorcycle cut. And a huge mountain of a man scrambling up from the asphalt, his boots hitting the street. She couldn't see his face behind his visor, just the straggled ends of a beard. Then he jumped into action, abandoning his bike and heading straight to the falls.

"Get the bike!" she shouted to Cat, and then she was off again.

Four blocks later, the biker cut south behind the Adventures in Mountainland storefront. He pulled himself up over the trash containers parked in a row, then leapt down the other side of a fence that had rusted from the damp, some of its links pulled free, the edges wiry and sharp.

Inaya clambered after him, the wires catching at her trousers and tearing through to her flesh. Panting, she disentangled herself and jumped, landing hard on the other side. The biker leapt to the other side of the creek in one bound. Inaya's legs weren't as long, and one was bleeding. She tried the jump and slipped just short of the other side, tumbling back into the creek. This time she fell on her knees, scraping her hands on stones in the creek bed. She pulled herself up, swiping creek water over her face to cool it from the burning heat.

How the biker was still running in his leathers, she couldn't imagine. Her entire body was slick with sweat. She might have turned her ankle when she slid into the creek, she couldn't feel it through the adrenaline, so she picked up the pace again.

The Disciple was still in sight. The streets of the old town led west to the pond and the falls. The biker had reached the gazebo that fronted the falls, pretty and picturesque, and she heard the squeal of a woman he'd barreled through, who was trying to capture a selfie. He came out around the far side of the gazebo, heading to the back of the falls. If he climbed up the stairs to the headland, Inaya wouldn't be able to catch him; he'd disappear into the woods.

She doubled her efforts, coming to a stop behind the falls. He was on one end, she was on the other, the water tumbling over their heads to the pond. The entire enclosure was dark. The Disciple paused, weighing the odds, as Inaya stood there shuddering. She ran five miles every other day, but that clearly wasn't enough.

She had a split second to see the man's eyes before he charged her.

She drew her gun and yelled, "Stop! Police!"

It didn't have any effect. Down the length of the barricade he came. With the full weight of his body behind him, he tackled her, and she went flying. She hit the barricade with one hip and tumbled over to the other side, her gun sailing from her hand and hitting the water with a thump. She followed it, bouncing against the embankment. Her head struck the painted railing. She sank into the murky depths of the pond, the falls roaring over her head.

The silence beneath the surface was perfect and cool. Her body relaxed into it, and she felt herself drift down, strands of algae brushing her face.

Just a rest, just a second to rest, black coolness all around her taking the pounding from her head. Her arms floated away from her body, her fingertips breaking the surface.

And then she heard Seif calling her name, his voice ragged with fear.

CHAPTER TWENTY-FOUR

Inaya coughed up some water and rolled over on the cement, Seif's arm hard around her shoulders. She hadn't drowned, nothing close to it, though you couldn't tell that from Seif's reaction. He'd called an ambulance and was waiting impatiently for the paramedics to check her out. Her blouse was plastered to her body, and catching Seif's eyes on her, she buttoned her blazer over it. Water squelched out of her sleeves.

"You need to get cleaned up," he said, helping her stand.

She put up a hand out of habit to tug her headscarf down, remembered she no longer wore one, and turned that into the gesture of smoothing water from her hair. Seif wasn't fooled. He followed the movement, looked like he wanted to say something, met her eyes, and held it back. A paramedic took over. She was led to an ambulance and had her vitals checked, a light shone into her eyes, her skull probed for signs of a concussion.

The paramedic was a man in his thirties, and she flinched from his handling of her body. Before she could say a word, Seif barked at the man's female partner to take over. The woman's name was Angie, and as Inaya told her about the bruise at her hip, Seif directed the other paramedic away.

Inaya refused to think about what this meant—his consideration, his knowledge of things that made her uncomfortable. She waited for the paramedics to leave, then asked for an update, giving Seif a quick rundown on the suspect she had chased.

"Disciples, sir. We should bring the rest of them in so I can identify my assailant."

"You need to change," he insisted. "Clean up. Get your head together."

Though she was dripping wet and felt queasy from the water she'd ingested, Inaya stubbornly refused.

"What about the bakery? Are Cat and Cyrine okay? Have we impounded the bike?"

"It's under control, Rahman. Not everything is your responsibility."

"At the very least, I'm a witness."

Or had she and Cat been the targets? And if they were, how had the Disciples known they were at the bakery? They kept the team informed of their whereabouts; no one else was privy to their movements.

Seif hesitated, uncharacteristic for him, his face turned to the side. Inaya found herself studying his profile, the sweep of thick lashes that she would give a kidney for. He turned back and caught her staring. His face changed in that instant, hard with hunger and demand. She blinked, and the expression she'd caught was gone. Neither spoke until Seif said, "Catalina and Webb can handle it. Come with me."

She blinked again at the abrupt change of subject. He led her to his car, where she balked at the thought of messing up the seats.

"Cat drove me out here. I can get back to the station with her." She wanted to check on Cyrine and Elias, too, offer her personal support. He wasn't having it.

"You're not going to the station. I'll drop you at your house. You can take a night off."

His tone was so firm that she knew better than to argue.

"What about your car? I'm still soaked." She was shivering under the blanket the paramedics had given her.

He didn't touch her, but somehow he crowded her into his car, throwing a blanket from the back onto her seat. As soon as she was in, he turned the heat up and slid the car into gear.

His eyes on the road—deliberately, she thought—he told her to summarize the incident. She described the attack for him, concluding with

"The bakery may not have been the target. It could have been Cat and me, seeing as we detained the Disciples' Sergeant-at-Arms."

He made a noncommittal sound, pulling up his GPS.

"Address."

She typed it in and he executed a smooth turn, rush-hour traffic building on the highway that ran parallel to the road. When they'd passed the Chatfield Reservoir, he said, "The sheriff will let us know if that's the case."

"You sound like you trust him." She'd just come to that realization. Seif was too easy with the attack, too unconcerned about yielding to the sheriff in the face of the complaint.

He shrugged. "He knows his job. His men respect him."

"There aren't any women on his team," Inaya observed.

"Maybe none applied."

They passed through the roundabout that led to Inaya's house. His eyes passed over the gracious homes with their wraparound porches, all with views of the distant reservoir, backing up against ranches to the west and the Cottonwood Club to the east.

"You live with your family?" he asked.

"Yes." She didn't explain or apologize. It was very much a part of who she was.

"I do too."

It was notably unlike Seif to share a confidence. Was it an opening? An indication of trust? Her heart began to thud against her ribs.

"You're looking after your parents?" she guessed.

The line of his lips firmed. "They're dead." He didn't give her space to express her condolences. "I live with my younger brothers." A wry smile twisted his mouth. "I'm supposed to be in charge of them."

So they had something in common. Inaya warmed to him at the thought.

"I live with my parents and younger sisters. I have two—Noor and Nadia."

"Your father's a criminal defense attorney."

He'd looked into her, then, because it wasn't a question.

A little defensively, she answered, "Yes. He's very successful."

"I know. He's been giving the DPD a hard time. You must be proud of him."

Inaya tried to decipher whether this was a sneer. It didn't sound like one. It sounded like the opposite—like Seif understood the interconnectedness of family.

They rounded a man-made lake and Inaya pointed to the gray and white house at the end of a meticulously maintained cul-de-sac. Seif pulled up in the drive beside her father's car, a silver Mercedes SUV that he'd bought at her mother's request. There was a car parked behind her father's car that she didn't recognize.

Inaya intended to thank him and make a quick getaway, but he was at her car door before she knew it, opening it for her, without offering his hand. She puzzled at the nuances. Courtesy stopping short of encroachment from the man who'd refused to respond to her salaam. She scrambled out, pulling the blanket he'd given her with her.

"I'll get this cleaned and return it to you."

He snagged the blanket from her hand and tossed it back onto the seat. "No need. I'll have the boys take care of it."

She made to thank him, but he was guiding her up the stairs to her house.

"I'll see you to the door."

Inaya's heart sank. That meant she had no choice but to introduce him to her parents in her current bedraggled state—her mother wouldn't hesitate to reproach him, boss or no boss.

"Beautiful house," he said pleasantly, ignoring her discomfort. Inaya wanted to kick him. She fished her keys from the purse Seif had returned to her and unlocked the door, while he took stock of the porch, hung with baskets of flowers. A set of cushioned loungers were framed by Golden Crane hydrangeas, and the air was rife with their perfume. Seif's head turned from the view of the fields where the horses next door were stabled. A gray foal was grazing in a pasture contained by a painted white fence.

"After you," he said politely.

They stepped into the gracious foyer, the floor marbled in white, delicate glass consoles framed in gold on both sides of the hall. A photograph hung on the wall by the entrance. It depicted the turquoise gate of a building worn away by time, the gate leading to the desert. It could have been a landscape of many places in the Muslim world, but it was a print of Afghanistan. Her father had purchased it as a reminder of a world that no longer existed for him, one deeply entrenched in his memories.

The end of the hall opened onto the two large rooms she had helped to decorate in her parents' understated style. From the sound of the noise in the house, they had guests. Suddenly, Inaya remembered her promise to her mother. Panicking, she turned to Seif, hoping to usher him out before he clued in to what was going on.

She caught sight of herself in the mirror at the end of the hall. Her hair was wet and flat, her clothing rumpled and soggy, and her mascara had failed to live up to its "waterproof" label. She looked like a drowned raccoon.

She would have attempted damage control, but it was already too late. Her mother, followed by Noor and Nadia, was advancing to the door, a beaming welcome on her face.

"*Beta*, you're late! Our guests are waiting. . . ." Her mother's voice trailed off as she took in Inaya's appearance. Her mouth opened and closed comically as she caught sight of Seif.

For no reason that Inaya could think of, unless she was warning Seif off, her mother gasped, "Look at the state you're in! Your *rishta* is here!"

How on earth could she have forgotten that tonight was the night?

She took in her mother and sisters: they were dressed in fashionable *shalwar kameez*, wearing long embroidered silk tunics with narrow trousers, chiffon *dupattas* artfully arranged over their shirtfronts. Her sisters were dripping in jewelry, beautifully made up, their hair long and curling, glass bangles on their wrists. Their jaws dropped at the sight of Seif.

Nonsensically, Noor teased, "Wrong night to bring home a man, Sis." She took a good look at Seif. "Not that you're not welcome."

"Things are going to get interesting," Nadia observed, her mood less dour than usual.

To Inaya's shock, Seif stepped around her and greeted her mother with a perfect salaam. Her mother returned the greeting. Inaya managed a sputtering introduction before her sisters could say anything more.

"My boss, Lieutenant Waqas Seif. Uh, sir, this is my mother, Sunober Rahman, and my sisters, Noor and Nadia."

His greeting to them was just as courteous.

"So *you're* the Big Bad Boss?" Noor's eyebrows shot up, her eyes sparkling with mischief. "You didn't do him justice," she chided Inaya. "Must be pretty fun to go on stakeouts with him for company." When she waggled her eyebrows, Inaya prayed a hole in the ground would open up and swallow her.

"No stakeouts yet," Seif said with good humor. "Mostly a lot of writing on whiteboards and community visits."

"If you'd visited *our* community, we would have remembered."

"*Budtameez!*" Inaya's mother gave Noor a smack to the back of her head.

"Ouch!" She gazed dreamily at Seif, whispering to Nadia, "Totally worth it."

Inaya's mother said something sharp to the girls in Urdu. Smiling broadly at Seif, they waved to him as they trailed back to the family room.

"*Beta*," her mother addressed Seif. "Are you Pakistani?"

Mortified that her mother had just called a police lieutenant "son," much less asked a personal question, Inaya stood frozen, still dripping water.

She had no idea how to bring this to an end. She barely heard Seif's answer. Two men came to join them. One was her father, the other could only be the man she had agreed to meet: Athif, the much-praised physician.

Clearly God wasn't planning to step in, because she was still present in the hall.

Mutual introductions were made. Athif examined Inaya's disheveled appearance.

He was attractive and reasonably tall with a birthmark at the corner of his jaw. His hair was smoothed back with product, and his teeth flashed at her, so white they must have been bleached. He was wearing a gray suit with a pink shirt and tie.

She realized everyone was waiting for her to somehow maneuver the situation, but she'd abandoned rational thought the minute Seif had followed her inside. She swallowed. The bruise at her hip was throbbing, and she wondered if she could pass off another faint.

Athif kept grinning that shiny smile at her. Finally, he said, "If you really didn't want to meet me, you could have just said no."

Everyone laughed. Inaya's eyes brightened with gratitude. She indicated her soaked clothing, "I thought you might like to see me in action." They all laughed again, but she felt her mother's elbow dig into her waist. On a smothered gasp, she added, "I'm *so* sorry about this. We had an incident at work. I'll just clean up."

"I'll wait for you," Seif told her. "We should be getting back to the team."

Inaya made her face blank. Was Seif attempting to *rescue* her? She grabbed at the excuse like a lifeline, turning to Athif to apologize.

"I'm sorry, I'll come and greet your parents, but we're working an urgent case."

Her father took her aside, holding her by the elbows to look into her eyes. "Are you all right, *beti*? Have you been hurt somehow?"

"No, no, I'm fine, Baba. Please don't worry."

But his concern for her in the midst of such awkwardness warmed her, as if he'd wrapped a layer of protection around her. He didn't berate her for being late or for her appearance, and he made no excuses to Athif for the nature of her job. Her father accepted it, accepted *her*, though she was a bird who had flown far from the nest indeed. She briefly rested her forehead against his chest. "I've messed up," she said into the fabric.

"Nonsense," her father answered. "We explained to Athif's parents you might get called out at any time. They were very understanding."

Inaya doubted that was true. It was more likely they were considering the dazzling possibility of marrying their son to Noor or Nadia, despite the age difference, in one of those "all's well that ends well" scenarios.

"I'd better get ready," she mumbled.

Her father let her go and she fled to the entrance of the stairs, not looking back, though she heard her father say to Seif, "Come and join us, Waqas. I'm sure you and Athif will find you have much in common."

"Yes," her mother added, though she sounded reluctant. "And perhaps you will explain to Athif's family why you have my daughter running around all over town."

Inaya's foot slipped on the stairs. She caught herself, not daring to look back.

The back of her neck felt hot, so she knew Seif was looking at her.

She was grateful she missed his reply.

CHAPTER TWENTY-FIVE

Other men might have found it funny; Seif didn't. Inaya was nearly thirty—why was she putting up with this? That guy whose hair stood up on its own, his cologne so musky Seif wanted to crack a window. Like Seif's parents, Inaya's parents were decent, respectable, polished in their conversation. But Athif, the supposed suitor, was an open book to Seif. He was a cardiologist, his parents nodding proudly as he told Seif about his job, and just beneath his easy conversation was a veneer of distaste as Seif answered questions about policing.

The word "police" was met with forced smiles. Athif challenged him about going over to the other side, but the challenge was so bland, he didn't answer. Besides, hadn't the doctor come here with a proposal for Inaya? Didn't he get that *she* was also police? She worked the same job as Seif, arguably with more tenacity. By sneering at Seif, he was sneering at his intended.

Then again, with the way his eyes kept returning to Noor, a little more dazzled each time, Seif began to doubt which woman he was here to propose to.

Seif liked Inaya's sisters—they were pretty and sweet, and their sense of fun amused him. They'd embarrassed Inaya in front of him, yet she hadn't reproached them, a sign the relationship between the sisters was close. Open, friendly, teasing. He liked that too. It reminded him of his rapport with the twins, up until this latest phase, where they were anti-everything about Seif's job.

The twins ferociously advocated defunding the police. Knowing the comprehensive scope of their arguments, arguments with which he sympathized, Seif played with them by saying, "If you put me out of a job, who's going to pay for college?"

The doctor made his skin itch. If he was here for Inaya, he wasn't showing her the respect she was due. He didn't rise when she entered the room, still caught up in chatting to Noor, and Seif wondered what that felt like for Inaya. The two younger sisters were knockouts, and they had youth on their side. No doubt the guy's mother would be thinking that made them more biddable, either one more suitable as a bride for her son. Inaya was about as biddable as a musk ox. She was tough, and no matter how clear he made his orders, she still found a way to bend them.

She came down in another of her smart pantsuits, this one a soft peach set off by a lacy cream blouse that flattered her complexion. She was wearing lip gloss to the match the suit, and eyeliner that made her eyes look as deep as a startled fawn's. She'd made an effort for the doctor, maybe conscious her sisters looked like princesses who'd escaped from the Arabian Nights.

Yet she wasn't self-conscious. She made small talk with practiced ease before extricating them from the situation with a polite apology. Her mother followed them into the hall, protesting Seif's half-finished cup of tea, though her concern was more over Inaya's departure.

"*Beta*," she said, unconcerned that Seif was listening, "You know how important this is."

Why? he wondered. Did her mother think that pompous ass was Inaya's last chance? She was only twenty-nine, for God's sake. Had she aged out of the market?

Inaya wasn't rattled. She soothed her mother with words she'd probably uttered a hundred times. Then, more practically, she added, "It's good he gets to see what my job entails."

"What if he doesn't like it? *I* don't like it, so how can he?"

Inaya grinned at her mother, whereas if Seif had been in her position, he'd have erupted.

"If he doesn't like it, then he doesn't like *me*, which means you'll have to cast your net a little wider. Because I don't think that, even for a cardiologist, you'd want me to make it work with a man who hated my job. Now, Ami, I have to go."

She was about to turn when her mother grabbed her by the shoulders. She prayed in an undertone, then blew out three breaths over Inaya's hair.

"There," she said with satisfaction. "Now my daughter will be safe."

Something twisted inside Seif's chest. How long had it been since his mother had prayed for him? He was forgetting her voice, forgetting the things she'd asked of him.

Come back. Return to us, my son.

She would have been disappointed in him for rejecting his heritage; by contrast, she would have loved Inaya.

The thought made him scowl. Inaya took the scowl as her cue.

When she was settled back in the car, she said, "I would apologize for all that, but I have no idea where to start."

Seif reversed out of her drive, glancing at her. She'd braced herself, expecting a reprimand, but he said, "We all have our crosses to bear."

He'd meant to sound sympathetic; instead he'd brought them back to Razan.

"Action items?" she asked him.

He was grateful she'd reestablished the boundaries of their relationship. It saved him from having to do it. He ran down the case with her.

"I'm waiting for an update from Dr. Stanger. He briefed me after he spoke with Cat. He's waiting on results from some tests he's running. Depending on what he says, we may be able to release the crime scene by the start of next week."

"That's good," she said. "It will give the community a place to mourn."

He'd seconded Inaya's request that a prayer space be found, but he hadn't had time to follow up. "Did Webb find them somewhere to pray?"

"Another business in the old town offered its second floor. It's not far from our mosque."

"It's not really a mosque," Seif noted idly. "Doesn't look like a community that couldn't raise money—why are they renting office space?"

It was an effort not to look at her when he could feel her gaze on him. He wanted to see her expression, though she'd give it all away with her voice.

She did, sounding surprised. "Even if you raise the money for a mosque, you know you have to get a zoning permit."

"So?"

She sighed. "Who do you think is in charge of those permits?"

"Town council, probably."

"Most of whom are members of the Resurrection Church. They voted the application down. The appeal gets decided by the sheriff, who said a mosque would cause traffic congestion."

"On Titan Road?" Seif scoffed. It was a long, blank, empty stretch, though with the new housing in the area, it wouldn't be for long. He forced his mind back to the point: another trail he could follow to the sheriff.

"I think we know it's not about traffic congestion."

"What did the council members say?"

"They took their lead from Switzerland," she said wryly. "'A skyline filled with minarets would not be in keeping with Blackwater's historic roots. It would create dissonance.'"

Fuck that, Seif thought. "Blackwater doesn't have a skyline, first off. Second, it also doesn't have enough history for dissonance to matter."

He could hear the smile in Inaya's voice when she answered pertly, "Not everyone hails from the capital of an ancient civilization."

He liked her humor too much, so now he delivered the set-down. "I hail from D.C., Rahman. Whatever you're trying to paint on me, that isn't who I am."

Her response was even better. "It was just a joke. I don't think about you all that much."

A harsh chuckle escaped him, then for some crazy reason, wanting the last word, he asked, "Then what was all that Big Bad Boss stuff?"

This time he looked at her when she said, "Well, aren't you?"

She'd had months of the sharp edge of his tongue, so he couldn't really argue.

"Yeah, I suppose I am."

They teamed up with Catalina and Webb at the station, a late evening for all of them, following a day of action. Inaya seemed to have lost track of time after her dunking in the pond, but he could tell the scene at her house was still bothering her. Seif had called the late meeting for her sake; the others didn't seem to mind.

Catalina and Jaime fussed over Inaya. Jaime, especially, was taking it hard, so he let Webb reassure himself that Inaya's near drowning wasn't serious. Once she'd satisfied herself that Inaya would be fine, Catalina took a napkin from her pocket and passed it to Inaya. She peered at the napkin, then let a soft whistle escape. Both women turned to look at Seif, and he felt the hairs at the back of his neck prickle. He called them to attention, asking for a report.

Catalina described the measures undertaken to protect the bakery. Webb had tracked Inaya's assailant down through the plate on his bike. He was cooling his heels in the tank, refusing to cooperate. They had a whole host of charges to arraign him on. He hadn't asked for a lawyer, but he'd demanded to see Ranger. Seif would have to finesse that. In the meantime, he asked Catalina to update the team on how Dr. Stanger's results affected her profile of the killer.

"The good doctor puts the time of death at roughly three or four days before her body was found. The cause of death is the wound to the side: it pierced the abdominal aorta. In other words, she bled out." She looked down at her notes. "Razan's body was preserved because it had been frozen almost immediately after death—we know this because crystals were found inside the wound. Dr. Stanger is doing cell deterioration tests to give us a more exact time of death."

"He had her for three days?" Inaya whispered.

Cat looked at her. "There was no interference with the body, no defensive wounds, no other injury except the one she died from."

"Then why keep her that long?"

"He may have needed time to make arrangements for the display. He'd also have to time his mock-crucifixion exactly. The mosque and the streets around it would have to be empty for him to have the time he needed."

"A hell of a risk," Webb muttered, his ruddy face pale.

"From the internal temperature of the body, Dr. Stanger estimates her body was removed from wherever it was frozen less than two hours before it was found."

"She was so pale," Inaya murmured. "I remember thinking she looked cold."

Seif looked to Jaime Webb. "What else does this tell us?"

Webb's bright blue eyes blinked back at him. To his credit, he didn't fidget.

"We focus on three things: finding the murder weapon, the kill site, and the storage site. There could still be significant forensic evidence at both sites, particularly evidence of Razan's blood. As for the murder weapon, did the doc have anything?"

Catalina pointed to the whiteboard, where a sketch demonstrated the dimensions of the blade. Webb got up to give it a closer look. He shrugged his big shoulders. "Haven't seen one like that before. I'll check with the hunting store in town; there's a military expert who works there who might be able to point us to other leads. Not likely they keep records, though, if this knife came through their store," he said glumly.

"Have a little faith, Jaime. Dr. Stanger said the weapon was more a tool than a knife. It's so unusual it might give itself away."

"Has Stanger tracked it down?" Seif asked.

"His team is working on it."

"And the profile?"

"I needed to talk to Dr. Stanger in more detail before I worked it up. Even now, the profile isn't complete, but I've given it some thought."

Catalina walked over to the whiteboard and flipped it. An enlarged photograph of Razan's body took up half of the board. Catalina used a pointer to highlight elements of the photo. "This is what I've come up with so far. He froze the body because he needed time; I'm assuming the killer was a man because of the strength required to raise the body up on the door. He's meticulous in the arrangement of the body, but not obsessive about details such as the distance from the ground to the door, or from the top of Razan's head to the lintel; Dr. Stanger measured the space, and the numbers are random. But looking at the placement of the body, you'll see the negative space *isn't* random—it's in proportion to how the killer positioned her. So the gold field of the door served as background—it's important in terms of how he arranged her, we just don't know why. I do think this is he what he wanted time for—the body is a message to be read. Each detail on it matters—the shawl, the red shoes, the little diamond brooches."

"What do we have on Razan's apparel?" Seif turned to Webb, who shuffled through notes on his desk. "Anything unusual like the knife?"

"Not quite. These items aren't sold at boutiques on Main. A check of local malls and stores in the neighboring areas also came up blank."

"So we're out of luck."

Webb looked eager. "Not quite. All of the items—shawl, shoes, pins—are sold online through Alibaba."

The giant Chinese retailer. Delivery would have taken some time, so . . . "They must have been ordered in advance. Any way to check?" he asked Webb.

"We're working on it."

He had to be satisfied with that.

"Is the message religious?" Inaya asked.

"It would seem so," Cat mused. "Though I think the more important element is the emulation of the Virgin. The crucifixion doesn't fit, and that isn't a mistake, it's deliberate. The choice of such a public display suggests a contempt for the police, though not for Razan. She's too lovingly arranged for that."

"'Lovingly'?" Webb made a choking sound.

"Lovingly," Catalina repeated. "I believe the killer knew Razan—knew her and cared for her, though he wasn't above using her to make his point. I don't know what that point was," she added before anyone could ask. "But what these contradictions suggest is that the killer was conflicted—this wasn't an easy or joyous kill for him, and we haven't found similar murders; if he's a serial, this *is* his first."

"Fair enough," Seif said. "Was there anything else?"

Catalina took time to weigh her answer. "The sophistication of his planning suggests he's confident and clever, not the type to panic. One element is especially notable."

The others didn't interrupt, letting Cat work it out.

"The murder is far too deliberate to be random. There had to be a precipitating event. And when we discover what that event was, that's how we'll find him."

Seif felt rage at the thought. Whoever the killer was, he'd had the patience to let Razan bleed out, find a place to store her body, then make the arrangements to display it. He couldn't fault Catalina's profile, yet his instincts told him part of the picture was still missing.

Inaya's hand shot up as if she'd read his mind.

"The real question is why he staged the body the way he did. If Razan was dressed as the Virgin Mary, that points a finger at the church, and from there to the Disciples. And let's not forget West's initiation tattoo. He may have chosen it, but the suggestion might have been planted. Or demanded. We should have been more thorough."

Sounding bored, Seif said, "We've covered this ground."

"All right, but none of us has ever seen the Virgin Mary, right? So how do we know about her?"

"From the Bible?" Webb put in, a serious comment on his part.

"The Bible *tells* us about her, it doesn't depict her. Neither does the Qur'an. So where do we get our sense of what the Virgin Mary looked like?"

"Is this a Black Jesus thing?" Seif interjected. "Because we shouldn't be politicizing this." He meant they couldn't address the murder only along racial lines.

"Give me some credit, sir. What I'm saying is that most of our knowledge of the Virgin Mary comes through historical depictions. Through art. Through *pictures* or paintings. The way Razan was posed—you called the murder 'artistic'—maybe the killer brought a painting to life. And if we knew what the painting is, we'd have some insight into his mind. What do you think?"

She wasn't asking Seif—she'd posed the question to Cat—but at some level, it made sense to him. He wasn't much for Western art, yet even for him, the mantle and ribbons suggested more than a sick pathology. There was order to the staging, a consonance in death that fit with the idea of a painting.

Who did they have on staff who could tell them more about art? He did a swift review, realized he'd have to turn to FBI resources.

Inaya had other ideas. "I have a friend who did her degree in art before she went on to medicine. Strange combination, I know, but she says it's made her a better physician. She might be available to chat tomorrow evening. It depends on her call schedule."

"Seems you have a penchant for doctors," Seif said before he could think better of it.

She looked at him, wide-eyed; then she burst out laughing. He stood there, arrested.

"The penchant is more my mother's." The others weren't in on their joke, so she continued, "My friend's name is Rupi Sandhu—*she* can at least point us in the right direction."

"Just a moment, sir." Since Catalina asked, he listened.

"We need to talk to Areesha first." Cat held up the napkin Inaya had forgotten at the bakery. "We've been out of the loop. Cyrine Haddad gave us the names of *two* Somali girls who are missing, not just one. If this *is* a serial killer, we need to be alert to any missing girls whose bodies may turn up, possibly arranged like Razan's. Areesha has insight into this community; she'll be able to help us."

Great, Seif thought. That was their first mistake—thinking their goals were aligned with Areesha's. He pivoted to the whiteboard, where five black squares were drawn. Inside each square was a name: Resurrection Church, Natural Foods, Blackwater Academy, Apex Dynamics, and Sheriff Addison Grant.

In the middle of the five squares was Razan Elkader's name.

From the church, a black arrow pointed down to the Disciples, and from there to Mercedes and Razan. For the Academy, "Principal Christine Nakamura" was written in, along with the names of the three boys who had harassed Razan: Campbell Kerr, Matthew Resnick, and Dylan Braun. Resnick and Braun had been interviewed; now their alibis would be checked against the time of death. That left Kerr to contend with, a task he'd set for himself.

They'd also look into Apex Dynamics; a third arrow connected the Academy to the aeronautics company where Razan had interned. Inside the Natural Foods square was the name Hassan Elkader. But under the box for the sheriff, there was a question mark underlined twice.

Inaya looked up from her notes at Seif, all bright-eyed innocence.

"What about the sheriff? He's the reason we're on this case in the first place. We know he's not thrilled about CRU oversight, but could you tell us whether you think there's any truth to the complaints against him?"

This time when he pushed back, it wasn't personal. His inquiries into the sheriff were something he needed to keep off the radar.

"I think you may have forgotten, Rahman. You report to me, not the other way around."

She dropped her notepad onto her desk. She signaled something to Catalina. Cat had the touch. It was hard to rebuff her gentle questions.

"We need to see the full picture, don't we, sir? Bring out all the information?"

"We will," he said, more reasonably. "When I think it's pertinent, and not a distraction from the lines of inquiry we're pursuing."

He had to give them something, before they stumbled into his op and undid a year of hard work.

"I've set up a meet with Grant to follow up. He mentioned there may have been some runaways in the county."

Inaya snorted. "I'd rather hear Areesha's side of things."

Seif rubbed the back of his head. Shutting down this lead would make no sense to his team. It would fix attention precisely where he didn't want it.

"Walk softly," he gave in. "And don't carry a stick."

CHAPTER TWENTY-SIX

They spent the next day doing as Seif had directed: putting a request in with the online retailer that sold apparel similar to Razan's; sending out patrols to check for abandoned or suspicious vehicles that could have been used to move Razan; making a list of factories that used industrial-sized appliances to try to determine where Razan's body had been stored. Jaime was making calls about the murder weapon, touching base with his military contacts, but so far they'd struck out with the knife: no one was able to identify it.

In the meantime, Inaya stopped in to speak with the artist who'd designed West's tattoo, a striking young woman named Tabby who worked at the Tattooed Rose, on the 16th Street Mall in Denver. She was dressed in a navy blue tank top and short shorts, colorful chrysanthemums decorating the upper curves of her breasts. They were the perfect advertisement: she'd designed the flowers, her partner in the business had applied them.

Tabby showed Inaya a tattoo artist's equivalent of a look book, an entire volume dedicated to fanciful religious art. There were several different workups of the Crucifixion, including the one on West's forearm. She confirmed that West had come to their parlor and chosen the design himself. The Tattooed Rose kept records: West's visit had been two years ago, but he was the kind of man who made an impression. Tabby noted that several of the Disciples had the same tat elsewhere on their bodies.

Inaya returned to headquarters to check in with the team, feeding the information into the investigation's database as they traded notes.

Cat collected her jacket, and Inaya looked up.

"Hassan Elkader called. He wants to return home, so we'd better get on with the search."

Though the house wasn't the kill site, they'd take a look in Razan's closet. The shawl must have been draped over her after her body was arranged, but the clothing underneath should have been soaked with blood. Which meant the killer had dressed the body in clothes he'd had on hand, which augured premeditation—but why? She put the question to Cat, who replied, "He must have been determined to keep his scene pristine. Blood spatter would have ruined its perfection."

That meant a set of Razan's clothes was also missing—something to add to the broader search, though her instincts told her the killer would have destroyed the evidence.

Inaya cut the tape at the Elkaders' house, letting Cat precede her into the musky air of the sitting room. She paused outside the door. The Syrian flag was missing from its place. It lay crumpled on the porch, reminding her of her first encounter with West.

She swallowed the lump in her throat and found her way to Cat, who beckoned her over to help search Razan's drawers. Meticulously, they went through her dresser and the clothes in her closet, finding nothing they hadn't expected. Her room was small, her possessions few. Her bed had a simple wooden frame; the bedspread was a pale lavender. A desk was crammed against one wall, a low bookcase beside it, where textbooks were grouped. On the bottom shelf was a collection of newspapers with thick, glossy pages. Cat sat down on the bed to page through them while Inaya continued to search.

On the wall above Razan's desk was a corkboard with a painted frame. A class schedule was tacked inside it, next to a series of photos. One was of Razan with a fine-featured boy who could only have been her twin. Another showed her smiling down at a toddler in her arms— the child who had drowned at sea? The third depicted a younger Razan in the center of a group of three boys. Her twin, Luqman, had his arm around her. The younger boys were clinging to her hands. Razan's head was turned toward Luqman, and both the twins were laughing.

Underneath this sparse montage, a handful of Polaroids gave a more recent picture of Razan. Photographs taken with Mercedes, both girls in their school uniforms. Razan with two smiling Somali girls. With Elias Haddad and Omar Abdi. A photograph with all the teens together, girls to one side with shy smiles, the boys attempting to look manly. Her gloved hands careful, Inaya collected the photos.

Cat was sifting through the newspapers, pausing from time to time.

"Anything?" Inaya asked.

"She was a good writer." Cat's voice was tight with emotion. "She wrote about borders. Her journey as a refugee. Some stuff about sermons at Resurrection—how they could lead to hate crimes. We should review them, if they were that bad." She bundled the papers together and held them up. "Sorting through these will take time."

Cat adjusted her leg, her boot knocking against wood. Inaya flipped up the quilt. The bed had two underdrawers for additional storage. Cat moved out of the way as Inaya opened the first. It held athletic wear. The second drawer was filled with Razan's one extravagance: a bright collection of headscarves. Inaya drew a deep breath, raising one to her face and drawing in the scent of perfume. Her heart clenched as she imagined Razan in front of her mirror, setting her scarf with jeweled pins, checking to make certain no tendrils of hair escaped.

Her own pain welled up; with an effort she choked it back. She'd coordinated her scarves with her clothing, just as Razan must have done.

She looked back at the open closet with a frown.

Razan's taste in clothing had run to muted blouses and long skirts, along with a few pairs of jeans. But on the Wednesday she'd vanished, she'd gone from school to the public library, and from there to the ice cream parlor.

Inaya rose to her feet. She pushed the skirts and jeans to the side, examining the empty space, awareness flooding her mind.

Razan's uniform was missing.

She'd been wearing it when she disappeared. And killed in it as well?

Her gaze swung back to the uncluttered surface of Razan's little desk.

No wallet, no laptop, no notebooks, no cell phone, nor anything to carry them in.

Her knapsack wasn't in the room.

CHAPTER TWENTY-SEVEN

They reported back to Seif, who told them to spend the rest of that day coordinating a search and interviewing witnesses who might know what had happened to Razan's knapsack.

Hassan Elkader, they had questioned at home. Next, they checked in with his wife at the hospital. Razan's extra school uniform was at the dry cleaners, which the team duly collected, but yes, one of her two uniforms was missing. Razan had left for school carrying her knapsack. She didn't bother with a purse; her wallet held her ID. Inaya wasn't surprised to learn that Razan didn't own a laptop, she was saving up for one; in the interim, she borrowed one from school or the public library. Her cell phone hadn't been seen since she'd been at the ice cream parlor, and once again they confirmed it hadn't been turned on since.

They were stymied for now, waiting for information to come in and be collated, or for new leads to chase down. Seif sent them home early; they'd regroup over the weekend.

Too frustrated to remain idle, Inaya and Cat arranged to meet Areesha Adams at a bookstore café the next morning. Inaya didn't think Cat's husband would approve of her working through the weekend, but at some point he'd have to accept the nature of Catalina's job.

Cat looked a little upset as they parked in front of the Book Mark; then, taking a breath, she set her mood aside to greet Maddalena, the lovely Italian woman who ran the store. Inaya enjoyed spending time at the little café, and often pleasurably browsed the bookshelves with her sisters before settling in to read in a nook at the back.

Areesha was waiting for them at a table squished up against the used-book shelf. It was fronted by mismatched chairs with cushions in bright colors, a selection of books open on the table before her. She had thoughtfully ordered iced lattes, and seeing Iyana and Cat, she gathered up the books and set them to one side.

Today, her bouncy curls were held back by a red silk band, with a bright red lipstick to match, her teeth startlingly white against her lips. Midsize earrings shaped like square locks dangled from her ears, winking in and out of her curls. She was dressed for the heat in a cool linen dress, her bronze sandals displaying her polished toes. She was chic, cool, and elegant as she gave them a measured nod.

Inaya smiled at her, thanking her for the drink, a smile she didn't return.

Her opening salvo was "Your boss is shutting me out of this case. I hope you intend to do better."

Another line Inaya would have to walk—obeying Seif's orders while getting to the heart of what Areesha wanted, in the hopes of an open exchange.

Before she could answer, Areesha turned her attention to Cat. "What are you doing here, Detective Hernandez?"

Cat's friendly smile vanished. "I'm a detective on this case."

Areesha made a clicking sound. "You know what I mean. You come from Nogales to this? You've always stood behind your community; now you're a cop? How do you justify that?"

Inaya sensed the anger beneath Cat's calm surface. Cat had done her own calibration of her duty, and how the objectives of her NGO work could be furthered by joining the police. That calculation was never easy; no matter how righteous her anger, Areesha couldn't know that.

Implacably, Catalina said, "I don't. Not to you. Now, you called us here for a reason, so why don't we get to that?"

Areesha took them both in. She didn't give off a sense of restless energy—she simply watched them. When the silence had gone on long enough, she offered, "I hope you know you're being played. They're not letting you near anything that matters."

The statement made Inaya uneasy. She waited Areesha out, using her straw to play with the ice in her glass.

"One, you haven't been told anything about missing Somali girls, am I right?" Areesha began to count on her fingers, the smooth oval nails the same bronze shade as her sandals. "Two, you haven't been to the Natural Foods plant. Three, you haven't made the connection between the sheriff and the plant. Four, you have no idea where those missing girls are."

Some of this was true. The rest, Inaya thought she'd better push back at it.

"We're here so you can tell us about those girls. Our lieutenant is speaking to the sheriff—he'll ask for his files. But at first blush he's said the missing girls could be runaways."

"Do you buy that, Detective?"

Areesha's eyes rested on Inaya's hair. Inaya held still.

"No," she said firmly. "It's not that it can't be true or that some families can't be strict, but unlike others, I don't take that as the default position."

"And why is that?"

Inaya set down her mug with a thud. A little of the liquid flowed over the edge. Cat passed her a tissue to mop it up.

"Don't play these games with us, Areesha. You know I'm connected to this community, and that I care about what's happened to these girls. Tell us what you know. Help us meet their families, and I'll do everything I can to find out what happened to them."

Unimpressed by this speech, Areesha said, "You've got eyes on this investigation only because of a white girl."

Suddenly, Inaya was angry. She leaned forward, lowering her voice.

"If this is just about the color of one's skin for you, then yes, Razan was light-skinned, but she wasn't white, and I think you know the difference. She was Syrian, Muslim, and a refugee. That puts her in a different category." She held up a hand. "Listen to me. I know we've put resources on this that those Somali girls didn't get. But it isn't just because Black girls get little to no attention when they disappear."

"Then why?" Areesha demanded.

This time, it was Inaya who counted out her reasons. "One, because we have a body. Two, because that body was arranged to suggest a crucifixion in a town with a church that preaches vocally against Muslims, using bikers as their enforcement arm. Three, because the Community Response Unit is new, and Lieutenant Seif wrestled this oversight for us."

"Then why keep me out of things? I'm a friend to the people here. I represent their legal *and* moral interests."

The claim sounded like an overreach.

"We don't know why Seif does things the way he does," Cat put in. "But preventing this from blowing up in the DPD's face is his responsibility, and you've threatened us with a lawsuit. Having said that, he's not going to give Sheriff Grant a pass. He deals with him because *we* can't. And you've had personal experience of that, so you should know what we mean."

Areesha nodded her agreement.

"Grant is a first-class dick. And I don't mean that in the complimentary sense."

The three women laughed.

"Jesus." This came from Jaime, who'd overheard. He pulled up a chair to join them, though they hadn't been expecting him. "No wonder men are scared of you women."

Areesha turned her smile on Jaime, who sat there for a minute, dazed. Then, like a spotlight shut off in a theater, Areesha dropped the smile. "You weren't invited to this meet."

"I'm never invited," Jaime grumbled good-naturedly. "Here." He passed a set of folders to Cat. "The doc asked me to pass this along for your review."

Areesha's eyebrow angled up. "You trust him to hear this?"

Jaime flushed, his expression strained. "I'm a DPD officer."

"That's why I asked."

Inaya cut things short. They couldn't sit here judging each other's politics—they had to focus on Razan. And if Areesha knew about other victims, she was ready to listen.

"I trust Jaime with my life. He's a good cop, and I don't say that easily, Areesha."

"Seconded." This from Cat in a tone that brooked no disagreement.

Though Jaime looked embarrassed by the praise, Areesha objected anyway.

"All cops are bastards." A dark glare at Inaya. "You know that better than anyone. So does Marcus McBride." The words were lethally delivered.

Marcus McBride.

At the sound of the name, a gaping hole opened in front of Inaya. In it was the sickening scent of blood, its taste metallic on her tongue. Wind whooshed at her ears; she hurtled down a tunnel to land on a tile floor, her scarf gone, her hair and face soaked with stench.

Her lips moved without sound.

Officer Danny Egan of the Chicago Police had beaten Marcus into a coma during a traffic stop. Marcus shouldn't have been a suspect; there were no grounds for the arrest, even though after the fact drugs had turned up in his car. Egan's body cam was off, but a witness named Zuri Chikondi had filmed not only the beating, but the planting of the drugs. Zuri made a statement on record, then released the video on social media, to a firestorm of response.

Egan had beaten Marcus because he'd known his rights and had asserted them, his hands at ten and two on the steering wheel, his confidence undaunted. He'd refused to show fear to someone who was used to cowing Black men; the beating was Egan's retaliation.

Jenella McBride, the victim's mother, made a complaint. Inaya took the case, naively optimistic that she could force a reckoning within the CPD. Her hubris had been knocked flat by the way the case had played out.

Foolishly, she hadn't anticipated how hard Egan would fight back. His friends dirtied the victim and the witness, they harassed Inaya at work, and when that failed to derail her efforts, they doxxed her, flooding right-wing blogs with her personal information. Egan's supporters began showing up at her home; rape and death threats soon followed. She'd pushed through it, knowing that her difficulties couldn't begin to compare to Jenella's. Jenella's community had closed ranks around her, but because of past misdemeanors, even as Marcus lay in a coma, he was reframed as a criminal.

Inaya had worked relentlessly to build a strong case against Egan, going through eleven years' worth of excessive-force complaints. There'd been no punitive action. Egan had been moved around, told to lay low, but he came back stronger than ever, free to act as he chose.

And after beating Marcus McBride, what Danny Egan chose to do was target Inaya, in a way she'd never forget.

Cat was calling her. Trapped by memory, Inaya's body was like stone. Still falling, yet she hadn't stirred at all. Everything she was feeling was reflected in Areesha's eyes.

She spoke woodenly to Areesha. "What do you think happened to those girls? And why is it connected to the plant?" When Areesha hesitated, maybe thinking she had hit at Inaya too hard, Inaya continued, "One of us needs to start to trust. Tell me what you know, and I give you my word, I'll follow it through."

Areesha gave in. "Fine. This is what I know. Two families are missing their daughters—two close-knit, loving, well-adjusted families, whose children were close. Two months ago, their daughters disappeared on the same day. The trail led to the reservoir at first. The sheriff suggested the girls were so miserable at home that they committed suicide, despite a lack of evidence to support his theory."

Cat closed her eyes. "What a terrible thing to say to the girls' families."

Areesha tapped the table. "Now you get it."

"Why 'at first'?" Inaya questioned, zeroing in on what mattered. Because if something had shifted the course of the investigation—

"Because after I got in Grant's face and asked him to dredge the reservoir, he came up with a different story. He claimed the girls had run away because he'd traced their cell phones."

"Then they're safe," Jaime said, looking stiff and uncomfortable with his big body shoved into the tiny space.

"He didn't show me the data. He didn't show me or the family any evidence at all."

"You don't show the public everything you have," Jaime said reasonably. "His deputies must have confirmed it."

"If Grant's men were told to confirm he was dead when he is very much alive, they would confirm that too. I don't think we want you here any longer, Officer Big Man."

Jaime blinked. Before he could say anything else to get Areesha's back up, Inaya asked him to check in with Seif. He was too polite to glare at Areesha, but he looked unhappy as he made his way to the counter for a drink. It was the compromise position between obeying orders and being kicked out of a club you'd failed to gain admission to.

Areesha picked up her story. "More importantly, Grant said he wouldn't give out the girls' information because they were fleeing abuse. Ask Lieutenant Seif if their new addresses show up in Grant's files." Areesha's mouth twisted. "They won't, because those girls didn't run."

Inaya didn't trust Grant, either, but so far Areesha hadn't given them anything they could act on. "How can you be sure of that without seeing the information for yourself?"

"You asked me about the plant, right?" Areesha's chair tipped back, the golden locks winking at them from within her curls. "You know Hassan Elkader was starting up a union to ask for safer working conditions, and for accommodation. *Religious* accommodation. You probably also know the workers around here didn't like that. Any more than these good Christian folk liked the idea of the workers raising funds for a mosque."

"I know permission to rezone the building site was denied," Inaya confirmed. "So?"

"Most of the workers at the plant are Somali, though fifteen years ago, they were mainly from Mexico and Guatemala." She flicked a glance at Cat. "You remember the ICE raid."

Cat shared a glance with Inaya. "We've talked about it before."

Inaya indicated that Areesha should proceed.

"So Latinos are out and refugees are in because refugees have papers and ICE can't target them in their raids. Natural Foods did a lot to support refugee resettlement here. They probably weren't counting on the reaction of the church. And they certainly didn't foresee what employees whose status wasn't in jeopardy might feel free to do, or they never would have brought Somali workers in." She paused to draw a breath. "Two of the Somali workers were key figures in unionizing Natural Foods. Those two men—Ahmed Abdi and Mustafa Diriye?" Her tapping became insistent. "They're the fathers of the missing girls."

Inaya sat all the way back in her chair, her drink forgotten on the table. She didn't respond at once, connecting the dots for herself. No profitable company wanted its employees to unionize. Unions meant higher wages, more benefits, and safer working conditions, which was important at a meat processing plant with dangerous machinery. Unions also meant collective bargaining power when it came to any employee grievances, such as lack of compensation for employees like Hassan Elkader.

And Elkader, Abdi, and Diriye were leaders in the movements to unionize. Abdi and Diriye's daughters had disappeared. Elkader's daughter was dead.

But why the altered crucifixion, then? And where were Abdi and Diriye's daughters?

Cat interrupted her thoughts. "Razan's body was cold, Inaya. Dr. Stanger said it was preserved by the cold despite significant cell deterioration."

Areesha looked mystified. Like every look on Areesha, it was a good look.

But Inaya caught on at once. "And there haven't been any other bodies. At least, none we've discovered."

"Exactly."

Inaya's eyes widened. "Where else could you keep a body so cold that it froze, then display it perfectly preserved when you needed to make a point? How about the locker at a meatpacking plant?"

They paused for a breath. Then Cat followed the suggestion to its natural conclusion. "If Razan was kept at the plant, how does that connect to the sheriff?"

Areesha ignored Cat's question. "We need a warrant for the plant." She got to her feet, abandoning her pile of books. She slung a sleek gold handbag on a long chain over her shoulder. "Are you coming?"

"You can't get a warrant just like that," Inaya told her. "You have to establish probable cause to search, or imminent danger to life."

"I know a judge." Areesha was on the move. Inaya and Cat scrambled to follow, Inaya thinking that this was a bad idea, one that would have Seif raking them over the coals.

On the sidewalk, she caught hold of Areesha's arm. "Wait. Please. Listen to me. There's a way we have to do things."

Jaime was sitting at an outdoor table, stuffing an enormous banana muffin into his mouth. He did a double take, crumbs falling from his lips.

He took in the three women poised on the edge of departure and said, "You three look like Charlie's Angels."

Cat made a motherly clucking sound; Jaime's artlessness inspired that in her. "You're much too young to know anything about that show. Now don't you have work to do?"

"Going, boss." He didn't forget his muffin. He just dumped it into a paper bag and gathered it up with his drink. Their byplay gave Inaya the chance to pull Areesha aside. "You didn't answer Cat. We haven't connected Natural Foods to the sheriff."

"It's like you're brand-new, just a lamb among wolves." She pointed to a patrol car that slowed down for a look as it passed the bookstore. It was a Blackwater Falls deputy. He made a strange gesture with his hand as he honked his horn and drifted by.

"What was that?" Inaya muttered. She heard pipes in the distance, high up the hills. For a moment it seemed like the pipes had answered the horn.

"Like I said, a lamb. Who do you think the higher-ups at Natural Foods sent around to make sure their employees got the message that there was to be no union? Who do you think has been intimidating the community into staying quiet? You didn't hear about the girls, did you?"

"No one would stay quiet about their girls. Even the sheriff couldn't stand in the way of that—the press . . ."

Areesha's eyes scanned Inaya's face, as if seeing her clearly for the first time.

"Inaya," she said gently, dispensing with titles. "What do you think happened to Hassan Elkader's hand?"

Shock froze Inaya in her seat.

"A workplace accident, he said. The sheriff wouldn't—"

"I think it's safe to say Addison Grant would."

CHAPTER TWENTY-EIGHT

Taking two cars, they pulled up at a small house in a tiny, overcrowded area on the fringes of the Falls. Here the views were interrupted by a scrapyard with colorful broken-down cars spilling onto dirt patches like streaks of poppies in a field. The families who resided here had done their best: painting over tin siding, keeping the dirt free of weeds, a line of white bricks forming a neat path to the door. Areesha had called ahead and both the Abdi and Diriye families were meeting them at the Abdis' house.

As soon as the initial introductions were made, Areesha summarized the purpose of their visit. While she was speaking, Inaya took note of the décor. The small living room was immaculate, clean and spare, not overstuffed with furniture, a wool prayer rug in one corner. There was a coffee cart resting against a wall that opened onto an equally tidy kitchen where scented coffee was boiling on the stove. On a display cabinet were framed pictures of the family's children. Two boys and a girl, all in their teens. A garland of fresh flowers was draped over the girl's photograph. This was Barkhudo, sixteen years old, joy shining from her eyes.

According to Fadumo, her devastated mother, she was energetic and mischievous, the baby of the family, indulged by her parents and brothers. Inaya recognized Fadumo as Omar's mother from the confrontation at the mosque. Waris was the mother of the other missing girl, Khadijah, also sixteen. Khadijah wore a headscarf, and in the photograph Waris showed them, she was smiling at her father, whose arm was around her waist. Khadijah was an only child, but studying the two women, Inaya knew Fadumo's grief wasn't any less for having other children, which reminded Inaya of the Elkaders' loss.

She gave her salaam to both women as soon as they entered the house, causing some confusion. She was law enforcement, a police officer, and yet she was something more, something the women didn't expect. Their liquid black eyes followed her as she took a seat on a dining chair that Omar brought into the room. He looked recovered from his encounter with the police, though the left side of his face was still swollen. He leaned against a wall, translating for the two women when their second, or perhaps third, language failed them.

Inaya studied him. He was tall and lean with a handsome face, his eyes almost amber, with a loose fall of curls he had tousled to frame a smooth forehead. He wore skinny jeans with a green T-shirt that said "Black Lives Matter" in bold letters. When he turned to one side to translate for his mother, she saw the back of his shirt: it featured a map shaped like dagger above the hashtag #FreePalestine. If he wore that T-shirt down Main Street in the Falls, trouble would definitely find him.

When Fadumo rose to make coffee, Omar stopped her, urging her back into her seat. He disappeared into the kitchen, where the sounds of a tray being assembled could be heard.

Fadumo's lips softened into a smile. "Omar is a good boy. He doesn't say 'This is man's work, this is woman's work.' He does everything for me."

Omar reappeared with the tray and served them coffee in delicately scrolled copper cups.

He said nothing to the others, but passing the tray to Inaya, he greeted her with a polite salaam. "Sister."

The amber eyes challenged her, the proud tilt to his head telling her he was torn between respect for her authority and anger at her failures. She apologized for the actions of Grant's men, asking if he was in pain, and suddenly he was an awkward youth, waving off her concern.

She sipped her coffee, listening to the two mothers describe the traits of their daughters. Barkhudo a bold thinker and a debate champion at her school, well-liked, a favorite of her teachers. Fadumo told them she'd even gone to the church one Sunday to hear what the pastor had to say. He'd broken off his tirade against migrants to tell her it wasn't too late for her soul to be saved. Barkhudo had stated that her soul belonged to God, and she trusted it to His care. A few of her classmates who attended the same service had cheered, and the pastor had turned to other subjects.

Khadijah, despite her vivid, smiling eyes, was more sheltered, quieter, but with an interest in photography and a noticeable artistic talent. Waris pointed to a painting of the falls that hung behind her head—a lovely phrasing of blues and greens across the depths of Blackwater Pond. In the alley beneath the falls, she had painted the figures of three girls holding hands, their faces indistinct. Two of the girls were wearing headscarves.

Omar followed her gaze. "Barkhudo, Khadijah, and Razan."

"They were friends?" Inaya asked him. "Did they go to the same school?"

He raised his smooth dark brows as if the question was a foolish one. Areesha and Cat continued to console Waris and Fadumo, so Inaya took the opportunity to move into the kitchen, setting her copper cup down on the melamine counter. As she'd hoped, Omar followed her, arms crossed over his chest, a pose meant to convey self-assurance, though he seemed oddly anxious.

"We can't afford that school. But Barkhudo and Khadijah knew Razan from the mosque. They were closer than sisters. Razan and Khadijah were always at our house."

His voice cracked when he mentioned Razan. Inaya raised her eyebrows. Was he moved by grief at her death—or was he thinking of his sister?

She couldn't tell how old he was. He could have been seventeen or eighteen, or he might have been in his twenties.

"Did you spend time with them too?"

Omar frowned at her. "With my sister, yes. Not alone with her friends." He looked at her curiously. "Do you not know this?"

Annoyed with herself, Inaya recognized that if someone put the same question to Nadia or Noor, they would deny hanging out with male friends. Whether that denial would be true was doubtful, but if the girls spent time at each other's homes, their parents would have acted as chaperones if there were young men present.

"Are you still in school, Omar?"

He drew up his shoulders. "I graduated last year."

Inaya suppressed the "Mashallah" she normally would have uttered, as Omar would probably be suspicious of her praise.

"So you're in college now?"

"I work at the plant," he said flatly.

"At Natural Foods like your father?"

"Yes."

"Your father wasn't happy there. I can't imagine he likes you working there instead of going to school."

His eyes flicked to her badge.

"He is happy. It's good paid work, and I need to do my part to support my family. College is a luxury not everyone can afford." He shrugged. "I would end up working at the plant anyway. It's somewhere that will hire us."

The unspoken implication was that a young man named Omar Abdi wouldn't be employable elsewhere.

"What about your father's efforts to unionize? It doesn't sound like something the plant was prepared to accept."

Omar opened his mouth, then closed it. He turned his head, staring out of the kitchen window at something Inaya couldn't see.

"The union was a bad idea. We didn't know how good we had it. We know better now."

Inaya went alert. "Why was it a bad idea?"

Before he could answer, Inaya felt a firm hand on her shoulder. She turned to face Fadumo, whose face was tight with anger. Her voice was steady as she said, "I have not given permission for you to ask questions of my son."

She hadn't needed an interpreter, then. Omar had been watching over her.

Cautiously, Inaya said, "Your son is an adult now. He can speak to me if he wishes."

Mother and son looked at each other, with Fadumo giving a small shake of her head.

"I have nothing more to say," he told Inaya.

"I want to help find your sister. That's why I'm asking."

Fadumo stepped between them, her head raised like a queen. "I insist you leave my son alone. We've dealt with police before; we know the way you operate. Your color does not excuse you. It makes you *more* accountable, not less."

Inaya should have been prepared for this. She had expected the bond of religion to buy her an easy way in. But she didn't know enough about Somalia to guess at how ordinary citizens fared in the hands of the police, and she confessed as much to them now.

Areesha entered the kitchen, catching Inaya's response.

"You think they're wary of law enforcement in *Somalia*? Pay attention to what's happening here!" A gold-tipped finger indicated Omar. "He's a Black kid in America. You can't ignore what that means."

"I'm also Somali," Omar said with dignity. "Don't erase that part of me."

Inaya apologized to Omar. "I shouldn't have made assumptions, but we need to know anything you can tell us about your sister's disappearance. We're not going to take it back to the sheriff—we're the Community Response Unit."

Fadumo ushered them back into the living room. She said something to Omar in Somali just as there was a knock at the side door in the kitchen. Omar shrugged, picking up his backpack from where it rested on a kitchen chair and slinging it across his shoulder. Inaya hung back a little to see who was at the door.

"Out, *Hooyo*, yeah?"

Fadumo nodded at her son. "Come back before dark."

It was an unlikely warning for a young man beginning to carve out his own path, but not if the family was on the sheriff's radar.

"Let's book it."

Inaya started at the familiar voice. It was Elias, Cyrine Haddad's son. He gave Inaya a quick nod before he was hustled out of view. Lingering at the window, Inaya caught their urgent whispers as they hurried around a bend in the road to Elias's car.

Blackwater was getting smaller by the day. Elias knew Razan and Omar. He was twice linked to their victim, but it made sense if the girls knew each other's families and Razan knew Elias through school. Kids were always connected, sometimes through social media, but here they were linked through family, school, and the mosque.

"Are you coming, Detective?"

The smooth skin of Fadumo's brow wrinkled as she watched her. When Inaya slipped past her back into the room, she added, "Nothing about my son should interest you."

Again, Inaya felt defensive. "I know Elias, actually. His mother is a friend of mine."

"You didn't help Mrs. Haddad any more than you helped us," Fadumo observed.

Which meant word about the bombing had spread.

"We've arrested the person responsible. We want to do the same for Barkhudo, but we can't without your help."

"They took my daughter. I won't allow them to take my sons."

"Who took your daughter, Fadumo?"

Fadumo pressed close to Waris on the small settee, her jaw set, her face turned away. Her cooperation was over. Areesha hadn't prepped them for this. In fact, she'd given them the opposite impression, that the parents of the missing girls were desperate for their help. Almost as if she'd set them up. Areesha caught the expression on her face and nodded to herself.

"I have Black sons," she said. "I wouldn't want them to run into Grant or his deputies."

Inaya's breath whistled through her teeth.

"I understand that. I still need to verify the allegations." She addressed Fadumo and Waris. "Do you believe Sheriff Grant genuinely tried to find your daughters?"

Waris rose from her seat, her movements stiff. Her English was less fluent than Fadumo's, but she made herself understood.

"I point at sheriff. What he points back at me?"

Catalina interjected. "What if we can find your girls?"

"Not stop." Waris shivered despite the heat. "He will do bad." She appealed to Fadumo for support. "We lose too much. Then this man take more."

Inaya's gaze moved between the two women. There had been undercurrents throughout the conversation she hadn't registered that now pinged against her mind.

What had Omar said?

The union was a bad idea. We know better now.

"You think your daughters are dead."

Waris brought a hand to her lips. Her strong fingers were trembling. "Like Razan," she said. "But for us, no *janazah*."

The Islamic funeral service and burial.

"Can you accept that?" Inaya asked.

Tears formed in Waris's eyes, slipping down her cheek.

She repeated her phrase. "The sheriff, he take more."

In the end, with Areesha's help, they persuaded Fadumo to allow them to search Barkhudo's room. Cat accompanied Waris to her home to search Khadijah's.

Barkhudo's room was bright and inviting, the walls painted white with a pale blue border, fairy lights strung across the bed. Not the proper, expensive ones you could purchase from Pottery Barn, but a leftover string of Christmas lights that Barkhudo had repurposed. There were anime posters on the wall, and a stack of books and other paraphernalia on a small white shelf.

Inaya executed the search swiftly, going through each drawer in the teenager's dresser, her night table, the clothes that hung in her closet. Nothing stood out. She paged through textbooks and novels, then took out items from Barkhudo's backpack, where again she found nothing of interest.

"Was her cell phone tracked?" she asked Areesha, who was watching her from the door. "Did the sheriff collect location data?"

"I told you what he gave us, and why I think it was falsified."

Inaya made a mental note to check those records for herself. She moved to Barkhudo's books. Her main reading consisted of manga and graphic novels. Inaya paged through each book. Expensive and in excellent condition, they weren't part of any library's collection.

"Did Barkhudo have a part-time job?" she asked Areesha.

"She had shifts at the ice cream parlor. One day a week."

Inaya tallied the cost of the books. If her brother was working at the plant to help out with the family finances, would Barkhudo have spent her earnings solely on herself?

She set the books aside, concentrating on a pile of newspapers she had missed—not *The Denver Post* or the *Blackwater Falls Herald*. It was the same newspaper she'd found in Razan's room. The Blackwater Academy's paper.

But Barkhudo attended the local public school. What was her interest in Razan's school? Was it the obvious one? Was she in a relationship with someone at the school? She was a pretty girl with sparkling eyes and a smile of some charm. And Muslim girls didn't always do as their parents told them. She knew that from Nadia and Noor's behavior, as well as from her own indiscretions. Of course, if the girls had become friends through the mosque, it was possible that Barkhudo was simply proud of Razan.

Inaya leafed through the pages, looking for a story that might have caught Barkhudo's interest. There was the standard school reporting—events, opportunities, a photography contest, a few literary exploits. Editor's notes related to administrative issues. Each volume's final page acknowledged the paper's sponsors. Inaya cast her eyes over these. The Resurrection Church was there. Natural Foods, Apex Dynamics, and several other local businesses. To her surprise, a small box at the lower left featured the Disciples' patch. Across from it was the sheriff's logo, like a deliberate choice, when the Disciples could have been paired with the church.

Who was the paper's editor? She flipped back to the masthead, but none of the names were familiar. No Campbell Kerr or his friends, no Razan, no Elias. Just an indistinguishable sea of Madisons, Taylors, and Kylies. So she checked the op-eds next and found a recurring name. Mercedes West. She scanned the columns quickly. Interesting. Mercedes wrote about diversity at the Academy. Her arguments were sound, and displayed a measured analysis.

Recalling her own high school days, Inaya flipped to the letters section. Just as she'd expected, most of the pushback was against the op-eds. Here she found the names of Matt Resnick and Dylan Braun, arguing against excessive wokeness, saying that scholarships to the Academy should be based on merit, not part of a diversity trend. Mercedes' op-eds began to appear in September. By the summer term, the boys' letters to the editor had become increasingly vicious, until last month, when they'd stopped writing in. They hadn't changed their minds, Inaya thought. They'd probably descended to the kind of rhetoric that was too poisonous to publish.

Still, why any of this would interest Barkhudo, Inaya couldn't guess. She paged through several columns by Razan, who, as Cat had described, wrote about borders and migration, as well as the racism faced by refugees. Her last column was sharper and more specific: it was an exposé on Apex Dynamics, the aeronautics company that had awarded Razan her internship.

Razan wrote about the arms industry in her article, connecting it to her personal plight as a refugee. She wrote about the bombing of Aleppo, singling out Russian armaments and attack helicopters. Only at the end did she mention Apex, pointing to the prevalence of arms and munitions manufacturers in the state of Colorado. Inaya lingered over the final paragraph.

"They sponsor our paper, they provide scholarships and internships, and they feed our students right back into the system, so that another generation grows up to deal with the world's most dangerous weapons, disconnected ethically and emotionally from the misery and destruction that those weapons cause."

The editor of the school paper must truly be independent, if the principal of the school had let this statement pass. Or had she?

Inaya flipped the page and found a well-researched rebuttal written by another student. Inaya read it closely. It was possible an honor student had written it, but it read more like arms industry propaganda, fed directly to a student in order to appease an influential sponsor.

She collected the things she wanted Cat and Seif to look over and wrote out a list of items she was removing for Fadumo, who accepted it without comment.

"I know you have no reason to trust me, but I'll do everything I can to find Barkhudo."

Fadumo startled her by moving to grasp her face. She held it steady between her hands while Areesha looked on.

"I do not want my daughter's remains in exchange for my living sons."

Fadumo's hands dropped. Her dark eyes turned to Areesha. "You gave me your word. If anything happens to my boys . . ."

"I won't rest until I've brought Grant down."

"May Allah guide you," Fadumo said, though to Inaya she offered only bitterness. "May Allah one day forgive you, sister, for turning your back on us."

CHAPTER TWENTY-NINE

"We need to speak to someone other than Waris and Fadumo—someone from the same community."

Inaya and Cat were in the car with Areesha, who was cruising through the streets on the outskirts of the grid. She and Cat shared their discoveries. Inaya had nothing apart from the articles written by Mercedes and Razan, Catalina had even less. She'd discovered that Waris had been too modest in describing her daughter's talents—Khadijah's paintings were remarkable. So much so that her father had built her a studio under a tin roof in the tiny backyard. Cat noted in passing that backyards in the neighborhood pushed up against each other. If Khadijah was out painting, her neighbors might have seen her and have something to report.

"What did she paint?" Inaya asked from the backseat.

"Seascapes from Mogadishu. The sites of Mecca and Medina, religious figures whose faces are obscured by ovals of light. I think you could identify them better than I can, Inaya. She also painted portraits; her insight was beyond her years. I found a painting of Omar rolled up inside her closet. He's even handsomer in paint."

But you had to sit for a portrait, which belied Omar's claim that he'd kept his distance from his sister's friends. Unless Khadijah had painted him from a photograph. She discussed the possibility with Cat, who didn't share Inaya's suspicion.

"Who wouldn't be flattered to be asked to sit for a portrait?"

Inaya was still doubtful. "Khadijah's parents wouldn't have approved."

"The kids could have hung out in a group while Khadijah painted Omar, and proximity could have worked its magic on the two of them. The portrait suggests as much."

"Isn't that assuming a great deal?" Areesha parked the car on a side street. She twisted in her seat to face Cat.

"I know next to nothing about art," Cat countered, "but this is so obvious no one could miss it. Young Omar looks like a hero on the cover of a romance novel. Larger than life and much too dreamy for such a pragmatic young man."

More secrets, Inaya thought. But were they relevant to the murder? She considered various scenarios. If Omar had been attracted to Razan, maybe Khadijah had resented her and the resentment had grown, despite the girls' closeness. Khadijah had been missing for two months before Razan was murdered—a tender, "artistic" murder—but what if she wasn't really missing? Suppose the sheriff was telling the truth, and Khadijah had fled her family to hide out with Barkhudo somewhere. And then . . . what? She'd come back to Blackwater Falls specifically to murder her friend, arranging Razan as the Virgin with the sensitive eye of a painter, and pinning her to the door of a mosque where the girls had prayed side by side? She might have even had access to a change of clothing for Razan, as girls often shared clothes.

The rest of it didn't hold up. Khadijah didn't have a vehicle, and she wasn't strong enough to maneuver a body. If she was capable of such a crime, she couldn't have done it alone.

The tension in her body seeped away. Though girls were sometimes jealous of each other, likening that to a motive for murder—*this* murder—was something she couldn't accept. It was a theory that had flitted through her mind in an instant, one she didn't share.

"Wait in the car," she said to Areesha. "I'm not letting you sabotage another interview."

Areesha's back went up. "I didn't—"

Cat touched Areesha's forearm. "You very much did. You took us there to make a point, but police work is about investigation."

"You needed to be reminded what this case is about."

"No," Cat said. "We didn't. I know, and Inaya definitely knows. We are looking for a killer who is probably also a kidnapper, and we are doing it under the shadow of police involvement. That's been very clear from the start. You may have fought your battles, but that doesn't mean we haven't been fighting ours. Now please. Stay in the car, and let us do our jobs. We're all on the same side."

Areesha straightened. Then she folded her long length out of the car so she was speaking to Catalina across the sun-warmed roof.

"I am *not* on the side of the police."

"I didn't mean the police," Cat shot back. "Aren't we all on the side of justice?"

Areesha settled herself against the car, unperturbed by the heat. She waved to the house she had parked in front of, indicating they should go.

Cat and Inaya climbed the stairs of a sunny yellow house with a makeshift roof that tilted at an angle.

Areesha wasn't done. "The jury's still out on whether you'll deliver."

Inaya rose on her tiptoes to peer through the window at the top of the door. "No one's home. Let's try the next house."

Cat sighed. "Door to door in ninety-degree heat. Where's Jaime when we need him?"

Inaya accepted the change of subject with a smile. "You take this side of the street, I'll go across. Less time in the heat that way."

They passed Areesha standing beside the car, cool in her white linen, as she watched them canvass. Some doors were opened to them, while others remained closed. No one invited them inside, but a few community members stood and chatted on their doorsteps. The entire process took a little over an hour as the sun glared down on the empty, potholed streets.

By the time they got back to the car, their clothes were plastered to their bodies.

Areesha ran the AC, giving them time to cool off before she asked, "Anything?"

Inaya blotted her forehead with the hem of her blouse.

"It seems there was more going on at the plant than we realized."

"You got them to talk? Well done."

Cat gave Areesha a crooked smile. "We promised we wouldn't take down their names. That loosened a few tongues."

"And the gist of it?"

"When they started at the plant, years ago, everything went well. The manager was grateful to find people who were willing to do the work, and she was willing to accommodate any special requests. Until the moment she wasn't. And that was due to the church hyping up anti-Muslim sentiment."

"The church has that much influence over a private business?" Areesha sounded skeptical.

"If they push for a boycott of Natural Foods products, you bet they do."

Areesha put the car in gear. "It's just a church. A big church, but still a church."

"With a televised Sunday sermon that reaches a massive audience," Cat put in. "Picture an episode of Fox News focused on Ilhan Omar or The Squad. It quadruples the hate they receive as members of Congress. So all the pastor here has to do is talk about the town being run over by 'infidel' practices." She looked sheepishly at Inaya. "Sorry, *hermana*."

Inaya shrugged. "I've heard it all before." She had. It was a wound she'd carried since her teens, a wound she didn't probe.

"So the plant manager was under some serious pressure," Areesha concluded.

"It's like you said. Religious accommodations that weren't controversial at first became a sticking point. And this came down from the top. No one talked about a union until accommodations were rescinded. *Then* the workers began to ask for better pay and safer working conditions. So Natural Foods created the monster they feared. Safer working conditions were important to the plant's employees, but not as important as having a place to pray, or flexible work hours during the month of Ramadan. They could have zoned a site near the plant as a mosque, but the church wasn't having that, either." Inaya rested her head against the back of Catalina's seat. "It's the same everywhere. Little men love to play God."

Areesha honked at a car that cut them off on the highway.

"So Resurrection is all over this."

"And let's not forget the Disciples," Cat added, "Or Ranger West."

Inaya shifted uncomfortably. She hadn't been allowed to disclose West's status as an undercover agent to either Jaime or Cat. She'd also forgotten to question Seif about West's assignment. She hadn't wanted to, after his sympathy the night of her disastrous *rishta*. She didn't like being at odds with him, yet he seemed determined to keep them on that footing.

They sat in silence for a while, until Areesha pulled up at the Book Mark.

"What's next?"

Inaya drummed her fingers on the back of Cat's headrest. "Next we tackle things we can't involve you in. A visit to the church, another to the plant. Maybe to the school again too. But if we move back into the community, you'll get a heads-up from us."

Areesha didn't fight this. "What about Catalina?" she asked.

Cat slipped her seat belt off. "Don't worry. I'm sure the lieutenant has something for me to do—he always does—and then sometime tonight I may get to see my patient and lonely husband." She grinned at Areesha. "Yours must be waiting for you too."

"And my boys," Areesha agreed. "Speaking of boys—whatever you find, go easy on Omar. He's trying to come to terms with the loss of his sister. He's not the villain here."

Maybe not, but he was hiding something. Perhaps a closer relationship with Razan or Khadijah than he was willing to admit. Still, Inaya had no interest in persecuting the young, when men with evil hearts abounded in the county.

"I'll keep that in mind." Exiting the car, she leaned in through the open window. "If you'll keep in mind that we have other lines of inquiry to pursue. Rushing things could ruin the investigation, or get us taken off it."

Areesha pushed her giant sunglasses to the top of her head so Inaya could see her eyes.

"You think I have a one-track mind," she said, "But I haven't forgotten Razan."

When she'd gone, Inaya and Cat headed home, though Inaya needed to call Seif. He answered on the first ring, patient with her recital. When she finished, he sounded thoughtful.

"These kids know each other well. If we can't find Razan's knapsack or her phone, and if her killer didn't take them, one of them may have an idea of where Razan might leave them. We know the phone was with her at the ice cream parlor—what about her knapsack? Mrs. Wendell confirmed that Mercedes and Razan were there—who else? I'll get Webb to find out if the parlor has a security camera, and to pull the footage if it does. Maybe we'll catch a break." He covered the phone to speak to someone else. He came back and asked, "You talk to your friend yet? The one who knows about art?"

"Not yet. Cat and I are planning to visit the church. I'll fit Rupi in after that."

"The church can wait. Talk to your friend first. Then prioritize Razan's school and her internship. We need to nail down her actions before we widen the investigation."

Though it irritated Inaya, she knew Seif was right. He'd sifted through her report to nail down their priorities with the sharp mind of an analyst. Yet he'd left the FBI to head up Community Response, which to her mind was a step down. Was he fleeing some kind of trouble? Was he keeping her away from Grant because he needed him on his side? Or was it as simple as Seif seeking a way to gain admission to an exclusive club—the old boys club?

"You all right, Rahman?"

She snapped back to attention. Seif's actions concerned her only insofar as they affected the investigation. Or if he let Grant back in.

"Yes, fine."

"No suitor waiting at home?"

The teasing note in his voice surprised her into laughter. "No, thank God. Unless my mother is secretly planning another embarrassing evening."

It was his turn to laugh, smooth and deep. Inaya warmed to the sound.

"Call me if you need a rescue." He hung up before she could speak.

Damn, she thought. They'd almost been flirting, and then he'd shut it down. The hollow pang that struck her felt too much like disappointment.

CHAPTER THIRTY

Seif dropped by the hospital on Sunday. All hospitals were noisy; he knew that from his own experience. He'd sat beside his mother's bed for nights on end as she died of pancreatic cancer, three years after his father was killed abroad, when Seif was seventeen. They'd caught it too late, and the cancer had proceeded aggressively, leaving only a ghost of the woman she'd been—remarkable in every way, and so warm. God, she'd been so warm, lighting up their home with her love. No surprise the twins had been lost in the aftermath of her death. No time to consider whether he'd been lost too, weighed down by what she'd asked of him.

Look after them.

Look after yourself.

Come back to your Creator, my son. Who else will pray for me?

He couldn't say he was observant in any way. He'd broken from faith to get what he wanted out of life, but he'd left wreckage in his wake. His parents, the twins, his former fiancée Lily. Inaya wasn't going to be another casualty of his anger at God.

But his mother . . . of course, he prayed for her. In his own way *and* hers. It was the least he owed her for not falling apart when his father was killed, and the authorities refused to return his body to the States. Had his father been cremated? Had he been buried with dignity or had he bled out somewhere in the desert? No way to know, no way to get answers, since he could never enter the country that should have been like home. Not unless he wanted to end up like his father.

He knew why he was having these thoughts. He was sitting beside

Mrs. Elkader's bed, waiting for her to awaken. She had an underlying heart condition, and her vitals were still erratic so the hospital had kept her. This had been Seif's first chance to get in and see her—to connect, as Inaya had advised.

Even in sleep, her scarf was loosely wrapped around her head, protecting her dignity from strangers. She was hooked up to an IV, an ugly bruise forming on the back of her hand, machines whirring in the background, but he noted that she didn't look frail. Life had forced resilience upon her. She'd survived the destruction of Aleppo, and the loss of two of her sons. To dream at night of your child being tortured by a merciless regime, of your infant son being pulled under the waves, then wake to the knowledge of your daughter's crucifixion—she let herself feel grief yet wouldn't break. She still had a child in Turkey, and he knew from the well-worn lines of determination in her face that she wouldn't give up until she'd brought him home.

A nurse came in to wake her, going through the routine of checking her blood pressure and her temperature. Fatima caught sight of him in the chair beside her bed, her fingers going to her scarf. When it was straightened to her liking, she asked the nurse to raise her bed.

No one from Al-Sham could mistake Seif's features, so he responded gravely to her salaam, not trying to deny her. Her anxious eyes searched his face. She spoke only four words.

"My husband? My daughter?"

"Your husband is outside, waiting to see you. We're still looking into Razan's death."

He expected her to do as his mother had done—entreat him, swear on his honor that he would not fail her family as so many others had done.

Instead she said with a grace he hadn't been able to muster in his own situation, "The people here have been so kind to us. The Baptists were our first contacts here, even before we found the mosque. They are people of such goodness—they are still trying to unite me with my son." She closed her eyes, the lines beneath them eloquent with sorrow. She'd done nothing to make over the signs of her suffering, yet she shared the beauty of her daughter.

It came from dignity, he realized. A quiet dignity that lit up her face, reminding him of *noor*—the light upon light that could illuminate the universe because it was the light of God. No, he wasn't being reminded, he was being *taught,* a thought that made him angry and restless. He hid both emotions from her.

"No one from this community could have done this, could they?"

"You know the cruelty in this world better than I do, Khaleh. What about the bikers? These so-called Disciples?"

"They are not from the Baptist church," she said quickly. Bitterness pursed her lips. "Though many men kill in the name of God, as *you* know better than I." In Arabic, she added, "Falasteeni?" She'd deduced it from his Arabic, so he nodded. A silent communication passed between them, the bonds of a shared history, a way of being in the world. The tension in her shoulders eased. She could have associated him with the lethal Mukhabarat of her own country, but in the curling of the Arabic language around his tongue, she'd found something else. The same thing he'd found when he listened to her accented English. Homecoming. The kind he'd known when his father was alive.

"So you know," she interrupted his thoughts. "But even these Disciples, yes, they bothered my husband sometimes. Made him angry and fearful for us. But they left my daughter alone because of her friend, Mercedes."

"Do you trust Mercedes, Khaleh?"

She made an expressive gesture with her long white fingers.

"She is a beautiful child. She was like a sister to Razan, as dear to me as a daughter." Her composure began to unravel. "My only daughter now."

Seif wasn't comfortable with a woman's tears; he wished he'd brought Catalina along. Not knowing what to say, he reached across the bed to the raised table at the side and passed the box of tissues to Fatima. She dabbed at her eyes, her head falling back against her pillow.

"Was there anything else you wanted to ask?"

He hesitated. He didn't want to insult this woman or bring to her mind new worries, but she was pliant now, unresisting, and she might answer differently than in her previous interview.

"To your knowledge, was Razan interested in anyone as a boyfriend, perhaps? Or was someone interested in her?"

Her answer gutted him.

"I wish she had been. I wish my daughter had known something of joy before her life was taken. But her heart was . . . burdened . . . is that the word?"

"Yes, Khaleh." Her English was excellent, her accent a stroke of grace. And for a Syrian mother to wish that for her daughter despite Islamic strictures . . . "What burden did Razan carry?"

"Luqman . . . Her twin," she continued at his puzzlement. "She was living only half a life because Luqman was the other half. She felt . . ."

"Lonely?" he guessed when Fatima didn't finish.

"Guilty." She crushed the tissue in her hands. "To have freedom and security, when Luqman didn't. She could enjoy things, my daughter. She could strive for things because she was striving for them both, but inside—inside, I think she knew very little joy." Her eyelids beginning to droop, she concluded, "Now the twins are reunited."

"What happened to your son, Khaleh?"

He asked this out of genuine curiosity, not because he thought it had anything to do with Razan's death. Catalina and Inaya had briefed him; he still wanted to know what this resilient and graceful woman thought of her family's fate.

"He fought with the Free Syrian Army." She shook her head. "Bombs were falling every day, East Aleppo crushed into ruin. The apartment buildings peeled, leaving the flesh exposed. Our flesh, our bones, our dreams. I don't know how my son thought he could fight Russian jets." Her eyes were made bleak by memory. "He believed it was cowardly to accept the killing of innocents as the dictator's right. As if it was Assad's country, not ours. So he became a fighter." She nodded briskly. "At the end, the gangs were roaming our neighborhoods looking for girls. My son was part of a patrol that tried to keep us safe."

"Did they hurt Razan?"

She shifted in the bed. "My daughter came to this country un-touched. Was she—"

"She wasn't interfered with," he said quickly. "No one touched her in that way."

His discomfort was acute. To speak to a woman his mother's age of matters of honor, matters she would deem intensely private, took more resolve than she knew.

Softly, so softly he wasn't certain she would hear, he murmured in Arabic, "Forgive my frankness, Khaleh."

She closed her eyes in acceptance. Perhaps she was even grateful, though his next question would shatter any illusion of gratitude.

"About your husband, Khaleh."

"Yes?" She didn't open her eyes. He couldn't leave the question unanswered, though he knew she needed her rest.

"How did he relate to Razan? We've heard he was angry she was working outside the home. Why was that? Was she too independent?"

She looked straight into his eyes, and he wasn't a good enough actor to hide his sense of distaste. It was a logical line of inquiry, one he couldn't neglect, yet bile surged in his throat.

"Do they make you ask things like this? Because they don't know who we are?"

His silence wasn't a tactic, he just couldn't pretend to disagree. He couldn't lie to her either, so he said, "It has to be asked, Khaleh."

She sighed. "Hassan loves Razan—loved her. She was the light of his eyes. The children's resistance—they learned it from their father. They wanted to make him proud—he *was* proud. He blames himself for it now. He thinks his example must have led to Razan's death."

This was what he wanted to know. "Why?"

She took him through the plant's efforts to unionize, and the role her husband had played, her voice turning bitter when she spoke about his injury.

Seif studied her so intently that she blushed. "Tell me about his hand. I thought his injury was the result of an accident."

She tilted her head toward him, her face much paler than when he'd entered the room. "You will keep this in confidence? You won't tell Hassan I told you?"

"I won't." An easy promise to make; he wondered if it would be as easy to keep.

With the bond of language between them, she must have decided to trust him. She drew a deep breath and began.

"A few days after he pushed for a union, Hassan was assigned to a new line. Another worker stumbled into him, his hand landed on the saw." Rage flared in her eyes. "The man wasn't there before that day, and he hasn't come back. He didn't stumble, he meant to do it."

"Do you remember the man's name?"

"Hassan didn't see his name tag. He was white. Thin. But he was tall and powerful, Hassan said."

"Tattooed?"

She gave him an exasperated look. "It wasn't a Disciple. They would never have the patience or skill to work in such a place."

Hassan didn't share his thought that a ringer could have been brought in. He needed to ask these questions of Hassan directly without, if he could manage it, violating Fatima's trust.

"When did the injury happen?"

There might have been a sedative in the IV, because her voice was growing fainter.

"Ten days ago."

"So not long before Razan went missing."

She closed her eyes. "Yes."

"Did you think Razan had gone camping by herself? Is that why you didn't report her disappearance to the police?"

Her answer was halting, tears seeping from beneath her eyelids. "We didn't like it when she went to the reservoir, but we didn't feel we could stop her. She was fearless on the journey from Syria, like a tiger freed from a cage. After everything she showed us she could do—getting us through checkpoints, keeping her younger brothers safe from harm—we didn't want her to feel trapped by our expectations. She had grown beyond us, somehow."

"But she told you if she was planning to camp out?"

"Yes. Always."

"So if you didn't hear from her or see her for three days, you must have been worried."

She brushed the tears from her face with the soft fabric of her scarf. Her fingers were so agitated in their movements that he knew she was seeking her prayer beads to mark off the attributes of God. To take refuge in familiar comforts.

"I will always blame myself," she said. "We should have acted." Her look at him was pleading. "But we have never been able to place our trust in men from the police."

He wanted to ask her for details, but she'd drifted back into sleep. So he turned to the man who had just come to the door. Maybe Hassan Elkader knew more than he thought he did.

He showed the husband the same patience he'd shown the wife, examining his face for signs of his Palestinian father without knowing it, searching for an anchor, or as Inaya had put it so unnervingly, a point of connection.

He made the usual assurances about the investigation, conducting the entire interview in Arabic, his voice low and soothing, his explanations generous. This man would know the Mukhabarat better than his wife. If his children had followed his example, had he fought to overthrow Assad? Did he blame himself for more than Razan, or for not reporting her missing? Was Luqman's disappearance on his conscience?

Bit by bit, he extracted the story of Hassan's injury. Hindered by his promise to Fatima, he led the man to the truth with gentle probing about the plant. Hassan didn't cry, didn't tremble. In fact, Seif was relieved to see a resurgence of anger in his eyes. It gave Seif confidence. For a moment he glimpsed a Syrian lion, a man who could lead others.

Hassan's voice growing stronger, he confirmed his wife's account.

"I know why they switched me to the other line. It was to put me near the saw."

Seif believed him. He knew what had gone on at the plant in the past—the ICE raid, the recruitment of refugees with very little experience to work around dangerous equipment. From what he'd heard, the refugees were hard workers, taking on jobs that no one else wanted because the pay was good, even if the safety conditions were dire.

Hassan described the new worker beside him in some detail. Tall, thin, and white, just as Fatima had said, with pale blue eyes set close together near the bony bridge of his nose.

"He was wearing a supervisor's badge. I think they must have promoted him because he was one of them."

"Maybe he earned that promotion."

Hassan blinked at him, surprised. "I did not envy him, Detective. I noticed he was slow. He was learning the slicer. And his hands were soft and pale, not strong and scarred like mine."

Hassan held out his uninjured hand, and he was right. The knuckles were broad, the tendons thick, his hands large and sturdy. In his mind's eye, Seif saw the image of a figure hoisting up a girl and pinning her to a door. Razan's parents had alibied each other for the period preceding the discovery of her body. When Fatima had been at work, her husband had been at the mosque. Inaya had been painstaking about checking every detail the couple had given her, perhaps because she needed to prove them innocent.

He buried the image, his gaze thoughtful on Elkader's hand. He didn't know much about the workings of a meat processing plant, except that space was limited on the line. One of the complaints brought against the plant during the pandemic was the lack of physical distance between employees, allowing for the spread of the virus.

Hassan had given him as thorough a description of the other man as he could, and confirmed that he'd never seen him before or since.

"You said he was wearing a supervisor's badge."

"Yes."

Probably a lost cause, but Seif asked, "Did you happen to see his name?"

Elkader held up his palm. "It was a nickname, Little Red. I thought it was strange."

Little Red. Something to ask the plant manager.

"Why was it strange?"

"Because the man didn't have red hair. His hair was curly and brown."

CHAPTER THIRTY-ONE

On Monday, Inaya parked at the Blackwater Academy. She was by herself. Cat was working on background material, Jaime was going through transcripts of the sermons of Resurrection's pastor. She didn't need backup to interview a school principal.

At the sound of the bell, teenagers spilled into the parking lot. The student body was mainly white and of a type, dressed in burgundy blazers and trousers. The girls wore skirts that had to be against dress code, rolled up at the waist to mid-thigh. They were fresh-faced and sweet, with lip-glossed lips and bouncy ponytails. The boys were tall and blond with ruddy skin and big shoulders. They drove off in luxury SUVs; no one here was hurting for money.

Inaya made her way through the throng, moving in the opposite direction. A security guard checked her ID and called in to the office to confirm her appointment. If his services were privately retained, the school fees had to be extortionate.

Her bona fides confirmed, the security guard unlocked the door. He was young and good-looking, with sharp cheekbones and a thick fall of chestnut hair. He attracted a lot of attention, but he seemed not to notice the students who tried to catch his eye.

He was otherwise quite receptive, so when she was done with the principal, she would come back and check his last sighting of Razan.

He escorted her to the principal's office, discreetly checking for her gun. She'd done the same, but the guard was unarmed. He carried a taser and a baton on his belt, but she guessed parents had drawn the line at a firearm on school property. Or maybe the principal had.

The principal was a well-groomed white woman who introduced herself as Christine Nakamura. She was the same height as Inaya, excessively slender, dressed in a green skirt-suit with sensible but elegant pumps on her feet and a patterned silk scarf at her neck that matched the suit. At her ears and wrists, she wore subtle emerald jewelry.

She invited Inaya into her office with a noncommittal smile. The office was spacious, with arched windows that opened out onto the green lawns of the quad. One wing of the school bookended the lawns, its architecture in the high-roofed Colorado ranch style. The quad was mainly empty, though a few students had gathered to chat on gold iron-wrought benches, the whole scene neatly arranged, much like Nakamura's desk. It was clean and uncluttered, with a beveled glass letter tray that was sitting empty and a photograph of the principal with a handsome Japanese man, his arm locked around her waist.

Ms. Nakamura—there was no invitation to use her first name—took control of the interview at once, evidently not a timid functionary anxious to accommodate police.

"When can we expect the police to release details that will enable us to make a statement to the Academy's family?"

Startled by this approach, Inaya repeated, "'Family'?"

"Our students, faculty, and staff. And of course, our students' parents. As I'm sure you can appreciate, Detective Rahman, uncertainty of this sort can be very bad for the reputation of an academy such as ours."

Prestigious, Inaya filled in. *And properly moneyed, to boot.*

Cautiously, Inaya said, "I can confirm for you that your student, Razan Elkader, was found murdered. I can't give you more information than that, as our investigation is ongoing."

"When and where was she found? Not on school property, I presume, given the absence of your colleagues or your failure to set up a cordon."

Inaya wanted to mull over Nakamura's choice of the word "failure," but she needed to stay sharp, or she'd be the one providing answers.

Time to put Nakamura on the defensive. "Why would you think Razan might have been killed at the Academy? Have you had trouble here?"

Nakamura's thin eyebrows arched up, two penciled-in triangles above equally sharp eyes.

"Absolutely not, Detective. The Academy is one of the most respected schools in the nation—why would you even suggest it!"

Inaya tried to appease her. "Wherever young men and women are thrown together, there are bound to be conflicts of some kind."

"Not at my school." She looked so dismissive that Inaya went straight to the point.

"What about the incident with Campbell Kerr and his friends? The assault upon Razan at your gym?" She hazarded a guess, waving her arm at the wing visible from the windows. "That's school property, right?"

Nakamura paused. The question had caught her off guard, and she deliberated over her response. She slid open a drawer of her polished wood desk, taking out a pen and notepad. The paper of the notepad was more like cardstock, inscribed with the school crest and Nakamura's name and title. The pen was even fancier, with a finely tooled gold nib, its black lacquer body overlaid with mother-of-pearl.

Christine Nakamura definitely enjoyed the finer things in life. Her cool poise, her style of dress, the immaculate office—they added up to a woman who insisted on control, yet was able to express herself through elegant details, like brushstrokes laid on a canvas.

She looked up at Inaya suddenly, the pen poised above her pad.

"That's a confidential school matter. How did you come to know about it, Detective?"

"I'm afraid that nothing is confidential in a murder inquiry, Ms. Nakamura. That's why I need to ask you about the assault on Razan."

Nakamura pursed her lips, her pen tapping the pad. Then, with a studied gesture, she laid the pen aside. "There's a nondisclosure agreement, Detective. Each of the students involved had to sign it, so I'm afraid I'll need to consult our legal counsel before I can answer your questions."

Pointless, Inaya thought, when the video had circulated everywhere. "Did *Razan* sign the agreement?" she pressed.

Nakamura's eyelids dipped. A pause before she admitted, "No."

"Were criminal charges brought against the young men involved in the assault?"

Nakamura quickly recovered. "Shouldn't *you* know more about that?"

"If charges were laid, the school would also be notified."

Inaya waited, letting her silence do its work.

"I think your questions would be better directed to the Blackwater sheriff's station."

"So you're not able to tell me if Razan was happy at your school?"

"She was very happy," Nakamura said firmly. "And why not? She had every opportunity to excel. And she made the most of it."

There was a note Inaya couldn't quite identify in Nakamura's voice, but it sounded like blame. She'd expressed no personal sympathy for the murdered girl, only that hectoring impatience at the inconvenience to the school.

"I've been wondering about that." She looked around the expensively furnished office. "The fees at Blackwater Academy must be quite high. I understand Razan was offered a scholarship. Can you tell me more about that?"

The phone on the principal's desk rang. Inaya indicated she should answer it. Nakamura let it ring. When it had rung off, she answered as if it was a shameful secret, "We offer several scholarships that are underwritten by our donors. Razan happened to qualify."

"It must have been a difficult transition for her from war refugee to student. How did she fit in with her classmates? Sometimes at private schools, scholarship students can be made to feel like they don't belong."

"I resent that accusation, Detective. Blackwater Academy is like an extended family. We welcome new students with open arms, and we treat each other with respect."

"Tearing a Muslim girl's headscarf from her head—three muscular teen boys pinning her down to do it—doesn't sound all that respectful."

Nakamura refused to concede that. "As I've said, I'm not at liberty to discuss that. But may I point out that if Razan wasn't popular and well-liked, she wouldn't have been elected president of at least two of our clubs?"

It was Inaya's turn to scribble on her notepad. "Can you confirm which clubs?"

Again, Nakamura was unwilling. "I can't have you bothering the students in those clubs."

"I'll take that under advisement, but for now, I'm trying to get a sense of Razan's interests. I can stick around and put these questions to your faculty, or you can simply tell me."

Nakamura clearly hadn't been expecting Inaya to be so persistent, or so underwhelmed by her authority. She gave a ladylike sniff. "Razan was president of the physics and math clubs, she was a contributor to the student newspaper, and she was involved in student drama on the technical side. She was also a favorite of her history and politics professors."

Inaya smiled a bright smile. "That wasn't so difficult, was it?"

But when she asked for the names of Razan's teachers, Nakamura put her foot down.

"There will be no further cooperation until I've spoken to counsel, as I've said."

Trying to get under Nakamura's skin, Inaya asked, "The school feels the need to retain criminal defense counsel?"

"*General* legal counsel," Nakamura said through gritted teeth. "I'll be seeking advice."

"I see."

Nakamura wanted her gone, so Inaya tried another line of questioning.

"As a matter of interest, how many students of color attend your academy?"

Her answer to that was pat. "A number that is representative of Blackwater's population."

"Including those from non-gated communities?" Though she was guilty of living in a gated community herself, the divide between the haves and have-nots, so deliberately designed, made Inaya uncomfortable. She pushed that discomfort onto Nakamura.

"I'm not sure what you're getting at."

"Then please let me make it clearer. What about the children of workers at the meatpacking plant—Natural Foods? Do any attend your school?"

"There was Razan, of course." Still no word of sympathy.

Inaya stood up, wandering over to the window. She glanced at the groups that had begun to collect in little cliques around the quad.

"So who received the other scholarships? I see only white students here."

"There are lower-income white families too, Detective." Briefly, Inaya considered whether Nakamura could be referring to children like Mercedes when she spoke of lower-income families—children of the Disciples.

"You mentioned donors. Would they include members of the Resurrection Church? Or Natural Foods?"

"We are affiliated with the church. The pastor conducts our chapel services."

"Have you heard of the Disciples, Ms. Nakamura?"

Her answer confounded Inaya.

"Certainly. They're a social riding club associated with the church. They frequently support school activities. And one of our school clubs is a motorcyclists' club. Members of the Disciples volunteer their time to teach our students."

Inaya thought of Hardtack. She'd hardly describe him as a member of a "social riding club." It wasn't for her to judge, but his rough-living lifestyle didn't fit with either this pristine campus or its haughty mistress. Or was she making an assumption? He might not be rough-living at all. She left it alone for now. They had another in to the Disciples, and Seif would be speaking to him. She asked about the plant instead.

Christine Nakamura checked her watch.

"They've been exceptionally generous in supporting our school. Two members of the board have their children enrolled here. They're a national chain, as you may know."

"Yet only one of their employees' children was enrolled at your academy. There must have been other lower-income families they were willing to sponsor. I know there are many Somali families who work at the plant, yet I don't see any Black students on your quad."

"I don't see why race matters in this instance. Razan was white herself. Her skin color wasn't an issue."

Inaya seized on the statement. "Then other things were? The scarf Campbell Kerr ripped from her head? Her Arabic accent, perhaps? What about the fact she was Muslim?"

"We have a diverse student body here. Razan faced no difficulty on any account. In fact, her teachers championed her."

"What about her classmates?" Inaya made an impatient gesture. "Set aside the incident in the gym. We've heard there was some resentment over Razan's internship."

Nakamura picked up her pen and made a note on her pad. "I can't imagine where you heard that, but I'd appreciate your giving me a name so we can face these allegations squarely."

Inaya wasn't able to rattle her, so Cat's gentler approach wouldn't work. They'd have to send in Seif or summon Nakamura to the station. It was better to accept her dismissal. She'd learned enough to know there were leads they'd be pursuing at the school, and she'd saved up a parting shot.

"Thank you for your time, Ms. Nakamura. I should notify you that we'll be interviewing your students, to inquire further into Razan's death. I'm sure one of them will be able to provide us with more information. The video of the attack is circulating freely, after all."

Nakamura's fine brows descended like thunder. Her own parting shot hit harder.

"You do as you must, Detective. The sheriff's children are registered at this school. We'll see what he has to say."

Inaya stopped back at the gate to speak to the security guard, who identified himself as Noah Alcorn. He took her questions seriously, though she realized that if he knew how Nakamura had shut her down, he would refuse to say more. So she kept things light, alluding to the fact that Nakamura was too busy to oversee the comings and goings of students, and that that was why Alcorn had been hired.

He explained to her that students had electronic key cards that allowed them access to the campus. They were linked to a student number, and he quickly pulled up Razan's. The last entry was for more than a week ago, the end of day on Friday, two days before her body had turned up. Inaya peered over Noah's shoulder to look at the screen. He was right—each of Razan's entries had been recorded. She asked for a printout, and while he saw to that, she tried to recall if Razan's key card had been found in her room with her personal belongings.

"Is Razan the only one who could use her key card?"

He looked up from the printout, puzzled. "Anyone can use a key card, but when I'm at the gate, even though I know most of the kids by sight, I check the card against the screen."

"Are you the only one on shift?"

"I trade off with Derek Prentiss."

"And is he as sharp as you are at keeping an eye on things?"

"I'd say so, yes."

"What happens when the kids all come at the same time in the morning? If you have to process the key cards individually, don't half of them end up being late?"

"We have ten stations open at the start of the day; the staff helps us run them. Same at the end of day, but end of day is faster because we're less concerned about who's leaving campus than who's coming on."

"So it's more likely that someone could slip out using Razan's key card than they could use it to enter onto campus."

Noah shrugged uneasily. "It's possible, but I hope nothing like that ever happens."

"What about video monitoring? To back up the key card system? Does the school have the budget for that?"

"I'm sure they do," Noah said drily. "But they don't see the need to waste it."

That seemed reasonable enough. The key cards would have to do.

"Could you give me the readout on the movements of these three students as well? Campbell Kerr, Matthew Resnick, and Dylan Braun?"

Noah's face closed down. He knew what she was asking and why.

"I'd better check with Ms. Nakamura."

But he didn't need to go far, because Nakamura was right behind them.

With a glare at Inaya, she informed them, "For information like that, you'll need to request a warrant. We don't cooperate with the surveillance of our students."

Perhaps if they did, and had, Razan would still be alive.

CHAPTER THIRTY-TWO

That evening, Inaya asked her friend Rupi to dinner. Her parents knew and loved Rupinder, and Inaya often cooked to give her mother a break, and also to remind herself there was more to her life than just work. Rupi was a vegetarian, so Inaya made potato kebabs, bhindi—okra sautéed with onions, tomatoes, and masala—and pilau with chickpeas and cloves. All the windows in the kitchen were open to let the scent of spices out, and she and Rupi chatted while Rupi set the table.

Any meal at home was a family meal, and Rupi enjoyed socializing with her family, as she'd come out to Denver on her own. Most people Inaya knew in Denver were transplants from somewhere else, and on meeting at a community presentation, she and Rupi had given each other the two-brown-girls-recognize-each-other-in-a-sea-of-whiteness nod.

They'd hit it off immediately—the same age, the same experiences, the same strong sense of family involvement in the choices they made. There was a shorthand to speaking with Rupi that made the friendship easy: they were starting from common ground.

Rupi had changed her clothes after work, and they'd both chosen to wear *shalwar kameez*. Rupi's long veil was pinned to her left shoulder, Inaya's was casually draped over the arm of her chair. They looked like twins in their pale cream suits, though Rupi's hair was cut to her shoulders while Inaya's spilled halfway down her back.

Their family dinner was its usual loud and convivial gathering, with Inaya's mother grilling Rupi on her romantic prospects. Rupi put Inaya in the hot seat, claiming Inaya was older and her situation more desperate.

Inaya kicked her under the table. Rupi grinned, her hands folded in prayer pose.

"Inaya has prospects," Noor put in, full of mischief. "A handsome cardiologist and a hot detective."

Inaya scowled at her sister. "My boss is not a prospect."

Sunober's scowl was even fiercer. "Indeed, he is not. We only marry among our own people."

"Afghan?" Rupi asked.

"Pakistani?" Noor offered helpfully.

Nadia stayed silent, and so escaped their mother's scorching glare.

"*Apne jaise*," she said pointedly. "*Pathan* *log*." Then, with a quick glance at her husband, she added, "Pashtun." After a pause, she offered "Sorry, *beta*" to Rupi, who only smiled.

Deciding to stir the waters, Inaya said solemnly, "It's my duty as the elder sister to make certain Noor and Nadia get married first."

Noor shot her a death glare, but Nadia didn't speak at all, strangely listless.

Inaya's mother sniffed at that. "If you're that concerned about your duty, hurry up and accept Athif's proposal so we can get on with your sisters."

Inaya thought of the man she thought she'd loved, until Yusuf had clarified his desire for her to set aside her career. His feelings hadn't run as deep as she'd hoped; refusing Yusuf had broken not his heart but her mother's, the radiologist who'd gotten away.

That wasn't what Inaya wanted. Or at least, it wasn't *all* she wanted. If she was looking for a partner at all, she was looking for someone who was sincere in his faith. She didn't care about his cultural background; she only needed him to love his family as fiercely as she loved hers, because then he would be capable of that same depth of loyalty when it came to their marriage. Other than that, her list wasn't long. He should be imaginative in his conception of his faith, and his masculinity shouldn't be threatened by the fact she carried a gun.

Before the conversation became focused on Inaya's prospects, she excused herself and Rupi, casting an older sister's eagle-eyed glance at Nadia as she did. She needed to push harder to find out why Nadia was so out of sorts, but for the moment, the case was the priority.

She'd filled Rupi in on the phone, and after dinner, they sat out on a porch strung with fairy lights, drinking ice-cold *lassi* while Kubo, the family cat, brushed around their ankles demanding Inaya's attention. Inaya called him Mr. Bojangles because of his bouncy gait.

She passed the crime scene photos of Razan over to Rupi, explaining that she was trying to uncover any artistic references that could explain the arrangement of the body.

When Rupi flipped the folder open, she fell silent.

After a while, she whispered, "Jesus."

"Literally."

Rupi drew the first photo out, holding it at arm's length. "I see what you mean. She's meant to be the Virgin, isn't she?"

Inaya bent down to stroke Kubo. "Except the Virgin Mary wasn't crucified."

"Still—the blue dress and the mantle over her hair. Gold and crimson aren't usually the Virgin's colors, yet there's no mistaking the posture. That red circle drawn on the door . . ."

Inaya's pulse quickened, catching Rupi's excitement. "Do you recognize it?"

"Something's off about the posture," Rupi said. "The body is depicted with the five wounds of Christ, but in the Crucifixion, Christ's arms are perpendicular to his body. Razan's aren't. It's like she has her hands raised in prayer."

"So?" Inaya shooed Kubo away from her lap. Like any contrary cat, he returned, butting her hand with his head.

"So this isn't really a depiction of the Crucifixion—it's almost like the arrangement is meant to distract you from the victim. The cloak has a crimson lining. There are diamonds pinned to her chest. That red circle—hang on a sec, I *know* these elements." Rupi picked up her phone and began typing. It took less than a minute for her to find the image she wanted.

"Does this look familiar?"

A solemn figure stared back at Inaya, her eyes large and pensive, her hands upraised in prayer. A gold cloak covered her head and shoulders, draped over a blue robe. Small white crosses were pinned to the cloak at the exact location of the pins fixed to Razan's scarf. And above the figure's head, against a background of blazing gold, was a perfectly centered red circle. The somberly composed figure was wearing red shoes.

"Who is she?" Inaya asked.

Rupi enlarged the picture on the phone, concentrating on the details.

"This is the Virgin Orans. It's a mosaic located in the Saint Sophia Cathedral in Kyiv. I don't know if this is going to confirm the involvement of your evangelical church, however."

"Why not?"

"This is an Orthodox depiction of Mary, influenced by Byzantine art—an amazing example of its kind. It's so large it nearly fills the vault of the chancel." She pointed to the red circle above the figure's head. "It seems obvious now, but that isn't blood, it's a halo."

"What about the wound?" Inaya asked.

Rupi pondered the image. "Can you get your tablet?"

With the tablet settled in Rupi's lap and Kubo settled in Inaya's, they examined the image again, this time crucially enlarged. New details came into view. Mary's stance was different in the mosaic, her feet slightly apart, unlike Razan's, which had been looped together.

Rupi made a choking sound. She pointed to the screen.

"It's a horrible bit of artistry, but look at the Virgin's waist."

A crimson belt was bound over the robe, a white handkerchief tucked inside it.

"See the way the belt loops up to the right?"

A cold finger slid down Inaya's spine. "The Crucifixion wound."

The two women sat there. Kubo leapt away, disturbed by their sudden stillness.

"I think I see what he did." Rupi's voice was a whisper.

"I don't," Inaya said blankly.

"It's an incredibly clever conflation of two images. Those are Greek Orthodox crosses on the Virgin's robe, meant to direct us to this near-Byzantine image. But the belt as the wound that killed Christ? The

Virgin Orans is meant to be an intercessor—which was the role Christ *himself* played before the Crucifixion, an intermediary between man and God. What's interesting is that when Mary stood by the cross before the Crucifixion, Jesus told her she would be the mother of his disciples, standing in his place with them. *She would be as Jesus to them.* So with the Crucifixion wound, your murderer points a finger at the church, knowing you'd follow that lead, and you have. Still, I think he made a mistake—he knows the story of Jesus and the Virgin Mary, but he doesn't necessarily know this church."

"Why not?"

"Because if he did, he'd know that most evangelical churches refuse to display common Christian iconography. Some may allow the bare cross, but a crucifix would be out of bounds." Rupi sat back in her chair, thoughtful. "Your murderer was trying to hoodwink you, but you might have the last laugh if he doesn't know about evangelism."

Inaya's body trembled, so great was her astonishment.

How had the whole team missed this detail about evangelical churches? Inaya had made assumptions about Resurrection because she'd seen West's tattoo; she hadn't talked to the pastor yet or visited the church, because Seif hadn't let her. She'd paid more attention to the Disciples and their record of hate crimes, seeing the crime through the lens of her own history.

"There's something else you should consider." Rupi was reading the details beside the image. "Mary is said to have used her kerchief to wipe away the tears of petitioners who came to her for help; it was a mark of her compassion."

Inaya thought back to the moment when she'd first seen Razan's body. Words tumbled into her mind, underlined by emotion.

"I did think there was almost a . . . tenderness . . . to how Razan's body was displayed. With a care that bordered on reverence."

"What does that tell you?"

"I'm not sure. I can't shake the feeling that this has to be someone who is comfortable with killing—at ease with the idea." Like a cop who'd stared death in the face.

The only person who seemed to fit that profile was Sheriff Grant, yet despite his overzealous policing, there was nothing in his background to suggest he was capable of murdering a young girl. And if he had, what was his motive?

Nor could she discern a motive among the others they had interviewed.

The murder *could* still be a hate crime, yet to kill a girl and clothe her like the Virgin didn't seem like hate.

She'd brief the team tomorrow, see if Seif agreed. Maybe then he'd finally permit her to tackle the pastor and his church.

CHAPTER THIRTY-THREE

The same evening that Inaya spoke to Rupi, Seif arranged to speak with Campbell Kerr. Grant had warned him to go easy.

"Kid's been through the wringer," he'd said. "Parents don't like it, and they've got plenty of say in this town."

Seif took that to mean they were major contributors to Grant's reelection campaign. He'd flagged that for Brandt, his boss at the FBI. But so far, everything he'd turned up on Grant suggested his campaign was clean. Seif knew there was dirty money, he just hadn't proven it yet. That didn't mean it wasn't there—he needed to get more creative, because something was brewing between the major players in this town, a rot beneath the slickness.

He pulled up to football practice, the glare of the floodlights illuminating the best field money could buy. The practice was wrapping up, the coach giving a few more instructions to the players before the team filed out to their locker room.

He had a word with the stocky, gray-haired coach, flashed his badge, and was directed to Campbell Kerr. He was the team's quarterback, and had the finely muscled body to go with it. He was handsome in the way of a young man yet to be formed, with ample Southwestern courtesy, not hard-edged like Seif had expected. Kerr didn't want to be alone with him, so the coach stayed on the field while the two of them took a seat on the bleachers facing the faded hills.

"Great place to play," Seif said as an opening. "I hear you're the local hero."

"My stats are good," Kerr said modestly, "but it's a team effort all the way."

"Have you been scouted?"

"The future's looking golden." The bitter note in Kerr's voice surprised him.

"You don't sound happy about it."

Kerr's blue eyes turned to him, a surprisingly candid look. "My classmate was just murdered. It takes the glow off any celebration."

He got off the bench, catching a ball that the coach tossed his way. He began doing tricks with it—spirals at the tip of his fingers, throwing it up and catching it between his legs—a range of actions that showed off his fitness and fluidity of motion.

Despite himself, Seif was impressed.

He raised an arm, and the football solidly met the flesh of his palm. He threw it back at Kerr in a smoothly delivered spiral. Kerr ran back a few steps, leapt up gracefully, and caught it at the tips of his fingers. Coming to his feet, Seif continued to question him through their play.

"I wasn't expecting you to be that concerned about Razan. I've seen the video of you tearing off her headscarf. I've seen her video too."

Kerr missed his catch, the football bouncing up to his knee. He held it between his hands, the pressure so intense that his knuckles and fingertips were white.

Seif waited, poised on the balls of his feet, expecting a hard throw. Kerr tossed the ball absently, all the way across the field through the posts. His talent, at least, was genuine.

"What I did was stupid and cruel, and now I can't take it back. Try living with that."

"Did you want to?"

"Wouldn't any decent person?"

So he wasn't an unreasoning jock. Unless Kerr was playing him, low voice, wrecked expression, and all. The coach gave a last whistle on the field, rounding up his referees. Kerr tore off his helmet, his blond hair damp with sweat.

"You don't believe me. No one who's seen the video does."

"What about your parents?"

Kerr gave him a rueful look. "They're my parents, so yeah. But it's not helpful."

"Why not?"

"They build me up at her expense. Razan's." He grimaced. "It's ugly. She doesn't deserve that."

With every word Kerr spoke, he sabotaged Seif's assumptions, his automatic anger toward the teen who'd so ruthlessly manhandled Razan. He wanted to stay angry, pin the kid to the mat, have him face the consequences. He couldn't. His brothers had come to him so often with that same shamefaced expression, expecting judgment, forcing him to temper it with grace.

He patted the bench. Kerr joined him, with obvious reluctance.

"Why did you do it, then?"

"I lead the youth group at Resurrection Church."

"So?"

"You ever hear our sermons?"

Seif shook his head. "That bad?"

"The pastor is always preaching about the enemy in our midst. The foreigners. How they cheat the system and then demand that we fit in to their culture, instead of the other way around." He spat at the ground. "The pastor told me he was counting on me to set an example, just like the Disciples. I didn't want to do it, but it was expected of me. Mercedes hated me for it." He dug into the ground with his cleats.

"Did that matter to you? Wouldn't your pastor consider Mercedes another . . . outsider?" He chose the word with care.

Kerr shrugged. "Yeah, probably. I didn't care. I used to date her. She's special, you know?"

"Like Razan?"

"In a different way, though both of them were different. More grown-up, somehow. They weren't into the stuff most of us are concerned about."

"Grades?" Seif asked. "Fitting in?"

There was pain at the back of Kerr's eyes. "Cliques. Popularity.

Who's dating who, crap like that. They cared about things like getting out the vote, helping refugees, health conditions at the plant. They were way ahead of the rest of us, taking on the real world."

"Have you ever been to the plant?" Seif asked idly. It was hard to ask about an alibi for the murder when the time of death was inexact. He'd had Jaime Webb check into cell phone location data for every person of interest. For the three days preceding the discovery of Razan's body, Kerr's placed him at a few specific locations: his home, school, and Main Street. And the location data failed to place Kerr near the mosque. Which could mean he'd left his phone at home or turned it off. Or that he had nothing to do with Razan's murder.

Kerr accepted a bottle of water from his coach, offered another to Seif, who took it with thanks. Kerr took a long pull of his drink before he answered.

"Never. No reason to."

"What about Apex Dynamics?"

Kerr paused in the act of lowering his water bottle. "Yeah, a few times. Once on a tour, then for my application for an internship."

"The one you lost out on to Razan?"

"I deserved to." He raised his chin to acknowledge the referees leaving the field with the coach. "She understood physics better than I ever will."

Seif remembered Kerr's casual toss of the ball through the goalposts. "I'm not sure I agree. You understand speed, velocity, force."

Unexpectedly, Kerr grinned. "Child's play, not rocket science."

"If it was child's play, we'd all have a full ride to college. You have one, right?"

A wistful expression sat oddly on Kerr's unfinished features. "Ohio State."

"Fitting for a local hero. Everyone says you've earned it. You haven't let your team down that I know of."

"I let myself down," Kerr said, a hitch in his deep bass. "I may have earned it, but I don't deserve it. Not after what I did."

This was serious, unreserved remorse. He wasn't playacting, or putting up a front. Seif didn't know if he would make the same confessions in front of his teammates or his parents, but here in the quiet and hallowed space of a high school football field, he was telling Seif the truth.

"Why do it, then? Were the others egging you on?"

Kerr swallowed. "It gets to be like a cult."

"The church group?"

"The church group, football. You're a god who can do no wrong. But that also means you can't show any weakness, especially in front of your . . . friends."

He stumbled a little on the last word, and Seif thought he'd almost said "fans," trapped between a muscular Christianity and a toxic form of masculinity.

"It wasn't your idea."

Kerr's shoulders hunched. "Maybe not, but I didn't push back against it when I was the only one who could."

A hell of a regret to carry. He could almost feel sorry for Kerr. Seif shifted in his seat so he could see Kerr better as he asked the crucial question.

"Did you kill Razan Elkader? Did you mount her body on the door of the mosque, displaying it like a crucifix?"

Kerr's eyes filled with tears, the clear irises reddening. Embarrassed, he wiped his eyes.

"No," he whispered. "I was stupid and misguided, but I couldn't kill anyone."

"You're saying the pastor is to blame for your actions?"

Kerr shoulders jerked. The look on his face could only be described as self-contempt.

"The pastor, my parents, Fox News, the president. I could pass the blame on to anyone. But no one forced me into that gym. No one made me yank off her scarf. *I* did that. And I have to hold myself accountable."

"You could have apologized to her," Seif suggested.

Kerr shook his head vigorously. "It wouldn't have meant much, after what I did. Besides, she deserved to have the last word."

Seif hadn't thought of it that way, hadn't even considered Kerr capable of such maturity.

"So what *will* you do?" he asked. "To make up for it?"

Kerr's breath soughed out of his body, the water bottle rolling to the grass.

"I'm helping Mercedes with Razan's memorial."

"Will that be enough?" Seif asked.

"No." Kerr got to his feet, wiping his hands on his pants. "I'll be trapped in that moment forever. The worst version of myself for the whole world to see. I'll never have the chance to grow out of it." His jaw firmed, no trace of self-pity in his voice. "That's the future I earned, the future I deserve."

He walked back across the field to retrieve the football he'd tossed, leaving Seif staring after him, the ache of Razan's death sharper and sweeter than before.

CHAPTER THIRTY-FOUR

The interview at Apex Dynamics took place early on Tuesday morning. Inaya and Cat found themselves in the tastefully furnished lobby of a steel and glass building with staggering views of the foothills. One wall was all glass, another held signed Mangelsen prints of lions on the hunt.

Apex then was perhaps a play on "apex predators," Inaya mused. There was a Mangelsen photograph called *Changing Lanes* that featured a pride guiding its cubs across a dirt road, the tawny cubs framed against red dirt and green grass. Inaya had inquired about purchasing it, only to find that it was priced at over seven thousand dollars.

Apex Dynamics must be doing well.

A pleasant security guard processed them through a separate gate for visitors, printing passes with their photographs on it, time-stamped strictly for the hour of their visit. Their firearms were checked at the gate and placed inside secure lockers.

The security guard smiled a white smile at them as he said, "Can't be too careful here."

It could have been a reference to Colorado's dismal record of mass shootings, or an indication that Apex Dynamics' secrets were well worth protecting.

The guard took them up to the eleventh floor and ushered them into a conference room where the views were even better. The room was spacious, the chairs just short of luxurious, the conference table a polished oval of Brazilian wood. Security *was* tight; the guard remained with them until they were joined by the man who had supervised Razan's internship, a man whose name was Linden Sych.

He was tall, lean, and bespectacled, with pale blue eyes and an air of charming diffidence, though Jaime's background search on him had revealed that the man was one of the brightest minds in the country, an engineer with advanced degrees in aeronautics, robotics, and computers. His understated suit was a Zegna, his tie and glasses Prada, with a pen so exclusive clipped to the outer pocket of his blazer that Inaya couldn't name the designer.

She noted the polished shoes and the less polished smile. He'd dressed to fit an image of success, yet gave the impression of wanting to be at his drafting board with his sleeves rolled up, his glasses low on his nose.

He offered them their choice of coffee, water, or freshly pressed juice, and to put him at his ease, Inaya asked for coffee for them both.

Once it was delivered, he eased into condolences for Razan, eager to assure them that a scholarship would be set up in her name for students from low-income families.

He looked at them anxiously as if he wasn't sure that was enough.

Inaya commended his efforts, offering a suggestion. "If Apex Dynamics wants to support the Elkaders through their tragedy, they left a son behind in Turkey. If you could assist them to bring him home, I'm sure it would be a great comfort. Perhaps the only comfort."

"Of course. I'll have my assistant make those arrangements at once."

Inaya glanced around the unrevealing conference room, all photographs and views. This time the photos were more subtle, tigers and leopards glimpsed in the green environs of the jungle—leaping from trees, taking their solitary strolls, looking up at a far-distant camera as they drank from a stream. Not just apex predators but part of an entire ecosystem. The photograph was discreetly watermarked in a corner with the name Shaaz Jung. Inaya made a mental note to look up the artist's work.

Cat took the opportunity to excuse herself to take a closer look at the photos. Like Inaya, she must have sensed that Linden Sych was taken aback by the presence of two detectives.

She gave him a friendly smile. The tightness of his body eased.

"Perhaps you could tell us a little about the work Razan did for you. I understand that she excelled in math and physics, and that this internship was prestigious."

Sych preened a little. "It's highly competitive. Razan's grades and her interview set her well above the other candidates."

Inaya took out a notepad. "Who were the other finalists?"

Sych offered those names at once. "They were also impressive, but they lacked a genuine passion for the work we do."

"Which Razan possessed."

"Absolutely."

"Yet she told her friends at school that she was basically a coffee girl. Could you comment on that?"

Sych had the grace to look sheepish. "Ah. The work we do here is classified, our materials highly sensitive. Government contracts, you understand. So there was a limit to the things we could put Razan on, or allow her to speak about." He looked beyond her to the view. "She was an ambitious young lady, so perhaps she felt a little thwarted."

There were two threads of equal interest here that Inaya wanted to pursue.

"You mentioned that the internship is prestigious. That means you must have been offering the students something of value to them."

"Absolutely," he said again. "We design experiments that test their aptitude for aeronautics and aerodynamics. I would have thought Razan found that challenging enough."

Cat's voice from behind them startled him. "Would you say she was dissatisfied with the nature of the internship? She might have thought it was a case of bait and switch."

"Not at all," Sych said with dignity. "We wouldn't offer the internship if we weren't looking to bring the best and brightest into our ranks. There may have been some difficulties because of the language barrier with highly technical work, but to me Razan seemed very happy. Always smiling and enthusiastic—she was a pleasure to work with. I don't know of any complaints, but you could check with my executive assistant. She handles those matters for me."

"Thank you," Inaya said. "We didn't mean to imply otherwise, we're just trying to rule out other possibilities. One of her friends told us that Razan was depressed."

Sych pushed his glasses back on his nose, his pale eyes wide and startled by the idea. "You think her death was a suicide?"

A reasonable question; the details of Razan's murder hadn't been made public.

"We've ruled that possibility out."

"Ah." He steepled his fingers beneath his chin, his elbows on the armrests of his chair. "Anyone in her position would feel sad, given Razan's losses. Her twin. Her young brother lost at sea. As for the crossing itself—I can't think of any words."

His tone was sincere, and Inaya found herself liking him. He was a little odd—perhaps that was the way of geniuses—yet he was also quite human.

"So she was comfortable enough to confide in you." Cat had rejoined them, speaking in her gentle way, such that Sych swallowed over a lump of emotion.

"I hope so," he said. "It's my job to mentor our students. That can end up being about more than just work."

"What is the work you do here, Mr. Sych? I understand this is an aerospace company." Cat gave a helpless shrug. "I'm not quite sure what that means. Do you design rockets? Or perhaps missiles, like Lockheed Martin?"

The air of the professional took over. He leaned forward in his enthusiasm.

"There's much more to the work of Lockheed Martin—they have a finger in every pie when it comes to munitions and national security, and of course, Apex has put in bids to subcontract work. The federal government awarded Lockheed a billion-dollar contract to enhance border security. Ah . . . homeland protection." An embarrassed smile tugged up his lips at the use of this lingo. "So far, we've been focused on developing a better product that might put us in the ranks of a Palantir or Anduril, companies that work on advanced technologies."

"I thought Lockheed was a major global arms developer." Inaya's puzzlement was reflected in her voice. Before Sych could respond, her cell rang. She excused herself to answer her mother, only half listening as mention was made of Noor's *rishta*. She could never get her mother to text her, so she murmured a soothing promise. She apologized to Sych with a helpless wave of her hand.

"Not at all." His narrow eyes beamed with warmth. "I may run this company, but even I take my mother's calls. Duty is as vital as success. Razan thought so too. That's why she fit in here so well." A shadow crossed his face. "I'm sorry, I've forgotten your question."

When Inaya asked about the arms industry again, he looked . . . not shamefaced exactly, but perhaps a little perturbed.

"The battle is at the border now, isn't it? Much though I support immigration—value it, in fact; it brought Razan to us—there's a difference between those who contribute to the building of this nation and those who come here for an easy ride, or hoping to peddle drugs. Open societies like ours need to secure their borders against an influx of undesirables."

He glanced at Catalina, suddenly divined that she was Latina, and flushed to the roots of his hair. "I'm sorry." He waved an abject hand. "I didn't mean—"

Cat didn't try to set him at ease. "Perhaps you should consider just what you did mean. Are people like me undesirable just because of who we are?"

His shoulders slumped in dismay, and to distract him from his thoughtless remark, Inaya picked up on Cat's earlier question.

"I'm still not clear on the work you do here, or the project Razan was hoping to work on that she might have felt disappointed about being excluded from."

"Oh, that's very easy. I can't get into details, of course, but it's no secret that Apex Dynamics is at the forefront of developing a better model of aerostat."

A lengthy explanation followed, mind-numbing in detail, and Inaya decided not to ask for further clarification. Cat knew a lot about the border; perhaps she would clue her in to aerostats.

When Sych was finished and gazing at them expectantly, Inaya murmured a polite "That's very impressive."

He beamed at them both. "The challenge is to best ourselves, to set the bar as high as we can." A tidy little homily on personal achievement followed. She had the sense he'd given it before. She listened closely anyway: the more people talked, the more they revealed themselves.

"Is there anything else you can tell us? When was the last time you saw Razan, for example?" He gave them the date she had left the intern-ship—a week before she'd disappeared.

"She had to turn in her security pass, of course. It seemed like such a shame."

"Could we check your logs? Just to make certain of the last time she was here."

He wasn't offended by the question. "I'll have my assistant confirm that for you."

"Did Razan have a locker here?" Cat remembered to ask. "Or an office of her own?"

Sych shook his head, embarrassed again. "She worked in my assis-tant's office, and I'm afraid our security protocols are so strict that non-permanent staff are not permitted to leave any of their belongings here. If I could have made an exception for Razan, I gladly would have."

That fit with the confiscation of their guns. Sych volunteered the aid of his assistant, whose name was Andrea Wong.

"Top of her class at MIT," Sych said. "One day she'll be running the company."

Sych didn't appear to have the usual prejudices about women work-ing in STEM. Still, she'd follow up with Wong.

She asked Sych her second question. "'A highly competitive intern-ship,' you said. Did you know that a few of the candidates who didn't qualify harbored some resentment toward Razan?"

Sych shook his head in disapproval. "Razan made light of it, but I knew. I saw the video," he explained. His mild face took on a censori-ous cast. "We made the right choice in rejecting Campbell Kerr."

"Did he complain to you?"

Sych sighed, turning his head to focus on Jung's photograph of a black panther climbing down a tree in a densely forested jungle. The jungle was a green blur, the panther a sleek line of beauty, the power of its shoulders on display.

"The Kerrs are county royalty, so they made their displeasure known. They thought Razan was an affirmative-action hire." He sounded outraged. "Kerr had a C in physics. He wouldn't know a vector from a warthog."

Both Inaya and Cat laughed, and after a moment, Sych joined in.

"It was an uncomfortable meeting, I suppose, but Apex Dynamics is one of the Academy's biggest sponsors. Ms. Nakamura—she's the principal there—wasn't about to allow the Kerrs to rally the troops. The Academy values our patronage too much."

So Nakamura had played a double role—cushioning the blows felt by their football star, while protecting Apex from the parents' wrath.

A difficult job, one requiring sensitivity and tact, and given what Inaya had seen of Nakamura, a quashing of her own ego that must have been difficult to swallow. And in both instances, Razan Elkader had been the cause of the problem.

She'd need to discuss that with Cat, but for now she had what she needed from Sych.

"Your photographs are beautiful," she said to smooth their departure.

He beamed at them again.

Warmly, he said, "Andrea has an eye. And the theme of these predators . . . well. That was inspired."

He showed them to Andrea's office, after giving them his card with the assurance that he was there to serve them in any way he could.

"Razan didn't deserve this. She was a shining example of the American dream."

It was an odd contrast with his earlier words about undesirables at the border. Like so many, Sych probably drew a line between legal immigrants and refugees and those who broke the law, without stopping to question the humanity of the law.

Some might have called Inaya a bleeding-heart liberal, but her father was a refugee, his life in Afghanistan uprooted, his youth passed in the crowded confines of the permanent camps in Peshawar. He hadn't been looking to the break the rules or grift his way to success at the expense of others. He'd been trying to survive war.

To have that in your history changed your outlook on the world.

And to abide by borders you hadn't drawn that cut your homeland in half, or that refused to acknowledge your historic ties to the land, wasn't easy to reconcile.

Cat's eyes sought hers in commiseration—it was one more thing they had in common.

Sych tapped Inaya lightly on the shoulder, and she stiffened. There was nothing sexual or predatory about the touch, yet she didn't like it. She guarded her personal boundaries. A woman could touch her, and if it was a friend, even embrace her. She preferred for men to keep their distance. He must have read her stiffness, because he dropped his hand.

"Could you let us know about the funeral? I'd like to be there for Razan. Andrea would as well, I'm sure."

He made the introductions and left the women to talk.

CHAPTER THIRTY-FIVE

Andrea Wong was a smartly dressed young woman with silky hair that she wore in wings and an expression of pleasant inquiry. Her office was attached to Linden Sych's, the door between the two offices closed. If the conference room had been an exercise in corporate opulence, Andrea Wong's office was more compact—even aerodynamic. Inaya grinned to herself at the pun.

The furniture lacked the stamp of any designer—it was cool black steel and glass, the desk featuring angles that gave it the appearance of forward motion, the chair compact and sleek, much like Wong herself. The office was obsessively tidy and organized, not a single folder out of place, the files themselves custom-designed with the Apex Dynamics logo on black folders with a silver edge. Inaya took note of all this with interest, but what struck her most, apart from the view—and clearly Wong was a favored employee to command an office like this—was the adjacent wall, which had been treated as a gallery wall. Expensively framed art hung in matching chrome frames from ceiling to floor.

Andrea Wong invited them to sit. Cat again demurred, taking her time looking over the prints. No leopards and tigers here, just a wild fantasy of electric Hong Kong nights, floating markets in Bangkok, Renaissance churches, bikers with lean, muscled bodies, the Challenger launch, the Shanghai skyline, and a fascinating array of images from the Hubble telescope, no rhyme or reason to any of it, except that, arranged with insight and an eye for color, they formed the outline of a dirigible.

Inaya took a seat across from Andrea Wong, leaning forward for a quick look at Andrea's burgeoning in-tray. The labels faced away from her, so she couldn't tell what the files contained. It wouldn't have mattered—Wong had adjusted her seat to cut off Inaya's view. Her smile was polite enough, but her eyes were laser-sharp.

She exuded cool femininity in a pale blue skirt and blazer, a mint green blouse beneath with a fashionably tied bow at the neck and a matching bracelet at her wrist. At her neck was a pendant with a Chinese symbol, not the ubiquitous cross. Inaya made a mental note to ask about it at the end of the interview.

"Linden mentioned that you're here about Razan."

"He said that you worked with her closely, Ms. Wong."

"Please call me Andrea. I did, of course. Linden's administrative work often falls to me," she said with a wry smile. "That includes oversight of our internship program. Choosing our intern is a committee decision, of course, but all three members were in favor of Razan. She was a delight to work with, so quick to learn."

"I understood she was a little frustrated by the nature of her work."

Wong's delicately penciled brows went up. "Not at all. It's just that she was ambitious. She completed her assignments here in record time, so she was keen to find new challenges."

Inaya ventured a guess. "Did you have her work on aerostat design?"

Wong covered her mouth to cut off a shocked laugh.

"Detective Rahman, I don't think you understand the nature of the work we do here. It's highly confidential national security work. Not only that, we always have bids in process on new designs, and those are multimillion-dollar contracts. The pressure to avoid leaks to our competitors is immense, not to mention the question of treason. Only employees with top-level security clearances are permitted to access the basement."

"What's in the basement?" Cat asked, turning from her perusal of the gallery wall.

"That's where our engineers work on our models. I'm afraid I can't say more than that."

In an apologetic tone that wasn't entirely feigned, Inaya said, "Mr. Sych did try to explain, but I'm not sure I understand what an aerostat is or how it could be classified as a national security interest."

Wong didn't condescend to her; her explanation was simple and concise.

"It's a light airship tethered to the ground with threat detection capabilities. It might remind you of a blimp."

"So Apex doesn't work on missiles. Aren't they more profitable than aerostats? Especially for a small company like yours, trying to make its name?"

Wong's eyes narrowed. "That's often the case, yes. But we focus on aerostats because they're Linden's area of expertise. Plus, you don't need missiles at the border."

Cat's scowl was fierce. "Does that mean aerostats have weapons capabilities?"

Wong shook her head. "No, aerostats were initially positioned along the southern border as part of TARS—the Tethered Aerostat Radar System. They were used to detect aircraft smuggling drugs across the border and to relay that information to operatives who could act to intercept. Now, of course, their reach is much more expansive."

"Mm-hm," Catalina murmured. Inaya heard the note of censure, even if Wong didn't.

"You know about these?"

Cat came away from the gallery wall, her movement almost like a threat. Andrea Wong sat up straight in her chair.

"We don't get into politics here," she warned the detectives.

"The truth is that these aerostats now monitor the border and relay that information to the Border Patrol. They're in hunt mode," Cat told Inaya. "And this is *always* about politics." She turned to confront Wong. "Politics is how you get paid. You said you're bidding for government contracts, right?"

Where Linden Sych might have been flustered by the unexpected attack, Wong wasn't. She didn't touch her hair or fidget in her chair.

"If we can assist the government in upholding the law, that is, of course, our priority."

"The amount of money spent on companies like yours to police the border could be better invested in easing the conditions that asylum seekers face at home."

Wong tilted her chin down a fraction.

"American security companies are not in the business of providing for foreign nationals who think they have the right to jump the queue."

Opinions like this surprised Inaya when they came from non-Indigenous people of color—people whose own parents must have come to the country as immigrants and suffered the concomitant trials. Now affluent, successful, and upwardly mobile, they took a certain pride in closing the door behind them, as if they were rightfully entitled and those following behind them cast a shadow on the prestige they'd obtained.

Inaya left that aside for the moment.

"Razan Elkader was a student activist, we're told. She was a refugee herself. So she may have had an issue with the work you're doing here. She may have brought unwanted publicity your way. She wrote an article about her internship here for her high school paper. You must have thought that the height of ingratitude."

"Razan was entitled to her opinions," Wong said warily.

Like her namesake, Cat pounced. "So you knew about it."

"I . . ." Wong trailed off, needing a moment to think.

Inaya hadn't moved from her chair, and now Wong sank down beside her. Cat turned back to the wall, and as she had intended, Inaya picked up her lead.

"When Razan first came on board here, did she know the nature of the work you do?"

Wong lifted a hand and let it drop. "She knew we were an aeronautics company and that we developed improved aerostat technology. She was eager to be a part of that, so we put her on some of our old designs, to take them apart and see how they worked."

"A high school student?" Wong had avoided the question. "She was capable of that?"

"She was advanced for her age," Wong said stiffly. "As I said, she was very bright."

Inaya could not picture Campbell Kerr remotely capable of the same kind of work. But maybe she had an ingrained prejudice against football jocks that she was just discovering.

"Improved aerostat technology," Cat said like she was thinking it over. She wasn't, and now she drew a piece of paper from her handbag and unfolded it with care. "The Holy Grail of aerostat design: it's unmanned, it stays in the air longer, it has more economical fuel consumption." She shook the page out so that it faced the others. "Oh yes, and it has better ground capabilities. Better for detecting and intercepting those you call illegal. This article in the student paper is by Razan; it was printed the week before she died. You knew that, didn't you, Ms. Wong? You had to put a stop to it, yet you knew you couldn't fire her after you'd used her so prominently in your diverse hiring campaign. 'Look, we've employed a refugee.'"

"So you think—what? We killed a teenage girl to silence her opinions? The mission here is hardly secret. Apex Dynamics is a well-established partner in border security. But it was news to Razan, probably because she was new here. She didn't know we were trying to acquire government contracts by working on a better aerostat."

"I think Razan had a fairly solid understanding of the arms industry: she experienced the bombing of Aleppo."

"We are not an arms and munitions company; we're not at war with anyone," Wong said through gritted teeth, her whole attention on Cat. Inaya took the opportunity to check the labels on the stack of files in her in-box. The first two stood out. Razan's name on the first, "Internal Review of System Weaknesses" written on the second. She was within her rights to ask for the first, but there was no way she could demand the second. And she had to know whether Razan's activism was one of the "weaknesses" in Apex Dynamics' systems.

Cat shook her head. "You militarize the border, so how are you not at war?"

A moment later, Wong asked them to leave. "I don't think I can help you any further. We weren't angry at Razan, we were disappointed. We weren't intending to fire her, but we did tell her that she couldn't continue to work for us and divulge company secrets. We take a strict view on that, and it can be a federal offense. After her article came out, she chose to resign."

"But you said the fact you work on border security is hardly a secret. Razan wasn't guilty of espionage, surely."

"No, not espionage. Just disloyalty. Linden was greatly disappointed—he thought they shared a similar vision, a love for the work itself."

Razan's essay would have rocked them, then.

Wong tried to move them to the door. Both she and Cat stayed where they were.

"Do I need to call security?"

"I hope not." Inaya pointed to the top file in Wong's tray. "We'd like to take a look at Razan's personnel records. And at your 'Internal Review.' Did you consider Razan a 'weakness'?"

Wong physically moved to block their access to the files, her delicate frame strung tight.

Then she seemed to reconsider. She reached behind her for the file on top and passed it to Inaya, ignoring Cat completely. "Please return it to us when you're finished with it. As for the second, that's a classified internal document that has nothing to do with Razan. It's about government compliance standards when we work on federal contracts."

Her eye contact was steady and direct, so Inaya let that slide. Instead, she asked about Razan's security pass. Wong pulled up the logs to show her proof the pass had been deactivated on the day Razan had resigned, with no further entries logged of her return to the building.

As Inaya's fingers closed around Razan's file, she thanked Wong for her cooperation. "I apologize for taking up so much of your time."

She was startled to see that Cat was back at the gallery wall, this time with her camera out, casually pointed at Wong. Wong opened her mouth to protest; Cat smoothly cut her off.

"Would you mind? It's like Mr. Sych said—you have an excellent eye—and I'm looking for something for my house. Your wall is giving me ideas."

"Well . . ." Andrea Wong hesitated. "That was kind of Mr. Sych, but . . ."

Cat snapped a dozen photos before she could finish. "Art isn't classified, right?"

Inaya ignored this exchange, her attention captured by a giant photograph framed in chrome beside the door. She'd had her back to it the entire time she'd been in Wong's office.

The photograph featured a group of smiling dignitaries under a heading stenciled in silver: "Blackwater Falls Steering Committee." The members of the committee included Andrea Wong and Linden Sych. It also included Christine Nakamura, a man in a pastor's robe, and, in the center, Sheriff Addison Grant. A cozy little club, indeed. Then she noticed Cyrine Haddad, snugly ensconced in the group. She was smiling up at the pastor, and beneath her shock, Inaya felt a little sick. Cyrine didn't belong with these people—she *couldn't*.

As she gazed at the picture, she experienced another shock.

Though the photograph was proudly displayed, the staging was a little off, the group not centered, the flash reflected in a mirror behind the group. Inaya peered at the mirror, where she could see the reflection of the photographer, tattoos swirling up his arms.

The picture had been taken by Lincoln "Ranger" West.

CHAPTER THIRTY-SIX

They pulled up outside the public library where Razan had spent her last day. The library was perched high in the hills, designed to look like it had been carved from the Rampart Range, a stone building with picture windows that looked down onto a Safeway, a gas mart, and a plaza filled with fast-food chains. Perfect for kids looking for a break from studying, with the added grace of a view that swept all the way out to the reservoir.

The heat was building, so both women left their blazers in the car, Cat in a sleeveless blue camisole, Inaya in a thin white blouse that buttoned at her wrists. It was a form of hijab without hijab; she was covered as much as she could be. The collar was high too, so for a moment she unbuttoned it to feel the little breeze there was.

"Hang on," Cat said. "Let's talk."

Inaya took in her friend. In Andrea Wong's office she had been cool and unperturbed, provocative without getting riled up in return. Now her brown eyes were fiery, her mouth set in the pout that denoted her rare temper. Inaya hoped it wasn't aimed at her.

"'Apolitical,'" Cat snorted. "As if anything is these days. Capitalism is an ugly creed."

Inaya and Catalina had argued this out on many occasions, though it wasn't much of an argument. They both thought their country was failing its most vulnerable citizens. But anything to do with the border and Cat could quote chapter and verse.

"What's gotten you so riled up? The aerostats?"

Cat ran a hand through her curly hair. Unlike Inaya, she didn't sweat at the first touch of heat. "Not the aerostats so much. More the whole setup, the way it's all taken for granted, that these are our immigration policies and trillions of dollars should be wasted on making life miserable for the poorest people on earth. The system isn't just sick, it's diseased. Companies like Apex lobby the government day and night—they don't just benefit from anti-immigration policies, they write those policies themselves."

Inaya patted Cat's arm in solidarity. Cat had listened to Inaya's raging thoughts over meals of *shami* kebabs and naan. At Inaya's house, they drowned their sorrows in mango juice or *lassi*. When Inaya went over to Cat's, it was *agua fresca* blended with watermelon and strawberry or cucumbers and lime.

Inaya canvassed the fast-food options and settled on a place that sold milkshakes. She bought strawberry for Cat and vanilla for herself. They took a few sips each, cooling off, before Inaya asked, "That was quick work with Razan's exposé."

Cat took a long sip. "I've been meaning to read it ever since we flagged it. I reviewed it when I went to the bathroom or I'd have told you I was planning to use it. I wonder if it's in her personnel file."

The file was locked in Inaya's case in the trunk.

"Probably redacted." She pressed her cold cup against her throat. God, she needed that cold in her bones on days like these, the pavement scorching beneath her shoes. "Though I think Wong was right. Why would they bother to silence a teenage girl when their mission is otherwise plain?" She would check the file regardless, but if there were answers to be found there, Wong wouldn't have passed it over. Whatever she'd given them would have been carefully curated.

Cat sighed, the last of her anger subdued by the taste of fresh strawberry. "Don't know how Campbell Kerr thought he had a shot at that internship."

"Did you see the photograph by the door?"

"Sych and Wong, you mean? Cliquey with the sheriff?"

"And with Nakamura. The church was represented too."

"It's quite a club. A powerful inner circle, with the sheriff at the center of it all."

"Cyrine, though?"

Cat sucked deeply at her straw. "What on earth was she doing there?"

"I don't know, but we need to talk to her and clear this up." Inaya set her milkshake down on the hood of the car, searching for her keys to pop the trunk. She was still digging out the folder when she said, "It never occurred to me to wonder how a town that doesn't exactly scream diversity supported Cyrine's bakery. Why didn't we question that? We've got bikers razzing refugees, and probably doing the same to workers at the plant, and then we have Cyrine's—functioning safely for how long?"

"Fifteen years," Cat replied. "They're Maronite Christians—that must have bought them some grace. Although they did get firebombed by the Disciples."

Inaya flicked pages in the file. "Not until after Razan's murder. If Cyrine was in the good graces of the sheriff and the pastor, maybe she put a foot wrong somehow after Razan's death."

Cat shared her sense of betrayal. It took an effort to push that feeling aside and return to the investigation. They would get to Cyrine in time.

"You're thinking Razan's murder and the firebombing are connected?" Cat asked.

"On the surface, they're both hate crimes. But why now, after Razan published that article? Why not before? I wonder if Razan ever snuck down to the basement." She shook her head. "There's nothing here. Just a list of assignments I can't understand." She looked up at Cat, smiling. "I know what you're going to say. 'Put Jaime on it.' Which reminds me—why did you photograph the gallery wall? Sych already told us that Wong had an eye for art."

"Yes, *chica*, he did." Cat finished her milkshake and dumped the cup in a nearby bin. "There was something about that wall. In Sych's office and the conference room the photographs were by famous photographers, each worth a fortune. Photographs of apex predators, as if to say they rule the border security jungle, when they're bit players compared to Lockheed Martin."

"Lockheed *does* contract out work. Share the wealth and all that."

"Make more money faster, more like. And they probably retain ownership of intellectual property and trade secrets even if they contract out the work."

"Apex isn't at their level," Inaya noted. "They don't work on missile design. Though missing out on the associated profits must be hard to swallow. Aerostats can't be in that league."

"Right, I'm getting off track. I was talking about impressions, trying to figure out the psychology of the players at Apex. So we see the predatory capitalism confidently displayed. And then in Wong's office, we see the other side. The mathematical precision of the photographs such that it doesn't matter what the individual art says—it's the cleverness of forming the aerostat."

Inaya dumped Razan's personnel file back in the open trunk.

"I'm not following you, Cat."

"What I'm saying is that art communicates something about the person who chose it. Andrea Wong is definitely an apex predator. She's also damnably clever and has the need to show that off with her gallery wall, but there's more to her than meets the eye."

Inaya remembered her fleeting impression of nightlife and the Shanghai skyline, which could be a nod to Wong's heritage. Something else the woman was proud of, despite the doors she closed on others. She'd all but shouted that she was a citizen.

"I need to look more closely at the pictures—get Jaime to blow them up and arrange them for us in an identical pattern on the wall."

Inaya waited, and was rewarded when Cat drew a deep breath.

"Did you notice the Renaissance church in that photo on the wall? There has to be a connection to Resurrection, no matter what your friend told you about the nature of the church."

CHAPTER THIRTY-SEVEN

Seif waited at the Chatfield Reservoir, where he'd been chasing a lead that came to nothing. His contact was a no-show, either frightened off even in the face of Seif's offer of protection or paid well to shut his mouth. He'd expected better, since his contact was the one who'd reached out and had up until now proven to be a reliable source. They usually spoke on the phone; this would have been their first meet.

Frustrated, he looked down over the two patches of man-made lake that disconnected from each other as they hit up against the edges of the dam. The view was good from the top of the reservoir, though the day was already hot, his hair sticking to the back of his neck. Dry heat, no humidity, the glare of the sun slashing against blue ripples in the lake. Very few trees for shelter; the ones that grew in a line up to the lake had been planted. You had to get deep into the bike path that circled the reservoir to get anything resembling shade, and that was a damp mossy shade where water had grown stagnant in the overgrowth of tree stumps and weeds.

The campgrounds were better kept, the brush pruned to prevent fires, though campfires had been banned in the summer and the ban had yet to be lifted. He'd double-checked Jaime's findings on Razan's camp reservations. Nothing for the week before her death, nothing after either. In the preceding months, as Mercedes had reported, Razan had camped up at Marina Point a couple of weekends—she hadn't missed any school.

He'd scouted Marina Point by himself, then sent a team to look for any indication that Marina Point had been the kill site. No blood had been found at the campground or on the beach. She could have been killed on the lake; there were far fewer campers in the fall—he'd followed that up himself. No boat slips had been rented that week, and no canoes were allowed to launch from Marina Point. No one had come up from the lake to kidnap and kill Razan. The reservoir was a dead end.

He shifted position impatiently. He could see as far as the highway from his vantage point, look down past the solid breastwork of the dam. Quiet as hell, no tourists around, no motorboats disturbing the calm. He turned the other way, and could just make out Blackwater's "historic" old town. Historic in Colorado meant the 1880s and the gold rush, old saloon facades stamped over newer buildings that were built solid behind their tourist-friendly storefronts. Local charm. Ice cream parlors, cutesy boutiques, adventure stores, salons, restaurants and bars. He'd hit the Lebanese bakery for lunch if it was up and running, should his lead came to nothing.

He checked the tiny shelter near the car park at the top again. Under its tin dome, environmentalists had put up posters in thin plastic frames describing the ecology of the reservoir. Tits, snakes, prairie dogs, and whatnot. Seif barely glanced at them, his mind on his contact's failure to appear.

He pulled out his secondary phone and called Jacob Brandt, his boss at the FBI.

"No show."

His boss swore. Asked his next move.

"The murder could be connected."

"Not seeing how," the voice in his ear said. "What do you have?"

Seif had nothing and he knew it. Still, he spun it out.

"There's been some talk of missing girls. Check your phone. I sent you a photo of the crime scene."

"Saw it. Looks like a dump site to me."

His boss was good at stating the obvious. Razan Elkader wasn't killed at the mosque—there was no blood trail to suggest it, and according to Stanger, the body had been frozen off-site. The search for a storage site was ongoing, though nothing had turned up so far.

"Not the point. The body was staged—if there's other girls, we need to look for a similar MO."

"Isn't your team doing that? Don't lose sight of what you're there for. We're on to something bigger than your murder."

Except they weren't on to it, if Seif's contact couldn't deliver.

"This is happening in Blackwater," he stressed. "And if it's happening in Grant's jurisdiction, you can bet that he knows about it."

"Like I said, not seeing how that's relative to your assignment. You're there to root out corruption."

"I need to talk to the sheriff. I can't put it off any longer."

"No!" The word came short and sharp. "You talk to him, you blow the whole last year. You do the job I sent you there to do. Prove that he's taking kickbacks. Show he's put his office up for sale."

Seif ran a hand through his hair, remembering that he sometimes caught Inaya's eyes on him when he did it. Too bad. He was sorely tempted, but nothing could happen there. There was a gulf of experience and a chasm of faith between them. Or so he'd convinced himself.

Seif huffed out a breath into the phone. "When you sent me here, you said it would be six months—I want out."

"You go nowhere until I say you do."

Being on Brandt's leash was an irritant like no other for Seif, who valued his independence. He liked his position on the outside. Now he was wedged deep inside an operation, and there was no getting out, his every move under surveillance by Brandt, by senior officers of the Denver police, and now, unfortunately, by Grant.

He'd sunk his teeth into this, so he didn't know why he was giving Brandt a hard time. Maybe because he didn't like the feeling that when this was done, it would be hard to leave to return to D.C. His brothers were settled now, and disrupting their lives again could mean splitting up the family. Not an option. Not for him, not for them. He'd made promises to his mother; no way in hell he'd go back on them.

That wasn't the only issue. He'd felt like settling down, like making a change since he'd met Inaya, when he never factored a woman into his plans. In the past, things had gone fine for a month or two, then the complications of his job became a deciding factor, and all his promises went south. The woman he was interested in wouldn't hang in there, wouldn't tough it out. She'd have demands that most people would find reasonable, and he'd feel like shit because he couldn't deliver what she had a right to expect. Togetherness. Loyalty. His protection. That she should come first, before he'd sorted out his brothers.

Only one had made it to the stage where she'd gotten to meet his family, and Lily was the one Seif had expected to take. To hold on for the ride. Otherwise, he'd have kept that sacrosanct. Family was something you didn't play around with.

Lily hadn't gotten that—how big it was that he'd allowed her past the door, keen to see how she fit in with Alireza and Mikhail. One had an Iranian name, the other's was Arab, and the boys—he still thought of them as boys—loved to confound people who couldn't figure out their background, even Lily. So he'd explained to her that his brothers would live under his roof until they went away to school or got married, or possibly both. He was looking forward to welcoming her into their small family.

Lily didn't get it, and he couldn't blame her for that. Until the day he'd introduced her to the boys, who were in their last year of high school, he'd made nothing of his identity, did nothing to make himself stand out as any different from her. She called him Cass; he drank with her sometimes. Said he didn't like meat so he'd never have to touch pork, and she bought it because she was a vegan. If she asked about his name or his origins, he'd push it off, saying the Seifs had been here five generations, everything else had bled away. He was American, just American, same as her.

Lily believed him. She wore short, tight dresses that showed a lot of skin, and he liked that, let her know he liked it. There was no reason to think that all at once everything would change, or that his hardwiring would kick in. That he was thinking he wanted someone who might make a home for his brothers, no matter what else she did. Someone he could take to a mosque he never remembered to visit. Someone who would say to him once a year, "Let's try fasting with the boys this Ramadan."

And his brothers would tease him and say, "Man, she's going to sort you out. All those things you wouldn't do for us, you're going to do for her." He'd get them in a headlock and taunt, "You do those things for God, not for a woman." They'd double-team him and he'd have to yield when they got his arms behind his back. They liked to get the last word in, so they'd say, "No, *habibi*, this woman is going to bring God into your life. She's going to rule you *and* this house, so you better watch your step."

He didn't know he wanted that until it all blew apart. His brothers were respectful, said nothing when Lily dressed the way she dressed or sat on his lap while she was talking to them. But the day she'd brought a bottle of wine over as a gift for them, Mikhail's eyes went sad and dark. He'd looked at Seif and pushed the bottle back at him.

"What are you doing?" he asked. "Doesn't she know who you are?"

That had precipitated the meltdown of all meltdowns, Lily hurt to the core, calling him out on his lies. He'd taken it, every word, because he knew he deserved it. He'd let her say her piece in the presence of the twins. But when she'd turned her anger on them, embarrassed by the way things had gone down, Seif had cut her dead. He'd put his blood and soul into the twins; he'd have sacrificed anyone for them.

In the end, it hadn't been a sacrifice, which probably made him a bastard. Lily hadn't deserved that—she'd loved him. She hadn't loved the lies he didn't know he was telling, and that had taught him something. He'd been pretending it would work, when it wasn't what he wanted at all. He just hadn't known that until Mikhail had called him out on his bullshit. The twins took him for who he was, but they never gave up on the hope he'd return to the path he'd forsaken. That night he'd done more than disappoint them. He'd shattered the illusion he was their all-knowing, all-virtuous big brother who couldn't do anything wrong. He didn't fall off his pedestal, he leapt, leaving it a crumbled heap.

Maybe it was messed up that the twins were the deal-breaker in his relationships, especially with women who never got to meet them, but that was Seif's hard line. He never wanted to see that look in Mikhail's eyes again.

Too late to recover what he'd lost—either with Lily or the twins. Lily, time had taught him not to mind, but the twins had turned into holy terrors. They'd become radical—not in FBI-speak, where every Arab or Iranian was a fifth columnist; the FBI called Black Lives Matter activists radicals too, when God knew, the least radical idea in history was that of preserving life. No, the twins had ramped up their activism, an additional headache he had to face if he wanted to hold on to his clearance.

They weren't in the mood to listen. He wasn't in the mood to speak.

It would work itself out in time. And he wouldn't make the same mistake, wouldn't invite another woman into the boys' home. He'd see the twins on their path, then figure out what he wanted for himself.

The man on the phone barked at him, bringing him back into the now. "You don't want out, Seif. You were made for this job."

Yeah. Deny it all he wanted, but he had a special skill set that meant he had to keep his head in the game. He didn't quit. He got things done.

"It's been a year," he repeated quietly. "We need to shake things up, which means I'm talking to the sheriff."

"We want him," Brandt said. "You blow this opportunity, we won't get another chance. So let me ask you—you sure he won't turn it around and play you at your own game?"

Seif followed the progress of a single canoe cleaving through the reservoir's no-wake zone. It wasn't his contact. But he still had cards to play.

"Grant isn't in the game. He doesn't even know it exists. We need to shake something loose; the murder is our way in. If he's involved, we figure out why. If he's not, our interference rattles his cage. When he gets nervous, he'll make a mistake. Then I'll get you what you need."

"You think the dead girl's important?"

"Yeah." He meant it in terms of his assignment. But he also meant because he'd seen Razan nailed to the door of the mosque, and a young girl named Mercedes weeping over her friend in a sterile interview room.

"Limited interference," the voice said. "If you find the link, good. If not, you pull out before you get made."

"Agreed."

He put the phone away, did another scan with his binoculars. No, his contact wasn't coming, so there was no point in sticking around, despite the view.

He got his car going, cranked the AC, and made a note in his log. He locked his backup phone in the glove compartment, and drove straight down Titan Road to the range. Time to get his head back in the game. Grant was taking bribes from contractors who were putting out bids on public works. He was also doing favors in exchange for campaign contributions, and his three biggest contributors were Apex Dynamics, Natural Foods, and the Resurrection Church. Seif knew the church had paid the sheriff to deny a zoning permit to the mosque—he'd followed that up after his conversation with Inaya. He had yet to establish the services given in exchange to Apex and Natural Foods. Maybe Razan's murder was the key to that.

In the meantime, Grant had established a whole system of kickbacks, and Seif's job was to prove it, knowing all the while that Addison Grant had branched out. He wasn't just guilty of overpolicing. He was getting kickbacks from private prisons for putting people into the system. His tentacles extended everywhere: he took money for arrests, he paid judges for convictions, he let probation officers off the hook on drug tests, he smoothed the way for contraband items to make their way into prison, including drugs.

Maybe Lincoln West was onto all that too. He knew West only by reputation, but that reputation was solid, though he hadn't known West was undercover. Maybe they could help each other out.

The key was to gain Grant's trust. That was why he'd delayed the interview, gone easy on the question of the missing girls, of total police incompetence or deliberate criminal neglect.

He'd score a few points at the town hall the following evening, and then he'd reel the sheriff in.

CHAPTER THIRTY-EIGHT

The town hall was one of the loveliest buildings in Blackwater, with a low-pitched roof, wide overhanging eaves, a rambling floor plan, and plenty of indoor and outdoor space. The style drew a little from the Spanish colonial heritage of the Southwest, with Craftsman accents and red-beamed wood. Most town hall meetings were held on the back patio, flagstoned in muted reds, with the Rampart Range as a spectacular backdrop. Tiny lights were strung along the lampposts, and other lights winked out at the audience from the hills, the scent of sagebrush mingling with a fresh mist off the falls.

It should have been the mayor's meeting, but it was conducted by the sheriff, several of his deputies stationed around the perimeter of the patio while he took the stage in uniform, looking almost subdued. The heavy brow was lowered, the genial face somber, as he expressed his sympathy to a crowd of fifty or so with well-worn phrases and assurances.

We ask you to put your trust in law enforcement a little longer.

This last was directed to the mix of workers from the plant, mainly Somali with a few Syrian and Afghan families at the fringes. Inaya's parents and sisters sat with them; she hadn't been able to discourage them from attending. Her mother was seated comfortably between Fadumo and Waris, while her father leaned forward in his chair, his eyes clear and alert, his big hands clasped between his knees. He was in defense-counsel mode, probing the sheriff for weaknesses. She knew, no matter what she said, he was going to do his best to protect her.

Seif had pointed out his brothers, who'd insisted on attending once Razan's murder had made the news. They wanted to support the community in Blackwater, and they often made friends at other mosques. They were seated at the very back of the patio, where they introduced themselves to the other young men, exchanging handshakes with Omar Abdi.

A few of the Disciples were present, including West and Hardtack. Cyrine from the local bakery was there too. She'd chosen a seat between the Muslim community at the rear and a group of parents from the school seated closer to the stage. Elias was with Omar at the back, and the two teens were whispering to each other. Christine Nakamura was present in the front row, accompanied by the dignified Japanese man Inaya had seen in the photograph on her desk. Beside her was the pastor of Resurrection Church.

Other faces caught her eye. A man with a high-bridged nose and pale, unwavering eyes stood behind the sheriff, so discreet he nearly faded into the hills. Dignitaries from Lockheed occupied the stage, Sych and Andrea Wong from Apex Dynamics seated near them. There was also an older white woman on the stage whom Inaya didn't recognize. Her thick gray hair shaded her face in a blunt cut. She was lean and wiry with strongly muscled shoulders, a detail Inaya paid attention to.

Cat elbowed her in the side, and she brought her attention back to the sheriff.

"We'll be doing plenty of consultation with community members. We intend to increase our patrols around neighborhoods where you feel unsafe. So let's open the floor for questions."

Grant's voice might have been soothing, but a ripple of protest murmured through the plant workers and Muslim families at the back.

She tried to interpret the statement. The fact that Grant was leading this town hall indicated he didn't intend to be sidelined. The protest was tepid at best, and she realized Grant's statement could be read as a threat.

Increased patrols in unsafe neighborhoods.

Additional policing of overpoliced communities. A dog whistle. Or a warning not to pressure the sheriff about Razan's murder or there would be consequences. No wonder Cat had nudged her. The desert climate meant the night was precipitately chill, the wind beginning to stir. The low growls of predators rumbled down from the foothills, and an uneasy, premonitory feeling skated down Inaya's spine. The crowd could break as swiftly as the weather.

Her gaze circled back to Seif. He was leaning against the patio doors that led inside the hall, not far from his brothers, unperturbed by the sheriff's statement. Maybe he hadn't clocked it, though he should be alert to signs of disturbance in the group that included the young men. That was where trouble would break out. She was about to warn Cat to be ready when she saw her father move to the microphone in the center of the audience.

"I thank you for your comments, Sheriff, though they raise some concerns. Many of your constituents already find themselves made uncomfortable by patrols in their neighborhoods." He adjusted his glasses on the bridge of his nose, his green eyes canny. "There is such a thing as overpolicing, one might even say targeted policing."

Grant put his hands on his hips, a frown creasing his forehead.

"And what does your daughter have to say about that, sir? Is she overpolicing too?"

Inaya froze, her gaze riveted on her father. He studied the sheriff calmly before he offered, "I am speaking as the legal representative of the mosque, not as Detective Rahman's father. She doesn't discuss her cases with me, and I wouldn't expect her to. I *can* tell you my daughter has great sensitivity when it comes to the people of this town. Can you say the same?"

The pinch-faced man behind the sheriff moved. A subtle, unintended movement that Inaya flagged at once, her spine straightening. He'd seemed like a bodyguard at first. Now he looked like a threat.

Her hands loose at her sides, she eased closer to her father.

He smiled at her, a gentle, giving smile familiar from her childhood, when he would ease her hurts away with some softly spoken lesson. A little of her wariness eased.

"I think the major employers in the county would appreciate your assurance that their employees won't be harassed by your patrols," her father continued.

The guests on the dais looked uncomfortable. Sych pulled at his tie. Andrea Wong's head was tipped up to the ceiling as though her valuable time were being wasted.

Grant made a conciliatory gesture to the VIPs. "How do you figure your clients are the victims? I don't see the Elkaders in that gang." His chin jerked at the small group at the back.

Rahman's reply was executed perfectly. "We're not a gang, we're a community. When one of us suffers, we all suffer."

The crowd erupted in cheers as Inaya's father took his seat. The next person who spoke didn't need the microphone. Her rich, resonant voice carried from the back.

"Areesha Adams, legal representative of the Abdi and Diriye families," she said. She strode to the front of the patio, the silk of her bright coral pantsuit billowing behind her. Omar leapt to his feet at the sight of her, following her to the mic.

Areesha grabbed the mic and turned it around to face the audience.

"You've filed complaints against the Blackwater sheriff's station, am I right?"

Half the crowd surged to their feet. Hardtack and West began to move toward Areesha.

"We should be hearing from the detectives at Community Response, as members of this community have no reason to trust you."

She pointed an elegant hand toward the back of the hall at Seif, then threw out her arm to indicate Inaya and Cat, her silk sleeve fluttering in the breeze.

Seif's deep voice brought the temperature down a notch. "I don't think the sheriff meant any harm. It's a credit to him that he doesn't take his responsibilities lightly."

"For God's sake, bro!" The cry came from Seif's brother Mikhail. He'd maneuvered his way to Omar's side. "Why are you kissing his ass?"

"Sit down!" Seif moved quickly to the mic.

While Inaya watched in horror, he gripped Mikhail, muttering to his brother in Arabic. Mikhail hesitated. Seif let him go. Mikhail grabbed Omar by the arm and stormed back to the rear of the crowd, where his twin joined them. All this was accomplished in silence, the three teens scowling at Seif. Seif leaned over and switched off the audience microphone.

Inaya couldn't take any more. Cat at her side, she came to stand with Areesha.

"What are you doing?" she demanded. "You can't silence a community representative."

Areesha draped herself around the microphone with the dexterity of a nightclub singer. "It's not me he wants to silence," she told Inaya. "It's Black voices period."

She switched the mic back on. Seif watched her with a curious expression, and only then did Inaya realize that he'd positioned himself to block Hardtack's path to Areesha. In a matter of minutes, he'd cleared his brother out of the path of danger and set himself up in his place. She stared at him, bewildered. What was he really up to?

"Areesha." Catalina's voice was gentle. "We're doing crowd control, that's all."

Areesha's head swiveled to Cat. "Oh?" she said aloofly. "Are you the voice of reason sent to calm down an angry Black woman?"

"No," Cat snapped at her. "I'm here to make sure you don't get your head bashed in by a biker."

Areesha caught sight of Hardtack. Her mouth dropped open before she recovered herself.

"I can handle him."

"You shouldn't have to." Seif stood firm.

A gentle tapping on the sheriff's mic pulled their attention to the stage.

A man cleared his throat, speaking tentatively. He offered an apology to the crowd at large, then to the Elkaders.

It was Linden Sych, a reluctant Andrea at his elbow. He was holding up what looked like a certificate framed in silver.

The crowd hushed, the noise vanishing into the hills like air escaping a balloon.

"Ah, Andrea and I wanted to present a posthumous award to Razan." Sych's gaze searched the crowd. "We were hoping the Elkaders would be here, but as I understand it Mrs. Elkader is still unwell." He glanced to the dais, where the other VIPs gave him encouraging signs. "In conjunction with Ally Jensen, manager at Natural Foods, we would like to announce a number of financial gifts in Razan's name."

Andrea took the certificate from him and passed him a tablet with a glowing screen.

"First, Apex Dynamics, Lockheed Martin, and Natural Foods have each endowed four-year scholarships for students from minority or refugee backgrounds at Blackwater Academy, arranged with the gracious assistance of principal Christine Nakamura."

A polite round of applause greeted these words. Inaya kept her back to the stage, her attention fixed on Seif's twin brothers. They were posturing in their anger, whereas Seif actually embodied the toughness they aspired to.

"Next," Sych interrupted her reflections on Seif, "Apex Dynamics will be inaugurating a fully paid internship in Razan's name."

Christine Nakamura turned around to offer a glamorous smile to the couple seated behind her. It took Inaya a moment to recognize the parents of Campbell Kerr—by no means the student to whom she would have granted the prize.

"Finally, in honor of our dedicated intern, we will of course be covering the expenses of Razan's funeral and hosting a memorial in our gardens next week. As Razan's father was an employee of Natural Foods, Ms. Ally Jensen will be working with us to help the Elkaders bring their son to America."

This time the applause was roundly delivered. Those who were still seated stood and cheered. Those who were already standing called out encouragement to Sych.

Only the Muslim contingent of the audience was silent. Ally Jensen took the mic from Sych, offering general thanks. Inaya let the words flow over her, keeping an eye on her sisters and her father. Noor had made her way over to Omar and the twins, where she introduced herself—she had a gift for making friends, particularly among her own age group. Nadia was folded in on herself in her seat, neither looking at nor speaking to anyone.

Fadumo came up to Areesha, her beautiful burgundy chador wound elegantly around her torso. She leaned in and whispered, "They can't buy our daughters."

Areesha tucked Fadumo's arm in hers. "They can't buy our silence, either."

The sheriff joined them on the floor. He made a grimace of distaste at the sight of Fadumo, covering it with a cough.

"There's no need to stir up trouble, Miz Adams."

Areesha tilted back her head, her coral earrings swaying. "This community needs to have confidence in the investigation. Does Lieutenant Seif need to remind you you're off this case?"

Again, Seif intervened. "That won't be necessary. The sheriff knows his remit, and you can trust we know ours."

"Two unsolved disappearances and one teenage murder victim don't engender a lot of trust." She turned to Seif. "Why are you allowing this? Does the sheriff have something on you?"

Seif's face hardened. "I suggest you resist the urge to slander law enforcement. We're all doing our best."

Inaya approached, intending to intervene. Seif cut her short. "Your duty is crowd control. Get back to it, Rahman."

She hesitated. Seif kept shielding Grant, yet he'd also stood between Areesha and Hardtack. Puzzled, yet not wanting to challenge him, she slipped back into the crowd.

Jaime was stationed at the exit, taking down names as people left the meeting. The members of the small mosque community had pushed their chairs into a circle. Someone brought thick and dark coffee over on a tray from a table at the side. Inaya slid into their midst, watching from the corner of her eye as Areesha continued to argue with the sheriff. No matter what Seif had said, it felt wrong to leave her on her own. She'd circle the crowd and head back.

Andrea Wong approached, drawing Fadumo away. A mask of reserve settled over Fadumo's face as she listened to Andrea's assurances, a sub-tle tightening that indicated a politeness Fadumo was offering against her better judgment.

Inaya touched Nadia's shoulder, leaning down.

"You okay, Nadia? Why don't you join Noor? I can introduce you to the boys."

Nadia huddled in on herself. "I'm not interested in boys."

Inaya grabbed two coffees from the tray, glad that her mother was still preoccupied with her own small group. She passed one to Nadia and took a sip from her own. Cyrine's brew. She found Cyrine in the crowd, chatting comfortably with Christine Nakamura and her husband.

All right, Cyrine had a son at the Academy, yet Inaya's sense of unease persisted. How had Cyrine gotten herself mixed up with these people? And why? A café was a place where people gathered and gossiped—had Cyrine facilitated that? Did she know more about Razan's murder than they'd suspected? Worse, could she be implicated?

"It's cold," Nadia said. "We should get going. We shouldn't even have come."

"You'll warm up if you drink your coffee," Inaya chided her. "Why did you come? Did Ami make you?"

Nadia grasped her cup, soaking up its heat.

"I'm not a kid, *baji*. I can make up my own mind."

That'll be the day, Inaya thought. No one could resist their mother's particular form of pressure. If she wanted you somewhere, you went.

"So what gives, then?" A warm bubble of noise floated their way from the rear. Noor had collected quite an entourage. Mercedes and a few other girls were chatting with her, eager to hang out with a group of attractive young men. The gathering had grown more relaxed, Mikhail's fiery temper subdued as quickly as it had erupted. "I think you'd like Lieutenant Seif's brothers. And you know Omar from the mosque. They're all very sweet."

"Sweet?" For a moment, Nadia shook off her funk. "They're hot, *baji*, not sweet. And I'm not interested in playing the role of some random guy's groupie."

"How about 'friend'? That's what Noor is doing, making new friends. You should try it."

Nadia pulled her knees up on her chair and buried her face in them, a posture that would have horrified their mother.

Concerned, Inaya stroked Nadia's hair. "What is it, sweetie, what's bothering you?"

Nadia didn't raise her head. Her voice was choked with tears when she said, "Why don't you go back to your policing? Don't investigate me."

Inaya's hand stilled for a moment before it resumed its stroking.

"I'm not investigating you, I'm big-sistering you. That's my full-time job."

She was rewarded with a muffled laugh.

"Maybe later, not now."

Inaya searched out her father. When she found him talking to Waris, she tipped her head at Nadia.

"We *will* talk later. I'm not letting this go."

She was reassured when Nadia muttered, "Don't I know it. But I'd appreciate it if you'd leave me alone right now."

"I'll try."

Not a promise she was likely to keep, even with murder on her mind. She caught Seif's eye and kept moving.

CHAPTER THIRTY-NINE

Leaving Nadia to sulk, Inaya worked her way through the crowd, winding up next to Sych. She thought he'd have left by now, difficult duty done.

"That was a kind gesture," she said.

"The scholarship?" He was less confident in this setting, fiddling with the buttons at his cuff, one of those brilliant minds who was far less adept with people. She wondered how he'd handled Razan's bright, probing curiosity.

"All of it, particularly getting the plant to help bring the Elkaders' son from Turkey."

"They're attempting to get a visa for Razan's uncle too—she loved him dearly—but it's difficult."

Inaya schooled her features into calmness. "She must have had a good working relationship with you to confide in you like that."

"You think so?" He sounded touched. "I'm glad."

"What else did she share?"

That brought him up short, and Inaya cursed herself for her abruptness.

"Mainly, she talked about her family, and the life she'd left behind in Syria. She was a generous girl, an artistic soul. She had a kind word for everybody."

More platitudes. She wouldn't get to the heart of Razan with platitudes.

"Generous how?"

He stumbled a bit, searching for examples. "She helped her friends with their homework. She let the thing with Campbell Kerr go, didn't persecute him the way she could have."

"Did you see the video she made?"

Sych nodded. "The video had so many interesting elements. Comedy, satire, feminism. But she released that video in self-defense and left it at that."

"Is that what she told you?"

Pride crept into his voice. "She asked my advice before she posted it."

"And you told her it was okay? You weren't worried it could be defamatory?"

"Not at all," he said firmly. "She had a perfect right to defend herself from that . . . goon."

Inaya was beginning to like Sych more and more. She'd thought of him as an intellect, removed from the concerns of others. Yet he'd call Campbell Kerr a "goon," and it was obvious he'd spared her blushes by not using coarser language.

But if that was the case, why had Christine Nakamura given the Kerrs that reassuring signal? She asked Sych that point-blank.

He frowned, his concern making him more attractive. "I don't know what you might have seen, but if we turned Kerr down once, we're unlikely to select him now."

Part of Inaya knew Campbell was just a kid with the potential to grow out of his bullying into someone with more consideration. He shouldn't be written off. The more suspicious side of her expected Kerr to turn out like her CPD colleagues. Better not to give him the chances that would help him gain influence. Chances that Black or brown kids wouldn't get.

She kept her thoughts to herself, asking, "Is it up to you?"

Sych was resolved on this point. "We vote on it. I hesitate to say my vote carries the most weight, but I'm hardly likely to bring on board someone who despised Razan."

So the parents were celebrating prematurely, which should have made Inaya happy. But for some reason she felt compelled to make a case for Campbell Kerr.

"According to my colleague who interviewed him, Campbell regrets his past actions. He admits he took it too far, and he's even worried that his actions may have led to Razan's death."

Sych surveyed her coolly.

"A guilty person *would* say that."

There was a lot of feeling there for a man who'd claimed he'd been nothing more than Razan's supervisor. Then again, it was a simple expression of humanity to be angered by murder.

Groping for answers, she asked Sych if he was married.

He couldn't mask his reaction—a haunting loneliness welled up in his eyes. "No spouse, no children, which I very much regret. I have family responsibilities—they take up some time."

Inaya understood. She put her parents' and sisters' needs before her own; it was a privilege to do so, yet she couldn't deny that it also took a toll. But if Sych wasn't married, was he referring to his parents?

Andrea Wong interrupted their tête-à-tête, placing her hand on Sych's arm. "I need to get home."

Sych gave her a rueful look. He offered his hand to Inaya, who shook it. He held on to her hand as he tipped his head at Andrea.

"I'm afraid Andrea is in charge of my schedule and my time, but I would be remiss not to thank you for your efforts on Razan's behalf. She shouldn't be forgotten."

Andrea's grip became more possessive as she led him away. If Sych was lonely, he wouldn't be for long.

CHAPTER FORTY

Noor was still chatting with her friends, so Inaya began to stack the outdoor patio chairs, surprised when Areesha joined her.

"Don't help me," she warned. "You're much too glamorous to sweat."

"Glamour doesn't get it done."

She began to work down the row from Inaya, still within speaking distance.

Inaya tried for a friendly opening. "You look like you've had a chance to rest."

Areesha snorted. "Then my face is lying to you."

"Is Grant getting to you? You could take a break from this, you know."

"If I don't stand up to Grant now, his power will only expand. Who do you think he was talking to about additional patrols? As long as he has this community in his sights, I won't be standing down."

Inaya shook her head. "Don't you ever get tired of having to fight all the time?"

Areesha shrugged. "My grandmother taught me that with the time I have on this planet, I have to build a little further than my ancestors did. I know I'm deeply loved and supported, not just in the present, but also by the past and future. There's a much bigger picture. So it may be terrible when you're in the middle of it, but it's an honor to be chosen for this work."

The impact of the words was staggering—a direct hit to a place hidden deep inside Inaya. She heard an echo of the Qur'anic call to justice.

More, she felt the call to community, rich and deep and lasting. Perhaps if she'd had it in Chicago, she could have persevered. Instead, she'd believed the system was too powerful to be taken on alone. She hadn't understood that she *wasn't* standing alone. She'd had Jenella McBride, and all the people Jenella had brought with her, yet she'd seen only herself. She blinked away her tears so Areesha wouldn't see.

"I never thought of it that way."

"You're new here," Areesha said gently. "You still have to build your bonds."

There wouldn't be a better opening. "You know this community well. They trust you."

"I earned that trust. I worked for it." Areesha tapped her fingers on her knees, her body humming with energy. "But I'm not some kind of savior. We all have to do our part to keep our community whole."

"*Can* it be whole after this?"

They looked over to the small Somali group.

"I don't know. Your daughter goes missing and you don't know why. It's like living in a nightmare. At least the Elkaders will have closure." She nodded at Fadumo. "They want to bury their daughters; they need to perform the *janazah* so their souls can be at peace."

Inaya's curiosity was stirred. "You believe in a soul?"

Areesha slapped her knee. "I was raised in the Gospel. I come from the Black church."

"I come from the brown mosque," Inaya teased.

The two women smiled at each other, then Areesha caught sight of Seif. He was talking to the man who'd been standing behind the sheriff like a bodyguard.

She frowned. "Why does your boss feel the need to keep caping for Sheriff Grant?"

Inaya was saved from having to reply when Cat beckoned to her across the hall. She'd buttonholed Cyrine, who seemed flustered by the attention, even as she cooed, "Is everything all right, my angels?"

Inaya asked her about the photograph she'd seen in Andrea's office.

Cyrine's hands fluttered at her sides as she said, "Christine is the principal at my son's school—she's very fond of Elias."

Inaya couldn't imagine the ice-cold principal expressing affection for anyone.

"Are you equally close with the sheriff and the pastor?"

Cyrine's long eyebrows pinched together. She studied Inaya and Cat.

"What are you really asking me, my loves?"

Inaya had the grace to look embarrassed. "They don't seem like your kind of people."

Cyrine's nervous fluttering ceased. Her eyes twinkled at Inaya.

"When your run a small business, my dears, *everyone* is your kind of people. The sheriff helps me with permits, and the pastor encourages his flock to visit my bakery." She fluffed her blond curls, no longer ill at ease. "I'm grateful for the patronage. Now, was there anything else?"

Even if there had been, she didn't linger, her farewells blithe and unconcerned, though her dark eyes were troubled as she made her way to Grant's side.

CHAPTER FORTY-ONE

Seif had asked to meet with Grant the next morning. He knew Grant liked him, because when Seif put himself out, he could be likable. They shook hands—friendly, man-to-man, not a pointless show of strength. Grant offered him coffee in his office, and though Seif wanted ice-cold water, he accepted, looking around.

A lot of money had come into the station, technically a substation, one of several in the county. But Blackwater Falls was tricked out. Everything was smooth and expensive—chrome fixtures, electronic signboards with police notices, and staff to spare. Patrol officers were sitting around doing not much more than chatting with a gorgeous red-haired receptionist, or maybe dispatcher, who was ensconced on a thousand-dollar chair behind the fortified glass at the reception desk. She wore a wireless headset and took her time talking to both patrol officers and the public. The bulletin board at her back laid out the particulars of the voting process, the hours that ballot boxes would be available. Leftovers from the last election that no one had taken down. At the bottom, a "Make America Great Again" sticker, and beneath that a Thin Blue Line flag.

On her side of the barrier, the redhead's desk was clear. He wondered if she had enough work to keep her busy, and why she had left up the signs.

"Julie, get Lieutenant Seif some coffee. Ask him how he takes it."

Julie smiled a lovely smile, not flirtatious, just warm. Something that made the public feel like they could trust her, that she would take their troubles to heart. He smiled back at her, something he rarely did with his own team.

"Black as my soul," he joked.

"Oh, hush now," she said like a good Christian woman, the smile tapering off. He looked for a cross at the neck of her lilac blouse and found it. She could be an evangelical—maybe a way into the Resurrection Church. Or maybe she *was* just a good Christian woman. One might not automatically exclude the other, but Seif somehow thought it did.

"A splash of milk, then," he confirmed, and the lovely smile came out again.

"Bring it into my office," Grant said, buzzing Seif through an electronic turnstile.

The sheriff's office was huge. There was ample room for a baronial desk and a smaller accompanying escritoire that doubled as a secretary's station. Unlike Julie's spotless reception area, Grant's desk was cluttered with files, news briefs, and more. His Moroccan leather chair rolled easily on gold casters. Two comfortable lounge chairs were placed on the opposite side. The vanity wall displayed photographs of Grant with all the major players in Starling County. In each one, Grant held the same pose: right foot forward, body angled out so that with his bearish shoulders primed he eclipsed the other party in the photo, his lips smiling, his eyes cold and clear.

On the opposite side of the wall, two chestnut bookcases framed a selection of guns. Hunting rifles and shotguns—these were for show. Coming through the barrier, Seif had glimpsed deputies in the armory, its steel door swung wide, its arsenal in a room-sized cage with electronic locks, firepower that would not have embarrassed an army captain at war.

The back wall of the office showcased a fantastic view of the foothills that Seif paused to admire. They were brown and parched in the full sun of daylight, blue-ridged and cool at dusk. Grant's assistant was also present, a middle-aged man with curly hair, his lips tucked in like a spinster about to cast judgment on the depraved. He wore owlish glasses and a trim blue suit with leather boots. This was Russell Pincher. Seif had met him the previous night.

"Don't mind Russell. He flags action items for me."

Seif knew all about Pincher. He wasn't Grant's assistant, he was the power behind the throne, methodically plotting the sheriff's rise and the expansion of his influence.

Seif took a seat in one of the lounge chairs as the sheriff crossed to his desk. He rose again to take the tray from Julie when she brought in the coffee, a gesture that startled the other men. Julie blushed with pleasure, closing the door behind her.

"Is Julie your station's call-taker? She must provide a lot of reassurance to the public."

"She isn't hard on the eyes, either," the sheriff chuckled, going on to say, "Yeah, Julie handles dispatch, and when she's off shift, a couple of my boys take over. They've got the training. They don't just listen to the public, they *hear*. Sympatico, you get me? Defusing things that could get out of hand."

Pincher gave a disapproving snort. Seif ignored it. The sheriff's words were unintentionally revealing.

"What kinds of things?"

Grant's amiability dissolved. He flicked a sharp glance at Seif.

"Why're you asking?"

"I'm curious if problems in largely crime-free suburbs are the same as the ones we deal with in the city."

"Blackwater isn't a suburb; get that out of your head. It's backcountry. And the people who live here are backcountry people. Except for the ones who come here chasing the 'American dream.'" He formed quotation marks with his fingers.

Seif took a sip of his coffee. Exclusive, mellow, with just a hint of bite. This wasn't station coffee, it was a cup of ambrosia.

"I'm not sure I understand the distinction," he said.

"We don't have the big cattle ranches like Wyoming, but folks here have small private ranches or farms. They have horses. They like to hunt. They climb the fourteeners; they hike. They pitch in for search and rescue. They go to football games and church. Everyone knows the high school quarterback and the homecoming queen."

There were three high schools in Blackwater Falls, and all of them had football teams. He took a guess, based on Inaya's report.

"The Blackwater Academy?"

It sat on beautiful grounds with fine views down the mountains.

"Campbell Kerr is a star," the sheriff confirmed. "He's the local hero."

"I thought that was you, sir." There was no need for Seif to flatter the sheriff, but he set the tone to expedite his mission.

That made the sheriff settle deeper into his chair. The two men drank coffee, Pincher hovering at the sheriff's elbow until Grant sent him to his desk with an irritated wave.

"Now what can I help you with, Lieutenant?"

"Just Seif, please, sir. Or Qas, if you prefer."

"Is that right."

Speculation in Grant's eyes, trying to place the name but coming up short. He'd set Pincher to digging, but Pincher wouldn't come up with much. Seif's cover was solid.

"A couple of things, actually. There's been some talk about girls going missing in Blackwater, which leads me to wonder whether Razan Elkader is the only victim of this killer?"

The sheriff sat straighter, the smile hitched up over features that had gone stiff.

"Who's been talking?"

Seif fielded this. "Community members who were at the mosque the morning we found the body. A few Somali families."

Grant relaxed again. "That all? We don't have bodies piling up here, just a couple of girls who flew the coop. Their families reported them missing, but you know those folks keep their girls locked up. We looked into the reports, even conducted searches. Nothing turned up. Those girls ran away from home. Right now, they're probably holed up together in a low-budget place in Aurora, living the dream."

Fuck. Seif's contact out of the loop. If he'd missed this, what else was he missing?

"I didn't see anything in the news. Seems like a couple of missing teens would be a bigger story."

Pincher intruded into the conversation. Seif looked over to his desk.

"The families were on the spot, getting bad press when rumors of honor killings started circulating. Sheriff Grant made things easy on them by quashing the story. He saved the parents a lot of embarrassment, I'm sure they're still grateful."

"And the girls?"

Pincher removed his glasses and dusted them with a cloth before setting them back on the bridge of his nose. Buying time, Seif thought, though Pincher said smoothly, "We left that to the parents to address."

"No follow-up?"

"They didn't ask for any."

"So that's why you didn't mention the earlier reports when we found Razan?"

"Correct." Grant peered into Seif's face. "No dereliction of duty in this county, as I'm sure you've heard."

"Of course. I'm just trying to square that with the complaint that asked for you and four of your officers to be removed from this investigation. What would you say is behind that if you looked into the missing girls to the families' satisfaction?"

"The Good Christ knows." The sheriff crossed himself, but it wasn't like Cat did it—sincere and devout. It was exaggerated, almost mocking. Seif didn't know enough about evangelicals. Did they cross themselves like Catholics or was Grant putting on a show? And for that matter, *was* Grant an evangelist?

Pincher spoke up again. "It's purely retaliatory. The people who come here to work are not our usual residents. They have demands and they make a lot of noise."

Seif began to play his hand. "Asking you to search for runaways doesn't seem unreasonable."

"Not that," Pincher said sharply. "They had other complaints."

"Such as?"

Seif ran through the list in his mind. Permits for the mosque and a Muslim cemetery, both denied. Prayer accommodations at the meatpacking plant that had also stirred up controversy. Various complaints about harassment by the Disciples, left unattended by the sheriff.

"These people don't know how to adapt. Rather than picking up our ways and being grateful, they expect us to accommodate a whole host of things that make people in this county uncomfortable. You know we passed the first anti-Sharia law in the country here in Blackwater."

Seif clasped his hands together, looking thoughtful. "Were they asking for Sharia law? The Somali workers who came here?"

Grant flashed him an irritated glance. "They would in time—just let them get a foot in the door. Preemptively, we closed that door. Churchgoing folk can't be expected to make their peace with folks who worship ISIS."

Seif shot him a keen look. "You mean Allah." He gave it the white pronunciation.

"Isn't that what I said?"

Seif let it go. "Doesn't the plant need these workers? I hear you had a raid a while back."

The sheriff grumbled a little. "New regulations, the boys at ICE doing some showboating so the president thinks there's movement on his immigration policies. We lost some damn fine workers when they booted the wets out." He gauged Seif's reaction to the term. "That make you uncomfortable, Seif? Me being politically incorrect?"

Seif shrugged, disguising his anger. "No skin off my back, I'm not one of them."

Grant nodded his approval. "So these new folks, they came as refugees, so they've got papers, and it's true, maybe we need them to take those jobs at the plant. But that sure as hell isn't the same thing as wanting them here."

"Understood." He'd softened Grant up; now it was time to turn to other subjects. "What about these complaints on file about the local MC—the Disciples? Any truth to those? I can't imagine it's easy having a biker gang running loose in your county."

Grant's reply was practiced. "The Disciples aren't a biker gang; they're not even a motorcycle club. They're a social riding club—nothing official, you get me? They don't cause us any problems."

Seif noted the "us."

"So there was no truth to these complaints? I ask because my detectives ran into them at the home of Razan Elkader's parents. They were buzzing the house with their bikes."

The sheriff didn't blink. "They were there to offer condolences. Nothing strange about that. We may not have a lot in common, but our people know the courtesies. Plus, I hear their daughters were friends. Also hear the father went AWOL when you tried to question him about the murder. Could be one of those shame killings, right? He pins her like she's crucified because she's been hanging out with kids who go to church. Poor thing." His sympathy sounded real. "She should have had a choice."

What this told Seif was that Grant had his own spies following CRU and leaking information about their activities to him. Apart from the public relations damage when they were trying to build trust, a leak could place his team in danger. He needed to make certain that Inaya was safe. And Cat. Jaime could handle himself, though even Jaime he wouldn't pit against a gang of thugs.

He returned to the sheriff's question. "He was overcome by grief. You seem to keep an eye on newcomers here; are you familiar with the Elkaders' story?"

The sheriff became expansive. He acted as if he had all the time in the world for Seif, though underneath it there was an edge. "Can't say that I am."

Seif turned to Pincher. "What about you?"

"I've done some research," Pincher admitted. "They came here as refugees from Syria, supposedly; their papers were in order. The man worked at the plant, the girl learned English quickly and earned a scholarship to Blackwater Academy."

"The man" . . . *"The girl."* Not "Hassan Elkader" or "Razan."

"She also worked at Wendy's Parlor," Pincher continued. "Maybe the father didn't like that—his girl out of the house. I admit it gave me a jolt to go in there with my children and see that girl working there. Don't know why Wendy hired her."

That would be Mrs. Wendell, who had offered a job to Razan.

"Why was that?"

Pincher gave him a derisive look.

"We don't care much for covering up our women. They're entitled to their rights."

He'd paced back to the sheriff's desk, having done no work that Seif could see in the interim, waiting for Seif's next question.

He spoke mildly to defuse Pincher's hostility, but the question was needle-sharp. "You don't think it's possible Razan made her own decision about wearing a headscarf?"

"Under that man's thumb?"

"You sound like you don't have much respect for Elkader."

Pincher's shoulders twitched. "He caused problems for our donors."

The sheriff cut his eyes at him, and Pincher subsided again. Stiff-necked, he wandered to the windows. Seif didn't think he was registering the view.

The lead was too promising to ignore. "Donors?"

Again, the sheriff's answer rolled right off his tongue. "My election campaign. Seems the folks at Natural Foods like me, same as all the other businesses in town."

Seif bet they did, because when the right palms were greased, law enforcement ceased to be an obstacle to getting your workers in, even if they didn't have papers.

"What trouble did Elkader cause at the plant? He injured his hand there, I'm told."

"Could have got that stringing up his daughter," the sheriff observed shrewdly.

Seif was patient. "Is that what you think happened?"

He caught Pincher shaking his head without speaking. "Maybe after his hand got caught in a slicer," Grant confirmed.

"So the problem was what? He wanted compensation for his injury, compensation he wasn't entitled to?"

"Oh no, much worse than that."

Seif set down his cup, his dark brows raised.

The sheriff didn't make him wait.

"Elkader wanted a union; he got the workers riled. The boss said if they unionized, he'd close down the whole plant."

Back at his car, Seif decided the plant had to be their top priority. He knew Inaya wanted to tackle the pastor and confirm her friend's insights into the church, but he'd direct her to wait until Sunday, when she and Cat could attend a sermon and watch the pastor in action. If Grant had been lying to him about Elkader's role at the plant—if he had something else to hide—this could be the break he was looking for.

CHAPTER FORTY-TWO

The first thing Inaya noticed was the smell. It came in waves, connected to the actions of the nearby abattoir. She didn't know how the workers of the plant could bear it; surely complaints had been raised by those who lived south of the slaughterhouse.

The Natural Foods plant was a massive beef processing complex, with holding pens leading to the abattoir where cattle were tagged and slaughtered. The smell of blood was always in the air. On hot days, the shed smelled like rotting flesh. On cooler days, the iron sweetness of blood covered some of the stink.

The central plant was where the carcasses were separated, heads and feet removed first, followed by dehiding and evisceration to remove offal, another ghastly odor. The carcasses would then be split and hung for primary inspection. If they passed, they'd be sent for chilling before quartering and deboning took place, a process that required quick and sturdy hands, deft time management, and the ability to wield heavy, dangerous equipment.

Inaya had done some basic research on the plant to prepare for her interview with Ally Jensen, the director of plant operations. Even then, she wasn't clear on the machinery Hassan Elkader had been operating when he suffered the damage to his hand.

She hadn't been permitted on the floor for health and safety reasons, but she'd asked Jaime to find a way to reconnoiter the central processing area. In the meantime, she was tucked into an office in a small outbuilding connected to the main plant. In addition to managerial offices, it included locker rooms for workers, public bathrooms, and a lounge. When she'd arrived, the lounge had been empty. It still was—all the activity was in the processing area. She noticed a third door some distance from the designated restrooms for men and women. There was an empty space on the door where a sign had been removed, leaving the trace of its outline. Unlike the restroom doors, this one featured a lock. She made a note to explore the room that lay behind the door.

She scanned Jensen's desk for the key. There were stacks of binders on the desk, plus a topped-up thermal coffee mug whose aroma mixed unpleasantly with the tang of offal and blood. No personal photographs or possessions, but beneath the binders was a laminated drawing.

Inaya moved swiftly, pushing the binders aside. She peered down to examine the drawing, which turned out to be a schematic of the plant. The printing on it was tiny—she could get a better copy from town records when she had time. For now, she made do, taking several pictures with her phone, then moving the binders back into place. Maybe the schematic would reveal what was behind the locked door.

She heard footsteps approaching down the hall, and took another quick look around the office. There were hooks behind a partially open door. On one of these hung a white lab coat, the word "MANAGER" stenciled over the breast pocket. On the other hung a lanyard with a sparse set of keys; Inaya counted five in all. She tipped the door back a little farther so that the keys were no longer visible. She had just slipped back into her seat when Jensen entered the room, looking harried. A perpetual expression, Inaya guessed, lines of worry etched deep into her face.

She rose and offered her hand. The other woman pulled off her glove and shook it.

"Ally," she barked when Inaya offered her name and rank.

She took her seat with a thump, her head diving to the clipboard in her hand. She glanced up, past Inaya's shoulder to the digital clock on the wall. She checked the time against her watch, then made a notation on the page.

"I've got fifteen minutes before my next walk-through, so whatever your questions are, I suggest you get going."

Inaya obliged her.

"What happened to Hassan Elkader?"

A pair of sharp gray eyes looked back at her. "Accident on the line," she said briefly.

"Mr. Elkader says he was pushed. By a man he'd never seen before." Inaya shared the description Seif had given her.

"News to me. Hassan didn't file a report."

"Do you think it's possible he was scared to? Intimidated against it?"

Jensen's gray eyes pierced hers. "By who? Me? I'm not the intimidating type."

Inaya looked at the woman's broad shoulders, at the strength in her stocky frame, and begged to differ. This woman could hoist a girl up on a door without breaking a sweat. The question was why she would want to.

"What about the union? Mr. Elkader was behind your employees' efforts to unionize. His accident could have been a form of retaliation."

Surprise flashed through Ally Jensen's eyes.

"That's not how I run my plant. Hassan was a good worker, a quick learner. A good manager knows better than to waste the skills of an employee like that." She glanced down at the time sheet on her clipboard, a faint blush on her weathered cheeks. "He's a good man, a *gentle* man; there aren't many like him these days. It's terrible what happened to his daughter."

Inaya took a moment to digest this. Ally Jensen and Hassan Elkader? She thought back. The man had been kind, handsome in a ravaged way—and Jensen was right, truly gentle. Jensen's voice softened when she spoke of him, as if the connection between them had been deeper and more personal than supervisor and employee.

"Yet when he was injured at work, Natural Foods fired him without compensation."

Jensen fidgeted with her clipboard. "We've made that right by underwriting the funeral and helping with his son's visa issues."

"Some would say that's just good PR."

"It is. It also had to be done. That it for your questions?"

Inaya studied her without speaking, letting the silence and Jensen's agitation build. There was a thread here she wanted to follow. Perhaps it was that Jensen had been at odds with her bosses on a matter of principle. Or perhaps she'd fallen in love with Elkader and done her best for him on the basis of that feeling.

Inaya went over the alibi window with little hope of confirmation—the window was overly broad; no one could possibly account for where they'd spent every minute. But Ally Jensen was operations manager, so she pulled down her schedule from a bracket on the wall. She'd been on shift, more or less continuously, and when not on shift, on call.

"At home. Asleep. The days on shift are grueling. Check my phone records if you want."

So she knew about cell phone location data. She could have left her phone at home. Inaya scribbled down the number. Her time was almost up and she still had two questions to ask.

"The daughters of two of your workers have been missing for some time. What can you tell me about that?"

Jensen sat back in her chair. "Heard about it," she admitted. "Don't know the details."

"Your employees didn't come to you? This was right about the time of the union activity. The fathers of these girls were at the forefront of that charge."

She waited for Jensen's reaction, the sound of machinery loud in the background, an antiseptic smell wafting through the open door. A chilly sterility covered the scent of blood.

Jensen's lips were pursed in concentration. The sturdy hands resting on her stomach were tensed, her clipboard forgotten. Everything in her posture told Inaya that Jensen was conflicted. She wanted to speak, yet couldn't.

Inaya leaned forward. "Anything you tell me will be kept in confidence unless it's critical to the investigation to reveal it."

"Not much of a promise."

"It's all I can offer, I'm afraid."

Another minute ticked by. Inaya coughed into the silence, the antiseptic in her lungs.

Jensen didn't react, used to her environment.

"I'll say this. The union wasn't that bad of an idea. These are good workers; they're highly skilled—they deserve workplace security. Management tends to treat them as disposable. We lost a lot of good people that way."

Inaya didn't comment on how rare it was for someone in management to endorse the push for unionization. She was too busy trying to figure out what Jensen wasn't telling her, shoulders squared, chin lifted, eyes bleak with regret.

She put that together with Jensen's earlier comments on Elkader.

"These workers are very vulnerable. Even with legal status, refugees often are." She tilted her head toward the sound of the plant in full operation. "I wonder how they even thought of putting their jobs on the line."

Jensen didn't answer, her gaze fixed on the digital clock.

"It was you, wasn't it? You put the idea into Hassan Elkader's head."

Jensen's composure cracked. She settled her palms on the desk.

"He wasn't supposed to get hurt. I thought they might fire him, I never imagined they'd do something worse."

"So you're saying there *was* an unknown man on the floor that day, that the accident wasn't an accident."

"Hassan said he saw him, and Hassan doesn't lie. But he may have been confused by things happening that fast." Her face went white at the memory. "If you're thinking you smell blood now, you should have been there that day. The arterial spray was sickening. I thought he might bleed out, right there on the floor."

The hollow expression in her eyes told Inaya more than words could have. Elkader meant something to her; the moment she'd grasped the fact of his imminent death still haunted her. But had she done anything about it since? Approached Elkader, made overtures?

"Who came to his aid?"

"I did. I was on a walk-through at the time."

Keeping a particular eye on Elkader perhaps. Sneaking glances at him when she could.

"Do you know all your employees by sight?"

"Of course. I hire them. And I fire them, when needed."

"So on your walk-through there was no one you didn't recognize on the floor."

She hesitated. "From the upstairs perimeter, you see hands and heads. Hands operating machinery or equipment, heads covered in helmets or net caps."

"Yet you recognized Hassan?"

"I knew his place on the line."

"What would he have been doing?"

"Quartering."

She explained in some detail the process of carcasses being removed from the hanging hall to be chilled in a refrigerated space, then quartered by mechanical saws.

"We observe all the safety precautions, of course."

"Time must be a factor. Maybe Mr. Elkader was injured because he had to meet a quota."

Jensen bristled at that. "We do have quotas, and time limits, for that matter, but those limits are determined with health and safety in mind. We know we're not dealing with robots."

Yet for all Jensen's stated concern about the plant's employees, most of the legal grievances against Natural Foods were stalled through the long machinery of court processes, rather than settled, something else Inaya had looked into, or given up on altogether because delay meant incurring legal fees that were unaffordable.

"Who makes the decisions at the top? About timing, compensation, lawsuits, and so on?"

Jensen eyed her cautiously. "There's a board of directors. And a CEO. They set policy at the top. And we have a pretty significant HR team to implement those policies."

Inaya looked up from her notebook. "Any names on the board I would recognize?"

She named a man in Kansas City as the CEO. Inaya made a note to have Jaime do a background check.

"And the board of directors?"

"It's public record," Jensen said stiffly. "There are six members of the board, including the mayor and the sheriff. One or two of the sheriff's people as well."

So the sheriff had a finger in this pie as well.

"That's not a conflict of interest?"

"If it is, that's not my responsibility. I operate within the plant."

Inaya didn't think this was precisely accurate, but she didn't want Jensen to get agitated. She returned to Elkader's accident.

"You were on the floor when the accident occurred, you administered first aid, but you claim not to have seen the accident take place."

"It's a big floor," she said drily. "And I watch all my workers, not just Hassan. I need to keep an eye on their knife skills—the work can be dangerous."

Inaya consulted her notebook. "You said, 'I never imagined they would do something worse.' Who's 'they'? Who are you blaming for the hit on Mr. Elkader?"

Jensen sank down in her chair. "It couldn't be a hit," she whispered, her gravelly voice a mere rasp. "No one on the board would order it. They're not capable of it."

"You don't think so?" Inaya asked gently. "Not even after Khadijah and Barkhudo, the daughters of two of your employees, went missing?"

Jensen's bewilderment cost Inaya a pang of conscience. Jensen was a simple, straightforward soul, trying to do her job well. These machinations seemed beyond her. Inaya smothered the pang and continued. "You didn't think these things could be connected—the push for unionization and retaliatory measures?"

Jensen shook her head, the wings of her gray hair feathering her cheeks.

"This is a meat processing plant. We're not gangsters. We don't kidnap young girls, we don't bring in assassins." But the look in her eyes suggested she was starting to have doubts.

A knock sounded on the door. A man's head in a hard hat popped in.

"Need to check emergency numbers with you, boss."

"Emergency?" Inaya asked, getting to her feet. "Has something happened?"

Jensen was already at the door. She spared Inaya a brief look. "Emergency slaughter," she explained. "Livestock culled from the herd because they're injured or unfit. Obviously, that's not good for business, because we have to put them down; we can't put tainted meat on the market. I'll have to cut this short."

Inaya saw her opportunity. "I have a few more questions—I'm afraid they can't wait."

Jensen picked up her gloves and put them on, her attention distracted.

"Fine. I'll be back in five minutes. Don't leave my office."

She shut the door behind her, and quick as a flash, Inaya snatched the keys on the lanyard from the wall. She waited until the hall was empty and she could no longer hear Jensen's voice.

Then she sprinted the short distance to the locked door that had captured her interest. Why was it locked? What was the sign on the door that had been taken down?

Keeping an eye out for Jensen's return, she tried the first three keys without success. They were growing slippery in her clammy palm. She dangled them from the lanyard, looking over her shoulder. The fourth key stubbornly stuck in the lock but didn't turn.

She could hear footsteps in the distance, growing closer.

Cursing under her breath, she fumbled for the fifth key, putting it in upside down.

"Dammit!"

Voices accompanied the footsteps. Any second now, someone would be turning into the hall and would see what she was up to. She yanked the key out and positioned it again.

It stuck in place. She couldn't turn it. Nor could she extract it.

The only other choice she had was to remove the key from the ring on the lanyard and dart back into Jensen's office before she was discovered. Her fingers slipped over the key ring, searching for the groove.

"Come on, come on," she muttered, working at the ring with her nail. She yanked the lanyard down hard in the process, and suddenly the key turned. She tried the door, praying under her breath. It opened, the key jiggled free, and in an instant she was on the other side of the door, the lanyard gripped in her hand, the door locked and closed behind her.

She stood still, leaning back against the door.

The voices came closer, so close that she could hear what they were saying.

"Cops still here?" a man asked.

"One up on the walkway; don't know where the other one is," another voice replied.

The first man grunted and said, "Fat lot of good that'll do 'em."

The voices moved away. Inaya slowly exhaled. Not that they could have done much, but Jensen would undoubtedly report her for purloining her keys.

She wasn't sure what she was looking for—possibly the bodies of two missing teenage girls—but what she found subverted her expectations. For a moment, she gaped in surprise.

She was in a largish room divided into two sections. On the left, a low bench ran the length of the room, positioned before a series of taps that allowed for the washing of one's feet. Against the back wall were six evenly spaced sinks.

On the right side of the room was a large prayer space. Inaya deduced this from a poster of Mecca that hung on the wall and the three long carpeted rows angled toward the poster. On the back wall, a low shelf included a selection of books both in English and Arabic, a handful of printed headscarves, and one large, rather musty Qur'an.

A flyer was resting beside it on the shelf, and Inaya read it without touching it.

It was a memo indicating that the prayer hall was to be closed, with a list of the reasons why—tedious, bureaucratic reasons that when examined made little sense.

The mystery of the locked door explained, there was nothing else in the room of any obvious interest. She checked her watch. She still had two minutes left, and it was time for the afternoon prayer. She'd washed up earlier, so she shucked her shoes, borrowed a headscarf from the shelf, and quickly performed the Zuhr prayer, mentally apologizing for the undignified speed at which she worshipped. At the end of her prayer, she included a special *dua* for Razan, Khadijah, and Barkhudo. She offered supplications on behalf of their families. As always, when she was finished, she found herself feeling more settled.

There was no sound from outside, but there was no need to prolong her risk.

She replaced the scarf, put on her shoes, and opened the door with the lanyard clenched in her hand. She locked the room behind her, impressed by her own daring.

When she turned around, Ally Jensen was waiting at the door.

CHAPTER FORTY-THREE

The two women stared at each other in silence. Inaya struggled for something to say; Jensen had no such problem.

"That room is out of bounds."

She didn't sound angry. Her voice was . . . empty.

Inaya reentered the office, hanging the lanyard up behind the door. She waited for Jensen to join her, and when she did, she said, "You closed the prayer room. Why?"

Jensen remained standing, stiff and straight, her gray eyes boring into Inaya. In that weary, weathered face was the desire to confide at war with an instinct for . . . what? Self-preservation? The unwillingness to condemn someone whose guilt she couldn't be sure of? Everything about the woman indicated her sincerity. She took pride in a difficult job. She bore no animus toward her workforce. She appeared to have developed a soft spot for Elkader. Maybe it was something more—a woman longing for a tender man's affection, his devotion even, though Elkader was married and unlikely to stray.

She checked the assumption at once. Just because he was Muslim didn't mean that Elkader hadn't responded to a sympathetic woman. A kind woman who wanted to protect him.

Did the two of them still see each other? And if they did, was that in any way relevant to the investigation? If Jensen had been the type she could see as jealous or possessive, her target would have been Elkader's wife, not his beloved daughter.

Inaya couldn't see it. This woman, with her lonely eyes and quiet competence, wasn't given to irrational acts of passion.

She considered Natural Foods' reputation as a place to work. The plant had accommodated its Muslim workers during Ramadan, rearranging their shifts to allow them time to break their fasts. A prayer space had also been created. Revoking these accommodations was the spark that had lit the push for a workers' union. So what had changed?

She put the question to Ally Jensen.

"You made a considerable effort to provide religious accommodation to your Muslim employees. So why is the room locked down?"

Jensen answered readily enough. "You can blame the church for that."

"The Resurrection Church?" Inaya clarified.

Jensen nodded grimly. "No employer in Blackwater can afford to be targeted by one of Pastor Wayne's sermons. If we hadn't fallen in line, Wayne would have called for a boycott of our products." She paused. "I've never been one for religion. Doesn't seem honest to me."

She could have meant the church. But Inaya thought she meant the pastor. "Do you think he also called for Razan Elkader's murder?"

"There are far more dangerous people in Blackwater than the pastor."

"Can you tell me who they are?"

"His Disciples, for one. The sheriff for another. The arms and munitions contractors."

This last was unexpected.

"How so? They're government contractors, aren't they? Working on top-security missile design and"—she reached for the word she'd learned from Sych—"aerostats and the like."

"Those are multimillion-dollar contracts," Jensen said simply. "People would do a lot to protect that."

But how that would factor into Razan's death, Inaya couldn't quite see. Yes, Razan had been an intern at Apex, but Barkhudo and Khadijah hadn't been. And there had to be something that tied the three girls together. Could this be the link? That they were daughters of the workers who'd pushed to unionize? Wouldn't Razan have been targeted first, as her father had led the effort to unionize?

"Do your Somali employees still work here? Ahmed Abdi and Mustafa Diriye? The ones whose daughters went missing?"

Grudgingly, Jensen told her they did.

Another anomaly, because Elkader no longer did. He'd been dismissed, yet surely there were other positions he could have been moved to at the plant. His disability wasn't permanent. Or was the fact that he'd been the chief force behind the union significant?

Something else caught her attention.

"Why mention the Disciples? You don't have personal interactions with them, do you?"

Unless the Disciples' harassment of some members of the plant's workforce constituted a link. If it did, that meant Jensen had a deeper connection with her employees than she had admitted to. One where they would confide the troubles they faced at home. Jensen wasn't *motherly*, exactly; that wasn't the word Inaya was searching for. She considered the other woman's physical strength, then matched it to the impression she gave of competence.

The word she was fishing for surfaced.

Jensen reeked of *integrity*.

Jensen ran her strong fingers over the grooves in her forehead, her patience at an end.

"Time's up," she said. "I'm due back on the floor."

"Answer my question first. What is the plant's connection, if any, to the Disciples?"

Jensen backed away from the door, indecision plain on her face.

"Trust me," Inaya said. "I'm not looking to hang you out to dry. I'm trying to do the same thing you did—protect the people who work here."

She moved back to Jensen's desk, openly studying the schematic of the floor plan. The walkway above the plant interested her. She needed access. She needed to see the operation for herself to determine how likely it was that Elkader's injury had been an accident.

Without a word, Jensen moved to her desk. She rolled up the schematic, secured it with a rubber band, and handed it over to Inaya.

Their eyes met as if they were conspirators in a scheme.

Then Jensen said, "After the talk about the union began to spread, the board of directors assigned security to the plant. *Additional* security, I mean."

Inaya gripped the rolled schematic in her fist, heart thudding.

"Now you get it," Jensen whispered. "We have Disciples on the floor."

CHAPTER FORTY-FOUR

The words "probable cause" kept running through Inaya's mind. Ally Jensen might allow her to take a look at the floor, but she'd need a reason to search every corner.

"How many Disciples?" she asked Jensen. "And who assigned them?"

"Three or four, usually." Jensen paused. "I don't know who exactly from the board made that call. I was told about it by upper management."

"And today?"

"Two. They walk around the floor, keep an eye on things."

"Are they disruptive?"

An anxious Jensen pressed her hands to her lips. "They have their ways of intimidating our employees. All the union talk has dropped, of course. They're here to make sure it doesn't start up again."

"How are Abdi and Diriye taking their presence?"

"Quietly. Like everyone else, they have their heads down."

Inaya unrolled the schematic between her hands, and scanned it, trying to understand the layout, looking for anything useful. For someone who'd been eager to get back on the floor, Jensen stood there watching her. When the silence went on too long, Jensen bent to rifle through her desk drawers. She came up with a small gold lock that she passed to Inaya.

"You can find scrubs in the women's locker room."

"Scrubs?"

"Safety gear for the floor. You can put a lab coat on over the scrubs. Grab a helmet and headphones, too. Lock the floor plan in a locker, collect it when you leave. Be discreet. Your colleague is up on the walkway. If you join him there, you'll be able to see the floor."

Inaya pocketed the lock. "Are you giving me permission to search the plant?"

Jensen braced her hands on her desk. "I can't do that. You'd have to see something suspicious or out of place."

Inaya grinned at her. "Like a Disciple in a lab coat?"

Jensen didn't smile back. "I can't do your job for you. You need to read the floor."

With her long white coat over the scrubs, the mask that hid her face, and the helmet on her head, Inaya looked like any other worker on the floor. Jensen escorted her to the steps to the walkway and left her there. She met Jaime at the top of the stairs. He was too tall for a lab coat to cover much, the blue of his pant legs exposed. Like her, he was wearing headphones to protect his ears from the noise. Inaya moved hers aside to ask Jaime if he'd seen anything.

They looked out over the noisy floor together. The scent of blood was everywhere, bloodstains on the floor at most stations, though workers with portable hoses moved across the floor, periodically spraying the blood down into the floor drains. There was so much machinery in motion, it was difficult to understand the layout. A thousand or more workers moved through an intricate pattern on the floor. Conveyor belts slanted down from a chute delivering sides of meat to trimmers on the floor, who faced each other in long rows across the belt. Knives flashed in their hands as they trimmed fat, bone, and glands from parcels of meat. A separate system of conveyors moved overhead, transporting collection boxes. Trimmed parcels floated down the belt to be packaged quickly by handlers.

Near the wall closest to Inaya, a section was cordoned off for deboning. Jaime gave her the same rundown he'd been given. Beef was frozen for twenty-four hours while it was inspected, tagged, and graded before being shifted to a huge array of hooks. Men and women shifted around the carcasses, expertly divesting the bones of flesh. Handheld saws were utilized by workers positioned at tables, and there were also mechanical saws, efficiently stationed in a line. Oddly enough, they reminded Inaya of sewing machines, slicing larger segments of meat into consumable portions. The meat had to be positioned by hand before the saw was operated, and though the operators were skilled, the potential for injury was there.

Jaime told her that all the workers were trained in knife skills, a point that Inaya flagged, but that a higher level of training was required for the operation of machinery. She could see why. Each step in the operation was reliant on the one before it—injuries not only disrupted that flow, they affected daily quotas.

As she watched the process play out, she realized two things. She didn't see a kill room or storage space on the floor. And it was impossible to pick out any specific worker from the walkway. Ally Jensen must have known exactly where Hassan was stationed.

She surveyed the floor again. From the deboning by hand with a knife to the mechanical saws, there was a gap. If Hassan Elkader had been one of the dexterous workers who moved around the hooks, a shove could have pushed him straight into the sharp teeth of one of the saws.

She scanned the floor again, unable to pick out Disciples.

"We need to find a cold storage room." She stretched up on tiptoes so she could whisper the words directly into Jaime's ears. He shook his head like a dog shaking off wet.

"No search warrant."

"We're just taking a stroll. You go right, I'll go left."

It made sense that cold storage would be closer to deboning operations. She couldn't see an easy source of transit to the hooks—there had to be something on the floor.

Jaime planted his big hands on Inaya's shoulders.

"We're not splitting up."

She didn't know why he was worried. The plant was operating in broad daylight—well, fluorescent lighting—there wasn't a dark corner on the floor, and she would stay out of everyone's way. That would be harder with Jaime at her back.

His mouth set in a stubborn line, he refused to listen. He dogged her footsteps as she moved from the end of one line to another, working her way back from the trimline to the hooks. Glancing up, she saw that the hooks were hung from a moving track that proceeded slowly down a line. She pointed it out to Jaime with a discreet nod.

They skirted around the outside of the deboning station, giving the workers plenty of space; the last thing she wanted was to cause a dangerous accident. No one stopped her until she got to a huge pair of swinging doors. Beyond the doors, in what looked like a large, closed space, workers who must have been chosen for their strength swung the skinned bodies of beef cattle from storage hooks onto the track. The air ushered out of the swinging doors was frigid. So cold that even with the mask on, Inaya's breath formed a mist.

"Back off!" a man yelled as he slung a carcass onto a hook. Inaya immediately obeyed, bumping into Jaime, who tried to drag her away. The doors closed again, shutting off her view.

She'd seen something. In that brief moment, she'd caught sight of a steel door at the end of the huge cold space. Inaya tugged Jaime's arm.

The doors swung open again, confirming what she'd suspected. There was another room behind the cold storage space. She waited for the doors to swing closed, then grabbed the "VISITOR" tag pinned to the pocket of Jaime's lab coat. Quickly, she slid the tag out of its plastic pocket and flipped it around. On the blank space at the back, she wrote the word "INSPECTOR," ignoring Jaime's protests. The next time the doors swung open, she pushed Jaime through the gap, following behind him.

The same man shouted a protest, his hands wrangling with the hook. Inaya pointed to Jaime's tag, and with a scowl the man swung the carcass around, moving out of their way.

Inaya stayed close to the wall, propelling Jaime forward. The smell in the enclosed space was nearly overpowering—it would be a long time before she thought of eating a burger again. The scent of blood lay like a film on her clothes, her face, and up the inside of her nose. She gagged, and Jaime stopped again, digging his heels in.

"We should go—you're not feeling well."

Inaya glared at him, prodding him with her clipboard. Not only was he obstructing her, he was ignoring her rank. She wanted to get out of this too, and she would have gladly taken any excuse but for the promises she'd made. If there was something to find at the Natural Foods plant, she was determined to find it.

The kill site, the weapon, Razan's blood. They could be here in this plant.

She scooted around Jaime, irritated by his lumbering pace. The long hall smelled endless, the floor slippery with blood.

Animal blood?

It was time to see for herself.

The door at the rear didn't budge. It wasn't locked—it was just too heavy to move.

"Help me, Jaime!"

Reluctantly, he lent her the support of his shoulder.

The door swung out, nearly clipping them both.

They were looking up at a burly man who was barring their entrance. He'd been guarding the room Inaya wanted to examine. He wore a loose plastic gown over his clothing, his broad face visible through a plastic shield, his beard clipped close to his jaw. Skull-and-bones rings glittered on his fists. A huge cross hung from his neck, visible through the plastic gown. His leather patch said "ENFORCER."

She was face-to-face with a Disciple.

"Let us pass," she said firmly. "This is police business." She fumbled her badge out from the pocket of her lab coat.

The Disciple pointed to Jaime's visitor tag. "You're not allowed back here."

He was still on guard, but what was there to guard in this cold, empty space? Why was the biker here, when Ally Jensen had told her Disciples patrolled the floor? She challenged his right to be there.

"Not looking to prove anything to the pigs," he said easily.

Inaya really hated being called a pig. "Step aside or my partner will remove you."

The Disciple backed up to block their path, the door half-open behind him. Jaime stayed where he was, looking torn.

"What's your name—I want to know who's obstructing me." A glance at his forearms revealed a giant tattoo of a rooster. "Is it Rooster?"

He nodded with a grin, leaning forward to jerk the helmet off Inaya's head. Her braid spilled out and he jerked her closer with a tug.

"Know who *you* are," he rumbled. "You put Hardtack away."

With a mighty shove of his arm, he flung her back down the row of hooks. She collided with a carcass, the impact cold and blunt and unbearable in its reminder of human flesh.

A whirring noise sounded above her head; the hooks were on a moving track.

"Contaminated," she gasped at Jaime. "Stop it, stop *him!*"

Though the track was programmed to operate on its own, there was a pair of buttons beside the door Rooster guarded. When Jaime hit the red button, the track shuddered to a halt.

Inaya made her way back to Rooster, lifting her cuffs from her pocket. When she approached, he bent to tackle her with his shoulder. Jaime didn't step in to help. She sidestepped Rooster, kicking hard at the back of his knee. He went down.

"Jaime," she snapped. It would take both of them to cuff Rooster.

His movements leaden, Jaime subbed in his cuffs for Inaya's, his knee in Rooster's back. Inaya had left her gun in the locker, and Jaime hadn't pulled his. He pushed Rooster back on his heels beside the door. Inaya moved through it, leaving Jaime to call for backup.

It was like stepping onto another planet, the temperature in the room was so cold. There were hooks in the wall, and from them hung monstrous, headless bodies, cattle slaughtered at its peak. In this room, the floor was spotless, the bodies tagged and separated by grade. Behind them, the walls were lined with glass-doored freezers.

She paused by each one, peering in. They contained things she'd have preferred not to see. Segments of flesh, a set of ribs here, hindquarters there, each stamped for disposal. The printing on the stamps was minuscule, but she thought she was getting better at identifying parts by sight. Flanks and shanks, briskets and ribs, the floors of the cases pristine. If Razan's blood had been spilled in this room, someone had washed it away.

The cold settled into her bones as she proceeded. Her teeth began to chatter, she briskly rubbed her arms. She'd come almost to the end of the room, finding nothing of interest. There was nothing in this cold dark tunnel that demanded a guard. Then why had Rooster been guarding it? Had someone warned him cops were at the plant? Was there a leak on her team?

She shuddered at the thought.

The fluorescent tubing overhead began to hum. A moment later, it shut off, leaving Inaya in total darkness. And she still hadn't come to the end of the room. She fished out her phone.

A sound caught her attention; she strained her ears to listen.

It was a slow, rumbling sound . . . a little creaky and high-pitched. That sound was overlaid with another—a distant buzzing noise; not the whine of the mechanical saw, something deeper and more powerful.

The hooks rattled on the line. The track moved above her head, and just as she turned to duck, the weight of a steer caught her shoulder. Her cell phone flew from her hand; she heard the crack as it landed on cement. The track sped up, a ghastly row of raw-smelling flesh shuttling toward her at high speed. Carried forward by momentum, the carcasses swung out at her, and she screamed as if ghosts were coming to life.

She ducked down, staying low, her fingers scrabbling for her phone. Her braid was caught by a low-hanging shank, her body yanked along. She tried to keep up with the track, feeling the sickening slide of something sticky as it slipped from her braid to her neck. With a grunt, she tore her braid free and threw herself on the floor.

As her eyes acclimated to the lack of light, she could pick out bands of fat, fleshy and white, against the darker color of the meat. She fought her way to the side with only those flashes to guide her, calling out for Jaime's help.

How far from the doors was she that she couldn't hear his answering call?

She was disoriented, stumbling forward with her hands out, touching nothing but emptiness. She had no idea where she was. Either she'd gone nose-blind to the smell, or the air in the room was fresher.

Her foot hit something hard before her hands did, a barrier of some kind. Then her hands met cold steel. She felt around the surface blindly, searching for something to grip, to open, a telltale hint of where she was. She encountered what felt like a giant pair of curving handles, cold, but not frozen to the touch. She yanked forward with all her might, and one of the doors came open, showering her with a blast of frozen air.

A light came on from the open space—another freezer, this one the size of an airport shuttle. Its doors were solid steel, its interior was empty, just blank white space waiting to be filled. She moved aside a little so the interior light would show something of the room.

Shuttle-sized freezers were plugged into the back wall through a grid protected from power surges. A generator hummed in the back— the sound she had heard earlier, a deep and powerful rumble from the far side of the room.

She circled around until she had a good view of the freezers' steel doors. She left the first door open, then one by one she checked the rest. Each one was empty, waiting for its cargo. The interiors were spotless, the air inside them free of the scent of blood or flesh. Either these freezers were new, or they'd been thoroughly cleaned.

She didn't know what tipped her off to a patch of blackness in the corner.

She couldn't see much, just a long cord plugged into the wall that disappeared into nowhere. She trudged to the end of the room, rounding the corner, then stopped. The cord led to another freezer, perhaps half the size of the ones in the outer room. There were others with it, stuffed into the room, and she could see from the dim light that these smaller freezers were damaged. Some were crushed, as if they'd been dropped. Others had a door hanging out of joint, or a dent that buckled the doors. Most of them weren't plugged in. Some of them were locked.

Breathing in harsh little puffs, she shivered at her sudden discovery. Only one of the freezers was both locked *and* plugged in. It was behind three others, shunted off to the side.

Again the floor was clean beneath her feet, and again she asked herself what on earth she hoped to find.

She came to the locked door and tested it. The lock was frozen solid.

She looked around for any left-behind tools. She didn't find any, but as she squeezed between industrial-sized appliances, she noticed a narrow steel panel hanging loose. She grabbed it, made her way back, and jammed it into the lock. As she bent it and snapped it free, the lock broke apart in two. The body of the padlock fell to the ground with a thud, the shackle springing free. Slowly, Inaya peeled back the door, using her weight to counter its resistance. It burst open from its plastic housing with a pop. She jumped, then laughed at herself.

It's nothing. Just an empty freezer.

She pulled the door wide and peered into the interior, where the light was muted by something solid in the way, hard and crusted with ice.

Inaya stepped aside so the outside light could find its way in.

She stared for a moment, unseeing.

And then the shadows resolved themselves, and she let out a silent scream.

Two faces encrusted with ice stared back at her, black and blue and cold.

CHAPTER FORTY-FIVE

Inaya watched Cat reach out a hand to the faces in the freezer. The processing of the scene was complete; Dr. Stanger had given Cat the time she'd asked for with the girls' bodies. Barkhudo Abdi and Khadijah Diriye had been found at last, two months after their disappearance.

Inaya couldn't see any damage to the bodies. They'd been placed in the freezer standing upright, their hands loose at their sides. There was no evidence of a wound, no blood coagulate frozen with the bodies. Unlike Razan, their eyes were closed, and they were dressed in the clothes they had last been seen wearing, jeans and long tops and runners. Nothing about them stood out, though each item of clothing would be examined for forensic data.

"Everything okay?" Inaya stood quietly beside Cat.

Cat's voice trembled with her discovery. "It wasn't the same killer."

Inaya stared at her, bewildered.

"If it was, his thoughts would be disjointed. That's not the case with the blunt and economical manner of these murders."

"This could be a case of manslaughter," Inaya said doubtfully. "An accident of some kind covered up."

"Perhaps. Julius will tell us if that's the case. The signs are distinct, though. The person who killed Razan didn't kill these girls. These murders are . . . efficient. Quick, cold, and necessary. Most likely committed by someone who had no personal relationship with the girls. Razan's killer knew her, maybe even cared for her. He's clever, poised, and deeply artistic. That's not what happened here."

Seif came up to join them. "I think you're right, Catalina." He put his hand under Cat's elbow, turning her away from the bodies. "There's no pattern here, which means we can't make assumptions. I'll get Jaime to notify the families. Dr. Stanger needs to get on with things."

"No!" Inaya caught hold of his arm, something she would never have done in normal circumstances. "I want to talk to you about Jaime." It was only the three of them in the frozen room, the lights cold and blaring, in contrast to the earlier darkness. "I think it's possible that Jaime is reporting to the sheriff."

Seif freed himself from her grasp, and she blushed. "I'm sorry."

He waved her apology aside. "Why?"

"Someone is watching us, following us, whether it's a Disciple or one of Grant's deputies. How do they know where we'll be? Either because Jaime's with us or because he's called them." She reviewed his actions at the plant. "He didn't want me to come in here."

"You think he knew the bodies were here? Or that the room could be Razan's kill site?"

"No," Cat said softly, by her side. "That's not Jaime, at all. He's not clever enough to dissemble; he can't hide the core of who he is. His face when he saw the girls—he was sick to his stomach."

Seif weighed in on Cat's side. "Maybe he didn't know about the bodies. Maybe he was trying to prevent Rahman from running into Rooster. That would account for his shock when Rahman made her discovery."

"He'd know Rooster was here, then." Inaya was having trouble accepting what the facts told her to be true: Jaime wasn't infatuated at all, he'd been keeping track of their progress.

"He was up on the walkway. He might have seen him head into the area."

"He was adamant about keeping me out, sir, and far too slow to come to my aid when I called for help."

Seif's brows lowered. He was angry, but not at her. At himself, Inaya guessed, for bringing Jaime onto their team—for placing him at the heart of the investigation.

"He doesn't know anything," Cat insisted. "Grant may have used him for inside information, that's all."

"That's more than enough. We'll have to go back and recheck every assignment we gave him, wasting time we don't have. You're right," he said to Inaya. "I won't have him notify the families. You're sure of the ID?"

Both women nodded.

"Call Adams. You and Catalina go with her, Rahman. I'll take care of Webb. We talk to the girls' families, and we find out who's in charge here. Whoever killed the union probably killed these girls."

CHAPTER FORTY-SIX

Seif released the scene to Stanger. He'd sent Webb down to the station with Rooster; he would head there now to deal with things himself. He must have missed something in Webb's past, a link that would tie him to Blackwater or make him vulnerable to Grant. DPD was riddled with Grant's cronies, people who'd come up with him or who owed him carefully cultivated favors. Grant knew how to put the screws on. And he needed officers on the ground to ensure his kickbacks were collected. Webb might be the link Seif was looking for, though he suspected Cat was right: Webb was naive enough to be of use, but that didn't mean he was corrupt.

Seif pictured the whiteboard where Cat had identified the players in this game. It had been too simple. They'd missed all the overlap, and the thought of it was giving him a headache. The Disciples were part of the church. And a Disciple had been guarding the entrance to the room where the bodies had been found, so the church was a more than interested party.

He'd take care of Webb. Inaya could handle the church.

Half an hour later, he knew it wasn't Webb's fault, it was his. He'd known Grant wouldn't tolerate being sidelined on the murder—he'd sent Pincher to intimidate Dr. Stanger—of course he'd find other ways inside their investigation. The question was why. Because Grant was somehow involved and needed to know when they were getting close? Or because it might have an impact on the sheriff's other activities? Did he suspect Seif's motives for cozying up to him?

He called Webb into his office, his face hard and closed.

Webb stood at attention, his blue eyes red from crying, his breath hitching in his throat as he waited for the hammer to come down.

"Have you been working with Grant from the first?"

Webb gave him a shamefaced nod, even as he tried to mitigate. "Not working with—just letting him know where we were on the case. He didn't want to be blindsided if his team took another hit. Morale is already low because we've taken over their case."

God, the kid was naive.

"It wasn't their case, Webb. Grant refused to investigate the disappearance of the girls whose bodies we've just found. His constituents don't trust him—that's why we took over."

Webb swallowed over what looked like a giant lump in his throat.

"I know that now, sir." Miserably, he asked, "What will happen to me?"

"That depends on what you do next. How did it work with Grant? How often did he have you check in? What else did he ask you to do—leak things to the press, destroy evidence, misdirect us . . . what?"

With great dignity, Jaime pushed back his shoulders. "None of that, sir. I wouldn't do anything like that, and the sheriff knows that." He looked confused for a moment. "I—ah—didn't actually deal with the sheriff, I spoke to Russell Pincher. He wanted updates on the case, he wanted to know who we were questioning and where we were on the ground—"

Seif cut his recital short.

"Which means if the Blackwater sheriff or his team were implicated in the murder of any of these girls, they'd have a head start when it came to destroying evidence. Maybe at the reservoir, where we searched for Razan. Maybe at the plant. Did you tell Pincher when our detectives were at the Lebanese bakery? Or on the floor at the plant?"

Webb hung his head, his breath shuddering through his lungs.

"So you know if Detective Rahman had been killed by that biker, or later at the plant by Rooster, that would have been on you. She said you were slow to come to her aid."

His head jerked up, tears pooled in his eyes. "I didn't mean for her to come to any harm. Pincher said they wanted to slow the investigation down."

"Did you consider why?"

The question Seif asked was meant to get him to think, to analyze Pincher's motives; it wasn't a judgment. Webb recognized his tone as a reprieve.

"If we solved the murder too quickly, it would show the sheriff up. It would humiliate Blackwater in front of the DPD. Sheriff Grant didn't deserve that."

Seif sighed, planting himself in his chair. He looked up at Webb, towering over his desk, his expression suddenly hopeful.

"What does Grant have on you?"

"I didn't think he had anything." Webb clasped his bony hands. "I believed him—believed *in* him. He helped my dad with some trouble. He recommended me for the DPD, when I wouldn't have had a chance—not with my dad on probation. He didn't say I'd have to do anything, he just talked about the fact that political correctness would put us out of work. We have families to support, people to protect—we couldn't let the city vote to defund the police. If Denver cut its budget, Blackwater would follow. The complaints against his team were malicious, he said; he wanted to keep serving the community he's worked for all his life." Webb looked away. "My dad . . . my dad used to beat on my mother, so I know the police can be the good guys."

The sheriff had a lot of pull with higher-ups if Webb had made it past the background check, but Seif already knew this. He wouldn't blame a child for his parent's actions—though Webb was no longer a child. He'd obstructed a murder investigation.

Despite this, Seif's anger at him had faded, finding a new target. Grant knew how to choose his victims. He'd appealed to Webb's sense of duty, the debt between them unspoken, while all the time he'd wielded the threat of Webb's past like a whip. He shoved a tissue box across his desk. Webb crumpled one in his hands.

"Did Grant help your mother?"

"She wouldn't press charges." Jaime wiped his eyes with the tissue.

"We didn't want Dad to go away, we just wanted him to stop. When the sheriff had a word, it got better."

"Your father did time, though?"

"For theft, not assault. When he came back, I was big enough to stand up for my mother."

And for himself, Seif guessed. He didn't like any part of this. He looked at Jaime and saw the twins, in desperate need of guidance, even as they fought him every step of the way. There'd been no older brother for Jaime to keep him out of trouble. Just a dirty cop who'd used him.

Seif barked a series of questions.

"Did you tamper with, destroy, or share evidence with Pincher?"

"Never!"

"Did you mislead members of this team about any aspect of this investigation?"

"No, sir. I wouldn't. I was slow with my work, that's all. And I kept Pincher in the loop."

"Did you knowingly place Detective Rahman in harm's way?"

Jaime's face crumpled. "I *should* be beaten for that."

With that admission, Seif couldn't take it any further. He stood up and opened the door, ushering Jaime out.

"The mistake you made wasn't entirely your fault. I should have shielded you from Grant." He met Jaime's gaze. "I'm giving you another chance. From this point on, you keep things locked down, and you *always* have your partner's back, are we clear?"

He recognized the look Jaime gave him as one he'd seen from the twins when he let them off the hook after they'd gotten into trouble.

Amazement underlined by joy.

CHAPTER FORTY-SEVEN

Areesha approached Barkhudo as Inaya watched. She'd refused to assist them with the notifications unless they allowed her to confirm the girls' identities herself. She'd met them at the plant, dressed all in black, as though she'd already begun to mourn.

"Is it all right to touch?" Her hand hovered above the crystals on Barkhudo's forehead.

Stanger had finished for now, so Inaya granted her permission.

Areesha brushed each girl's cheek with her palm, resting her forehead against theirs.

"My sweet girls. You've had no justice, no peace, but I swear to you, you'll have both."

"Ameen," Inaya murmured to herself.

Areesha's eyes were dazed with grief, her sparkling aura dimmed. It hurt to see her so shaken. When Inaya patted her shoulder, she didn't shake the comfort off.

"My boys are younger than Barkhudo and Khadijah. I've talked to them, made them understand about police—that they're guilty until proven innocent. I've wrapped them up as safely as I can, but one day—" She broke off, swallowing tears. "One day they'll be somewhere I can't protect them, and God forbid I find them like this—abandoned like they didn't matter."

She gave Inaya a watery smile. "Clay is an artist like Khadijah—he says he'll be a sculptor one day. Kareem wants to be a lawyer so he can take over my work. He says his mama needs a chance to rest." Her eyes dropped to Inaya's badge. "How can any of us rest when our children can be taken from us and no one is held accountable?" She turned back to the girls. "Please treat them with dignity. That's more than they had in life."

The visit to Fadumo's home was every bit as wrenching as Inaya expected it to be. In hindsight, what she'd asked of Areesha was unfair: to serve as an informal liaison, to soothe inconsolable grief with her hard-won right to be with Fadumo and Waris. Inaya should have seen that Areesha carried too much, *shouldered* too much, as part of her commitment to a community in such deep pain that it could only be expressed through anger. She thought back to the morning they'd met when Omar Abdi had been beaten by the police, when all he'd done was ask about his sister.

Please tell me. Is that my sister in there?

At Fadumo's house, Khadijah's painting of Omar now hung in pride of place, given as a gift to the family by Khadijah's mother. The families tied together in life, in grief, and in death. Omar stood beside his portrait, his chin trembling, his fists clenched as he fought his body's grief, and Inaya watched Areesha examine his reaction, knowing what was coming for her boys: joy that could be defiant, an act of resistance in itself, set against generational rage at a system that wouldn't change.

Inaya couldn't stand in her place, couldn't add up the heaviness of names like Laquan and Elijah and Tamir and Trayvon and Sandra and Breonna and George and Marcus, couldn't look at Omar's bereavement and see the killing of her own child.

Omar's mother, Fadumo, hadn't cried, her posture sturdy as she took in the news. She exhaled like she'd been waiting a lifetime to do it, her ravaged gaze on Inaya.

"The *janazah* for my daughter?"

Inaya bent her head. "As soon as we can manage it. I'll push as hard as I can." She bit her lip, wanting to offer comfort yet conscious that anything she said would be weighed against the badge she wore. "My mother will want to come and see you. My whole family will."

"And you?" Fadumo asked, with a grace that pierced Inaya.

She knelt and pressed her forehead to Fadumo's knee. "And me." She cried the tears Fadumo wouldn't. "Don't you know my prayers are with you?"

Fadumo patted her hair, her fingers stiff.

Her reply was steady. "I hope your gun is too."

With Cat beside her, Inaya followed Areesha's car into town. They parked near the gazebo, needing fresh air after the horrors of the day. The stink of the plant still clung to Inaya's body. The sharp brightness of the Colorado evening washed some of that stink away, the sky cloudless and starry, the falls muted and deep.

They strolled around the pond, avoiding the alley behind the falls, Areesha taking a minute to call her boys while Cat made excuses to her husband: the women needed to talk.

They came to a halt at a picturesque spot. Inaya gathered a handful of stones and skipped them across the pond.

"Thank you for helping us, Areesha."

"Thank you for letting me come to the plant. I didn't expect to have the chance."

It was Cat's turn to gather stones. She didn't know how to skip them, so she flung a few as far as she could. A tiny splash rippled through the pond.

"You said something to Fadumo before we left. Can I ask what it was, if we're sharing?"

Areesha's smile glimmered in the dark. "We have no choice but to share."

"So? Tell us, then." The stones in Cat's hand fell into the pond with a plop.

"I promised Fadumo the sheriff would answer for his failure to investigate the girls' disappearance. I've found evidence that will help."

Inaya looked at her warily. "What kind of evidence?"

"I hired a private investigator to follow up on the sheriff's claim that, based on cell phone data, the girls must have run away or gone up to the reservoir."

The fine hairs on the back of Inaya's neck stood up. "And?"

When Areesha skipped a stone, it sailed halfway across the pond.

"The sheriff slipped up. The Chatfield Reservoir was on his mind for a reason. My investigator tracked the girls' cell phones to the lookout above the dam. Their phones went dead after that: they were never turned on again."

CHAPTER FORTY-EIGHT

Inaya wanted to charge at Grant, put him away for good—and if they couldn't achieve that, at least get him out of law enforcement. She reported in to Seif, trying to convey her sense of urgency. He told her to wait—he'd talk to Areesha himself. He'd already assigned a separate team to the murders at the plant: the team would keep them up-to-date. They needed more on the sheriff, Seif argued; forensics from the plant might help.

In the meantime, he'd given her the go-ahead to interview Pastor Wayne. So on Sunday, Inaya dragged Cat with her to the church, astounded by the show they put on.

The interior of the church could have served as the set of *American Idol*. Giant screens flanked the stage, and a complex sound and lighting setup made the most of the large auditorium. There was a live band on the stage behind the pastor, a choir seated on a raised dais at the back, and assistants at hand to cater to the needs of Pastor Gentleman Jack John Wayne. His real name was John Waalfort; Gentleman Jack John Wayne was a stage personality.

Inaya took a good look at the pastor's toothsome assistants. The men were clean-shaven in matching dress shirts with perfectly creased khakis. The women looked as if they'd just stripped off yoga wear to step into their tight blue dresses.

Inaya and Catalina were at the back of the auditorium, taking note of the large families in attendance, cowboys and beauty queens, with four or five children each.

John Wayne, a hearty and earnest man, was wearing a headset as he worked the stage, his voice pitched to the rafters. The lights turned a soft gold, spotlighting him with a halo over his chestnut brown hair, his audience rapt as they listened.

It was a performance in every sense of the word, a canny commercial artistry behind it.

Cat nudged her waist. "Holy Lord, he's seen us."

Cameras turned to Inaya and Cat, their images splashed across the screen.

A murmur went through the crowd. Pastor Wayne held up his hand.

"Brothers and sisters, children of God, I ask you to welcome these sinners into our midst. Guide them with your grace and forgiveness."

"Sinners?" Inaya mouthed to Cat, entertained.

Catalina crossed herself. Inaya raised an index finger, shrugging. She did indeed sin, but her god was forgiving.

"We appreciate the police being here," Wayne continued. "And we always appreciate sinners joining us inside the fold. However, sins must be confessed to be redeemed."

"I thought confessionals were Catholic," Inaya whispered to Cat.

"Nondenominational evangelism. It's a little bit of everything."

Inaya tensed as the pastor picked up volume.

"But we have to ask ourselves about these police. Are they part of our community? Are they loyal to America—we know that eighty-two percent of them are not. They're not willing to fight and die for America. Does that sound like loyalty to you?"

Eighty-two percent was an oddly specific number. As the pastor built up steam, Inaya sorted through the background the team had gathered on Gentleman Jack John Wayne. He'd modeled his ministry on a familiar combination of anti-Muslim and anti-refugee sentiments, sentiments that had gained strength and speed in the months after 9/11. Muslims had been the bogeyman back then, just as those at the border were now. Pastor Wayne must have background on her. He knew she was Muslim, and along with diving into habitual tropes, he was connecting her to Razan, the association rife with racism. Yet he did so in the calmest, most benign tones, a smile on his florid face.

"We are very sorry indeed that a young girl came to this country only to lose her life. That's a tragedy by any measure."

The crowd murmured its assent.

"But let's not stop there, brothers and sisters. We know why they come. They think they'll earn the rewards of Heaven. Suppose this poor girl had died on the way from Syria—she'd get the same reward as if she'd died as a terrorist."

The crowd rumbled.

"She wouldn't have died here if she'd stayed in her own country. Think about *that,* my friends. This was deliberate; this was planned."

Inaya's scalp tightened. Where was Wayne going with this?

"Could it be this young girl died in America because her people are trying to change our beliefs? If you try to control the culture of America through Sharia law, could it be Christ the Redeemer answered? Look at the meatpacking plant. Generous to take in migrants as workers, and what do they get in return? Requests for 'accommodation.'" He turned the word into an insult. The congregation booed on cue. "*Religious* accommodation. They start praying to Allah on our dime; they demand time off for Ramadan. That's where they begin, but where does it end, my friends? It ends up with them breaking up this Christian nation."

He pointed triumphantly at a figure in the crowd. "Ask our friend. *She* knows. They did it in her country too. You know what the Lebanese civil war was? Muslim militias hunting decent God-fearing Christians."

With a sense of horror, Inaya realized he was pointing at Cyrine. The band played the *Jaws* theme in accompaniment to his words. Cyrine's body swayed to the music.

"Bless you, my sister. Your prayers will be heard. Your people will be avenged." His voice began to build to a crescendo. "We will not let our nation fall! We will not become servants of Al-lah—we worship Christ the Redeemer! If you attack the beliefs of this great nation, if you invade, we won't stand by and take it! When you strike at America, America strikes back!" His pudgy fists punched the air. The congregants were on their feet, many turning to point at Inaya and Cat, the atmosphere so charged that they began to edge toward the exit.

The audience cheered, the young children frightened as wildness swept the crowd.

"Poor child, poor child." He lowered his voice as he spoke of Razan. A hush fell over the crowd. "Maybe she thinks she was destined for Heaven. Such a sad thing, isn't it, my friends? I pity her." And indeed, he looked pityingly at Inaya. "Because don't we know that unless you accept salvation through Jesus Christ Our Lord, there can be no redemption?"

He bowed his head. "Think of where the poor child must be."

A few women cried out in sympathy.

He raised his leonine head to glare at Inaya. "It's time for you to accept that some folks belong here, some don't: take that message to heart." He signaled two security guards.

A threat, pure and simple, but though her heart was racing, Inaya had faced down harder men than Pastor John Wayne. She would turn the congregation on its head.

"Pastor," she said innocently, "what if I want to be redeemed?"

He was sharp enough to know she wasn't the slightest bit interested in the Resurrection Church, except in a professional capacity, but the mission behind evangelism was to bring people to the word of Christ; he could hardly reject her. He was a showman, so he mastered the moment with a joyous cry of "Hallelujah!"

The congregants cheered with him, and the tension in the hall dissipated.

"Close call." Inaya took one long breath, followed by another.

Cat touched her shoulder. "Look." She pointed to television cameras aimed at the stage. "They're filming this. I think it's a livestream."

"It's a multimillion-dollar empire built off his personal charisma. There's a huge appetite for evangelism in this corner of the country."

"You're thinking Colorado Springs and the Ramadan pork barbecue back in 2015?"

Inaya grinned. Though the advertised barbecue held by a chapter of the Infidels Motorcycle Club had been intended to anger and offend, it was also undeniably funny. The ban on pork was a dietary restriction, not a sacred taboo.

"That," she agreed, "and the fact there are six megachurches between the foothills and downtown Denver."

Cat snorted. "As a Christian, I can tell you this is a very aggressive form of worship—that's not why I mentioned the cameras. Think about the fact that this sermon is being televised."

Cat was studying Inaya's face, her expression grave. "You don't get it. You've lived with it so long, you don't pay attention." She tugged Inaya to a pair of seats at the end of an empty row.

The sermon continued, the pastor a master of pitch, his voice rising and falling in rhythms that could lull you to sleep, or possibly to tears, regardless of what he preached.

"We need to protect ourselves, our culture, our country, and our church," he was saying. "Sharia is now in effect in some American cities where the Muslims have high numbers and outvote regular Americans. If you think it can't happen here, it's already happened. Remember the unionizing effort at Natural Foods? Migrants pioneered that—why? Because a good Christian employer wasn't about to have his employees washing their feet in the sink so they could bow down to Al-lah on the company's dime. So we've got two problems. We have enemies of Christ in our midst. And we have socialists acting up. Enemies of Christ, enemies of capitalism."

He nodded sagely, and someone shouted, "Preach!"

Cat leaned in and whispered, "Anti-Muslim racism gets such a pass in this country that they can televise it without consequences. No one's going to rein them in—not journalists, not politicians, not local civic leaders. It's only going to spread."

Inaya sighed. She knew what Cat was saying; she had intimate experience of it, and community-wide experience too. She knew it was a network, an intense web of connections and conspiracy theories, well-funded and professionally disseminated. But she refused to let it be the only thought on her mind. It made her a victim, when she knew she held within her the capacity to change things. Yes, rampant hatred was a threat, and God alone knew where it was heading, but she couldn't live her life constrained by misery, especially when she was privy to more than her share of joy. She had safety, family, education, work, and more than her share of privilege. And she had friends like Cat.

Her secret devotional self also had words, so many words she clung to.

Do they think they will be left alone after saying "We believe" without being put to the test?

She personalized the Qur'anic verse to reflect upon her own convictions: Do I think I won't be tested in my belief? Wasn't this a test of the faithful? A test she passed on some days, failed on others, but always exerted herself toward.

She grabbed Cat's hand and squeezed it.

"I've been reading the background the team put together on the church. It seems that of late the pastor has been fixated on border security. That's a life-and-death matter for kids separated from their families and detained in cages. So it's not all about Muslims."

"Border security." Cat winced. "He's doing his part to keep the coffers of Apex full."

She caught Inaya's querying glance. "These big companies don't just profit off policies that militarize our borders, they *make* those policies themselves. And who better than a pastor to preach the morality that squares it all away?"

"You've gotten cynical," Inaya observed, not without sympathy.

"I've gotten practical. How do a handful of struggling NGOs go up against the power of massive arms manufacturers in the fight to treat others as human?" She motioned at the stage. "I reject the kind of Christianity that despises the poor. Christianity without Christ's compassion?" Her eyebrows came together in a frown. "Make it make sense, *hermana*."

"I wish I could," Inaya replied. "People make their careers off calculated fear and loathing—the pastor is just another player in a burgeoning industry."

"Don't underestimate him." They both watched as he wound down the sermon by hugging his attractive assistants, kissing them on both cheeks. They smiled back at him—but could the shine be wearing off those smiles? "He said Razan died because she and her family were invaders. He likened her to terrorists. I think he'd be quite adept at directing others to kill. All in the name of Christ, of course."

"He wouldn't do it himself?"

"Oh no. Not when he can cast that charisma far and wide. It's a naked use of power, emphasis on the 'naked.'"

"You caught that too? You think he's a charlatan behind the Christian piety, getting it on with his handpicked few?"

They watched the pastor exit the stage after the choir stepped down, followed by his personal coterie. The house lights came up, chatter rising in the hall on a swell of goodwill.

Nothing like the specter of foreign enemies to stir the blood, Inaya thought with a touch of Cat's skepticism.

When the hall had emptied, Cat answered her. "Men like that often acquire a sense of infallibility. The world is their oyster and so on, because they think they innately deserve it as members of a privileged class. Think Eliot Spitzer, or more recently Matt Gaetz."

"Carl Lentz, Ted Haggard, Jimmy Swaggart," Inaya added.

"Wayne is a swaggart, all right."

Inaya laughed out loud. "Should we confront him in his den?"

Cat rose with a flourish. "After you, *chica*."

When a security guard tried to stop their approach to the pastor's office, Inaya flashed her ID with a little bit of swagger herself.

"Don't you want to spread the good word?"

Flustered, the guard knocked on the door. With a doubtful look at the two of them, an attractive young woman let them in.

CHAPTER FORTY-NINE

The pastor wasn't in his office, a young woman with the remarkable name of Mary Jane Templar explained. They could sit in the reception area and wait, alongside dozens of others attempting to receive the pastor's personal blessing.

Catalina took charge. She ordered the security guards to bar the door, advising them that their pastor would likely prefer as few witnesses as possible to his police interview. When the guards demurred, Cat pulled back her blazer so her handcuffs and gun were in view. Their preferred option of an interview at the station was declined, just as she intended. The pastor's office was less threatening.

They were left alone with Mary Jane Templar, who said nervously, "Pastor Wayne will be along any moment. There are a few exceptional members who require special attention."

For "members," Inaya subbed in "donors" as she took a good look around the room. The reception area was lavish, heavy on the ranching motif, with the whitened antlers of elk decorating the walls. The rustic coffee tables were burdened with platters of food—charcuterie, imported cheese with wafer-thin crackers, fruits and sweets in abundance, boxes and boxes of gourmet chocolates and pretzels. And in one corner, under the picture window, was a giant open bar, specialty ales on one side, crystal champagne flutes on the other.

The door to the pastor's office was open, and it had even better views, the back wall made of glass, the hills dark green in the bright glare of day with withered patches where grass and shrubs had died in the semi-drought conditions. With a silent signal to Cat to distract Mary Jane Templar, Inaya slipped through the door.

The room didn't signal piety to her. The only adequate descriptor would be "opulence." A pair of velvet sofas flanked an Azizi walnut desk. No papers on the desk, just a handful of photographs in crystal frames, the pastor with his Stepford brood: dainty wife, wholesome children, even a matching beagle. No ego wall of the pastor with smiling luminaries like in Wong's office, though she was expecting it, and no art or music at all, speaking to the essential blandness of the pastor's personality. She was looking for something, was mystified by its absence, but she couldn't quite pin down what it was.

She moved closer to the wall that held two bookcases with locked cabinets, also crafted by Azizi, an Iranian-American furniture maker of increasing fame. The choosing of these pieces suggested a sensitivity to beauty she hadn't expected from Wayne—almost an artistic appreciation. Of course, Azizi's early pieces would be worth a fortune in coming years, though Inaya wondered how the pastor squared his possessions with his anti-Muslim vitriol. Had no one thought to call him on it? Did it suggest some kind of interface between Islam and Christianity?

She tried the cabinet doors. Locked, as she'd guessed they would be. Probably where the church's financial records were kept. It would be worth it to have a look. See if the church was concretely linked to the Disciples' drug trade.

Voices sounded in the reception area—Cat greeting the pastor, Mary Jane desperate to explain why she'd permitted the police access to the pastor's private chambers. Inaya strolled over to the windows, unhurried, and that was where he found her.

"Praise Jesus," he said heartily. "What do we have here?"

Inaya swung around, realizing what it was that she'd missed. On the bare walls. On the desk. In the bookcases she'd tested, with their leather-bound volumes.

There were no icons in the room. Rupi's reading had been correct. Nonetheless, after that sermon, the pastor's involvement in Razan's death merited serious consideration.

"I'd be grateful for a few minutes of your time, Pastor."

His indeterminate blue eyes did a quick scan of her body.

Wayne closed the door behind him with a thump, shutting Catalina out. It locked with an audible click, and Inaya pitied the young women who worked for him. It was becoming clear that it was only a matter of time before a sex scandal hit the church.

He sat down heavily on one of the sofas, patting the space beside him. He'd spread his legs, his hands dangling between them, in that posture men so often adopted, as if they were claiming territory in the wild. Taking up space they weren't entitled to, though she supposed it *was* his office. She stayed where she was, one eyebrow coolly raised.

Wayne reached into the pocket of his very expensive suit, fumbling for a cigar. He lit it with practiced ease, the tang of bitter cherry filling the room. Inaya walked over to a small window on the opposite wall and opened it so the smoke could escape. She was closer to the pastor now, but not within touching distance, unless he decided to lunge at her.

He pointed to the slick telephone on his desk. A landline. Maybe he knew that cell phones could be hacked.

"Addison and I go way back. I pick up that phone and call him, you're in a world of hurt, young lady."

"Sheriff Grant has been removed from the case."

Wayne's grimace was contemptuous.

"You newcomers don't know enough to know who the real power in this town is."

She could have gone along with this, but she decided to dispense with games.

"A nice little club you have here. Grant, Nakamura, Apex. Even Cyrine Haddad."

He took a long draw on his cigar, staring at her through a veil of smoke. He wanted her to feel ill at ease, unsettled by his open carnality. She shrugged it off. She knew which kind of men to fear. Gentleman Jack John Wayne was a clown.

"Tell me about your sermon, Pastor."

"What about it?"

"You put the blame for Razan's murder on Razan. You said she earned it by coming here as part of an unwanted invasion. Your sermons contain their fair share of agitation, even incitement, I would say. Weren't you worried that one of your congregants might act?"

"Now that's just where you're wrong," he said. "I never tell them to do anything. I just keep them informed about what's going on in America."

She stepped out of the path of the smoke, fanning it toward the open window.

"So you genuinely believe the things you say? It's not just for ratings?"

"I believe we have a Christian mission—" he began. Inaya cut him off.

"I heard all that onstage. But you don't seem like the most Christian of men."

"Why do you say that?"

His smile had a thousand sharp teeth.

Inaya waved at the photos on his desk. "You're a married man with a beautiful family, yet you haven't stopped staring at my chest."

His eyes shot to hers. "Are you going to charge me with sexual harassment?"

"I don't think I'll need to. Eventually, your assistants are going to come clean. Women tolerate predators for only so long."

"You think I'm into other women?"

Inaya reflected on the handsome young men who'd flocked the stage.

"So you're an equal opportunity abuser?"

Wayne stood up, calmly stubbing out his cigar in a crystal ashtray on the desk.

"You're barking up the wrong tree. I look because the Lord loves beauty. But I never, ever touch."

It was said with great solemnity. Inaya didn't believe it, but he'd successfully diverted her attention.

"What's the right tree, Pastor?"

"The girl was a pain in my ass," he said frankly. "What with her articles against the church, accusing us of 'Islamophobia,' a made-up case of victimization if ever I heard one."

"So you weren't responsible for stopping the Muslim community for obtaining a permit for their mosque? You didn't have the land re-zoned?"

His shrug was over-casual. "There's a difference between speaking up for your own and victimizing others. We're out there to proselytize; we don't need to breed new enemies."

"Was a girl like Razan your enemy?"

"Like I said, she was a pain in my ass. She wasn't significant enough to be an enemy. She was, however, a convenient target, though I didn't ask my flock to murder her. That's not something I would do."

With every word, he was edging closer to Inaya. She didn't move, preoccupied by the view, by lights blinking from the hills. She repeated her question idly.

"What's the right tree, Pastor?"

He breathed into her ear. "If you're worried about sexual harass-ment, you should be looking at Apex Dynamics."

"Why?"

His hand landed on her shoulder.

"Heard the girl was unhappy there. You should look into that."

Because that was where the pastor's thoughts would naturally take him? Or because he'd had his ear to the ground and had heard a rumor?

"We know about the op-ed she wrote, opposing weapons of war."

"You don't know enough, it sounds like."

"Meaning?"

"Your job to figure it out, not mine to hand it to you."

"You're not concerned about the community you serve?"

He looked affronted. "The girl wasn't a member of my flock."

He approached Inaya by the window, his hand clamping down on her shoulder. "You interested in joining?" He whispered the words into her ear, his breath hot and moist. "I could make it worth your while. Teach you to look the other way when my Disciples get rowdy."

Inaya remained cool and undisturbed, shrugging his hand away. "I think you've forgotten that I listened to your sermon. Your style of worship isn't mine."

He tried to grasp her shoulder again. She evaded him neatly, and his momentum carried him forward into the window. He hit his head hard.

"Raghead bitch," he spat. He would have turned on her then, but anticipating it, she twisted one arm behind his back and held him against the window.

A little sigh left her body. It was good to have the truth confirmed. He may have been a pretender, stirring up his congregation for the benefit of ratings or what passed for fame and influence in his world. But it wasn't merely charlatanism—there was a core belief there. He'd sipped the Kool-Aid himself.

There was a pounding on the door, a rough male voice calling out.

"Get in here," Wayne shouted, sweating beneath the increased pressure of her arm.

The door flew open beneath the hard pressure of a man's shoulder. Lincoln West. He slammed the door behind him, swearing.

He was dressed as a Disciple, wearing his club colors. The rage in his eyes was very real.

"What the *fuck* do you think you're doing?"

He strode over to her, shoving her aside.

"You all right, Pastor? You need me to deal with her?"

Wayne held himself stiffly, his eyes gleaming with fury.

He shook his head. "Not this time. Grant will deal with it. It's an open-and-shut case of police brutality." He jabbed a finger at Inaya, a mark showing up on his wrist. "You'll be charged with assault."

Inaya edged around West, careful not to brush against him. If he was playing a part, he was doing it very well.

She slid her phone from her pocket, showing it to them. The recording function was on.

"And you'll be charged with offering me a bribe. Not to mention you resorted to racial slurs, and pointed the finger at one of your church's major corporate donors."

Wayne fell for it. "It's illegal to record someone without their knowledge," he blustered, subsiding into his chair.

"So sue me."

Wayne jerked his chin at West. "Deal with her, Ranger."

West seized her by the shoulders, lifted her up, and set her down on the opposite side of the desk in a stunning display of brute strength.

"Get the fuck out of here. If I see you around this church again, you won't be dealing with a man of God. You'll be dealing with me."

She ignored the threat, despite the fact that her shoulders were aching. He was looking out for her, but getting to Wayne was more important. She put her weight into her hands on the desk, eye to eye with Wayne.

"You said you didn't ask a congregant to murder Razan. But you've just told me about your Disciples." She turned her head to indicate West. "Did you ask them instead?"

Wayne didn't answer. West marched her to the door. As he pushed her through it with unwarranted force, she heard him whisper, "You're going to get yourself killed."

CHAPTER FIFTY

Late Sunday night, Inaya shut down her work on the case. She was tired, and she wanted to pray. She took the time to shower and change into clean clothes, wrapping her *shisha-lawn* prayer shawl around her head and torso. She'd made a space for prayer in the corner of her room facing the *qibla*. On a low table beside it was a much-loved copy of the Qur'an beside a vase filled with fresh flowers. Her mother-of-pearl *tasbih* rested on top of the Qur'an.

When her prayer was complete, she settled in on her carpet, her hands held up in supplication. She added a special *dua* for the murdered girls and asked for guidance in solving their murders. As a feeling of peace washed over her, she heard the doorbell ring.

She ignored it. Her cousin had once told her rituals couldn't be harmed when they were sacrificed for the ideals they stood for, yet she preferred to complete her prayer with total focus.

Someone else answered the door, voices fading into the background.

Nadia paused at her door, a glum expression on her face.

Inaya finished her *dua*, gracefully rising to her feet.

"Why do you look like someone who's just lost her best friend?"

Nadia shrugged, moving away. Inaya caught at her hand, dragging her sister inside. Reluctantly, Nadia perched on Inaya's bed, her posture defeated. Inaya sat down beside her.

"Tell me what's going on."

"There's nothing to tell," Nadia sniffed.

Inaya stroked her hair. "I *am* a detective, you know. You've hardly spoken in the last few weeks; you go to school late and you come back early—that's if you go at all. So tell me what gives. You know I'll keep it between us. Are you upset about some boy?"

Nadia's lower lip trembled. A sob broke from her chest.

Inaya hugged her shoulders. "You want to date someone and Baba won't let you?"

Nadia pushed her arms away. "It's not always about boys." Her voice was low and bitter. "At least not the way you think."

Inaya's stomach clenched, her instincts on alert. "Someone hurt you? Harassed you?"

Nadia nodded, rubbing her eyes with her hands. She met Inaya's gaze defiantly.

"It wasn't my fault. I didn't do anything to deserve it!"

"Of course you didn't." Inaya kept her voice soft and soothing. "You aren't to blame, Nadia, but you need to tell me what happened."

It burst from her sister, the pressure erupting at last. Inaya's cell phone buzzed, but not for a minute did Inaya think of the case. She was listening to Nadia's recital with a cold and furious anger, already making plans.

A classmate named Tyler Whitlock had been harassing Nadia, demanding her attention and resorting to crude remarks when she ignored him. And then one night after night class, he'd cornered her in the parking lot and put his hands on her. Not just on her but all over her. When she'd screamed and tried to fight him off, he'd punched her in the ribs. She'd been saved by her classmates, but hadn't filed a report. All of this had happened last month.

No wonder Nadia dreaded returning to class. No wonder she'd been miserable and silent.

Inaya rose from the bed and collected her notepad, her phone, and some tissues, then came back to sit beside her sister. Nadia took the tissues with a muffled thanks. When she'd cleaned her face and blown her nose, Inaya handed her the notepad with a pen.

"Write down the names of the witnesses for me."

Nadia looked at her, alarmed. "What are you going to do?"

"*You're* going to file a report. And I'm going to send officers to interview the witnesses who helped you, and to bring this dirtbag in."

Despite herself, Nadia laughed at Inaya's use of the word "dirtbag."

"I don't know," she said hesitantly. "I don't want to make a whole big thing of this."

Inaya knelt in front of her sister. "I know, sweetheart, I get it. But he could escalate, or he could do this to other girls, so we need to get it on record. We can't let him get away with violence. If you don't report this, he'll think he's safe."

She wiped her sister's face with a tissue, catching her own reflection in the mirror near the bed, the hardness behind her eyes. "He's not going to feel that way for long."

Nadia hiccupped over another sob. "Baba will kill him," she whispered.

Inaya clasped her sister's hands. "We won't tell Baba until after everything is sorted."

"What if he thinks I encouraged him?"

"Baba would never think that. He knows no woman is responsible for a man assaulting her, do you hear me, Nadia?"

Nadia's eyes were red and puffy, but some of the strain eased from her expression.

She began to scratch names down on the pad, Inaya standing over her shoulder.

"Does he follow you on social media?"

"I blocked him," Nadia whispered. "That made him mad. He used a fake account to get to me, and he's been following me around."

Shit, Inaya thought. Whitlock was a stalker. She made Nadia show her a picture of her assailant, screenshotting it for future reference. Then she took the list of names from her sister and tucked them into her purse.

"I'll deal with this, I promise. And I'll keep you informed every step of the way. Nothing about the process is going to take you by surprise. Your comfort and safety are my first priority."

Inaya slid her handbag over her shoulder, checked that her phone was charged, and then hugged Nadia again. "I've been called out, but we'll talk more when I get back. And in the meantime, talk to Noor. She's been worried about you too."

A little of the weight lifted, Nadia eyed Inaya. "You're something of a badass, *baji*."

Inaya knew otherwise.

But this was something she could handle, so she said, "There's nothing I wouldn't do for you and Noor."

Silence stretched between them. A deep voice could be heard from the foyer, speaking to their father. Inaya recognized it as Seif's, as did Nadia, whose delicate eyebrows lifted. "Lieutenant Seif came here to get you? What's up? Does he need some one-on-one time?"

"Nothing's up, so for God's sake, don't embarrass me."

Nadia grinned with a hint of her old mischief.

"No need—you've already gone red, but I'd blush too if my boss was that hot."

Inaya mock-growled at Nadia, secretly relieved that her sense of mischief had returned.

CHAPTER FIFTY-ONE

"You look upset."

Seif drove them up the long road to the church. He'd gotten a tip that Pastor Wayne was holding a meeting with the Disciples there, a meeting that had been hastily arranged in the wake of her interview with the pastor.

The hills dashed up against the horizon, ominous in the dark, the air smelling of the falls. Inaya loved evenings in the Falls. The chill of the desert climate, the stars pinned to bands of blue on the lower horizon, the howl of a coyote on the wind.

"Should I not have come to your house?"

Inaya's thoughts were still on Nadia. "You could have texted me and saved yourself a drive," she said.

"I did. Twice. You didn't answer."

Inaya looked down at her phone, switching between the photograph of Tyler Whitlock and her messages. Seif was right. He'd texted twice telling her to meet him at the church.

He shrugged, an easy ripple of his shoulders. "You were praying."

When his eyes had widened at the sight of Inaya covered by her shawl, she'd fidgeted with her chador, not sure how to respond to his evident interest.

Her hand slipped on her phone, pulling up the screenshot again.

"Who's that?" Seif asked. "One of Kerr's friends?"

With an effort, Inaya focused on his question. She guessed that

Whitlock would be in his early twenties like Nadia, a few years older than Campbell Kerr and his friends.

"No. He's just—"

"Someone who upset you," Seif guessed.

She'd forgotten how perceptive he was. Wondering if she should, she told him about Nadia. She didn't downplay the incident, and listening to her, neither did Seif.

He let her finish, then a wall of heat hit her. It took her a moment to recognize that it was coming from Seif.

In clipped tones, he made her go over her planned response.

When she was done, he directed, "You turn this over to the Sexual Assault Unit; they'll see it through, get the witnesses on record. You'll need to bring your sister in. No arrest tomorrow, but the day after, we'll see."

She was a little disappointed in his response until he added, "Forward his name and photograph to me. I'll check for priors."

"I can do that myself."

He pulled the car into a parking spot behind the church, opposite a row of Harleys.

"Get me, Inaya."

She sat up at his tone, giving him her full attention.

His black eyes burned into hers. "I don't like it when men assault women. So you work the system, let me take care of the rest."

Her mouth dropped open. Was he suggesting that he planned to do something to Whitlock?

"I can—" she began.

"Whitlock's not getting within fifty feet of you."

He exited the car, leaving her with no choice but to do the same. His gaze was fixed on the Harleys. There were twelve bikes and two cars in the lot; the outer lights were dimmed and very little light was showing from the interior of the church. Seif made for the side door, the only door that was lit. He pushed it open, letting Inaya precede him.

They were huddled together in a small vestibule, but the pastor's voice reached them from the stage of the auditorium where he'd given his sermon. The house lights were down, the screens blanked out, only the pastor on the stage.

"You go ahead." Seif indicated the aisle that led down to the stage.

Inaya peeked around the corner. The Disciples were there in their club leathers, occupying the first few rows, Hardtack out on bail, and Ranger West spread out across three chairs, bored by the pastor's ramblings, keeping an eye on his phone. The sheriff wasn't seated with them. He was leaning against the wall opposite the stage, close to the Disciples, his arms crossed over his burly chest, his jaw clamped tight. There were no women in the audience, and no other congregants in the huge, empty hall. Inaya widened her eyes at Seif.

"By myself?" she whispered, reassuring herself that her gun was in its holster.

"You'll be covered." He jerked his chin at West. "I'll come down the other aisle."

He disappeared behind the booth that housed the sound system.

Keeping close to the shadows, Inaya edged into the aisle farthest from the group. She remembered that the chairs didn't creak, so she slipped silently into one to the right of the sound booth. The stage lights held the pastor in their glare, the auditorium otherwise dark.

"This isn't the time for hell-raising, boys," Wayne was saying. His bland, good-looking face was red. "You need to lie low until these fucking foreigners get the hell out of our town." He grimaced at West. "Apologies on account of your kid."

Hardtack snorted. "She's a half-breed, not a foreigner."

West punched Hardtack hard in the arm. "No one calls my kid a half-breed."

The punch sounded like it had cracked bones, and Inaya was amazed that Hardtack hadn't doubled over. Wayne made soothing sounds. Hardtack put his hands up in apology.

"Shit, man, didn't mean nothing by it."

West shrugged. "Don't mix my kid up with fucking ragheads."

"Of course, of course." Wayne looked bewildered by the confrontation he'd provoked, but there was a gleam to his eye that made Inaya wonder if he was trying to draw West out, get him to betray himself.

Or maybe she was extra-anxious because she knew West was undercover. He'd slouched back into his chair, idly swiping at his phone.

Inaya's teeth scored her underlip. She sent West a mental warning, turning her head to the left. There was no sign of Seif prowling down the aisle yet, so she stayed in place.

"Two things," Wayne went on. "We got nothing to do with this murder, though they're trying to pin it on us. But you guys"—he pinned Hardtack with his gaze—"buzzing the enemy's house, blowing up Cyrine's café . . . Cyrine didn't like that, and neither do I. Cyrine's one of us."

"Bullshit." Hardtack stormed the stage, light glaring off his cut. The sheriff shifted his position minutely, but both Hardtack and Inaya caught it. The movement was a threat. Hardtack subsided. "You see those pictures in her store? Fucking Beirut. You remember Beirut? Two hundred and twenty Marines dead." He spat into his palm, wiping it on the arm of his chair.

Inaya was surprised that his memory was so fresh. The barracks bombing in Beirut had taken place in 1982.

"She's a good Christian woman," Wayne appealed to the sheriff. "Isn't she?"

The sheriff joined him on the stage. "It would seem so." He studied Wayne for a moment, a curl to his lip, as if the pastor was more trouble than he was worth. Wayne, expansive and genial moments before, shrank into himself a little, pale beneath his Colorado tan. "Get your youth volunteers out to help Cyrine at the bakery. I've got a reporter who will cover it."

He swept off his hat, a thick swath of hair falling over his forehead. When he tipped back his head to shift it, his gaze landed on Inaya at the back of the auditorium.

"*You.*" He pointed a finger with lethal intent. "What the *fuck* are you doing here?"

Inaya thought of saying "Attending church" as a cheeky response, but the Disciples had turned as one, a dozen tattooed, brawny men who were looking for a fight. She made eye contact with the sheriff, then deliberately looked up at the surveillance cameras that covered every inch of the hall. Seif's absence was notable and had her panicking, but though every instinct was screaming that she ease her way back to the door, she made her way down the aisle instead, stopping before she reached the bikers.

"I thought I might learn something relevant to my investigation. I'm wondering what *you're* doing here, Sheriff." She itched to confront him with the evidence Areesha had gathered. She controlled herself—when they tackled Grant, they'd have to make it stick.

She ignored the Disciples as if she couldn't hear their angry rumbling, speaking directly to the sheriff. If she had a prayer of getting out of there unharmed, it lay in the sheriff's hands.

"My job," he said bluntly. "Staying in touch with my constituents. Making sure their needs are met."

She didn't buy it. He was here to do damage control. But just how much influence did the sheriff have over the pastor and his bikers?

"This is a private meeting," Wayne sputtered. "You've got no right to trespass."

Inaya crossed over the auditorium to the far side of the stage, closer to Addison Grant. Closer to West too. He was still slouched in his seat in his indolent pose, but his eyes were sharp and alert beneath their heavy lids. Fixed on her. Tracking her. A slight shake of his head condemned her for getting herself into this situation.

Seif had brought her here, she wanted to protest, but Seif was nowhere around. And West couldn't act as her backup without blowing his cover. She let her eyes sweep the depths of the stage, noting the huge television screens and the billboards of Wayne with his shiny white smile, his arms draped around his twentysomething volunteers. This time she paid attention to the absence of a cross or crucifix.

Oh well. In for a penny, in for a pound. "Just to confirm, Pastor, it *was* the Disciples who firebombed Cyrine's bakery? Was that at your direction?"

West sliced another look at her, his face hard with warning.

Wayne's oily facade dropped over him like a cloak. "Now, now, Little Miss Big Britches, I think you heard me say the opposite. That members of this congregation"—a wide sweep of his arm indicated the Disciples—"shouldn't be bothering the good folks of this community."

"You called the Elkaders 'the enemy.'"

She could see Wayne thinking back on his words. "Not *our* enemies—enemies of Christ. Enemies of God's salvation."

"How do you figure that?"

God help her, why was she taunting Wayne in a roomful of rabble-rousing bikers?

"If you don't accept Jesus Christ as your Lord and Savior, what else can you be?"

Wayne's voice was getting stronger. He was gaining confidence as he spoke. Inaya cut him off before he could work himself up.

"I think you can be assured the Elkaders love Jesus."

Wayne squinted down at her from the stage. "How would you know that?" He wet his lips with a fleshy tongue. "Unless you're tight with them. On the inside, so to speak."

The hall went wired. She'd underestimated her predicament.

A handful of the Disciples moved, circling her on the floor. Taller and broader than her, they blocked any route of escape. Their shoulders brushed together, hiding the sheriff from her view. She stayed calm, doing a slow rotation until she'd made eye contact with each one of them.

These weren't part-timers, they were all the way in. They weren't frightened of authority: they relished the challenge she posed.

They ran drugs and guns, West had said. And they were equipped with the know-how and equipment to launch firebombs. But were they so far gone as to have committed murder? Could these men have abducted the two Somali teens?

She decided to ask them.

"Did you kill Razan Elkader? Or Barkhudo Abdi and Khadijah Diriye?"

She placed her hands on her waist, easing her blazer back to reveal the fact that she was armed.

A Disciple spat at her feet. She didn't flinch, keeping her gun hand loose. It wasn't Hardtack. She didn't know this one. Like West, he possessed a certain attraction. Symmetrical features, a thick head of hair, blue eyes, three black teardrops tattooed under his left eye. His eyes were cold and dead. Did the teardrops represent his kills?

"You're a biker bigot," he told her. "Fucking coming in here and accusing us of that."

So maybe not, then. And it was true. Except for the casual bikers who rode the Rockies, she assumed most bikers were criminals, whether they belonged to a gang or a motorcycle club.

"One of you firebombed a café while I was in it. A whole group of you came to the Elkaders' home to harass them, again while I was there. I'm my own eyewitness, so forgive me if I don't share your interpretation of Christian charity."

The cold, dead eyes bored through her.

Taking a chance, she asked, "If it wasn't you, then who? Bikers have their ear to the ground. They know all the bad apples."

Low and rough, he said, "That don't mean we share info with the pigs."

The threat of the men at her back became electric, but she told herself she was holding three aces: Seif, the sheriff, and West.

They couldn't kill her in front of so many witnesses—in front of the pastor of a church, for God's sake. It would come back on the sheriff, and she'd clearly heard him say he didn't want another shitstorm. She had her phone on her. Seif probably did as well, so they could track them to the same spot by triangulating their phones.

So no, they wouldn't kill her. Rough her up a little, maybe. She refused to consider that they might do other things. Seif was her backup. He'd never let it happen.

Get me, Inaya. Whitlock isn't getting within fifty feet of you.

All right. If he was so protective of her, then where the hell was he?

She didn't have to wait for Seif. Another big man cut through the circle. West, thank God. He shoved her back up the aisle with an ungentle hand.

"Wanna get back to my kid. The pastor doesn't want trouble. Neither does the sheriff. That's the gist of this meeting, yeah? So why are we hassling a pig?"

He gave Inaya another shove that sent her stumbling. Fleeting eye contact with West told her he was furious with her. He backed her up the aisle, one belligerent step at a time, and when she was far enough away from the others, he muttered, "They don't know anything. If they did, I would have passed it to Seif. Get yourself out of here, Brazil. These men are not playing."

"Get your hands off me!" she yelled for effect, but she scrambled back to the vestibule while the men's derisive laughter echoed after her.

West had left off his pursuit, but another pair of boots dogged her. She put her hand on the door. A male arm reached over her head to slam it shut again.

Grant. And unlike Wayne or the Disciples, he wasn't a man to be fooled.

"My jurisdiction," he rumbled at her.

"My investigation," she fought back. His chin dipped. His hand snaked inside her blazer, a movement so quick and skillful he had her gun in his hand before she knew it. He flipped it and ejected the clip. "Seems like you don't know what boundaries not to cross."

He crowded her against the door. She gave him a furious scowl, shoving one hand in his chest. He picked up her hand and bent it back at the wrist. She let out a little cry.

"The police commissioner and I go way back. A word in his ear and this parody of a policing unit . . . Community Response, for Christ's sake, gets folded up like a tent." He tapped her nose with the butt of her gun. "Know your place. Run around town if you must, but don't try to play our game." He let his eyes roam her face. "You don't belong here, princess."

"Razan Elkader's murder isn't a game. I'm here to do a job, and I won't let you stop me."

He twisted her wrist sharply.

The door opened behind her. She fell back as Grant released her.

A hard arm reached around her. Not to steady her, but to take her gun from the sheriff, who proffered it butt-first.

"I've got this, Grant." Seif's voice, just above her ear. He tucked her gun into her back.

She grappled with hearing that tone from Seif. Deferential. Almost ingratiating. She whipped around to turn her fury on him. Seif's hand crushed the point of her shoulder. She gasped and kicked him in the shin.

"You've got a spitfire there," Grant observed. His man-to-man mockery was the last straw for Inaya. She turned back to give him a piece of her mind. Seif caught her around the waist so that her back was to his chest.

"She's not that easy to control," he said in the same dismissive tone the sheriff had used. His fingers bit into her ribs. "Don't know how she found out about your meeting, but I'm here to collect her. Sorry to bother you, Grant. It won't happen again."

Grant eased back on the balls of his feet, his gaze still watchful.

"See that it doesn't."

Seif jerked Inaya back out the door. Grant tossed him the clip.

"Last warning, Seif, or you'll be hearing from the commissioner."

"Understood. Like I said, she's not easy to control."

"Then find another way to burn her out."

He shut the door in their faces. Inaya heard the lock turn.

Frustrated and furious, she turned her anger on Seif. "Where did you disappear to? You brought me here, then left me to that pack of wolves!"

"Quiet."

He jogged back to the car, not waiting for her to follow. Inaya took her time joining him, even when he flashed the lights at her.

She was mulling his words. *Don't know how she found out about your meeting, but I'm here to collect her.*

He'd lied to Grant. And his attitude was different from his typical effortless authority. She'd seen him use that same air of deference with senior officers at their station. It made him seem like an opportunist. Humbling himself like he knew his place with the men in charge.

Not the way she knew him to be.

Get me, Inaya.

She didn't get him at all. She slid into her seat, leaving her belt unbuckled.

"Fasten your seat belt, Rahman." He sounded as if the very sight of her irritated him, which it would if she'd fumbled his game. Whatever game he was playing, on a board she couldn't see. Just like Lincoln West.

She froze in her seat.

Just like Lincoln West.

Her hand reached out to the gearshift, putting the car back in park.

"Not until you tell me what op you're running on the side."

CHAPTER FIFTY-TWO

He concentrated on the road rather than Inaya, his thoughts ticking over. He wasn't authorized to tell her the truth. She might keep it to herself, she might use it against him, she might hold it in reserve, a card to play at a later date so she could refuse his orders. Or so she could get something she wanted out of him.

He told himself this even though he knew better. Inaya had integrity. It was her recklessness that made her unpredictable. He'd told her to pay attention to the meeting. He hadn't told her to challenge Wayne, the sheriff, or a dozen Disciples. She'd done all three.

It might have gone better if he'd been up front with her, instead of ducking out to Wayne's office. The locks were easy to pick, both on his door and his desk. He'd gone through Wayne's papers in meticulous detail, finding no proof of kickbacks. Then he'd discovered a safe he had no chance of accessing because he had to get back to Inaya. Too late, as it turned out. She'd gotten herself into plenty of trouble in the time he'd left her alone.

Thirty minutes later he turned off the highway onto University, where the neighborhoods merged with fast-food joints that served the student community. He bypassed these to go to Bonnie Brae. Here, trees extended their branches across the road, dappling his car with shadows.

"Where are you taking me?"

There was unease in her voice. Good. Maybe she'd stop charging into new scenarios like she was indestructible. West being on site when Seif wasn't covering her was no guarantee she'd be safe. West was in deep with the Disciples. He might not be willing to sacrifice the work he'd put in to keep Inaya safe.

If he hadn't needed to keep the sheriff and the pastor distracted, he wouldn't have called on her for backup. If he'd still trusted him, he would have called on Jaime, or possibly on Cat. But favoritism or not, he did his best to keep Catalina out of high-risk situations. She'd been battered by her dealings with ICE, and was under family pressure to leave the police. He did what he could to make her feel safe; he didn't want to lose her.

The risk he'd taken with Inaya—he might as well admit he wanted her with him. He wanted to see her again, and not at the shop, where he had to maintain his distance. He was close to getting the goods on Grant, yet here he was risking it for a shot at a woman who wouldn't be interested in something less than permanent. He respected that, but it was a hell of an inconvenience.

He angled his jaw so he could keep her in view.

Her sisters, he could see; anyone would want in there. But Inaya wasn't like them. She was . . . *extraordinary,* his mind supplied.

He'd planned to say the opposite, but what was the point of lying to himself any longer. He wouldn't be making moves on her if she weren't.

"Why are we at the university?" she persisted.

He pulled in opposite the new library of the University of Denver. The campus had beautiful grounds. The older buildings were approached through a circular drive, Admissions on the right, the refurbished library behind it, two other old-stone buildings at the bottom of the circle and to the left. Stately buildings that had grown old together, trees giving much-needed shade in the sunlight, dull red ivy on the buildings. Good signage, lights on the path.

"Which building does your sister have her classes in?"

He turned to look at her, taking in her surprise.

"You can't see it from here, but it's the law building. Ricketson." She seemed to be having difficulty coming up with what to say next, so he came to the point.

"Just want to canvass the places where Whitlock thinks she's vulnerable."

"You can't . . . *do* anything."

"Forewarned is forearmed." He left it at that, getting down to business. With what he had planned for Whitlock, he didn't want her involved. He'd also made up his mind about confiding in her. He wasn't coming clean. "I'm not running an op. I thought it would be worthwhile to search the pastor's study."

"Without a warrant?" Her eyes and mouth went round, and his gut registered just how much he liked that expression on her face, her quickness not as much.

"If I'd found anything incriminating, I'd have come up with reasonable grounds."

"No wonder people don't like the police. You've just proved we can't be trusted."

He laughed, surprising himself, but when Inaya joined in he thought, *God, what a beautiful sound.*

The car enclosed them in an atmosphere of intimacy, warm and dark, breathing in each other's air, near enough to touch, though he'd kept himself in check out of respect for her. Not as easy as he thought it would be.

"So you came up with nothing."

"There's a safe in the office I couldn't get into. Maybe there's something there."

"Like what?" she sounded suspicious. "Written orders to Hardtack and company on executing Razan? Doesn't seem likely."

She spent the next few minutes repeating Rupi Sandhu's conclusions about the Virgin Orans, giving them greater emphasis than the first time she'd briefed the team. She told him about the mosaic in a cathedral in Ukraine. He gathered that the gist of it was that the Crucifixion was a blind, but the Virgin Orans mosaic might help them find their killer.

"The person who'll have the most insight into the mosaic vis-à-vis the murder is Catalina. If you haven't already, bring her up to speed in the morning."

He noticed Inaya's frown. It tweaked a velvety mole at the corner of her eyebrow that fascinated him, a fascination he covered by speaking.

"If Rupi thinks Razan's killer deliberately misled us, that means he wasn't expecting us to find out about the mosaic. If we want to play that angle against him, the fewer people who know about it, the better. But ask Catalina for her thoughts. Now, show me the law building."

Inaya looked at him doubtfully. "I don't think—"

He gentled his voice. "You can trust me, Inaya."

"It's not that." Her voice was so soft, he leaned in to hear her, gratified she didn't retreat. "There's very few of us in a position like yours, because we're still seen as untrustworthy. If you do something to Whitlock—warn him off, hurt him—it could blow back on you, but it doesn't just affect *you*. It will affect all of us, including Cat."

He knew that in one sense she was talking about cops from minority communities. But in another, her reference was strictly to Muslims.

Instead of staying on that track, he asked, "Why are you singling out Catalina?"

"Because *you* single her out. You do it all the time."

She sounded jealous. The thought pleased him, even though she was off base. He had no romantic interest in Catalina: he'd hired her because of the work she'd done with the undocumented. He'd read through her history with ICE and asked her to confide in him, as a condition of bringing her on board. He liked to know his people, and his respect for Catalina was unequivocal. He hadn't felt the same about Inaya, ambivalent about her from the start. He'd wanted her to have another chance, knew she'd be good at the job, but he'd been wary of getting too close—wary of things he refused to admit they shared.

Inaya didn't elaborate, and the silence began to eat at him, though he pretended to be scoping out the law building, before he turned back the way they'd come. Down the leafy parade of University that connected with the exit to Blackwater, his sense of being unfairly accused building up inside. Rahman wasn't some paragon who could sit in judgment. Everyone who did this job had lines they were willing to cross.

Nervously, her fingers tapped out a rhythm on her knee. "You can't deny you give Cat extra consideration."

"Consideration you want? You need me to take it easy on you, Rahman?"

"Not at all, *sir*." He felt the heat of her glare singe his cheek. "Favor Cat, don't favor Cat, it's all the same to me."

He grunted. "You think you had it rough?" He felt her freeze. "Catalina came to us from Nogales. Do you know what that means?"

"I know she's spent most of her life working on behalf of undocumented workers. I think that's amazing." Her words rang with pride in her friend.

He set about deflating it. "That's as far as you got?"

Inaya didn't get angry. She slumped back in her seat, and when she spoke, there was a tinge of horror in her voice.

"What did I miss?"

"You missed the Border Patrol. You missed her encounters with ICE." He wasn't angry anymore, because Inaya's expressive face showed the depths of her dismay. "If I'm kind to Catalina, it's because I know what she's been through at their hands. Maybe one day she'll tell you about it herself—she had no choice with me."

She gave this some thought, so silent he could hear his own heartbeat.

"Can I ask you something?"

"Go ahead." He tried to sound calm, though his heart was thumping.

"When am I 'Inaya,' and when am I 'Rahman'?"

He pulled over short of her driveway, out of sight of her house. He exited the car and she did the same, facing him across the hood. The trees in her development were saplings, the streetlamps clean and angular, casting a glow on her face.

"You know the answer to that."

"I do?"

"It lines up with those times you call me Qas." He smiled to himself, liking the way her accent modified the Arabic "Q" so it was softer on the ear.

She held his gaze, letting him see what she wanted.

He didn't know how to respond. He didn't know what he was doing here, lingering with her after dark, when he knew down to his bones he wasn't the kind of man she needed.

"I can't make you any promises."

Now the shield came down. "I didn't ask you to."

Oh, she'd asked him with that look, but he let her have that. "Nothing else from the meeting?"

She was too proud to press him, and maybe when he was done with Grant, he'd knock some sense into himself.

"There *was* something." The eager light that warmed her brown eyes appeared again. "Not from Wayne or the sheriff, apart from the standard sexism." She shot him a droll look, and he grinned. He motioned for her to continue.

"If you were to ask me, I'd say the pastor was telling the truth. They don't want attention. They don't want the Disciples to bring it to them. Proselytizing, yes. Harassment, yes. But he doesn't sound as if he's up for escalation, and so far I can't see a motive."

"Areesha will give you plenty of motive."

"For the Black community, maybe. But Razan's body wasn't hidden, which makes it hard to buy racism as the motive. How would that fit with the mosaic?" She pursed her lips and stared into the distance. "Unless you have some other reason to suspect the pastor?"

Seif hesitated. He had to be careful here. "The church is one of the main donors to Grant's reelection campaign. If Grant is caught up in this, it could be that Wayne is too."

He knew his excuse was weak as soon as the words came out of his mouth.

"Maybe." She gave him another chance. "It doesn't sound like reason enough to conduct a search without a warrant."

"I was playing all the angles."

That wasn't true. And from her obvious disappointment, Inaya knew it too.

She said good night quietly, and didn't turn back to wave.

Just as well. He was in too deep with her.

CHAPTER FIFTY-THREE

As promised, Inaya took Nadia with her to the station in the morning. Her sister wasn't wearing makeup, and she'd dressed to avoid attention in a baggy brown jumpsuit. Inaya hated seeing her like this, her confidence damaged by Whitlock. They'd gone back and forth over Inaya's insistence that she report the assault; eventually Inaya had overcome her sister's fears.

But Nadia's doubts surfaced again. She tried to hang back at the station, so Inaya slid an arm around her shoulders. "It's all right, I won't leave you. And I promise you, my colleagues will be gentle. If it gets to be too much, you can take a break."

"Please, *baji*. Don't make me do this. It's not worth ruining someone's life."

"I'm not making you do this—your conscience is making you do this." Inaya could be as patient as Nadia needed her to be, she was still going to see this through. "I know you have a soft heart, honey, but you need to focus on his actions—Whitlock isn't innocent." She put steel into her voice. "Your life is just as valuable as his."

Nadia began to cry as beautifully as she did everything else, tears pooling in her gem-like eyes. Sighing at this part of the process, Inaya passed her a tissue. "Tears don't work on me, kid." She brushed a strand of hair from Nadia's pale cheek. "Think about the next girl, and the next. You have a duty here. Now are you a Pathan, or not?"

The reminder of their warrior ancestors was meant to make Nadia laugh.

Nadia sniffed, dabbing her eyes with graceful fingers. "You know you're a bully, right?" But her jaw had firmed. As frightening as it was, she'd see it through.

Inaya's lips quirked. "I can't watch you suffer if I can do something about it. That's in the big-sister manual."

Nadia arched a perfect brow. "I'd like to see that manual some-time."

Inaya pretended to zip her lips. "Top secret, kid."

She hustled Nadia through the doors, ignoring her muttered threats.

God willing, her sister would be fine.

After Nadia made her report, Inaya dropped her back home. Her next appointment was at the falls, and she enjoyed the peaceful drive, relieved that the interview was behind them.

Blackwater lay in the shadow of the Front Range, and it was almost impossible to believe that dark deeds like the murder of three young girls, or the assault on her sister, had taken place in its environs. She'd thought to herself many times that the town was too shiny, too per-fect, a vision of Americana, with fern-green pastures unfurling north of the reservoir, and pickup trucks and ranches that spoke of a vanished dream: the hardworking people of the heartland.

But there were hate crimes and harassment in this heartland, com-munities who lived at the mercy of their employers, and vigilantes and cops who were there to make them obey. In Chicago, the exercise of power was naked and direct; she knew that all too well. Blackwater's old-fashioned gentility masked its insistence on the status quo, an in-sight that made her uneasy.

She was getting morbid, forgetting the welcome of people like Mad-dalena and Cyrine, the dedication of Julius Stanger to his work, the friend-ship she had forged with Catalina and Jaime. Her thoughts turned around again: how could Jaime have abandoned her at the plant? She had given her word to Areesha that Jaime was someone she could trust. What could have motivated him? He was nothing like the sheriff's men. She hated it for all of them that Jaime had proven her wrong. He'd shattered any last illusions she might have held, and when Areesha came to know of it, her belief that the police were incapable of reform would be handily confirmed.

But maybe West had something to tell her that would help. She parked near the gazebo where she was meeting Lincoln West. She'd been headed in to work, dreading seeing Seif the morning after their confrontation, and she welcomed the chance to delay follow-up.

The air held the presentiment of heat, though a chill lay over the pale glare of the sun. West stood in the shadows, out of sight of the street. When he saw her, he strode down the path behind the falls. The current was heavy in the mornings, the noise from the falls drowning out secondary noise. The last time she'd been here, she'd been chasing the Disciple who had thrown her in the pond. She wondered what West had in mind, why he'd called her and not Seif. Did she strike him as more vulnerable? More amenable to pressure? Last night, she thought he'd threatened her out of concern for her safety—what if he had other motives?

West had shaved this morning, and instead of his leather vest, he was wearing a denim jacket over a white T-shirt that did little to disguise his tattoos. Inaya caught a glimpse of a black holster under the bulky jacket; he'd come to their meeting armed.

She didn't bother with pleasantries. "What if someone sees you with me?"

He bent his head down to hear her under the roar of the falls, stepping a little too close. Inaya backed away.

"You're jumpy, Brazil. Not wearing a wire, are you?"

The way he said it made her look around. No one could see them from the street. She was alone with a man she didn't really know, and she'd told no one about the meeting. Her fears were distorted, Nadia's testimony fresh in her mind.

"Answer me!"

Her voice dried up in her throat. West's easygoing demeanor was wiped out by sheer fury. She backed away from him, coming up against the railing.

"Hell with this," West growled. "I've put too much time in to risk you blowing my cover. Seif said I could trust you—looks like he's a fool."

He grasped her shoulders with his big hands, jerking her close, one hand sliding down to yank her shirt free from her trousers, his hand brushing naked skin. The touch electrified her.

The roar of the falls filled her ears, water swirling everywhere. A stench rose up from the pond—*No, wait, the pond didn't stink, the water was fresh and clear*—but she could smell it, feel it in her nose and mouth—why? A hard hand jerked her back by the hair. Her hair—why was her hair uncovered? A brute of a man crowded her, his size overwhelming, and her mind went blank. She was falling, spiraling away. . . .

She was in the women's bathroom. She finished washing her hands and tidied her headscarf in the mirror. The lights flickered on and off. Dread filled her as she turned to face the door.

Six CPD officers were barricading the exit.

She didn't hesitate. There was no way past them, so she locked herself in one of the stalls, her hands shaking as she searched for her phone. She made a 911 call and in a low voice stated the nature of her emergency, getting it on record. She left the line open and texted a friend in her unit, then sent another text to her father. She didn't know who to call when the cops were dirty, and she had a sudden sharp understanding of her constituents' complaints.

Where did you turn when those who were meant to help you were the ones you needed to be saved from?

Someone hammered at the door, the blow so powerful that Inaya fell against the toilet.

"You have the fucking nerve to try to bring down Egan?"

Her voice high-pitched with terror, she squeaked, "I'm just doing my job."

The hammer blow came again, but worse, the doors to the stalls on either side of hers were wrenched open. Since they couldn't rip her door off the hinge, they were scrambling up on the toilets. The door went all the way to the ground, they couldn't drag her out from under it, so she shrunk down as small as she could beside the toilet.

A cop named Dixon who was lean and wiry jumped down into the stall.

Inaya began to shout names into her phone.

She was snatched up, and dropped the phone on the floor. Now she began to scream as Dixon boosted her up to another cop named Schierholtz, a strong, beefy man who pulled her up by her arms. They wrestled her out of the stall into the open space.

She headbutted Schierholtz and scrambled all the way back to the dryers. Two other cops were barring the door, the rest advancing on her.

She planted her feet and grabbed her gun.

She aimed it at John Broda, the one who had to be the ringleader.

"You shoot, we shoot back. That would solve the problem."

They hadn't picked up her phone, so she spoke overloud, naming each man she could see, finishing with "You're good cops. Why do you want to go down because of Egan? We have to stand for something better."

Broda moved forward until he was within arm's reach of her gun.

He was going to try to grab it. She fired past his shoulder, the bullet scoring straight to a wall. Chunks of plaster rained down near the exit.

Broda flinched; everyone else stood still.

"We're just here for a chat."

Inaya didn't believe them, but a little of her tension eased. She'd considered the worst: a gang rape or six bullets in her body, one of them drilled between her eyes, or in the back of her head, execution-style, while she was on her knees.

"A chat?" She looked to Dixon. "You put your hands on me."

"You put Egan in the hole," Broda fired back.

Inaya's free hand wiped her forehead. She was strangely cold, yet she could feel sweat on her forehead. Dixon and Schierholtz were inching forward. She fired another shot—somebody would hear it and come running.

They stopped again.

She turned her gun back on Broda. "Marcus isn't Egan's only victim. You know he's bad, he's dragging the whole force down—why are you covering for him, when we're meant to serve these communities?"

Even as she said it, she knew how foolish it was. Schierholtz smirked, but it was Broda who said, "Where've you been, Rahman? The community is the fucking enemy. I get home at night, my wife and kids breathe easy. They don't take my safety for granted."

Inaya wrapped both hands around the grip of her gun. Her shoulder was getting tired, her eyes pinned to Broda's.

"Marcus McBride was someone's son. His parents don't take it for granted their kids are coming home, either. None of our complainants do, and that shouldn't be because of us."

"Fuck," Broda said to the others. "Will you listen to this bitch? She's been here five years, and she still doesn't know how it works."

The others laughed.

Inaya's gun wavered. "Please," she said. "Look, I'll drop it. I'll do what you want me to do, just let me out of here."

"Yeah you will," Broda answered, right before he rushed her.

The gun flew from her hand, spiraling across the floor until a cop at the door stopped it with his boot.

Broda dragged her forward. Dixon pinned her arms.

"No!" she screamed, her fears resurgent. Broda shoved her down to the sink.

Hands scrabbled at the back of her head. With stunning force, her headscarf was wrenched from her head, her face pressed so hard to the granite that she thought her cheekbone would shatter. She tried to kick behind her. Someone caught at her legs and she was airborne, and then she was back in the stall, her head shoved down the toilet while the flush ran and ran, her face totally submerged.

She choked and they yanked her back, spluttering water, then immersed her again, epithets flying thick and furious in the air as hard hands subdued her struggles. Red bubbles burst behind her eyes. She blacked out, but came to again when she was heaved up bodily, then flung down on the floor.

Boots came at her, but they didn't kick her. There was total silence as she coughed her way back to life, her torso racked by the need to breathe.

And then she realized they were filming her, playing with her hair, tugging off her ponytail holder, her hair flying everywhere. It was black, thick, and straight. And now it was made obscene by her dunking in the toilet.

Their eyes and hands were on her and all of it was obscene.

All of it made her feel unclean.

"Fucking raghead," Broda said. He pulled her hair once and let it go.

Wearily, she slid up against the wall, every inch of her body aching, her ribs either bruised or broken, her lungs still heaving as she spat out water.

Broda knelt down so they were face-to-face; Schierholtz held the camera.

"Now you get it," he told her. "Next time you stay down."

She was reckless enough to venture, "I'll report you. You're all going down with Egan."

Broda kicked her hard in the ribs, so hard that she almost blacked out again. In all her training, no one had told her that violence could be so intimate that it would burrow down inside you and make you forget who you were. She was stunned into silence.

Broda gestured to Dixon, who gave him another phone. This one was held up to her face as water dripped into her eyes. She wiped it with a sleeve, knowing there was worse to come.

"Pretty," Broda said.

He was talking about her sisters, their pictures displayed on his phone.

"They're young but still fuckable, and my boys have appetites." He leaned in close, his breath hot and heavy on her cheek. She began to tremble again. "We know where they go to school. We know the routes they take to come and go. We know they say they're at the library when they're with their friends." He snapped his fingers in her face. Her body jerked in response. "They can go missing in the blink of an eye. And when we send them back to you—if we don't leave them in a ditch—they won't be anywhere near as pretty as they are right now."

Inaya stared into the eyes under the jutting brow and knew he meant every word. Her insides sagged. Her heart sank like a stone.

"Gun," he barked, and she jumped again, hating herself for her cowardice.

Her gun slid across the floor. Broda placed it in her hands.

A toilet flushed and then choked like it had been plugged by something thick.

"Your rag," Broda said. His thick fingers trailed down the length of her long hair. "Funny." He grinned to the others. "Rahman gives new meaning to 'being on the rag.'"

The others laughed again, the sound a little forced.

Her eyelids drooping, her ribs burning with pain, she realized they were getting agitated. She'd fired two shots, and they'd been with her too long.

"You get me now?" Broda asked, shoving the phone in her face.

"I get you," she panted. "Please don't hurt my family."

"That depends on you, Rahman. You know what you need to do."

She did. She might have a recording on her phone, but she knew she would never use it. If anything happened to her sisters, her family would never recover.

The platitudes she had offered to Jenella McBride now tasted like chaff in her mouth. How could she have thought she knew the other woman's suffering? The terror and dread became so routine, they left a person numb. You stripped a person's humanity away, and all you had left was the acceptance of loss, the banality of tragedy.

She thought courage was baked into her skin, her image of herself pompous and overblown. Now she knew otherwise, sunk by the fear of harm done and further violence promised. She wasn't worthy of standing in the same room as Jenella, whose dignity remained unimpaired even when there was no one to fight her corner. If courage was baked into anyone's skin, it was Jenella's. No wonder she'd turned to her own community rather than to Inaya.

To her horror, she realized she was crying when Broda wiped his palm across her cheek. Inaya shuddered at the touch, at his brutal yet easy handling of her body.

Watching her face, he knew he had won this round.

Dixon stomped to a stall and gathered up her cell phone. He'd seen it after all; he'd just let her think she had a chance. She'd been a quixotic fool, thinking she could take them on.

Dixon kicked open a second door and dropped the phone in the toilet on top of her scarf. Then he flushed it again.

They left her in the bathroom. No one else came in. Despite the gunshots, word must have gone around that a lesson was being taught to the fiery young crusader at COPA. The one who thought that accountability had some meaning in their work.

She stopped wasting time on self-pity.

She needed to get out of there. She touched a hand to her ribs and groaned. Broken, for sure. Even getting off the floor would be hard, but she did it, breathing harshly at every jolt.

For a moment, she simply rested, taking stock of her situation. She inched toward the paper towel rolls—thank God, they hadn't given way to air dryers, and as quickly as her body would allow her to move, she wiped her face and patted down her hair.

Her ribs let her know she couldn't bend over the sink to wash it, so instead she moved at a snail's pace to the stall where Dixon had flushed down her scarf.

She didn't care about the scarf, she was focused on her phone. She peered at the toilet. The scarf had clogged the basin, her phone resting on top. She fished it out with a wad of paper towel. Then she wrapped it up and tucked it deep into her pocket.

No point in rescuing the scarf. Let them keep their petty victory.

She stumbled from the bathroom, her back as straight as Jenella McBride's, her head held high, so that it was others who turned away, unable to meet her eyes.

A minor act of courage the night before she resigned.

CHAPTER FIFTY-FOUR

When Inaya came back to herself, she was in the gazebo, her head pushed down between her knees, a man's strong arm around her.

"That's it," West said in a low rumble. "Just breathe."

She tried to scramble to her feet and failed.

"Hey, hey, hey," he crooned. His hand was on the back of her head, lightly stroking her hair. "Take it easy. Take a few deep breaths."

Shuddering, she obeyed. One breath, two, a third.

Her face and hair were dry. Her ribs didn't ache. She wasn't with Broda and the others. She was safe, in Blackwater Falls.

She looked up into the face of the man trying to comfort her.

His color was off, concern creasing his brow.

"I'm sorry." She was embarrassed by her weakness, embarrassed she'd confused West with a criminal like Broda.

"No, Brazil, my fault." West helped her to her feet, then quickly backed away. "No way I should have touched you like that, even if I thought you were wired. I scared the hell out of you." A careful pause as he weighed his words. "I'm guessing you've had trouble in the past."

She wouldn't confess her humiliation to West, but her mouth trembled with a smile when she saw the distance he was keeping, his big hands jammed into his pockets.

"I think the sun was too much for me. Maybe I should have eaten breakfast."

West frowned, as if telling her not to bother with a lie.

"That looked more like PTSD." His bulky shoulders shrugged. "I'm no stranger to that."

His admission made her feel a little better, his eyes grave as he studied her.

"You need a shoulder, I'm here." He shook his head at himself. "Don't know why I thought you were trying to trip me up. Being undercover messes with your head—you get antsy around everyone, even your own kid." He gave her a slow once-over, as if to reassure himself he hadn't harmed her. "I wouldn't hurt you for the world."

"I think I knew that." Her legs were still shaky, so she sank back down onto the bench. "Can we pretend it didn't happen?"

He took the bench across from her, the look in his eyes gentle. "Pretending is all I do."

Suddenly warm, Inaya stared out over the pond. Seeing her blush, West grinned.

"Why did you want to meet?"

He fell in with the change of subject.

"You need to stay away from the Disciples. I already told you—they weren't involved in Razan's murder."

"What about the girls at the plant? Rooster was guarding the entry to the room where I found their bodies. Don't tell me he didn't know."

"He didn't. The Disciples are muscle for hire. He was asked to keep an eye on the cold storage rooms at the plant; he didn't know about the bodies."

"Who asked him to do that—the sheriff?"

"You won't find a paper trail connecting Grant to anything," he told her. "Our president would know, but asking him would make him suspicious. He keeps information on a need-to-know basis. He's well-paid for it, and whoever picks up the work gets their cut."

"Your president?"

West smiled an oddly sweet smile at her. "It isn't Rooster, I can tell you that. Our president's club name is Boulder."

"Because he's built like one?"

West laughed outright. "No, because he lives there. That's why you don't see him much in Blackwater. Headquarters are up in Boulder; he runs operations from there."

Inaya remembered the photograph that hung in Andrea Wong's office, the picture of the town's power players taken by Lincoln West. She asked him about the connection.

His laughter faded. "My safety, my kid's safety when I'm undercover depend on getting strangers to trust me. On knowing anyone who might be in a position to blow my operation, and convincing them I'm a true believer." The spurs on one boot scraped against the floor. "The folks in this town are closely connected, so I insinuate myself into their relationships."

"Is that what you're doing with me? Confiding in me so I don't blow your cover?"

He concentrated on convincing her. "I need something else from you. You're letting the Disciples distract you from finding out who really killed Razan. I'm trying to save you some time, because my kid's been crying herself to sleep."

Inaya's face softened at West's concern. "Help me then. Tell me who paid for muscle at the plant." The link could still be relevant: there was Hassan Elkader's injury to consider, and the knife skills she'd seen on display on the processing floor made her think of the precision of the crucifixion wound, a connection she needed to examine.

"That's what I came to tell you. Look at who's on the plant's board and check for calls to this number." He held up a slip of paper.

"This is Rooster's cell?"

He nodded. He put the slip of paper on the bench beside her, settling back. His deep voice rumbled, "You and Seif looking at suspects?"

He'd earned a little trust from her, so she answered, "I have to admit, the Disciples topped the list. Without them, all we have are people connected to Razan. Campbell Kerr and his friends. People at the school. Her bosses at the place she interned. Unfortunately, there's no motive that narrows things down—and nothing explains the way the body was arranged."

"Don't want to tell you your job, Brazil, but have you tried showing the girl's father pictures of your persons of interest? He might be able to identify the person who caused his injury." At her quick look of surprise, he said, "Mercedes told me about it. Which brings me to the second reason I'm here."

Concerned, she asked, "How is Mercedes coping?"

"She isn't. And I know my kid well enough to know it's not just because her friend was murdered. Mercedes *knows* something, but she won't tell me what's bothering her and her friends." He looked uncomfortable. "I thought, maybe a woman's touch could help."

"The last official sighting we have of Razan is by Mercedes. They were together at the ice cream place on Wednesday afternoon."

"With Elias Haddad."

"I'll see what I can do."

He linked his hands. The words "JESUS SAVES" stood out on his broad knuckles.

Inaya studied the ink that covered him. "Will you want to keep your tattoos once your assignment is over? They're quite . . . distinctive."

He rubbed his hand across his face, the movement cracking the pattern of the ink.

"They've always been part of me, but God knows when this is over I want nothing to do with Resurrection or the Disciples. It depends on how long the FBI wants me here, I suppose." His voice dropped in pitch. "You might have to get used to seeing me around."

Her lips curved at his obvious teasing, and his eyes brightened at her answer.

"That doesn't sound so bad."

CHAPTER FIFTY-FIVE

Catalina and Jaime were waiting for her at headquarters when she arrived, Seif nowhere in sight. She raised her eyebrows at Jaime, not knowing what to say. His face was a study in misery, his skin blotchy and red. She looked over at the whiteboard, for the first time noticing the work Jaime had left undone. The security footage from the ice cream parlor hadn't been collected, nor had he printed out Cat's photographs of Andrea Wong's gallery wall.

"You're still here?" she asked, feeling queasy.

"I wouldn't have let anything happen to you," he said fervently. "I was under orders not to interfere with the Disciples. I didn't know—I didn't know . . ."

Inaya dropped her purse on her desk. "You didn't know we'd find the girls at the plant?"

He stammered out an answer. "I d-d-didn't, I swear."

Inaya shifted into her seat, grabbing the folder that contained Dr. Stanger's most recent findings. Full results would take time; he was conscientious enough to send them his thoughts at every step. "Who gave the orders for you to spy on Community Response? Were you planted?"

He swallowed. "No! The sheriff made a call. He said I could undo a lot of damage by doing some honest policing. I thought he meant it. I was trying to do the right thing."

Inaya kept her head down, focused on Stanger's report. "Instead, you did the opposite. You left critical work undone, and you let the sheriff into our investigation when we needed to keep him out of it. We defended you to Areesha. We staked our credibility on you."

A series of texts came in on her phone, probably from Seif. She left her phone in her purse, waiting for Jaime's answer.

"We don't answer to Ms. Adams," he burst out.

She looked up, eyes cold. "Is that the best you can come up with? We answer to the community. Areesha is part of that community— *she's* someone we can trust." She dropped the folder. She'd scanned Stanger's report without taking in a word, her gut churning with anger.

Jaime backed down. He sat down heavily, his hands clenched together in his lap.

Seif came into the office, rolling in a blank whiteboard, his face set and angry. He'd heard what she'd said to Jaime.

"Leave Webb alone—he didn't have a chance against Grant."

Inaya ignored the gruff note in Seif's voice. She didn't look at him. Leaning forward on her knuckles, she repeated her question.

Jaime stood up straight, taking over the whiteboard.

Inaya didn't back down. "I want to know who gave the orders to intercept us at the plant. Who put Rooster on us? Who knew we would be on site?"

Jaime tacked a photo to the whiteboard, hands unsteady, his back to the others. The words left his throat in a strangled gasp.

"It wasn't Grant. I didn't report to the sheriff—I took orders from Little Red."

They converged on Webb, speaking over each other until Seif demanded silence.

"Who the *hell* is Little Red?"

Webb blinked at him, confused. "I thought you knew. You went to see the sheriff, you met him."

"A name, Webb."

"Rusty—Russell Pincher. We call him Rusty, the sheriff calls him Little Red."

"Why the nickname?" Inaya asked. "Was it to protect his identity?"

Webb seemed to clue in at last that the information he'd tossed out was critical. "No, nothing like that. It's because that's what the name Russell means: Little Red."

"Julius told me Pincher is Grant's fixer," Cat advised.

"The power behind the throne," Seif said grimly, not happy to have overlooked this. "Was this more obstruction?" he asked Webb.

Webb spread his hands like a guileless teen, his blue eyes wide with fear. "No. I did tell you I was reporting to him. You asked me to keep that line open. Is the name important?"

"Rahman," Seif snapped. She'd know what he wanted, she wasn't obtuse like Webb. She sifted through a stack of reports, handing him the notes on his interview with Hassan Elkader.

"Little Red was the name of the man who damaged Elkader's hand," he told the others, reading the notes to himself.

"Why would he use his own name?" Inaya asked, appalled. "Why not get a Disciple to do his dirty work?"

"A fixer is hands-on," Seif explained. "He wouldn't trust anyone else to do his job."

"He must be on the board of the plant. If we check his phone records, we'll probably find a link to Rooster." Inaya connected the dots at full speed. "Unionizing would have hurt his bottom line. So he stopped Elkader when the threats against Abdi and Diriye didn't work."

Cat went to the board, where Barkhudo's and Khadijah's pictures had been placed beside Razan's. "They dropped the idea of a union when their daughters went missing—they must have hoped Barkhudo and Khadijah would be returned in exchange for their cooperation."

"Elkader kept at it," Seif agreed. "So his lesson was personal."

Catalina continued to stare at the picture of Razan. Seif came to stand beside her.

"What is it?"

"'A fixer is hands-on,'" she said, quoting him. "If he killed Barkhudo and Khadijah, he held on to their bodies to keep their families in line—as long as they had hope, they'd forget the union. I think if we dig deeper, we'll find they told Elkader to keep his head down too."

"He didn't listen," Seif offered, knowing Catalina wasn't finished.

She turned to look at Inaya. "What did Stanger say about cause of death? Were the girls stabbed?"

"They were strangled. There was no blood on their bodies, and none on site. Either theirs or Razan's. Beyond that, Dr. Stanger is still running tests."

"So it wasn't Razan's kill site."

Catalina couldn't know that for sure, Seif thought. It would take time to check the entire plant. If he considered where else the girls' bodies might have been kept, he couldn't think of many options. Industrial-sized freezers weren't run-of-the-mill appliances; there were a limited number of businesses where they would be used. They were behind on this line of inquiry, now, of course; he'd asked Webb to oversee the search to run those places down, and, under orders from Pincher probably, Webb hadn't followed through. Seif had checked.

He wondered if Webb could be as gullible as he seemed. Catalina and Inaya could make connections in a heartbeat; Webb couldn't see what was right under his nose.

He agreed with Catalina—Pincher *must* have murdered Barkhudo and Khadijah, which likely meant he had also killed Razan. Catalina had called the murder clever, artistic. Pincher was clever, all right. And maybe he had a side to him they hadn't uncovered yet. The murder weapon was obscure, the Virgin Orans unknown to most nonspecialists. He should have Webb check into the origins of Pincher's surname, it wasn't common, and he hadn't heard it before. Russell Pincher, kingmaker—he'd been so focused on Grant that even when he knew Pincher was his operative, he hadn't paid enough attention.

Razan, cleverly arranged as the Virgin Orans, the crucifixion a blind to point them at the church. No, that wasn't right. It didn't fit. If Pincher was so clever . . .

"What?" Inaya was watching him.

Pincher should have known, as they'd learned from Rupi Sandhu, that the Christian iconography so typical of the Catholic Church wasn't used by evangelicals. There was no crucifix on display at Resurrection; they hadn't even mounted a cross.

In this one instance, Razan's killer had shared their ignorance.

"You're right," he said to Catalina. "Someone else murdered Razan." He nodded at Inaya. "Your friend Dr. Sandhu told you the crucifix was a blind. *But it was a blind created by someone who didn't know the church.* He knew the Virgin Orans; he didn't know about Resurrection. He's probably never been to a sermon."

Inaya stared at him as though struck.

"'I've never been one for religion. It doesn't seem honest to me.'"

"Who said that?" he demanded, wanting that look off her face.

"Ally Jensen, at the plant. All these connections to the church—the sheriff, the Disciples, the plant—but not Jensen herself. We've always thought it must have been a man who killed her, but Ally Jensen could have done it. She's strong." Inaya's forehead was pinched in distress.

"What's her motive? How did she know Razan—how did she get her alone?"

Catalina stood between them, a reluctant referee. "Perhaps through Razan's father?"

"Yes," Inaya whispered. "She was in love with him."

"So she kills his daughter—why? So his wife would leave him for daring to push for a union and bringing her death about? Jensen couldn't have done it to protect the plant—you told me *she* suggested the union to Elkader and the others."

Inaya kept her gaze on his face, though she seemed distracted, and he felt a piercing need to focus her attention on him. After a moment, she said, "Jensen claimed not to know Pincher was on the floor."

Webb came to life, sounding eager. "I was up on that walkway for a while. I know Pincher, and I wouldn't have recognized him among the other workers. There are too many people on the floor, too much action. Jensen could be telling the truth."

"I hope you're right," Inaya said. "What now?"

"Now we work the evidence," Seif said. "If Pincher dealt with the injury to Elkader, he may have taken care of Barkhudo and Khadijah. We place him at the plant; that's a start. Forensics may give us more. When we have that evidence, we make our move." And maybe in the process, he'd be able to bring Grant down.

Inaya interrupted. "I have Rooster's cell number. If he called Pincher or vice versa, that gives us leverage." She thought a moment. "Ally Jensen also told me one or two of the sheriff's people are on the board of Natural Foods. What if Pincher is one of them?"

Seif gave her an approving nod. "Let's take care of that now."

He put each of them on a separate task, and sent a team member to show Elkader a photograph of Russell Pincher. Inaya put out a call for Rooster's phone records, Catalina began a search for National Foods' registration: articles of incorporation would list members of the board. That done, he turned to Webb. "What else have you been sitting on?"

Desperate to redeem himself, Webb held up a thumb drive. "I followed up with Mrs. Wendell. I collected the footage from her security camera, but I haven't watched it yet."

"Did you give it to the sheriff?"

Inaya's question deflated Webb's excitement. His face fell. "He wasn't interested."

Because as Areesha had said, he'd never tried to find the girls.

"Jaime." Catalina put her computer search on pause. "Where are the photographs from Andrea Wong's office? Were you able to dig up any background?"

Webb's face turned red. "I printed the pictures from your phone, but I didn't do much digging on the original photographs. Pincher told me to leave Apex alone—their campaign contributions are important to the sheriff."

Seif took control again before either of his detectives could puncture Webb with a few well-chosen words.

"Take the photographs when you're done your search, Catalina. Webb can help you. Rahman and I will go over the footage." He checked with Inaya. "Anything on Rooster?"

"His cell service provider will call me back."

"Good." He grabbed the thumb drive from Webb, hurrying Inaya along. She looked back at Catalina, a puzzled frown on her face.

"What is it?"

Inaya shook her head. She'd forgotten her anger at Webb.

"I want to know what's bothering Cat about that wall."

CHAPTER FIFTY-SIX

Seif gave Inaya his chair, leaning against the wall while they waited for the drive to load. Unlike Webb's, his desk was spotless—confidential materials locked in a cabinet, the glass top free of streaks or personal photos. Senior officers sometimes came in to chat, so he kept his brothers under wrap. Now he realized that it wasn't just his bosses he'd been deflecting.

He wanted to explain his actions, but maybe the less said, the better. She knew he'd lied about the op. If he started to talk about their visit to the church, that would be the first thing she'd raise. She'd also remind him about the evidence Areesha's investigator had collected; she'd ask why he was delaying when the pieces were falling into place. He didn't resent her tenacity—it kept him sharp. If he couldn't sideline his own detectives, he shouldn't be undercover.

"Why are you smiling?" She swiveled in the chair to look at him. "With the wrench Jaime's thrown into the investigation, I wouldn't think you'd be feeling cheerful."

He was going to get Pincher or Grant; it was unlikely he'd get both. Either way he'd be answering to Brandt, and yet—what in hell was wrong with him that he couldn't make up his mind?

"Maybe I'm happy."

To his astonishment, she blushed, turning her chair back around.

She tapped at the keyboard. "Fill me in. What is there to be happy about?"

He came to stand behind her chair, leaning down to look at the screen. The feed was clear, the images black and white.

"Progress," he murmured into her ear. "I think we're making progress."

She could take that any way she liked—if he was out of his depth, why shouldn't she be as well? She was breathing a little faster, so he put his hands on her shoulders, pretending to watch the screen.

In a tight little voice, she said, "You shouldn't touch me."

"Am I trespassing?" he asked.

The air in the room felt warm and heavy. Actions played out on the screen. Seif didn't catch them, waiting for Inaya's response. When she still didn't speak, he said, "The way you watch me—I thought it meant something. Did I misread you?"

She paused the action on the screen, giving him a snippy look.

"You fascinate me," she admitted coolly.

He was inches away from doing something reckless in an office with a glass wall.

"I'll take that as a compliment."

"You shouldn't. It's like watching a penned-up leopard."

She was aiming for indifference, but at the glimmer of uncertainty in her eyes, Seif's resistance dissolved. He couldn't fight her any longer. He didn't want to.

She reached up and patted his hand, and even a touch as simple as that seared him.

"Inaya—" He was poised on the brink of an offer. Unconcerned, she cut him off.

"I know what you're doing," she said.

"You do?" His heart began to pound.

"I know why you've been giving Grant cover."

Her words put out the fire. He straightened away from her, his back to the glass wall.

"You used to be FBI. You're still working for them, aren't you? You're looking into something big, something to do with Grant. That's why you took your eye off this, why you couldn't keep track of Jaime. Whatever your assignment is, it isn't about Razan."

He locked the door to his office. He picked up the small remote on his desk and activated the blinds, each movement precise. Next, he took a piece of paper from the printer near his desk, unclipping the expensive pen from his jacket to write down a single sentence.

My office could be bugged.

He'd swept it the day before, but he wasn't taking any chances. Aloud he said, "Who is that with Razan? I recognize Mercedes—I don't know the boy."

She caught on, letting the video play.

"That's Elias Haddad. He and Razan were both at Blackwater Academy. You read my report, remember?"

"Play it again."

She dragged the cursor to the beginning. Then she plucked his pen from his hand.

We need to talk about this. By now, you should know you can trust me.

This time she watched the video while he scribbled on the sheet of paper. It was an innocuous scene. Three bright and happy teens enjoying a break on a hot summer day, Mercedes and Elias laughing at something Razan said. The security camera was in line with the table where the teens were seated. There was a queue at the door—it snaked around the corner out of sight, shadows dark against the glass.

That's why I put you in charge at the mosque. I knew you could handle things.

Inaya ignored his message. Her hand trembling, she set the cursor back and watched part of the video again. And again. When she looked up at him, fear was stark on her face. She pushed the chair back clumsily, as if she'd lost control of her movements.

"What is it?"

She shifted the cursor again, this time pointing to the screen.

"We have to hurry. We need to talk to Elias."

Seif caught it on the last replay. When Razan entered the ice cream parlor, a navy blue knapsack was slung around her shoulder. The strap was covered with pins that glittered in the sun. They hadn't been able to find it. The video told them why. As the teens left the parlor, Razan gave it to Elias.

CHAPTER FIFTY-SEVEN

They made their way to the elevators. Seif was checking his phone for missed calls; Inaya had the drive in her pocket. She didn't trust Jaime with the knowledge, so she couldn't stop to bring Cat up to speed.

Cat caught up to them as the elevator doors opened. Her hand covered her phone. "Julius wants to talk to you—he has something."

"Handle it," Seif barked. They were at his car in seconds while he spoke to West on the phone. "Keep Mercedes with you. Don't let her out of your sight." To Inaya, he said, "Call Cyrine Haddad."

Teenagers were unpredictable. If they called them in, they might run. Better to get to them. Sounding wary, Cyrine agreed to keep Elias at the bakery. Inaya wondered if she'd been right to warn her. She kept thinking of the unexpected places where she'd found Cyrine. In the front row at the church. Chatting with the pastor at the town hall. In a photograph at Apex Dynamics with both the sheriff and the pastor.

Yes, her bakery had been attacked by Disciples, but from what she'd heard at their meeting with the pastor, that had been a rogue move. The pastor had described Cyrine as a member of his flock. Yet Cyrine was a Maronite Christian.

What explanation could there be for Cyrine's failing to mention that not only did Elias and Razan attend the same school, their relationship had been close? Close enough that when Razan could have given her knapsack to Mercedes, she'd trusted Elias instead. Then again, as far as Razan knew, Mercedes was linked to the Disciples.

She was startled out of her thoughts when Seif placed his hand on hers.

"If you're worried about Elias because he has the knapsack, don't be. There's no reason to think Razan's knapsack places him in danger."

His hand was rough and strong. She wanted to hold on to it, seize its comfort for herself. And not just comfort, but more. She'd felt this pull from the start. Something in Seif called to her. His history, his expressive dark eyes, the struggle she read in his face. That rush of feeling when he looked at her and she thought, *I know him, he's one of ours.*

She forced herself to think of Razan, of the way the girl's face had lit up as Elias teased her, though she knew he was out of reach, the distance between them too great. Just like the distance between Inaya and Seif.

Not only did she want to keep her job, she wouldn't act outside the limits of her beliefs. She'd already permitted liberties she shouldn't have, affected by his touch, *wanting* it. The conflict inside her burned, too harsh and demanding to ignore.

He pulled the car to a stop across the street from the bakery, and she eased her hand free to release her seat belt.

"Please don't," she said, sad and serious. "I'm accountable to my Creator."

He was silent as they left the car, silent as he pushed past her to the door of the boarded-up bakery, a thoughtful silence without anger. Cyrine was waiting for them, her beautiful eyebrows raised nearly to her hairline.

"You scared the life out of me."

It wasn't an exaggeration. Under the heavy makeup, she looked shocked. She was wearing an apron over her elegant clothes, a bucket at her side. The stink of smoke was still in the walls, but most of the damage had been cleared out of the space. The bakery cases were empty, the posters taken down to be cleaned.

Elias entered from the back, cleaning supplies in his hands. He saw them and stopped in his tracks.

Cyrine spoke to him in a combination of Arabic and French. A warning or a set of instructions?

Elias dropped the supplies.

He made it as far as the door. Seif called him back and he stopped, responding to the authority in Seif's voice, and now he sat across from Inaya, a cup of strong coffee in his hands. He was pale with shock like his mother, whom Seif had taken aside so Inaya could speak to him alone.

"I need to call someone before I speak to you."

"A lawyer?" Inaya asked gently.

"Mercedes."

"Mercedes is with her father. You'll have to decide on your own."

"Decide what?" He sounded surly.

"Whether to speak to me or not. I'm your mother's friend; you know you can trust me."

"I don't know that at all."

His bleak honesty set her back.

"Why not? You've known me a long time."

"I know you when you're nice to my mother, not when you act like a cop."

"Can you tell me how that changes things?"

He gave her a sullen look. "I was there that day at the mosque. The day you found Razan. You let the cops beat Omar. You didn't do anything to stop them."

That's why I put you in charge at the mosque. I knew you could handle things.

Elias was right. She hadn't helped Marcus McBride. She hadn't stopped the sheriff's men from assaulting Omar Abdi. Areesha Adams had done that, while Inaya hadn't even suggested that Omar should file a complaint. She'd expected the boy to take it in stride, and he had.

An institution incapable of reform.

As long as you don't abandon me when I start to speak about systems instead of people.

"You're right, and I'm sorry. But you're wrong if you think I don't care about Razan." She lowered her voice, made it confiding. "We didn't give up on Barkhudo and Khadijah. I promised Omar justice, just like I'm promising you."

She could tell he didn't believe her. He shrugged his lean shoulders, his gaze fixed on his coffee cup. Mercedes might have convinced him, but in her own interview, Mercedes hadn't told them about Razan's knapsack.

"What do you want from me?"

"I want you to stop running. I want you to tell me why Razan gave you her knapsack, and where it is now."

"I don't know what you mean."

"You were caught on camera with it. I can show you if you wish."

The boy's face sagged. "I have to make a call. It's not just up to me."

Inaya passed him her phone. He called Mercedes, his knuckles white where he gripped the phone.

"They know," he said. "What do you want me to do?"

She heard the girl sobbing through the phone. Elias murmured to her, then paused to listen to Mercedes.

"I promise." He ended the call, tossing Inaya the phone. "She said to make sure you return Razan's things to us when you're finished with them."

The pressure in her chest easing, Inaya took a pair of gloves from her bag. She fitted them on and waited. Elias went into the back of the shop, returning with Cyrine and Seif.

Cyrine was carrying a blue knapsack with a long, glittering strap. She passed it to Inaya, who took note of the pins. Blackwater Falls with the town logo of the gazebo and the falls. Blackwater Academy. The Syrian flag, the Lebanese flag, the Somali flag. The Black Lives Matter logo. A No Borders pin. A small and stylish rocket. The biohazard symbol. A pin that read "Hands Across the Sea." And another that was personalized, one Razan must have had designed. Two names twined together under a set of laurels: Luqman&Razan.

God, she couldn't bear it.

She looked up at Cyrine, bewildered. "You've had Razan's knapsack all this time?"

Seif was sharper with her. "You've obstructed a murder investigation by withholding and tampering with evidence. We could have you charged."

Cyrine ignored Seif's temper. "I wore gloves. There's nothing in

Razan's knapsack that ties her to the sheriff, just textbooks and notes, otherwise I would have been in touch."

Seif froze where he stood, one black eyebrow shooting up. "That wasn't your call to make—do you have any idea how long we've been looking for it?"

With a keen sense of her son's welfare, Cyrine told Elias to leave. He left his cup on the table, his lean body turned toward the knapsack as if it were a lodestone.

"We're trusting you," he said bitterly. "But only because we have no other choice."

His words rang inside Inaya's head, reminding her of her mother's words: *the public hates you*. These were children steeped in the history of harm done.

"Why did she give it to you? Did she know she was in danger?"

His sullen face crumpled. Angrily, he brushed the back of his hand over his eyes. For the first time, Inaya noticed a tattoo on the outside of his wrist—a delicate Maronite cross.

"Razan just asked me for a favor: she warned us not to tell anyone we had it. She told me not to go through it. She said she'd pick it up on Thursday."

"So she didn't go camping."

"No." A sob caught in his throat. "If we knew—if we knew, do you think we would have left her alone? That was the last time we saw her."

The little café was silent, giving space to his grief.

Then Inaya asked, "Where did she go, Elias? The last time you saw her?"

"Down the street to the bus stop. Mercedes and I wanted to check out the bookstore—it's at the opposite end. When we came out again, the bus was approaching the stop. We crossed the street to hang with Razan, but she was already gone."

Seif stood toe to toe with Cyrine, his face set in hard lines that would have warned off anyone else, the groove at his mouth cut deep. Cyrine placed her hands on her hips.

"I'm not as easy to frighten as my son."

"You're my source," he said flatly. "You were supposed to meet me at the reservoir, but you didn't show. All those times you called me to tip me off, I thought I was talking to a man."

She gave him a diffident smile. "I used a voice distortion app."

He scowled at how easily he'd been fooled. "Why didn't you come forward if you knew I was tracking Grant?"

Cyrine glanced at Inaya, who was watching the scene unfold with astonishment.

"I'm sorry, my darling girl. If I talked to anyone, it should have been you. But as I said, I know your mother, and I couldn't involve you in this." She shook a finger at Seif, who backed up a step or two. "Why do you think they bombed my café? I tried to gain traction with the players in this town because I didn't want to pay for the sheriff's 'protection.' I thought they would leave me alone if they considered me a friend." She grimaced. "Why else do you think I listened to those dreadful sermons at the church?"

She moved back behind the counter, reappearing with a ledger in her hands.

"I underestimated Grant. The bombing was his way of telling me I wasn't off the hook."

Seif took the ledger from her hands. "Do your records implicate Grant?"

She made a sound of regret. "I'm sorry, no. Only his attack dog, Pincher. He sets the terms and collects the money. If he can't come himself, he sends a Blackwater deputy or one of the Disciples. I do have dates and amounts. You should check with Maddalena at the Book Mark and the other old town boutiques."

Seif blew out a breath, coming to terms with his failings. You could get so focused on a single lead that the rest of the picture faded. Not once had he guessed that Cyrine Haddad would be willing to take such a chance. And now he had something on Pincher, something concrete.

"Is this what you were going to give me at the reservoir when you didn't show?"

"I'm sorry. I thought I was being watched."

"Then why now? What's changed?"

"When you called, I thought you had figured out I was your source."

Inaya was holding the knapsack by its strap like it was about to detonate. He knew how she felt. His whole op had blown up—he could get Pincher with Cyrine's help, and maybe Pincher could be turned. On his own, he couldn't trace Grant's payoffs; the man was too clever for that. He was out of leads. He believed Cyrine: Razan's knapsack wouldn't give him anything relevant to his op. That didn't mean they couldn't use it to find her killer.

He should thank Cyrine instead of snapping at her. "I'll be back to talk to you."

"And my son?"

He felt like making a point about obstruction. Inaya answered for him.

"Elias knows Blackwater. If he doesn't trust us, who can blame him? He was respecting Razan's wishes by holding on to her secrets." She hugged Cyrine. "I'm so sorry about the café."

"Me too, *habibti*. We will rebuild, and you will help me, yes?"

They moved apart. "Of course I will." Inaya's slender fingers massaged her delicate nape, and a stab of lust hit Seif. He wanted to run his fingers over the skin her action had exposed, and he was shaken by the knowledge that he was helpless against her. He needed a break from Inaya. He'd liaise with the team on the plant murders and see what they could do about Pincher. While he made his report to Brandt, Inaya could work out the rest with Catalina.

He excused himself to answer his phone. Not Brandt—Areesha Adams, the last thing he needed, though in another life, a life where he could gather his history inward, and inhabit the space his brothers lived in, he would have been on her side of the tape when Grant's officers had gone for Omar. She didn't know he was cheering her efforts, and she didn't owe him the benefit of the doubt. Why would he expect welcome from her when he'd only recently joined the battle she'd been waging for decades?

When they spoke now, she wasn't as hostile as he'd expected—Inaya's influence.

A little fearfully, she asked him, "You've confirmed the police are involved?"

She was asking about the deaths of Barkhudo and Khadijah. Two young girls cut off at the knees, their bodies discarded like carcasses—a metaphor that made his gorge rise.

"Yes." He summarized their suspicions about Pincher. He was just as candid when he told her they were still gathering evidence against him.

By the way her breath sighed out in his ear, she hadn't expected him to be so forthright.

"What about Grant?"

He pressed his forehead against a window that had survived the bombing. His free hand traced out his thoughts on the pane, the rhythmic sentences painful. He wrote in Arabic, the language of his retreat.

"I don't know if we have enough to go all the way to the top. I'll do what I can."

She didn't push him, so he made a request.

"Ms. Adams—don't tell the families yet. I don't want to let them down again."

"Call me Areesha," she said, and hung up.

Inaya was waiting for him by the car, still dangling the knapsack by its strap. Her expression gave him pause—he liked it when she gave as she good as she got; this quiet compassion unnerved him. Ice settled in his veins. Did she read Arabic? Was she pitying him?

"Can you handle things with Catalina?" he asked evenly.

"If you need me to."

She'd seen through him. His coldness had given way to stumbling attempts at seduction, finesse burned off in the crucible of raw desire. He thought it wouldn't happen unless he made it happen. Not if she could see what it cost him to strip away the things that belonged to a man with a name like Waqas Seif, a name he'd had to truncate, like severing a limb or disavowing his history. The twins so boldly, blissfully free while he—not Inaya—spent his life in camouflage. Now he knew he had no power against her.

She knew his dance by now—he'd show her some things, keep what mattered to himself when she pushed, then do it all again. But if he wanted to shut her out, she'd shown him where her boundaries lay, giving him permission to withdraw.

Like a coward, he took it and ran.

CHAPTER FIFTY-EIGHT

Jaime had used the pictures from Cat's phone to separate out the individual photos from Andrea Wong's gallery wall. The pictures he'd printed were pinned to the whiteboard in an arrangement that replicated Andrea Wong's outline of an aerostat, an airship shaped like a zeppelin.

Cat stood transfixed before the board, poised at the edge of discovery.

It was *there;* she could feel it.

"Jaime."

He appeared at her side, so eager to please that her heart turned over.

"Can I help you, boss?"

"You stood up for us against Grant's men. Was that so we wouldn't suspect you?"

She heard his painful swallow, felt the heat of his hand as it hovered above her shoulder before it fell to his side.

"You know who I am at the core."

He wasn't bitter. He was too naive for Grant's poison to have spread. She'd been observing Jaime for months, working with him close at hand, trusting in his basic decency.

"I'm sorry you were under so much pressure. I wish you could have come to me."

"I do too." He rubbed a fist against his heart like it was aching, and Cat's arm stole around his waist. A maternal warmth crept through her—wasn't Jaime just another lost stray in a world so brutal and deceptive that kindness couldn't survive?

"I do know who you are at the core."

They studied the whiteboard together, Jaime's chest rising and falling with emotion. He hugged Catalina back, then asked her, "What are you looking for there?"

His broad hand sketched the outline of the aerostat.

"I don't have an eye for art. Yet something about the arrangement of these photographs is itching at the corner of my mind."

She thought of Khadijah's talent, the love-inspired painting of the young man Omar, who had accepted his fate as a worker without the protection of the law. Resigned to his restricted choices. Her mind added another stroke of color to the painting: Areesha's regal head bent over her hands as she listened to the mothers of the missing girls, the grief shared, the killings distinct yet the trauma generational. She ached to offer her services as a counselor, to speak to Waris of the sensitive, insightful daughter she had raised, wondering all the time if Khadijah's artistic eye would have picked out what the photographs on the wall were silently trying to tell her.

You know me, Catalina, you see me.

Why wouldn't it come? Why should the wide-ranging photographs in their aerodynamic arrangement speak to her of Razan?

She studied the photographs she'd taken on her phone, compared them to the order on the whiteboard.

"Did we arrange them correctly?" she asked Jaime. "Maybe we got something wrong."

The mistake would be Jaime's; she'd included herself as a matter of grace, of kindness extended to a friend when the nature of friendship mattered.

Jaime applied himself to the task. She pitied him his new self-knowledge, wanted to smooth a road only he could travel, knew her husband, Emiliano, would be angry there was no one her empathy spared.

"For God's sake," he would rail at her. "Save something for yourself."

She closed her eyes, willing the truth to come, willing Razan to speak.

Inaya rejoined them before Cat could come to an answer. She was holding up a knapsack, explaining she'd located it through the footage on the security camera. Cat didn't look at Jaime—if they'd found it weeks earlier, the case might already be closed. Not voicing that aloud was how she let him know there was still a chance for him to make things right. Inaya, her *hermana*, had taken a little longer but had reached the same conclusion. What was friendship truly worth if they threw Jaime away?

She cleared a space on Jaime's crowded desk, setting the knapsack down after a quick look at the whiteboard. Her phone buzzed with a text just as Jaime shifted two of the photos.

"Sorry," she said to Cat. "Rupi's been texting. She's been digging into the mosaic."

His darkness eclipsed me. Her first thought on seeing the display of Razan's body.

The crucifixion pose had eclipsed the Virgin Orans.

So slowly it felt like it was taking her a year to move, her head shifted back to the board, her eyes searching for a single image.

Jaime had repositioned it at the center of the design.

It wasn't just an aerostat, she saw now. Andrea Wong had arranged the pictures so that the colors and shade formed a halo around the center, drawing the eye to a single photograph.

"Why?" she asked aloud.

Inaya raised her head, tilting up the screen of her phone.

Rupi had sent her a photograph—it was the same image.

"It wasn't a Renaissance church," Cat said. "How could we have missed that?"

"Rupi thought we might want to see the Saint Sophia Cathedral."

The site of the Virgin Orans.

CHAPTER FIFTY-NINE

Inaya upended Razan's knapsack out onto Jaime's desk. Keen to assist, Jaime cleared his things out of the way. She explained about the mosaic as she sifted through Razan's knapsack.

Textbooks, a binder where she'd taken notes for school, a pamphlet advertising School Spirit Day, and her wallet. All that was missing was her phone.

The textbooks covered calculus, physics, and drafting. She passed them to Cat and Jaime.

"Look for anything Razan might have written, something she tried to hide."

Pages turned in a tense silence. Inaya opened the binder. Colorful dividers separated the subjects Razan had taken at school. At the back of the binder was the insert envelope, and this was crammed with additional papers. Notes between Razan and Mercedes, the harmless teasing of girls. A letter still in its envelope that contained a tortured apology from Kerr. Razan had kept it, cherished it, held it safe, and protected Kerr's privacy. There was a photograph among the papers, smoothed over by loving fingers, of Razan with her twin Luqman. The innocence of youth, their arms slung around each other's shoulders, finding joy in a war zone.

We have to live before we die.

A copy of the school paper, the same issue that had contained Razan's op-ed on weapons of war . . . *they feed our students right back into the system, so that another generation grows up to deal with the world's most dangerous weapons, disconnected ethically and emotionally from the misery and destruction that those weapons cause.* Razan had highlighted the passage, and in tiny print beside it she had written: "What is my responsibility here?"

Inaya's pulse sped up. Andrea Wong was at the center of this, and she was seconds away from knowing why. She shook out the school paper: two drawings fluttered to the floor.

She picked them up with care and set them side by side.

Different designs of an aerostat marked "CLASSIFIED."

Inaya's untutored eye swept over them. Each design was distinct; she wouldn't have known she was looking at the same border security technology. How and why had Razan managed to get her hands on these classified blueprints? The security procedures at Apex were exhaustive, and Andrea Wong had confirmed that a high school student wouldn't be allowed into the basement where the engineers worked.

Ink bled through the page of one of the designs. Inaya flipped it over, and in the same tiny printing, she read: "I have to speak to Andrea. I can't let this go on."

Below this, Razan had made a notation. "Wed. 6 p.m."

She had it. They had it. A meeting with Andrea Wong just after the last time anyone had seen Razan, a meeting Wong had lied about. The blueprints, the photograph of the cathedral on Andrea's gallery wall—it all fit. She didn't know what the Virgin Orans meant to Wong, but she was going to find out.

"Jaime!" At the snap in her voice, Jaime jumped to attention. "Get Seif to meet us at Apex. Cat and I are going in."

CHAPTER SIXTY

They prepared for the confrontation. Cat placed the school paper and the aerostat schematics into separate evidence bags, and tucked them into her purse. Inaya was counting on the fact that Wong was too arrogant to expect she'd be found out.

"Was she strong enough?" Catalina asked. "To pin Razan to that door? And after all, why position Razan to re-create the mosaic?"

"Maybe if she wanted something badly enough, or if she felt threatened by Razan. She might have wanted fame, money, success. Linden Sych's job. A woman with those credentials should never have been an executive assistant. Even Sych said she should be running the place."

They were waved through the security gate. Inaya parked the car with an angry flourish. When they were asked to turn over their guns at the desk, she and Cat refused.

"Don't call up," she warned the guard. "We're here to make an arrest." She told him to expect armed officers, and to send them up when they arrived. She hoped Seif made it in time.

This time she paid attention to the apex predators, to the jade green eyes of the panther in the jungle, the elusive creature captured by photographer Shaaz Jung, who knew a killer when he saw one. Panthers killed to survive. Was that what Andrea had done?

They knocked on her office door, not waiting for an answer.

Andrea came to her feet as Cat strode to the gallery wall.

Her voice was sharp. It carried a note of fear. Inaya watched her hands.

"Step away from your desk, please."

Andrea didn't listen. She braced her hands on the desk and spluttered at them, "What are you doing here? How dare you breach a secure facility?"

Inaya didn't try to disguise her rage. Why had this woman murdered a teenage girl? Had she seen Razan as a rival to her brilliance? The pastor had hinted at some kind of trouble at Apex. Like a fool, she hadn't listened, her prejudice against him bone-deep. Was Andrea the source of that trouble?

I have to speak to Andrea. I can't let this go on.

"Move away from your desk. I won't ask you again."

Faltering, Wong obeyed. A pair of mother-of-pearl prongs fastened her silky black hair into a simple chignon. They matched the black-and-white dress she wore beneath a blazer. Inaya reached out and captured the prongs, testing the tips as Andrea spat out an objection.

The tips tapered to a dull point; they weren't right-angle triangles. They could still serve as a weapon, so Inaya pocketed them.

Andrea recovered her cool. In a scornful tone, she demanded, "Explain yourselves."

Inaya kept one hand poised just above her Glock, the other at her handcuffs.

"You met with Razan Elkader on the night she disappeared. On Wednesday, at six p.m. You failed to tell us you were the last person to see Razan alive."

Andrea spoke quickly, the words tumbling over each other.

"Because we didn't meet. She didn't show up for the appointment. I wasn't the last person to see her, and I certainly didn't kill her."

Inaya unhooked her handcuffs, her gun hand relaxing. "Turn around, please."

"No! Wait!" Andrea stood up straight, pushing the wings of her hair behind her ears. "I can prove it to you."

"How?"

"Our building logs. They register each swipe of our security passes. You can also admit someone as a guest, but that request has to be logged, as we did with your interview here. We have to sign out visitors as well. I was here. You'll see that Razan wasn't."

Inaya glanced over at Cat. She'd removed the photograph of the Saint Sophia Cathedral from the wall.

"You could have met her somewhere else."

"The logs record exit times, too. You can see for yourself."

Inaya hesitated. The security guard Noah Alcorn had told her the same thing about key cards at the Academy. The system at Apex Dynamics would be much more sophisticated.

Wong was no longer panicked. She'd managed to recover her composure, and Inaya would at least have to let her establish the proof of her alibi.

"Show me."

Her voice was rough with grief. She hadn't let herself dwell on the image of Razan, arranged in a parody of the Crucifixion, the posture of the Virgin Orans reminding her of her own hands raised in *dua*.

Andrea didn't wait for permission to boot up her computer. She placed a call on her internal phone.

"Can you send me security logs for . . . ?" She raised an eyebrow at Inaya, who told her the date.

The three women waited in silence, until Cat advanced with the frame that held the photograph of the cathedral, laying it on the desk.

"Why did you choose this photograph? What significance does it have?"

Distracted, Wong stared at the computer, pulling up her email files. "What? Why does it matter?"

Cat persisted. "The cathedral matters because it's the site of a mosaic called the Virgin Orans. Razan's body was arranged to imitate the Virgin."

Wong's eyes snapped to hers in shock. "You can't be serious—you can't believe I would hurt Razan, especially based on such tenuous evidence." She stared at the photograph, one hand pressing the pendant at her neck as if to reassure herself.

Inaya heard the ring of truth in the words, as Andrea went on, "I was proud of her, delighted to be her mentor. I wanted to see her succeed. We need more women working in STEM. We're less . . . rapacious . . . somehow." She nodded at Catalina. "I thought about what you said to me, about border security measures. I realized you were right—we can't divorce the human side of things from the work we do here."

She'd given Cat an opening. Cat laid the bag with Razan's op-ed in it on Wong's desk.

"So you came around to Razan's point of view. Was that what she wanted to discuss?"

Wong shrugged. She turned her giant monitor around, showing them the logs. She unsnapped her security tag from her lanyard—Inaya studied the barcode, compared it to the one on the screen, to the dates and times displayed. Andrea Wong was right: she'd been here most of that night. Inaya asked her about the possibility of someone else using her pass. Andrea explained that in addition to the pass, there was a fingerprint scanner. Any discrepancies between the name on the pass and the user's fingerprint would flag an immediate response. That seemed clear enough, so Inaya repeated her question about what Razan had wanted to discuss.

Wong was preoccupied by something on the screen. She answered Inaya absently. "Actually, she said she wanted to discuss something personal."

"The choice of the Virgin Orans was certainly personal."

"What?" Wong was still distracted. She ran a finger along the screen. "There's something not quite right here."

Catalina's phone rang.

"Julius," she said to Inaya. Inaya nodded, and she took the call. Covering the phone with her hand, she mouthed, "He can't get ahold of Seif, so he's calling us."

Excitement thrummed through Inaya's veins. Andrea wouldn't escape. Dr. Stanger held the final pieces.

"Put it on speaker."

"You have us both, Dr. Stanger," Inaya said to the pathologist. "And a third party in the room. We're about to make an arrest."

Andrea's mouth gaped as Stanger's tinny voice came through.

"Then this will help. Several of our tests have come back. Cell deterioration results put Razan's death at some time during the evening of the Wednesday she was last seen."

Andrea blinked, her finger jerking on the screen.

"Excellent," Inaya said. "Was there anything else?"

"You've been trying to pin down a location where Razan was held before her body was found at the mosque."

"Yes, we have."

"Then this might help. We found nanoparticles in Razan's lungs. They're unusual. They're aluminum particles that normally produce hydrogen gas and aluminum oxide."

Inaya frowned at Cat, peripherally aware that Andrea's hand had slipped from the screen.

"I'm not following."

"Oh, let me explain!" Stanger sounded far too cheerful for his job. "These specific nanoparticles remain extremely stable and safe while frozen. They're experimental at present—you may have heard of ALICE? The aluminum-ice model?"

Inaya had no idea what he was telling them, but he finally got to the point.

"It's a new type of rocket fuel used in aerospace design."

Andrea Wong put her head down on her desk. When Inaya checked to see if she had fainted, she found her pulse was racing, the skin at her wrists ice-cold.

Wong raised her head. Tonelessly, she said, "We store rocket fuel in the basement for our experimental needs." She pointed to the screen. "There's a discrepancy here—a guest was admitted that night, but their name wasn't logged in." She used her keyboard to scroll down. "What if the guest was Razan?"

Wong was playing innocent, but they almost had it all now. The security logs placed Wong and an unknown guest in the building at the same time. Wong could have killed her before she logged her exit. The particles found in Razan's lungs meant she'd met her fate in the basement.

"How big is your storage facility? Could it hold a body?"

"Yes, yes." Wong admitted the truth with a strained echo of her normal manner, her expression bemused, her hands smoothing her hair in a continuous gesture.

Cat showed her the photograph again. "Tell us about the cathedral. And about the Virgin Orans. Was she special to you?" She pointed to Wong's necklace. "You're a Christian, aren't you? The characters on your pendant—they say 'Our Lady of China.'"

Wong's lips moved without sound. Then she whispered, "How did you know that?"

"I took a picture of it during our interview and matched it through an image search."

Inaya marveled at Cat's initiative. She'd mentioned the pendant to Catalina, then deprioritized it on her list of urgent follow-up tasks. She remembered now that Cat had aimed her camera at Wong.

Cat now removed the other evidence bags from her purse, laying them on Wong's desk, shunting Razan's op-ed to the side.

Wong squinted at the documents. "These are classified! How did you—"

"This is what Razan wanted to talk to you about. You've been trying to distract us with your belated recognition of *human* security at the border."

Andrea's head dropped to study the documents more closely. Her gaze went to the photograph of the cathedral, then back to her computer monitor. Her full lips flattened into a tight line. She went on the attack.

"I don't know anything about a cathedral—I don't even know where it is. I have no idea what the words 'Virgin Orans' mean. I'm a Christian, but so what? So is nearly everyone else."

Her eyes skittered away from Inaya's.

"So you chose the photograph at random? The cathedral is in Kyiv."

The noise of a man's polite interruption came over the speakerphone. Inaya had forgotten the line to Stanger was open.

"That reminds me," he said. "I traced the knife that was used to kill Razan. It's a Mikov. A customized weapon in the Czech Republic. It originates in the Ukraine."

Chilled to the core, Inaya remembered where she'd last seen the Mikov's exclusive logo.

"Oh my God." Wong's whisper was shattered, the color leached from her face. Her trembling finger pointed at the list of IDs on the screen. "*He* was here that night."

The three women turned as they heard the ominous click of the communicating door.

CHAPTER SIXTY-ONE

Linden Sych stepped in from his office, his Mikov pen clipped to the pocket of his blazer.

His gun was the latest American model of the Walther PPQ. He used it to marshal the women together behind Andrea's desk.

"I hoped it wouldn't come to this."

Her heart pounding, Inaya said, "Mr. Sych—"

He gave her a pained look, correcting her pronunciation. "You didn't know I was Ukrainian, did you?"

She'd stopped thinking about people's names, more interested in their actions. Instinctively, she and Cat moved to shield Andrea. Sych made a warning sound.

"I must ask you not to move. Guns here, please. Now."

They had no choice but to cooperate, though Inaya was thinking at light speed. She placed her phone facedown beside her gun, the line still open.

"Mr. Sych." She repeated his name for Stanger's benefit. "Please give me the gun."

How could it be Sych? *Why* would it be Sych, unless he and Andrea—who chose this moment to be voluble—were working together.

"I was trying to tell you," Andrea said. "*I* didn't choose the photographs for our wall. Linden is the expert—he selected each print in the building."

Though his gun hand was steady, Sych's shoulders sank in. "I couldn't take the risk that one of you might spot the cathedral. I had to misdirect you." In a reverent whisper, he asked, "You found the mosaic, then?"

Inaya nodded. "Why did you pose Razan as the Virgin?"

"I spent my childhood in Kyiv with my mother—we lived near the cathedral, and I grew up under the Virgin's protection. I *revered* her. She was my guardian, my protector—my inspiration. Razan's gentleness—her compassion—reminded me of the dignity of the Virgin Orans." He turned his gun on Cat. "I'm sorry, but I must ask you to handcuff your partner."

At once, Inaya placed her hands behind her back. Cat sidled close, clicking the handcuffs into place. But only one was around Inaya's wrist. Her other hand was free.

Sych waved the gun at Andrea, who stared at him like he'd grown another head.

"Please cuff Detective Hernandez. You won't try to hurt me, I know."

Andrea's hands were shaking. She hadn't noticed Cat's maneuver and locked both cuffs into place.

"I didn't plan this. I didn't want to hurt Razan, any more than I planned to hurt you."

He used the gun to wipe the sweat from his forehead. Inaya paid attention to the tremor in his hand. Was he ill? Overwhelmed? Or was it another attempt to mislead them?

She remembered the light in his eyes when he'd spoken of Razan.

"If you didn't want to hurt her, why did you? You told me the two of you were close. Were you punishing her for the article she wrote? Or were you angry because she resigned?"

He brought the gun to bear on her again.

"I—no. Is that what you think? If there was any way around it, I would have let Razan live. I *wanted* her to live, to take her light into the future. She was brilliant; she could see right into my mind. She would argue with me about the aerostats, try to convince me to get Apex out of border security, but she didn't know how much we depended on government contracts."

His gun sketched the outline of the gallery wall. "Have you ever noticed how beautiful aerostats are? How perfectly they're balanced?"

He sighed, his head down, and Inaya inched closer to Andrea, trying to give her some cover. "How could they have cost me so much?"

Sych had left the door open behind him. Through it, Inaya caught the shadow of a movement. She kept her face impassive. She had to keep him talking; the motive behind Razan's murder was still unclear.

"What did they cost you, Linden? Tell me, I'd like to understand."

"Yes, you've been kind to me, Detective. As kind in your own way as Razan."

Naked emotion deepened Sych's voice, pointing her to the truth.

"If you loved her, why did you kill her?"

"It wasn't wrong," he said quickly, not denying the charge. "The pastor saw us together, and he put an ugly rumor out there, but I didn't love her in that way. Razan's bright spirit, the liveliness of her mind—they were a joy to be around. I was lonely—I found myself soaking up her warmth. If I had to kill her, at least I could honor her in death." His head swiveled to the photograph of the cathedral. "I didn't think you would see past the crucifixion. I hoped you'd suspect the pastor." His grip on the gun firmed, a deadly look in his eyes. "The *mudak* deserved it for the way his sermons targeted people like Razan."

"Yet you're the one who killed her. And you still haven't told us why."

Sych flinched.

Her voice soft and low, Inaya added, "You've never been to Resurrection, have you? Evangelicals object to the crucifix—they refuse to display it."

He listened, running the Walther under his chin, and Inaya tensed. The manual safety was off, the gun ready to fire.

"I didn't know that." Grief colored his voice. "I didn't have to lie about it, then."

"Why did you? Why do any of it?"

He ran one hand through his hair. He betrayed his inexperience when he turned his gun sideways to threaten Andrea. She'd slipped the aerostat designs out of the bags, the line of her mouth slack with shock.

"Tell them," he said.

"Did Razan find these?" she asked him, dazed.

He responded by raising the gun, and Andrea stumbled into speech, holding up the blueprints so Inaya and Cat could see them.

"This is an aerostat. *This* is a missile." She raised one of the blueprints. "This design is trademarked—it belongs to Lockheed Martin. You stole it," she whispered. "You committed treason. *That's* why you killed Razan—because she must have found out."

Tears trickled down Sych's face; he rubbed them with the back of one hand. The shadow behind him edged closer. Inaya held her breath. One more second.

"Our aerostat was rejected—a competitor came in with a lower bid. The only way to salvage the contract was to expand into missile design. Apex would fold if we didn't. Our employees, our shareholders, my mother's place in her nursing home—everything depended on it." A sob shook his body. "Razan was going to tell Andrea—that would have been the end."

He took another step, righting the gun in his hand.

"I'm sorry, I have no choice." Without further warning, he fired.

Inaya shoved Andrea to her knees. The bullet whizzed by Inaya's temple, burning her skin. Sych raised his hand to fire again. She yanked Cat forward and threw her down to the floor in the tight space behind the desk.

And in that whisper of time before life ended, Inaya recited the *kalima*, her final testimony to the Oneness of God. Yet the hot blast left her exempt from death, the prayer running on a loop. She was crying, speaking it aloud.

Sych toppled forward. His body hit the desk, then slipped down to the ground.

Seif had used a taser. He handcuffed Sych, kicking his body away. His arm came up to catch Inaya close, his other hand smoothing the tears from her face. It lingered at the spot on her forehead where the bullet had brushed her skin.

"Thank God, he didn't shoot the mole," he tried to tease her, but his hands were shaking badly. His fingers traced the velvety mark at the corner of her eyebrow. She buried her face in his throat, whispering his name. He stroked her back as he held her.

Their preoccupation lasted for a second. Then they turned to Cat.

Inaya left the shelter of Seif's arms, freeing Catalina from the cuffs.

"Dammit!" Cat was in a rare temper. "Don't you ever risk yourself for me again!"

Inaya dangled the open cuff on her wrist. "You tried to save me first."

They hugged each other as Seif shook his head, his thoughts centered on Inaya. A remorseless light had exposed the truth. The lies fell away, the things he'd lost surged back. He didn't know his way forward, didn't know *siraat-al-mustaqeem*, the straight path. But he had somewhere to begin.

Andrea Wong tugged at his sleeve. "I wasn't part of this, you have to believe me. Apex doesn't develop missiles. I would never be part of that."

Seif turned away, securing the evidence. What he wanted to say was said by Catalina, with her singular empathy and insight.

"The distance between a weapon and its victim exists only in your mind. To build it, you have to be comfortable with killing; you have to accept the consequences of what the weapon is meant to do—whether it's to take a life or to destroy the chance to seek asylum at the border. Your weapons have killed before. It's just a matter of time before they do again."

Team members were waiting for Seif's word outside the door. He had only a moment to act before they'd swarm into the room. He turned to Cat. "Take Ms. Wong downstairs."

He turned Sych's body over, his knee on Sych's chest. "Where's the kill site?"

Unable to move, Sych wheezed, "The basement. Razan was planning to tell Andrea about the blueprints; I told her Andrea wanted to take a look at the models in the basement, so the three of us could work things out."

Seif increased the pressure from his knee.

"Where'd you grab her? What'd you do with her phone?"

Sych's cough came from his lungs.

"Qas." Inaya's soft protest warned him. He wrapped one hand around Sych's throat.

"Answer me!"

Sych gasped out each word. "Bus stop. Her phone was off. I took it when she tried to turn it on. Destroyed it. Brought her into Apex as my guest and I—I took care of her there. I put her body in the freezer, and kept the basement clear until it was safe to move her."

Seif squeezed hard, then let him go. He looked up at Inaya, took in the shock on her face, her hand resting on his shoulder, the restraint so gentle it killed him.

That murdering bastard Sych didn't know the meaning of love.

CHAPTER SIXTY-TWO

In contrast to how dangerous the arrest had been, the aftermath was smooth. Faced with a raft of charges, Sych made a full confession. Maybe later he'd work up some anger at Seif's methods, but for now his grief had taken over—his most pressing concern, apart from Razan's death, was that with his arrest he could no longer pay for his mother's care at her exclusive nursing home. Sych's only remaining family, she'd been suffering from dementia for years.

There was also the fact that Stanger had witnessed Sych's confession. That he hadn't recorded it was a mark in Seif's favor. So far no one had questioned his methods, though he sensed Inaya's apprehension. She was right to worry about the anger he kept concealed at the injustices of both his past and his present, the incursions that chipped away at his pride in who he was. He studied his bandaged hands. Under the dressings, his knuckles were bloody and bruised. He'd taken care of another problem last night.

He'd come out of the shadows in the parking garage to tackle Whitlock, taking him to the ground, feeding him the fury of his fists.

"Touch Nadia Rahman again, and you won't be getting up."

Whitlock had stared at his masked face in terror. "I swear, man, I won't."

Seif would be waiting if he did.

Two days after the arrest, he called Brandt at the FBI. With Elkader's identification of Pincher as the man who'd attacked him, and the pay-offs recorded by Cyrine, the evidence had piled up. Add in the fact that as a member of the board of Natural Foods, Pincher had a stake in the failure of the union, and they had him dead to rights.

Seif was calling to tell Brandt what they *didn't* have.

"You get Grant?" Brandt asked, though he was too sharp to have missed the news.

Pincher had confessed to the murders of Barkhudo and Khadijah. They'd been taken to put pressure on the men behind the union; he'd had a Disciple follow them, and grabbed them when they'd gone hiking at the reservoir. It was too dangerous to hold them, so he'd strangled them the same night, holding out hope they might be returned if talk of the union died. He could have targeted Razan, but he'd maimed Elkader instead. In a small mosque community, perhaps it was inevitable that the girls had been friends. Their deaths weren't otherwise linked.

Indeed, Grant and Pincher had counted on the fact that Black girls were easier to disappear: they didn't capture headlines, and it wasn't hard to convince the public they'd run away from home. Black Lives Matter protests may have pushed police brutality onto the national agenda, but they hadn't yet made an impact in a town like Blackwater Falls.

By contrast, white-skinned Razan had been an outspoken student at a well-known school, and she'd held a prestigious internship: her death would have stirred up a storm. Community Response's involvement in her murder proved as much. They hadn't been brought on board for Barkhudo or Khadijah.

That wasn't the worst of what he had to share.

"No. Pincher wanted to make a deal, tried to turn on Grant, but it's Pincher's name on the paper trail, Pincher acting as fixer—we still have nothing on Grant. The prison kickback operation might yield a payoff down the road, but Grant's been very careful. When Pincher pointed the finger at him, he showed me Pincher's logs. Dates, times, meetings, written by Pincher himself. Pincher wasn't smart enough to get proof he was acting on Grant's orders."

Brandt spat out a colorful curse. Then he sighed.

"Your cover's blown, Seif. You might as well come home."

"It's not as bad as that. Grant thinks we stumbled onto Pincher's activities in the course of our murder inquiry. He doesn't know he was the target."

"He must have his suspicions."

Seif braced one arm above his head on the glass.

"Maybe, but he can't prove it. He's never met me before, the murder investigation was legitimate, and we made an arrest. None of that was a front."

"That's not all you have," Brandt said shrewdly.

Seif grinned to himself. Yeah, he liked working with the man. He told Brandt about Lincoln West's undercover op. West was another way in.

Brandt listened with interest, asking at the end, "Who else knows about West?"

Seif closed his eyes. "Only Detective Rahman. She guessed I might be working an op. Push comes to shove, I'll find a way to use her. West likes her, so she could liaise with him."

He knew Brandt wouldn't hesitate. He'd sacrifice Inaya and West without a thought, if it would net him Grant. Seif would have to watch out for them, now that he'd offered them up.

"Talk to West, find out who his handler is. Let's make this official. Oh, and Seif?"

Seif pulled in a breath. "Yes, sir?"

"My condolences. Glad you got the man who killed that girl."

That sweet girl, Razan.

It was time for her *janazah*.

CHAPTER SIXTY-THREE

On Friday at noon, Inaya, Cat, and Areesha had coffee together at Cyrine's bakery. Cyrine had served them a new flavor of coffee, the roast smelling of cedar. Or maybe Inaya was imagining it, beguiled by the poster of the tall and sturdy trees.

Elias, Mercedes, and Omar were gathered together at another table, speaking in low voices. Omar looked over to the women and said, "We'll be attending Razan's *janazah* today."

Inaya reached inside her purse. She carried extra scarves for whenever she needed to pray. She passed a pale blue one to Mercedes, thinking of how she had first imagined Mercedes as the Virgin. "You're always welcome at our mosque."

The door to the bakery chimed. Campbell Kerr walked in, head down, glancing over and nodding at the three women before making his way to Mercedes. He evidently didn't know who to ask, so he just asked Mercedes. "Can I come with you? I'd like to pay my respects."

Omar glared at him, surging to his feet. Cyrine brought another cup of coffee. Mercedes wound the scarf around her hair. Inaya and Cat watched the moment play out. Areesha didn't intervene, her hands folded in the prayer pose.

Elias reached over and helped Mercedes tuck a few strands of hair into her scarf.

Cyrine set the cup down on the table, saying to Kerr, "For you." Her fingers played over her shiny Maronite cross. Elias stood up, shoulder to shoulder with Omar, who glanced over at Inaya, waiting to see what she'd do.

She did nothing, thinking of Barkhudo and Khadijah, whose funerals had taken place yesterday. She had prayed at each of them.

The boys didn't shake hands, but Omar looked around, grabbed a chair from another table, and placed it before the extra cup. Sinking into his seat, he echoed, "You are always welcome at our mosque."

Listening to them, Areesha said, "A change is going to come." She was wearing a green turban, styled to leave her neck exposed. She was a woman who built bridges, who wasn't threatened by difference, whose struggle for justice found room for joy in ordinary things. The turban was a sign of respect. It was also just Areesha.

"Things look hopeful for their generation, even if we didn't get Grant," she observed.

She was right. They'd arrested Pincher, the Disciples who were on his payroll, and a number of Grant's deputies, whom Pincher had named as working with the Disciples to harass the workers at the plant. Grant had turned over everything he had on Pincher; his own hands were clean. But they'd keep their eye on him. Leopards didn't change their spots: one day soon he'd go too far. When he did, the three of them would be waiting.

Inaya said as much to Areesha, who unfolded her prayerful hands and reached out to Cat and her. The three women held hands.

"We brought the truth out into the open, and we made people see that Barkhudo and Khadijah matter—that we wouldn't let them be forgotten, or let their lives be cast aside. We gained our girls a little justice: the man who killed them is going to jail. If we have to settle in and wait for Grant, well then, welcome to the struggle." She squeezed their hands. "We won't always be on the same side, but we *see* each other, and that's a start. We can build something together, if we extend a little grace." Areesha thought for a moment. "I'm talking about the three of us; I don't mean the police."

Cat's dimples came out. "I hear you, *hermana*. I promise you, I'm with you."

Inaya simply said, *"Ameen."*

The door opened again, and a breathtakingly handsome man came to collect Areesha.

"Meet my partner," she said. "David Fortunate Adams."

"That's fortunate, all right," Cat agreed, and the man gave a booming laugh.

Areesha winked at them as the couple turned to leave. "You two would look amazing in any color but blue."

Inaya's smile was a little sad. She'd taken a step forward when it came to her job, but the real reckoning remained. She didn't know if reform *could* be achieved from the inside.

"It's time for the *janazah*," she told Cat. They helped Cyrine pull the shades, then walked out with the kids as Cyrine locked up, Kerr drifting to the back. West was waiting on the sidewalk, his bulky shoulders leaning against a red pickup. A decal at the back of the cab read "CHRISTIAN WARRIOR," and a steel-plated fish was anchored to the bumper.

"Come on, kids. I'll give you a ride."

West jerked his chin at Inaya, who considered his fierce appearance. She lowered her voice so Mercedes wouldn't hear.

"Ah, I wouldn't go to the mosque if I were you. You'll scare them."

He grinned at her. "You're the expert on that."

She blushed at the reminder of their encounter under the falls.

West waited to say more until the kids were in the truck, nodding a greeting at Kerr.

"You going to the mosque, Brazil?"

"Yes, to pray. And to extend my solidarity"

"You're good at that, Inaya. Remember it when my time comes."

He was still undercover, so she made her stance confrontational, while she whispered, "Be careful, won't you, West?"

He smiled his sweet smile at her. "Thank you for helping my kid. I never forget a friend."

CHAPTER SIXTY-FOUR

When West and the kids departed, Inaya took a moment to pin her headscarf in place on the street outside the mosque, where she and Cat had parked at the front. The lonely stoicism she'd been practicing wasn't strength: she was strong because of Cat. Because of all the people who loved her. In the search to come to this conclusion, she'd unearthed a fundamental truth. She was dearly loved by the God she worshipped, the One whose hands kept her safe.

Inside the mosque, she embraced her mother and sisters. They were soberly attired, with not a lick of makeup to be seen. They met and mingled with the rest of the community, Nadia as lively as Noor. Inaya pulled her to one side, curious at the difference in her. Nadia's mood had improved after she'd pressed charges against Whitlock, but she still wasn't sleeping well. If Whitlock didn't plead down, there was still the trial to face, and Inaya wondered if Nadia blamed her for not letting things slide.

Both Nadia and Noor were keeping their eyes on Seif's brothers on the other side of the prayer space. Inaya would have her hands full if Blackwater became the twins' mosque. She smiled, thinking she would welcome the closeness. She would view it as the legacy of the three young girls: Barkhudo, Khadijah, and Razan.

"Who's got you so excited?" she asked in the chiding tone of an older sister. "I hope it's Alireza, because I think you might have competition for Mikhail."

"*Baji*, please. Take a look at Lieutenant Seif."

Inaya swallowed. "What? Why?"

Nadia caught on to Inaya's discomfort. "His hands, *baji*. Look closely."

She'd been trying to focus on Razan's *janazah*, so she'd ignored the men's prayer space. Now her gaze instinctively found Seif. Both his hands were bandaged around the knuckles.

Nadia whispered industriously into Inaya's ear. "When Tyler came to class the other day, his eyes were swollen, and I think his nose might be broken. He was holding himself funny too, like his ribs were hurting." Her voice was awed. "I think someone beat him up."

Inaya nearly swallowed her tongue. Seif caught her looking at him. He raised his bandaged hands and dipped his head to her, like a warrior dedicating a victory. She couldn't reward him for this, yet how could she ignore the fact that he'd put himself on the line for her.

Get me, Inaya.

Was it possible she did?

Nadia dug her elbow into Inaya's side. "He's acting like he could be my older brother." A saucy grin tweaked her lips.

Inaya spoke in her strictest voice. "First off, Lieutenant Seif is an officer of the law—he doesn't condone violence. Even suggesting such a thing could place him under review. Second, I need you and Noor to remember—and I cannot stress this enough—*the lieutenant is my boss.*"

Nadia rolled her eyes, muttering under her breath, "You're so clueless, *baji*."

Inaya grinned at the little troublemaker as she wandered off to find her friends.

She ran into Ally Jensen near the door of the mosque. The golden Moroccan door had been replaced by steel-reinforced panels connected to an alarm. Inaya's father had donated the money for a comprehensive security system, with cameras and motion sensors, for the mosque.

Jensen grabbed her arm, overcome by emotion. "We have the best news, Detective Rahman! I still can't believe it."

Seif joined them, standing so close it felt like a touch. "Tell us," he invited.

Jensen bounced a little on her feet. "It doesn't make up for Razan, nothing could, but I think you'll be glad to know the Elkaders' family in Turkey will be arriving here soon."

Inaya quite couldn't take in the news. By rote, she said, "May God reward you."

Jensen signaled to someone over her shoulder. Inaya heard her father's voice at her ear, and turned to him.

"Baba, did you help—"

"My child, a refugee is someone who carries his home wherever he goes, even as he finds a new place of belonging. It was the least I could do for the family, may God offer His mercy."

There were tears in her father's eyes. She pressed herself close to him, alarmed.

"What is it? Did something happen, Baba?"

Holding her safe in his arms, he touched his lips to her scarf.

"They buried their daughter today. I could not face going on if I had to bury mine."

CHAPTER SIXTY-FIVE

If Seif had thought Fatima Elkader beautiful before, her face was radiant now. Five days after Razan's *janazah*, her brother-in-law had arrived at the airport with her son, Uthman, who'd been left behind in Turkey because his birth certificate was missing when they made the decision to flee. His papers couldn't be processed, and so at ten years of age Uthman had been separated from his parents.

But there was another boy, his musculature skeletal, the cavern of his chest sunken in. His hair was thick and curly, his face prematurely aged. This was Razan's twin, Luqman, who'd been tortured by the regime until a friend had paid for his release and he'd then made a journey to his uncle in Izmir, Turkey.

One son clasped Fatima's legs, and she rained kisses on the head of the other, dumbfounded in her joy. Others had come to the Elkaders' home to welcome the family—Areesha Adams, Fadumo and Omar Abdi, Khadijah's mother, Waris, Cyrine and Elias Haddad, Ally Jensen, and surprisingly, Andrea Wong. Inaya and Cat, Inaya's mother with them. The small living room was crowded with guests, and each visitor had brought a gift. The small table in the center of the room was cheerfully burdened with food.

Introductions made, Seif had reassured the family, Uthman listening to his Arabic with large, wondering eyes.

Luqman raised his emaciated face, the skin drawn tight over his battered cheekbones. His haunted blue eyes met Seif's. He was looking around the room, baffled by the presence of so many strangers, and the absence of one he loved. One whose breath and blood were woven through his own. Seif knew about twins, the way they were part of each other. Inaya understood too. She bit her lip until it bled.

Luqman's voice was hoarse, ruined by his torture, but he spoke in the lyrical Arabic that Seif hadn't known he hungered for, the words striking clean to the bone.

"Tell me, my friend, Waqas. Where is my sister, Razan?"

ACKNOWLEDGMENTS

A wonderful group of people have taken me on this journey to the publication of my tenth novel, and I'd like to thank them all. Thank you to my wonderful Minotaur family—it's fabulous to be working with all of you again. Thank you, Catherine, for your amazing insights and your incredible collaborative spirit. You have the twin titanic gifts of wisdom and tact, and I'm so, so blessed to be working with you! Thank you to Hector, Nettie, and Allison, as well as Minotaur's superb creative and sales and marketing teams—you make my life so much easier, and you keep these books shining and in the hands of readers. Nettie, you are truly a wonder in everything you do for me! My very grateful thanks also to Kelley Ragland and Andrew Martin for seeing the worth of stories like these.

As for those who helped me research this book, where do I begin? Thank you to the very kind Scott Graham for helping me understand Colorado water issues, and for giving me the go-ahead to create Blackwater's famous falls in a state suffering semi-drought conditions.

Thank you to Jonas Apala for devoting so much time to a series of interviews that gave me a better picture of policing in Colorado, and answering the most difficult and sensitive questions with such honesty and empathy. I could not have written this book without your help. I have definitely taken liberties, with all the mistakes those entail—please do forgive me. (Also, Jonas and Cati, thank you for letting me borrow Kubo for Inaya. I continue to adore him!)

Thank you to Border Patrol Agent Matt Dover for an in-depth

discussion of issues at the southern border, and for not minding an interview that may have turned into an interrogation. You were so gracious and forthright, and forced me to grapple with many difficult questions.

My deepest thanks to Téo, Juan, and Deisy for agreeing to speak with me about your experiences at the border, and the life-changing journeys you've made. Your courage and humanity are deeply humbling.

My very sincere thanks to Councilwoman Candi CdeBaca of District 9. Your time and insights were infinitely valuable to me, and I remain awed by your dedication to the communities you continue to serve against all odds. I hope you write a memoir one day.

Thank you, as always, to my dear friend Ardo Omer, for such helpful advice on Somali customs and names. Despite our different heritages, we have so much in common. And dearest Yara, thank you for always coming through in a pinch to solve my Arabic language difficulties.

Thank you very much to Margaret Mizushima and the Rocky Mountain Mystery Writers Association for respecting my point of view on policing while I was writing a difficult book on police violence and racial profiling. You were wonderfully gracious.

Thank you to Crime Writers of Color and the inestimable Kellye Garret for doing so much to support writers like me. Though challenges remain, CWoC has given us all a marvelous sense of community.

Thank you also to a group of incredibly generous and versatile writers: Uzma Jalaluddin, Alex Segura, Hank Phillippi Ryan, Hannah Mary McKinnon, Hilary Davidson, and Jennifer Hillier. I adore you all, and will forever remain grateful for your kindness.

Thank you also, dearest Uzma for digging into the heart of Blackwater with me, and being the best critique partner I could ask for. You have the sharpest eye and the kindest heart. Hopefully, we will reunite soon at the Starving Artist for waffles.

And finally, to Danielle Burby, my deepest gratitude and admiration. *Blackwater Falls* would not exist without you. Thank you for championing me, for guiding every step of my writing journey, and for our wonderful partnership. Can you believe we're ten books in? Thank you for absolutely *everything*.

To my family and to my friends who are also family, thank you for everything you did to help me through such a sad and challenging year. Your support through months of grief is something I treasure. Nozzie, you are my foundation, and because of you, I was able to see my father again. Thank you to my unstintingly kind childhood friend Saima: you offered such gentle and wise guidance through so many unexpected challenges. Nader, you made so many sacrifices for me, and I will always love you for them.

This is the year we lost my beloved father, but I hope you will see his gentle spirit resurrected in Haseeb Rahman, a man who loves his daughters as much as my father loved his.